AN ORIGINAL NOVEL OF THE MARVEL UNIVERSE

COLLECT THEM ALL

CORINNE DUYVIS

MARVEL

AN ORIGINAL NOVEL OF THE MARVEL UNIVERSE

GUARDIANS OF THE GALAXY

COLLECT THEM ALL

CORINNE DUYVIS

MARVEL

GUARDIANS OF THE GALAXY: COLLECT THEM ALL PROSE NOVEL. Published by MARVEL WORLDWIDE, INC., a subsidiary of MARVEL ENTERTAINMENT, LLC. OFFICE OF PUBLICATION: 135 West 50th Street, New York, NY 10020. Copyright © 2017 MARVEL

ISBN# 978-1-302-90272-8

Printed in the U.S.A.

ALAN FINE, President, Marvel Entertainment; DAN BUCKLEY, President, TV, Publishing & Brand Management; JOE QUESADA, Chief Creative Officer; TOM BREVOORT, SVP of Publishing; DAVID BOGART, SVP of Business Affairs & Operations, Publishing & Partnership; C.B. CEBULSKI, VP of Brand Management & Development, Asia; DAVID GABRIEL, SVP of Sales & Marketing, Publishing; JEFF YOUNGQUIST, VP of Production & Special Projects; DAN CARR, Executive Director of Publishing Technology; ALEX MORALES, Director of Publishing Operations; SUSAN CRESPI, Production Manager; STAN LEE, Chairman Emeritus. For information regarding advertising in Marvel Comics or on Marvel.com, please contact Vit DeBellis, Integrated Sales Manager, at vdebellis@marvel.com. For Marvel subscription inquiries, please call 888-511-5480. **Manufactured between 2/10/2017 and 3/14/2017 by SHERIDAN, CHELSEA, MI, USA.**

First printing 2017
10 9 8 7 6 5 4 3 2 1

Cover art by Dale Keown and Jason Keith
Interior art by Joe Madureira and Peter Steigerwald

Stuart Moore with Joan Hilty, Editors
Design by Jay Bowen with Salena Johnson

VP Production & Special Projects: Jeff Youngquist
Assistant Editor: Caitlin O'Connell
Associate Editor: Sarah Brunstad
SVP Print, Sales & Marketing: David Gabriel
Editor in Chief: Axel Alonso
Chief Creative Officer: Joe Quesada
Publisher: Dan Buckley
Executive Producer: Alan Fine

To Suzanne,
for opening up new worlds.
Pinky hug.

AN ORIGINAL NOVEL OF THE MARVEL UNIVERSE

CORINNE DUYVIS

MARVEL

1

THE PLANET Levet wasn't, strictly speaking, uninhabitable.

On paper, it ranked a solid 5.1 out of 7 on the Az-Moris scale. It had breathable air, significant landmass, and scads of fresh water.

That ranking, however, did not go into detail about said air (putrid), said landmass (90 percent swamp), or said water (chunky).

Between those elements and the fact that the surface was devoid of life aside from the criminals banished there by the Kree, Levet was, in all honesty, a terrible excuse for a planet.

"Gotta admit," Rocket said, "that space debris is choosing the right hunk of rock to destroy."

"Yeah, I won't lose sleep over this one." Peter Quill scanned the observation screens from the pilot's seat. They were taking slow sweeps across the planet's surface, making occasional—so far futile—stops to search for life at the rare encampments they encountered. "Does it even have a decent bar?"

"Does it even have *people?* They could be long gone. You sure we ain't wasting our time, Quill?"

"We did come across those fly-infested corpses with their heads bashed in," Gamora pointed out. "They looked fresh."

Drax nodded. "I admire their assailants' resilience. It takes gusto to kill in this heat."

"There." Gamora jammed a finger at one of the screens. "Movement."

The five of them—Rocket, Quill, Gamora, Groot, and Drax—stood on the bridge and squinted at the screen.

"Nah, that's another cloud of stormflies," Rocket growled.

Groot looked out the viewport, holding one splayed, branched hand to the glass. "I am Groot?"

"Let's check." Quill flicked a switch. His voice boomed down over the planet below. "Ahoy there, Levet! If anyone is listening, you'll want to make yourselves known right about now. We'll make it worth your while."

Gamora sighed and leaned in. "Space debris has entered your solar system, and some of it is headed for impact. We know the Kree left before everyone was evacuated; we're here to get you out."

"We apologize about the debris," Drax added.

"Yeah, that was…" Quill flicked off the microphone. He spun his seat to face the others, leaving the ship on autopilot. "Come on, the debris didn't have much to do with us. This time."

"Most of the interstellar fiascos of the month have at least a little to do with us, Quill," Rocket said. "Have some pride in what we do."

Groot tapped the glass. "I am Groot?"

"Hey, what do you know." Rocket stretched to peer at the screens. "There really is life out here."

Quill swiveled his seat. "Let's get to work."

GAMORA'S fierce reputation meant she rarely experienced stubbornness. People either cooperated with her, fled, or attacked.

They did not *argue*.

Her patience, as a result, was underdeveloped.

Gamora extended a long, green finger toward the Guardians' ship, which loomed over her, Drax, Rocket, and a pair of convicts. Its worn, patchwork-metal hull looked fantastically out of place in the swamp-and-bog landscape around them. The hatch was still wide open; most of the convicts were already cuffed and inside. The two left out here had other priorities.

"For the last time—" Gamora snapped.

The convicts went right on squabbling. One yapped on about honor. The other refused to set foot on board the same ship as the first convict, out of principle.

"Hey!" Rocket prodded the nearest one's shoulder, reaching up with a gun twice his size. His banded tail swished in annoyance. "Gamora was talking to you. I think she was planning to say, *Shut up and get on board before I toss your broken body on instead.*"

"Close enough." Gamora pushed sweat-drenched, deep green locks from her face for the hundredth time. *Saving lives is important,* she told herself. Saving lives was the mission. Saving lives was what heroes like the Guardians of the Galaxy were all about. There was a reason she'd dedicated herself to the group: Saving lives was a small step toward making amends.

Also?

Saving lives was damn frustrating sometimes.

Especially when she had to do it on a planet like Levet. Even though the air was technically breathable, the swamp fumes were just the right consistency to hover around the head of the average biped. Rocket was lucky. His nose might outperform theirs, but he was also short enough to escape the worst of the smell.

She pointed again at the ship's open hatch, holding her breath as she spoke. "If you want to kill each other, do it after we drop you at the Kyln."

"The Kyln?" A DiMavi stuck his head out of the ship. He'd been the first to let himself be cuffed and climb on board, but now he leaned out, his green skin dark in the evening gloom. "No way. Send me to any other prison. Or I'll take my chances here! Do you know what that place is like?"

"Yes," Drax said.

"They'll eat me alive!"

"Most prisoners are not interested in consuming each other's flesh."

"They'll kill me!"

"They might do that," Drax admitted.

Gamora nodded her agreement. It *was* a distinct possibility.

"You don't understand, I'm really not made for that kind of place, I'm just—"

"An activist," Gamora finished. "We know. Likely story."

"Gamora means it is *un*-likely," Drax clarified. He was holding onto one of the convicts to prevent them attacking each other, with arms roughly the size of the convict's torso. Judging from the way Drax's green skin had veered rapidly toward gray—even his intricate tattoos had lost their red hue—Gamora wasn't the only one bothered by the fumes.

Rocket waved a dismissive, clawed hand at the DiMavi. "Boohoo. You ain't the only 'activist' here. Get back on board."

Gamora turned away from the DiMavi, ignoring the wet squelch of the grass underfoot. She held the cuffs up to the nearer convict's face. "Do you want to put these on yourself? You have two seconds."

"—ooo-oooot."

"Was that Groot?" Rocket's head shot up and turned south, where Quill and Groot had gone to pick up the last remaining stray criminals. Gamora followed his lead, scrutinizing the landscape. Drab marshland stretched out before them. A hundred feet ahead, the grass gave way to shallow swamp water and willowy trees.

No trace of their teammates.

Gamora raised her hand to her communicator. "Quill?"

His voice crackled. "*Star-Lord* when we're on official Guardians business, will you?"

"What's happening?" Without looking, she tossed another set of cuffs at the grass by the convict's feet.

"Don't know. Groot and I separated. Groot, come in."

"I am Groot? I…am Groot."

"A booby trap? Are you kidding me?" Rocket said. "You okay?"

"I am Groot?"

"I don't care if it's a tiny one! I'm on my way."

"Need help?" Gamora said.

He slung his gun over his shoulder. "Nah. Go have fun with these guys. Don't kill anyone till I'm back to watch."

With that, he bounded off.

ROCKET approached through the sparsely planted trees. He'd gone around to avoid the swamp, but even the regular paths were soggy and squishy. Every step resulted in an unsteady bounce, sending gross mud drops splashing up to cling to his fur. In this gravity, he was light enough that each step practically launched him up into the air—his gun was probably the only thing weighing him down.

"I am Groot?" Groot said, seeing him coming.

"Whaddaya mean, am I okay? Are *you* okay?"

Groot would be fine—he'd recovered from worse—but he didn't look it right now. His legs were splintered, the bark rubbed off to reveal fresh, pale wood. His movements wobbled in a way that had nothing to do with the ground underfoot.

Quill approached from the other side. At every step, he had to yank his feet free with a horrendous squelch. "This is so much worse than Earth swamps," he said, grimacing. The mud was everywhere, from the drenched hem of his long. red trenchcoat to splashes on his pale hair and paler face.

"I am Groot," Groot answered Rocket.

"Well, then, don't go yelling like that." Rocket crossed his arms and scanned the area. Trees. More trees. Squishy ground. Leafy tree trunk. Hidden tree house. An exploded mine—"Are you kidding? You fell for *that?*" He wrinkled his nose. "That's embarrassing. I'm embarrassed for you, man. We just grew you back from a splinter after last time you got blown up. And these traps aren't even hidden that well! I already spotted four. Two mines around the base. And two camouflaged explosives there, on the tree trunk, pressure-activated. You see 'em? Hey, there's a snare behind those bushes. That one's not awful, actually."

"I am Groot."

"There ain't nothing wrong with my priorities!"

Quill shook his head, then looked up at the tree house, masked by the massive yellow leaves furling directly from the tree trunk. "Hey! Anyone alive up there?"

"Get out of here!" a voice called back—low, gruff. "I know you're after my house!"

"You know about that incoming space debris, right?"

"I said, get *out!*"

Rocket shrugged. They'd tried their best. "All right. Quill, Groot, let's go."

"I am Groot." Groot didn't move.

"What? We tried. Let's bail. They could be having an awesome riot at the ship! We're gonna miss out!"

Groot shook his head. "I am Groot." Then, looking up, he said, "I am Groot?"

"What, you're gonna have a nice conversation?" Rocket said. "He almost blew you up!"

"Speaking of getting blown up," Quill said loudly, "that's about to happen to Levet. Want to save us some trouble and come down? We're not after your tree, man! It's a great tree, don't get me wrong, but we're a little busy saving the day."

After a moment, the voice said, "How am I supposed to trust that?"

"Don't you know us?" Rocket said. "We're the Guardians of the Galaxy, c'mon."

"Never heard of you."

"That hurts," Quill called up. "We saved the universe a few times. But in your defense, you've probably been on Levet a while. Listen, I'm Star-Lord. *The* Star-Lord? Team leader? I'm kind of a big deal. This is Rocket—tactician, technician, definitely not a genetically modified Earth raccoon."

"One of a kind," Rocket added. "Also, I'm not a flarking raccoon. You take that back."

Quill went on, unperturbed. "At the ship, we have Gamora, the deadliest—I mean, greenest—woman in the galaxy, last of the Zen-Whoberians, definitely not a reformed assassin. And there's Drax the… Discourager. Hell of a guy—impressively honorable, definitely not someone who would ever go on a murderous, vengeful rampage through the galaxy. Or have a nickname like 'Destroyer.' It's for *sure* Discourager."

"I am Groot," Groot said, sounding dubious.

"What?" Quill peered sideways. "I'm trying!"

"Try harder." Rocket glared.

"I am Groot," Groot agreed.

"And then there's Groot!" Quill continued, projecting a cheerful voice. "You met Groot when you almost blew him up! He's a living tree, you live *inside* a tree—I'm sure you'd get along."

"I am Groot," Groot said eagerly. "I am Groot?"

"Stop trying to befriend subpar murderous criminals," Rocket groaned.

Gamora's voice came in over their earpieces. "We have a Kree ship incoming."

Quill made a face. "I thought they'd abandoned Levet."

"Bastards," Gamora said.

"*Bastards.*" Quill shook his head. "Why am I not surprised? All right. Groot, get our new friend out of that tree."

Groot pushed himself to his full height, wavering as he caught his balance on the soggy ground. The branches of his toes dug deep in the mud, squelching with every step toward the tree. He reached up. Snakelike vines twisted around the bark on his arms, shifting and stretching. The process was slow—slower than usual; maybe the mine had damaged him more than he let on—but he'd almost reached the lowest of the leaves. He stepped closer to the trunk, adjusting his weight—

"Careful!" Quill yelled.

Rocket bolted forward on all fours. "Groot, you don't listen, do you? Booby trap! Left, step left—"

Groot half-turned, both massive arms still raised. His leg shifted.

Rocket was on top of the trap just in time, claws prying into the device, piercing its chip a fraction of a second before the bomb would've exploded. He glared up. His tail lashed in agitation. "I *warned* you, you barked buffoon."

"I am Groot," he mumbled.

"You should be."

"I am Groot. I am Groot."

"Don't get all dramatic. I knew I could deactivate that bomb in time." Rocket shifted his glare to the tree house above and groped for his blaster. Even if they rescued the guy minus a few limbs, it'd still be a rescue, right?

"Rocket," Quill said, his voice a warning.

"Don't you come up here! I have a gun!" the guy yelled.

"Yeah? Wanna compare?" Rocket aimed his weapon up at the tree. Cocked his head, squinted one eye shut.

"*Rocket!*"

Groot pushed the gun aside, then reached up into the tree with elongated arms. For a few moments, there was just the sound of leaves rustling, branches snapping. A muffled yell. Then Groot pulled his arms back, his long fingers wrapped around a middle-aged Kree wriggling for freedom.

"Are you having fun?" Gamora said sharply over the comms. "That ship is getting too close for comfort."

"We're on our way," Quill said.

"Put me down!" the Kree yelled. "Put me down!"

"I am Groot?" Groot said amiably, shifting him to carry him under one arm.

"You don't even know how lucky you are to be dealing with Groot instead of the rest of us," Quill said.

Rocket bared his teeth. "Now let's go fight some Kree."

2

HIS STORY actually does check out," Gamora said as she and Quill stalked toward the bridge. Drax had taken them into the air seconds after Quill and the others made it on board.

"What's that?" Quill asked.

"The DiMavi's story. Well, his, and those of the two pink Kree and the Spartoi. They really are activists. The arrest records claimed they were violent terrorists, but nothing backs up that account. They might be thorns in the Kree's side, nothing more. They were probably banished instead of put to work because they might've riled up the other inmates." Prisoner uprisings could be entertaining, and were often necessary—Gamora would give them that. Uprisings were also messy. The Kree did not like messy.

"Forward me what you found. I'll take a look after I lose that ship on our tail."

A smile tugged at her lips. "I know what you're thinking. And the Kree will *not* like it."

"Why? Because those poor activists never made it to the Kyln? They must've been left behind on Levet to die, unbeknownst to us. It's tragic, you're right, but what could *we* have done about it?"

"Very tragic." She followed Quill in silence, glad to be back in the ship: Metal support beams recessed into the walls at her side, the ground under her feet was firm with the occasional bolt or crooked floor plate pressing into her soles. The mild smell of rust and sweat was a lot better than the swamp.

It didn't look like Quill was planning to bring up what had happened with Groot. Gamora had caught enough on comms—and from Rocket's ranting as he boarded—to have a rough idea of the events, though.

"Groot?" she prompted.

"Maybe it's nothing," Quill said immediately, so fast that he must've been waiting for the question. He didn't face her as he talked.

Coward, Gamora thought, not unkindly.

"It's not nothing," she said. "Groot is too smart to fall for a booby trap twice. Especially immediately after it was pointed out to him. And he's taking too long to recover. Same as last week, after that dustup with the Badoon."

He didn't respond. The door to the bridge slid open. Rocket came up from behind and burst past them, but Quill lingered in the doorway, turning to Gamora.

"Go...do your thing," she said, the words she'd borrowed from Quill feeling alien on her tongue. "I'll check on the prisoners and Groot." *Especially Groot,* she thought.

Quill cracked his neck. "Time to pick a fight."

WHAT'RE they doing?" Rocket bolted to the pilot's seat, leaning over the screens to see what Drax and their new Kree friends had been up to. He tapped the sensor output with a clawed finger. "Ha! Scanning us. Trying to identify bio-signatures, I bet. Good luck with that, losers."

"Do not encourage our enemies, Rocket." Drax, sitting in the navigator's seat, was shifting between possible courses projected in front of him.

"You want me to make a run for it, Quill?" Rocket asked. It had been ages since he'd had a good space chase. Well, days. In any case, he could use this opportunity to try out a new maneuver he'd come up with.

"Would there be any point?" Quill grabbed a ceiling cord to steady himself as he leaned over Rocket's shoulder and studied the screens.

"Speed-wise, no." The Guardians' ship was fast. The Kree ship was faster. It was a Perennian A-TH2—nimble, swift, and sharp. It wasn't much in the weapons department—a couple of lousy serin blasters, with only the dual-focus laser as an actual threat—but it was agile enough in a fight to land a dozen shots before it ever got hit itself. "Challenge-wise, though…"

"Slow us down. Let's stick around. You're in my seat, by the way."

"You want me to pilot, I'm sitting in the pilot's seat." He flashed a sharp-toothed smile. "Want to make something of it, co-pilot?"

"My team, my ship, my seats, all I'm saying. Drax? Go help Gamora— I'll take over." A moment later, Quill slid into the vacated seat. "Oh, look. They tried to say hi again. Open her up."

The projector between them sprang to life, the lower half fizzling amid the plastic fighter-pilot toys Quill had glued onto the dash. A blue Kree face glared at the both of them. "This is Lieutenant An-Kell, speaking from ship *X-A Supremor*. You are in Kree territory, *Guardians*." The word dripped with skepticism.

"Oh, good, at least *you* know us," Quill said. "I was getting a complex after what happened with Blondie."

Rocket perked up. He'd suspected Quill would pull a "Blondie" after he suggested they slow down, but it might've been a "Joplin" instead, or he might even have wanted to try—*gross*—boring diplomacy without any kind of secret maneuvers, code words, or violence involved.

It wasn't up to the ranks of pulling a "Jackson Five," but still: This could get fun.

"You did not have permission to access Levet. State your business."

"We were just passing by—we're in Kree territory? Really?" He turned to Rocket. "Did you know that? Wow, I am so sorry, man. We'll be right out of your hair."

An-Kell let out an irritated sigh. "I'm scanning 19 life-forms on board, and you've suspiciously activated a bio-scrambler preventing us from identifying the signatures. Unless you can prove otherwise, we've determined you're carrying our prisoners, in addition to entering a registered banishment planet without permission. We hereby arrest you—"

"Whoa, hold on now." Quill leaned in. "Let's say we *were* carrying prisoners. Hypothetically. Maybe we'd only drop them off at Kree-Pama like you should've done—since otherwise they would, you know, die. You want to explain why you half-assed your evacuation?"

"We don't owe you an explanation."

Rocket half-listened to the conversation. He was moments from positioning the ship correctly—beneath the X-A Supremor, a couple yards farther starboard, at just the right angle—but he'd need more time to do it without the Kree noticing anything funny.

Twenty seconds, he signaled, flashing his fingers by his side where only Quill could see.

"Let me guess, An-Kell—"

"Lieutenant An-Kell."

"—the other day, your colleagues landed on Levet and put out an emergency alert, and anyone who didn't hear it or didn't make it to the designated meeting spots on time was out of luck. Your colleagues tripped over themselves to get out because the big bad space debris was coming— which, for the record, you probably could've stopped in the first damn place. Here's what I'm scratching my head over, though: What are you doing here *now?* I thought you'd all stay safe and far away."

An-Kell bristled. "We're here to arrest you, Star-Lord."

"Which is apparently more important," Quill spat, "than sending a ship to evacuate the remaining prisoners? You could've been doing your actual job instead of having us pick up your leftovers! I mean, hypothetically!"

"We are not set up to transport prisoners," An-Kell said stiffly.

Rocket gave a thumbs-up.

Quill's eyes flicked over, but he didn't give the go-ahead yet. "So to be clear: You're arresting us for doing your job. Hypothetically."

"We're arresting you for carrying our prisoners and for entering a registered—"

Quill thumped back in his seat, disgusted. "Go for it," he told Rocket.

"*Pew.*" Rocket hit the button.

Quill waved his hand through the projection. It fizzled out.

"Hit!" Rocket crowed as the blast connected smack-dab in the triangular area on the bottom of the Perennian's forward wing. That was the thing about the Perennian line. For all their agility in battle, the ships were so narrow that their weak spots were close to the surface. And that agility wouldn't do any good with a damaged equibrilator.

"All right, let's zip it—" Rocket started. Then the ship jolted, slamming him back into his seat. "What the heck?"

Quill gaped. "Did they just—?"

"They just *chained our fricking ship!*" Rocket yelled. "Chain! What is this? Did we slip through time again? Is it three thousand years ago? A chain! A physical! Metal! *Chain!*"

"Can you—?"

"What do you think I'm trying to do?" He furiously tugged at the controls and tried to get a clear shot at either the Kree ship or the chains. One of the chains had half-wrapped around their primary blasters. If they fired, they'd be close to blowing up their own ship.

"The equibrilator hit made them spin too far overhead...I can't—"

Without their equibrilator, the Kree couldn't dodge or navigate properly—but now, neither could the Guardians. Worse: Nothing was wrong with the *Kree* weapons. Even a pathetic serin blast was a threat when you had to absorb a couple dozen of them.

And the first of those had already landed. Rocket buckled in before launching back at the controls. Maybe if he shut off the tertiary engines and double-timed the portside thrusters, the ship would tilt enough to slacken the chains and put the target back within reach...

"Stay on comms." Quill sprinted off the bridge. "We're going out there."

3

DRAX would have preferred to guard the prisoners rather than leave the ship. That tall, purple one looked especially shifty. He had made sure to inform Gamora, however, and he trusted her impressive capacity for murder.

"Drax, tail end," Quill instructed as they floated out beneath the ship. The red lights of his helmet glowed. "Stay out of sight. Groot, with me. We're taking the wings." He signaled—Groot did not have the benefit of a linked-up helmet—and pulled himself toward the wings, floating over.

Drax kicked off the side of the ship to propel himself toward the tail end. Overhead, a few lights blinked. Far to his left and right, the wings of the Guardians' ship were sharply lit against the dark of space—they were high enough over Levet that the sun, which had been close to setting when they were on Levet's surface, now struck their ship from below with relentless brightness.

Drax could not see the Kree ship that hovered above—their own ship blocked it from sight. Good. It meant the three of them were out of sight from the Kree, as well.

"We're taking damage," Rocket shouted over the comms. "Gam! Gamora! Engine room, now!"

The ship strained against the chains with every Kree blast. The metal links were stark white, almost glowing, the chain as thick as Drax's wrist. Three or four were wrapped around the ship at different locations. Drax grabbed one, pulling himself to a stop. Even through his suit, the metal was hot to the touch—a result of time in the sun without the benefit of an atmosphere.

There was just enough slack to grab hold of the chain with both hands. His fingers wound into the links. He spun himself around in a slow somersault, letting his feet find the ship, and planted himself for leverage. He pulled.

He clenched his jaw.

He pulled harder.

The metal didn't even *move*.

"Drax, any luck?" Quill asked.

He tried again, yanking the chain this way and that. He felt the ship shift under him. When he looked down, he saw two dents where he had planted his feet.

"I am not experiencing luck," he admitted darkly.

"Must be some Kree alloy. The cutter and my element blaster aren't doing much, either."

Drax had been about to take his own cutter from his belt, but he abandoned that plan. He narrowed his eyes at the chain before him. It was wound around the ship twice, the lines criss-crossing. As hard as he pulled, it gave him no slack, and the ship's tail was too irregular to simply slide the chains off.

"Are you having fun picking your noses out there?" Rocket growled over comms. "I need my blasters, guys!"

"Rocket. Quill. I am going to break the ship."

"What? Don't break my ship!" Quill said.

"Don't break the ship, you idiot!" Rocket agreed. "Negative! Don't break the ship! What's the matter with you?"

"If I break off this triangular object, I can slide off the chains."

"Don't—break—" Rocket snarled. "Actually, never mind. Break it. Have fun."

"What? No!" Quill said. "My ship!"

"A stabilizer wing is easy to fix, Quill, and we need to move," Rocket said. "Our shields won't hold much longer. The Kree are taunting us, by the way. You want me to patch you in? They're real smug."

"Drax, I have an idea. Get close to their ship. Break the winches," Quill said. "I'll distract them. Groot will keep trying the chains."

"Understood," Drax said.

"Destroy those serin blasters while you're at it," Rocket added.

"Understood."

"And their ugly faces!"

"Understood."

"Groot is saying something, too," Quill offered. "I think it's 'I am Groot.'"

Drax couldn't see Groot or Quill from his position. He moved toward the edge of the ship, looking over for the first time. The Kree ship hovered overhead—sleek, narrow, smaller than the Guardians'. The sun cast the stark shadow of the Guardians' ship across part of its hull.

Several lines of chain stood tautly between the two ships, spanning at least 40, 50 feet. A blob of mud hurtled upward, following the same path as the chains, splashing on the Kree ship a hair's breadth from one of the blasters protruding from its hull.

Quill's element gun, no doubt. It would be a sufficient distraction. Within seconds, Quill had changed modes, and a hail of ice rained up.

The nearest Kree weapon shifted position to focus on Quill.

Drax used the moment to pull himself over the edge of the Guardians' ship. He hunched low against the hull, and leapt up. Twenty feet, fifteen, ten… He twisted in zero gravity, landing on the Kree ship in a crouch. He looked up to scan for Groot—there, working to loosen a chain on the wing— and Quill—there, firing another shot as his boot thrusters flared brightly.

Drax clambered across the Kree ship, finding handholds and pulling himself along, going straight for the nearest chain.

The Kree inside had detected him. A serin blaster twisted to take aim. Drax pressed close enough to the Kree hull that the blaster could not hit him without risking damage to their own ship.

"They stopped with the taunting," Rocket informed him. "I think they're coming out."

There: The chain disappeared into a funnel-like opening in the hull, its controlling winch hidden inside. Drax made his way closer.

"Yoo-hoo," Quill sang. "Focus on me, you big, blue babies. Let Drax work in peace."

Drax aimed the cutter at the funnel, right where the chain exited. The metal bubbled and blackened, but did not budge. It did not matter. He only needed to weaken it. He pounded a fist against the ship. Again. Again. The metal dented, then cracked. Again. He laughed, feeling the structure weaken under his strikes.

He could make a hole large enough to climb inside and disable the winch—but it would take too long. Their ship would suffer heavy damage.

Drax waved to catch Groot's attention, then pointed at the twisted metal.

As Groot made his way over, wooden hands and fingers already extending to reach inside the gap Drax had made, Drax surveyed the situation. Groot had worked one chain loose. Another two—the one on the tail end and the one around the ship's body—remained. The Guardians' ship's blaster, which had been twisted aside by one chain, was free and aiming at the Kree ship. Nearby, Quill was keeping two suited-up Kree busy.

Make that one.

Make that—

What was he doing?

"Quill?" Drax asked. "I do not think this is the time for dancing."

"They're shooting at my boots!" Quill's voice yelled into his ears.

Quill struggled to keep still as his one functional boot sent him veering left and right and up and down. He barely managed to keep the remaining Kree attacker at a distance with his element gun. "Wait, I can fix this. I just need to turn off my—"

His functioning boot thruster cut out.

The other sputtered. Flashed bright flame. Sputtered again.

The functional one sprang back to life, but weakly.

Quill spiraled and cartwheeled, spinning away from both ships. "*Guys!* A little help!"

"Remove your boot," Drax instructed. "Use the functioning boot to propel back."

"That'll compromise my suit!"

"Most likely."

"I'll *die!*"

"Ah. Yes. I forgot how fragile humans are."

"*Half* human!"

"Human enough," Rocket pitched in. "Don't make excuses."

Drax grabbed hold of Groot and pushed off from the Kree ship. The winch came with them, pulling free from the damaged hull.

Once near the Guardians' bridge, Drax released Groot, who latched onto a rim of the Guardians' ship with one hand to hold himself steady. His other hand reached for Quill, vines stretching from his fingers.

Drax landed in a crouch on the hull outside the Guardians' bridge. He looked up. Another Kree had exited the enemy ship, aiming a weapon at Groot. Eyes narrowing, Drax took a blade from his belt and flung it. It hit the Kree's hand. The Kree jolted away, the gun slipping from his grip.

Drax was momentarily disappointed to have to miss out on the screams of his enemies. The vacuum of space had its drawbacks.

Air and blood flushed from the rip in the Kree's glove. Within a moment, the Kree had slapped a patch on the tear, sealing himself back up.

By that time, Drax had launched himself at the Kree. He wanted his knife back.

Drax against a single Kree was not a fair fight.

Nor was it a long one.

"Drax!" Rocket and Quill yelled at the same time.

He looked up. Quill was whirling farther away; worse, Groot floated nearby, also untethered. Shards of wood drifted near the rim of the ship. His hand had splintered.

"Mind helping out?" Quill's voice went higher.

"We've got all power diverted to shields," Rocket said. "We fly, shields go down. With that d'ast Kree ship still attached, they could blow us to tiny bits from up close. They're"—the Guardians' ship trembled as another shot hit—"working on it already."

"Groot loosened the chain on the wing," Drax said. He left the unconscious Kree floating for his colleagues to retrieve and pushed himself toward the Guardians' ship. "If I remove the stabilizer on the tail, we should be able to escape."

"If you remove the stabilizer, we can't steer ourselves close enough to Quill and Groot to grab 'em. We'd smush 'em trying."

"Do *not* smush us!" Quill said. "That's an order!"

"Understood." Drax landed against the Guardians' ship in a crouch. "I will break the stabilizer."

Drax sped toward the tail end, alternately kicking off and pulling. The ship shook as it absorbed another hit.

"Did you not hear—" Rocket yelled.

He was already pounding on the stabilizer wing to weaken it. "We do not need"—*thump*—"to be close." *Thump.* "We have chains."

"I—ahhh. I gotcha."

"Precisely."

Drax broke off the stabilizer with a satisfying crack.

4

WHAT exactly happened out there?" Gamora asked. "The view from inside the engine room is limited."

Peter was slumped on the couch in the leisure area, the seven-sided room at the center of the crew quarters. He felt relieved to have solid ground underfoot and breathable air around him again, but he wasn't in the mood to celebrate. Groot sat with his back against the door to his quarters, examining his torn-up hand.

They had left the Kree ship far behind: With its damaged equibrilator, it was useless in a chase. Now that they were out of reach, Rocket had suited up and gone outside. He had to repair the stabilizer before they attempted any landings.

"They broke my boot," Peter said miserably.

Gamora nodded. "I got that part. I vividly pictured that part, in fact."

"I am Groot."

"No, it wasn't. Don't blame yourself." Peter sat upright and half-turned to look at Groot.

"I *am* Groot." He held up both hands to show them. The fingers on his splintered hand had grown back, but they were only twigs, notably fresher than his other hand. The legs damaged in the earlier mine explosion had recovered fully, but it had taken at least three times longer than usual.

Peter rubbed his forehead. "I shouldn't have taken you outside. I knew you weren't okay yet."

"Of course you should've," Gamora said. She leaned against the couch armrest. "Don't play martyr. No one is better suited to working in a vacuum or taking direct hits than Groot. He took out the winch, didn't he?"

Gamora was right, of course. And Peter hadn't made the decision lightly: He'd known the risks. Mostly, anyway—he hadn't expected to spend 10 minutes drifting. He'd spent a lot of those 10 minutes asking himself the same thing Gamora probably was now.

What was going on with Groot?

"I am Groot—I am Groot. I am Groot." He started off lively, but grew quiet. He curled up against the door and looked away, as if scared or ashamed.

"You really don't have a clue why your hand splintered so easily?" Peter pressed.

He shook his head.

"It's not just that you haven't grown back properly yet since you had to regrow last month?"

Another shake of his head.

"Of course not," Gamora said. "He's been in the field when he was smaller than this."

"I am Groot."

"You're right. It's not just the splintering," Peter said. Groot had grown forgetful, sluggish, ever since he'd been blown to bits and planted again. He hadn't been in the field often enough for it to be a problem, but it seemed to be getting worse. Had they grown him back wrong, somehow?

"Poison?" Gamora suggested.

"I am Groot."

"How could we check?" Peter asked.

"I don't suppose we know a doctor who specializes in *Flora colossi*."

"I sure don't."

"I am Groot."

"I'll put out a call," Gamora said.

"Yeah. We'll drop off those political activists at the Teer-XI station and go straight to the Kyln, before Drax starts cracking prisoner skulls and the Kree realize we're not actually at Kree-Pama like we told them. You know, there's a downside to sending people on a wild goose chase: You don't get to see their faces when they figure it out." Peter stretched. "I need to go and fix my boot. And see if Rocket needs help."

"I have him on comms. He's been yelling about wanting an assistant."

They glanced at Groot at the same time. Normally, he was the one to help Rocket with repairs.

He wasn't even paying attention. As if he hadn't heard Gamora at all.

"I'll play lovely assistant for the day," Peter said, moving past Gamora to the exit. "And Groot…"

He looked up. "I am Groot?"

Peter already regretted saying something. "I don't know, man. We'll figure this out."

FINALLY, we're done," Rocket growled, hours later, as the massive doors of the Kyln closed behind them. "I saw how those guards were watching me. They can't wait to lock me up again. What's the problem? I ain't even wanted! Currently."

Mostly for lack of proof, but still. Didn't those guards have anything better to do?

"I am Groot," Groot said quietly as they walked along the open port bridge to where they'd docked their ship. Instead of paying attention to the group or the ships ahead—a crude, blockish Spartaxan one was just arriving—Groot was staring up. Rocket followed his gaze. The multileveled docking area of the Kyln exterior had an artificial atmosphere that allowed an unobstructed view of the galaxy stretching out around them. The lilac surface of a nearby moon obscured part of the Tneric arm, which spiraled on their left, a galaxy cluster so bright it had to be more star than not. A stretch of sky pulsed—the almost imperceptible sign of a ship going past at warp speed.

"Buncha stars, big deal," Rocket scoffed. "We got a lot of them, you know."

Groot sighed. "I am Groot."

"Can we hurry up?" Quill kept looking nervously back at the Kyln looming overhead. "I don't trust the guards not to tip off the Kree. Or the prisoners to keep quiet about the activists missing from the group."

"We'll need to deal with the Kree soon, anyway," Gamora frowned.

"I'd like to fix up the ship first," Quill said. "Maybe save the galaxy a couple more times so they'll remember they owe us? Just a thought."

"I like this thought." Drax punched one palm with his fist. "I am ready."

Groot was still looking up; he bumped into Gamora. She spun, one hand up, the other already on the sword at her belt. Then, relaxing, she said, "Groot. Eyes up front."

"I am Groot." He winced.

"Whats'a matter with you today? Eesh." Unease twisted in Rocket's stomach.

"Friends," Drax said. "Look."

The blockish ship had docked one level up and was unloading its cargo in a straight line onto the walkway: at least two dozen prisoners, shackled at feet and hands—and occasionally claws, tentacles, pincers, and extra pairs of hands. They shuffled toward the Kyln. One or two prisoners glanced over the edge of the walkway, as if considering leaping off until the art-grav no longer held them, but the guards only had to wave their prodders to make them snap back in line.

And at the back of that line—

"Is that…?" Quill started.

Holy crap, Rocket thought, *it's another Groot.* Right there. The other *Flora colossus*—almost Groot's size, but a little thinner and shorter—trudged along with the rest of the prisoners. "Hey, an ex-girlfriend of yours, Groot?"

Drax frowned. "I thought Groot was the only *Flora colossus* in this part of the galaxy."

"Looks like he's got competition," Rocket snickered. "Wonder what this one's in for."

"I am Groot," Groot said, staring. "I am Groot?"

"Are you sure?" Quill said.

Rocket sent Groot a sidelong frown. "Yeah, who says you're the only one? Some other *Flora colossus* might've gotten adventurous and wanted to check out the galaxy. They can't *all* be stick-in-the-mud tree supremacists."

"Your people do not care very much for you anymore, Groot, do they?" Drax asked.

"We're checking it out." Quill fired up his boots, hovering a few feet above the walkway—the gouts of flame weak but even—and shot off toward the next walkway, a ship-length away.

Drax took a couple of steps back, then made the jump.

"I do like shortcuts." Gamora ran ahead, then swerved sideways, leaping onto the nearest parked ship and clambering up as easy as running.

"Oh, sure, sure," Rocket said as he scuttled up Groot's back, claws hooking into the bark. "No need to wait for us. Why bother?"

"I am Groot," Groot said, distracted.

Once properly installed on Groot's shoulder, Rocket patted the side of his head. "Let's move."

"I am Groot?"

"Nah, I don't trust you one bit after your shoddy performance today, but who else am I gonna hitch a ride with?" Rocket bared his teeth at the prisoners above. "Let's go visit the fam."

5

HEYYY," Quill drawled. Gamora could see him just ahead, slowing down to hover near the prisoner walkway. Already, four guards of varying species had their guns drawn and pointed. One yelled orders over comms—calling for backup, probably.

Gamora skidded to a stop on a transport ship. Drax slid in beside her. She wanted to move closer, but these guards would be shooting to kill.

(They would miss, of course.)

The one who had been talking over comms gestured at her, rough but authoritative. Within half a second, two guns were pointed at her and Drax. That was the highest-ranking officer on site, then. She would take him out first if it came to it.

"State your business, Star-Lord," the commander said. He kept his face largely neutral, but the way his feet parted marginally indicated he was alert, ready to jump into action if needed—the man was smart enough not to underestimate them. "Any closer and we *will* shoot."

Behind the commander, the dozen or so prisoners looked up at the Guardians with interest. That included the *Flora colossus* at the back, whose eyes widened at the sight of them. They widened farther when Groot and

Rocket arrived on the ship behind Gamora—she felt the vibrations, heard the ticktack of wood on metal. She didn't need to turn.

She cocked her head a fraction to the side as she observed the *Flora colossus.* His expression didn't show interest or wariness, like those of the other prisoners.

It was shock.

Quill was still hovering, hands open and spread wide in order to look less threatening. He did, Gamora admitted, excel at looking nonthreatening. It was a skill.

"Mind if we have a quick chat with one of your prisoners?" he asked.

"We really do, in fact."

"I am Groot— I am Groot—" the prisoner-Groot was saying, but between the buzz around them and the distance, Gamora couldn't translate.

"See, your tall, leafy friend there," Quill went on unperturbed, "isn't a common sight around these parts. We'd really like to have a talk. Supervised, if you want. Five minutes."

"You *are* aware it's a tree that can only speak three words?" the commander said slowly. "Regardless. The answer is no. Step away, Guardians. We *will* engage if necessary. If you want to talk to one of the prisoners, you'll need to go through official channels and request—"

"That'll take *weeks*—"

"Months," Gamora muttered.

"Look out!" one guard shouted.

It happened in the space of a second:

One prisoner, a bulky Stenth woman, dashed forward. Her elbow smashed into the guard's face (good technique, given her cuffs) as her other hand went for his gun. It blasted harmlessly against the reinforced walkway. Then she had it in her hands.

The next blast was aimed at the guard's torso. It wasn't harmless this time. An orange flash, a splatter of red, and he went down.

The situation had changed.

Two more prisoners turned on the nearest guards. More orange flashes. Other prisoners scattered, yelling. Some tried to get away from the gunfire. Others tried to get away, period.

"D'ast it, Quill!" the commander screamed. "It's never easy with you around, is it?"

"Permission to assist?" Quill yelled back. Every one of his muscles was tense, his hand already on his element gun, but he waited for the go-ahead.

A split second of hesitation. "Granted." Then the commander turned, yelled something into his microphone, and entered the fray.

Gamora took a second to assess the situation. The guards had their hands full with the prisoners who had chosen to fight. That meant the Guardians should—

"Focus on the escapees," she called. "Before the guards take them out the hard way!"

Quill was already swerving after a Shi'ar couple scuttling away across the transport ship's hull. "Groot, Rocket, get anyone who isn't fighting out of harm's way. Injured guards, scared prisoners."

They fanned out. Drax took the Stenth who'd started the mess—she'd grabbed the dead guard's body as a cushion and dropped herself over the edge of the walkway, probably aiming to land on one of the ships or walkways on the lower levels. She left a trail of blood in the air from a shot to the shoulder. Quill took the Shi'ar. Groot and Rocket were crawling along the bottom side of the walkway, Groot's arms and vines winding around to pluck people up out of the fray.

Gamora went after another pair of escapees: the prisoner-Groot and a tall, frail Kree. They ran side by side, past the transport ship, as fast as their cuffed feet would carry them. The Kree fell, but the Groot hooked a finger into the back of his jacket and yanked him upright without slowing down.

Shouldn't call him Groot, Gamora thought as she landed in front of them in a crouch. But up close like this, she couldn't think of him as anything else. This Groot and their own looked *so* much alike. She could even swear that he recognized her, the way he looked at her now.

"Listen—" she said.

An orange flash.

The Groot exploded into splinters. They scraped past Gamora's face and clattered down on the walkway behind her. Two legs, still stuck in their cuffs, thunked down.

For a second, she stood immobile.

It wasn't as if she'd never seen a Groot die—if you could call it that.

It had just rarely happened two feet away from her.

She snapped out of it. With one hand, she grabbed a chunk of wood. With the other, she took the Kree's wrist. She darted to the side, pulling him along. Just in time. A second orange flash went past them, right where the Kree had stood.

She sped up, sliding behind the nearest ship, where she pulled the Kree down in a crouch. "Stay," she snarled into his ear. She listened for footsteps. Nothing.

"They—they just shot—he wasn't even—" the Kree babbled, staring at the scattered splinters.

"He'll be fine." She held up the splinter she'd taken, a shard of wood the size of her hand. "Plant this. Learn botany. You'll have plenty of time on the inside. This Groot will be…" She stared at the shard. Turned it over. Her eyes narrowed. "How did you meet him?"

"What? They just…"

"Answer me."

For the first time, the Kree looked at her. He swallowed a gasp. His eyes bulged out. "You're Gamora! Oh, flark, you're Gamora."

"Yes."

"The—the deadliest woman in the galaxy?"

"More than one galaxy, but yes."

It was nice to have a reputation.

If inconvenient, sometimes.

He scrambled away on his hands and knees. "Oh, flark, oh—"

She grabbed the cuff connector between his feet and dragged him effortlessly back. "Do you really want to go back to the spot where they were shooting at you?"

"Yes!" he yelped.

"Poor decision-making. Where did you meet Groot?"

"Will you let me live if I answer?"

She suppressed the urge to roll her eyes. That would be too Quill of her. Sometimes, though, it was the perfect way to express her thoughts. "You *are* aware I am saving your life?"

He looked at her with such fear she couldn't tell whether he was aware of much of anything.

She rubbed her forehead. "Answer."

"I—I bought him, all right? I bought him at the Knowhere market, that's all, he was just a sapling, still in a pot and everything, they had a bigger model there to show—"

"Model? Who is 'they'?"

"Uh, some woman. Green."

"Be more specific." Could mean Skrull, DiMavi, Froma, Insectivorid, Inhuman, Earth mutant—

"I don't know, all right? Green, like you. I mean, not—obviously not like *you*, not Zen-Whoberian—"

"Tell me about her before you embarrass yourself further."

He swallowed audibly. "She had a hood on. I could barely see her. Didn't have a stall, neither. I knew it was shady, but that tree creature she showed off looked real practical. I bought it and got out. I just needed someone to help me with, uh…"

"Crime."

"*Small* crime," he said. "*Little* crime. Groot didn't mind doing it, neither. We were friends. You know, I really shouldn't even be here. I'm practically innocent."

"Where on the market?"

"Near the Skrull performers. But when I went back—twice; I had questions—she wasn't there anymore."

"Gamora?" Quill's voice came in through comms. "Situation is under control. Where are you?"

"Coming now. Prisoner in tow. Tell those trigger-happy bastards to hold their fire, all right?"

"Hey, where'd that other Groot…" Rocket's voice—coming through comms—fell silent as Gamora stepped out of hiding and back within view of the group. Farther down the walkway, nearer to the guards and remaining prisoners, Rocket was wiping his gun down on his shirt. He glanced up at her approach—first looking at her, then lowering his gaze to the splintered mess scattered on the walkway around her feet. For a moment, Rocket stood unmoving. Even from this distance, she saw his hands around the gun going still, forming frozen claws. Then he shot into motion, sprinting for the guards. "You krutacking—"

Quill was closer than Gamora. He jumped forward, grabbing the collar of Rocket's jacket just in time. "Rocket. Don't."

Groot crouched. He placed a single hand on Rocket's shoulder, large enough to cover half his torso. "I am Groot."

If they said anything else, it was too soft for Gamora to hear. With the Kree prisoner by her side, she approached the others, keeping a wary eye out for anything else that might escalate the situation. The group was smaller than before. Fewer guards, fewer prisoners—the rest were either dead or inside the Kyln or both, Gamora supposed. Multicolored blood spatter and scorch marks stained the area.

The commander stood in front of Quill, shoulders slumped, but eyes sharp. "You realize we're not thanking you for your assistance."

"Fair," he agreed. Quill didn't sound cheerful about it, though. His eyes lingered on the wood in Gamora's hands as she came to stand by his side. She hadn't given the shard to the Kree prisoner yet. She didn't think she would now.

She held it up to the commander. "This Groot wasn't fighting. Was this necessary?"

"Was he running?"

"Yes. But he wasn't violent. He wasn't a threat, he—"

"Look, he was a prisoner, he tried to run. We're authorized to use lethal force to prevent escape."

"Authorized! Doesn't mean you *should!*"

Even when she raised her voice, the commander wasn't intimidated. If he knew of Star-Lord, he knew of Gamora, too, yet he didn't bat an eyelash.

Now, she would have preferred some cowering.

One guard took the Kree prisoner by her side back into custody. Good, Gamora thought. One less worry. She turned to Groot. "Groot?" She didn't know how to phrase it. "Did you recognize that *Flora colossus?*"

Because he had recognized *them.* She was certain of it.

"I am Groot." The words came deliberate, unsure. He looked up, still crouching beside Rocket, and nodded. "I…am Groot."

Rocket had skepticism written all over his face. "The other Groot was *what* now?"

"I am Groot."

"It was you?" Gamora repeated carefully. "Not simply another *Flora colossus*. Not simply a relative. But *you?*"

"Are you certain?" Drax asked. "Perhaps he simply looked similar."

Rocket snorted. "Yeah, no offense, but you all got a similar kinda arboreal look going on."

"Would you recognize yourself if you looked in a mirror?" Gamora said. "Give Groot some credit." She held up the shard of wood again. She studied it with equal parts guilt—she hadn't been able to keep him safe, hadn't even had a chance to talk to him—and wonder.

How was this *possible?*

"Could he be a genetic duplicate? A twin? Or grown from"—Quill made a vague, animated sort of gesture—"I don't know, some acorns you dropped by accident? Acorns are seeds, right? You know, I actually have no idea how *Flora colossi* work. Or acorns. Never mind. Carry on."

"There was a second, older *Flora colossus* at the market, according to the prisoner." Gamora narrowed her eyes in thought. "Someone is selling *Flora colossi?* Found this younger Groot duplicate and added him to their wares?"

"All this fuss over some tree," a guard muttered. "What's going on lately?"

Gamora had been nearly ready to jump him over the first comment. The second one made her pause. "*Lately?* What do you mean?"

The guard glanced at his commander, who nodded. "We got…well, several guards received an attempt at bribery this week. Someone wanted a heads-up if any *Flora colossi* turned up."

"Why?" Quill demanded.

The guard shrugged.

"Who?" Gamora asked.

The guard hesitated until the commander cut in. "If we tell you, do you agree to be gone within the next five minutes?"

"You know what? We'll even make it three," Quill said.

Drax crossed his arms. "It is a generous offer."

The commander smiled wryly. "It was the Collector."

6

I NEVER liked that guy." Rocket grouchily worked the navigation controls as he talked. "You guys seen the way he looks at me and Groot? He's all *fascinated.*"

A shudder ran down his spine. He'd seen that look on a handful of faces in his life, and it never spelled anything good. It was the kind of fascination a person showed right before cutting you open to see how well you worked.

If the Collector had his way, the best Rocket could hope for was to at least get a *comfortable* cage in the Collector's private museum of curiosities, antiquities, and monstrosities. As an Elder of the Universe, the Collector took full advantage of his immortality to ignore pesky mortal morality and indulge in his messed-up hobby.

What Rocket wouldn't give for a one-hour shopping spree in the guy's museum, though. The Collector had amassed some sweet gadgets over the years. Rocket could upgrade the ship, the weapons—probably whip up a couple of nice loud explosives—

"We don't have to like him," Gamora said. "We only need answers from him."

"Gotta say, I am seriously curious about those answers." Quill turned over the boot in his lap and wiggled his bare toes against the dashboard.

With the ship on autopilot, he was taking time to fine-tune the boots' propulsion system. And stink up the cabin. *Real nice, Quill.*

Gamora sat backwards in the gunner's seat, her arms across its backrest. "My best guess: The Collector got wind of *Flora colossi* in this part of the galaxy, and is sniffing around because he wants one for his collection. They're uncommon, they're interesting, they're powerful. Right up his alley."

"Think he knows about the duplicate?" Quill asked.

Gamora just shrugged.

"I still say we should hit up the Knowhere market," Rocket said. "And not *just* 'cause I want a new octrical finner."

"Based on what that prisoner said, the seller's long gone," Quill said. "We're better off seeing what the Collector knows. I don't trust him, but I do trust he does his research if he's after something."

"I know that! I'm just *saying.*" Rocket leaned back in the co-pilot's seat. "Our octrical finner is a piece of junk, is all. Don't blame me if we're spinning in circles by next week."

"I am Groot," Groot mumbled. He seemed to have only half-followed the conversation.

"We did not know either, friend," Drax said.

Rocket snickered. "Yeah, I mean, if I'd *known* you could be duplicated, I'd've grown a whole army of Groots years ago. Come at me now, Badoon. Let's see whatcha got. Me? I got a *forest.*"

"There's no way the normal *Flora colossus* reproductive process can lead to genetic duplicates, is there?" Gamora asked.

Groot shook his head.

Quill looked up from his boot. "So it's more like cloning. Do we think the older *Flora colossus* the seller apparently had at the market was a duplicate, too? Did they sell other saplings? I mean, jeez, how many Groots could we have running around? This one hooked up with a bad character and got dragged into petty crime, which…" He trailed off with a glance at Rocket.

He shrugged his agreement. "It's in character. No argument there."

"There are many reasons one might purchase a *Flora colossus,* duplicate or no duplicate." Drax had a dark look. "These reasons are not all pleasant."

"That's what I'm worried about," Quill said.

"I am Groot," Groot said miserably.

Rocket made a "psh" sound. "Come on, buddy. Quit your moping. We'll find whoever sold those Groots and fling them out the airlock, then round up any other *Flora colossi* they might've sold. Easy."

"There are refreshingly few galaxies at stake," Gamora agreed.

"I am Groot."

"Is that the plan?" Drax asked. "Find the seller, and save the Groots?"

"Um, *yeah,*" Rocket said, side-eying him. "Can't have lowlifes running around with Groot knockoffs. It's a matter of principle. That *is* the plan, right, Quill?"

"That, and figure out if it's connected to what's been happening with *our* Groot. There has to be a reason he's so fragile all of a sudden."

"Yeah, that. Easy."

"Easy," Gamora echoed.

She still looked worried, though. So did Quill and Drax. Groot, most of all.

Whiners.

The sight of those splinters on the walkway flashed before Rocket's eyes. He cringed.

"Gimme that." Rocket crawled over the armrest of the navigator's seat and perched there to snatch the boot from Quill's lap. "It's a micro-propulsor, not a warship. You need delicacy."

"Go for it, man." Quill raised both hands. "I asked hours ago if you wanted a stab at it."

"Yeah, well, 'scuse me for having faith in your skills," he grumbled.

Quill spun his chair to face the others and continued on about the Collector and Groot and whatever else they were fretting about.

No reason to be fretting, Rocket thought, bowed over the boot and furiously poking at Quill's sloppy handiwork. *No reason at all. Jeez.*

Groot would be just fine.

THE COLLECTOR'S latest museum was located in an isolated arm of the galaxy, far from civilized life and farther still from any notion of common sense.

The *shape* of said museum was a prime example of that: a gigantic frog floating in space.

"Gotta say, I'll never get tired of that," Rocket said.

"I am already tired of it." Drax said, his face near the viewport as the ship approached. Gamora could practically see the frog reflected in his eyes. "*Why.*"

"Of all my questions for the Collector, that ranks low," Gamora said. A moment later, she admitted: "It does rank, however."

The Collector let them dock and enter so fast, she wondered whether he'd expected them. Within minutes, he had kissed the backs of their hands in welcome, and they were trailing him through the halls.

"Sooo. Tivan. I see you've redecorated." Quill stealthily wiped his hand on his pants.

Drax was still staring at his own hand in horror.

"You like?" The Collector swept an arm at the massive gilded walls. They sparkled so brightly that Gamora was tempted to shade her eyes. A floral-themed relief pattern stretched the length of the hall.

It was almost—but not quite—as tacky as the Collector's clothes, which currently consisted of gold-sequined pants and a metallic, sparkling cape lined with purple fur.

"It's, uh…very…" Quill fumbled.

"Is it real gold?" Rocket tapped the wall with a knuckle. "'Cause then, yes, I seriously like."

"It sparkles," Drax added helpfully.

"I am Groot," Groot agreed.

The Collector watched the five of them with something that resembled fondness. Good: He might actually give them answers. Their history with the Collector was long and complicated enough that it could've gone either way, depending on his mood—or theirs, to be fair.

"So, tell me, my friends," he asked, warm yet wary, "to what do I owe the pleasure?"

"You get any Groots in, lately?" Rocket cocked his head at the Elder, abandoning his inspection of the walls.

"Pardon?"

"*Flora colossi,*" Gamora said. "We know you've been asking around. Why?"

"I see. Interesting." He folded his hands before him. His cloak glistened with the movement.

"I am Groot." Groot stepped forward. He narrowed his eyes. "I am *Groot.*"

"Could someone perhaps…translate?"

"He's sayin' you ought to answer our questions, or he'll jam his fingers into your skull and wriggle them around a bit." Rocket helpfully motioned his claws to illustrate.

"He did *not* say that," Quill said.

"I paraphrased!"

The Collector raised an eyebrow.

"We encountered a *Flora colossus* that appears to be a duplicate of Groot. Your name came up. We would"—Drax crossed his arms—"*prefer* to discuss the situation as friends."

"Have we ever been anything else?" The Collector tapped his chin thoughtfully, as though recalling their previous interactions. "Very well. Given our close, trusting relationship—"

Gamora kept a passive face, but only barely.

"—I would be happy to explain my part in this. Come, my friends. Allow me to offer you a drink—a zengrita?"

Rocket and Drax perked up. So did Quill, but Gamora knew there was more behind it. Quill was savvier than he let on. "Now there's an idea," he said sunnily.

They followed the Collector through the aquatic wing, past a display of kaleidoscopic shells to a crystal tunnel running through bright, gray-green water. Coral lay scattered across the aquarium floor, growing several inches in the time it took them to walk past; a winged creature soared by in a self made air bubble, snatching fish from the water in five-pronged claws. An opaque dust cloud clung to the curved tunnel glass, shifting sideways as they went. From a certain angle, Gamora could swear she saw a set of eyes within,following their every move.

"Are those seahorses?" Quill asked, walking at the front of the group alongside the Collector. "Are those *sardines?*"

The two of them extolled the virtues of what Gamora assumed were aquatic Earth species. No doubt the Collector knew Quill's intent, but he was prideful enough to enjoy the attention regardless.

"This is taking too long," Rocket said. He and Groot had lagged behind to walk beside Gamora.

"I am Groot."

"Since when is Quill so interested in a buncha fish?"

"You know he isn't," Gamora said.

"Yeah, yeah, diplomacy, whatever."

"I don't enjoy it, either."

Gamora knew that she contributed more to the team than brute strength and a fearsome reputation. She acknowledged those strengths, of course— took pride in them—but they were only tools. Fighting was not always the solution, but it was an option they usually kept in mind.

Not so with the Collector.

An uppercut would do little to a practically immortal Elder of the Universe like the Collector. Their only means of leverage was the threat of destroying his museum—and they shouldn't play that card first thing. They had never gone up against the Collector without a good reason, and Gamora suspected that was part of why he'd never sought payback. He'd simply taken their conflicts in stride. As far as she could tell, he had a twisted sort of respect—even admiration—for the Guardians of the Galaxy, and it wasn't worth endangering that simply to get their answers sooner. Better to accept his drinks, indulge his fish-related interests, and leave on good terms with their information.

Having their usual go-to plan—violence—eliminated made Gamora uneasy, but the Guardians had enough enemies already. They didn't need to add the Collector to that list. Besides: Between Levet, the Kree ship, and the Kyln, they'd had a long day. They deserved a drink.

She tore her eyes away from a diamond-like creature that seemed to shatter and reform with every breath, and followed the Collector into his office. The space was as ludicrous as the rest of the museum: one wall a high-tech console featuring numerous screens, the opposite wall covered in mounted skulls of species Gamora did not recognize. A number of peculiarities littered the rest of the room, the most normal of which was a floating red-gold settee.

The Collector disappeared through a door, returning with a serving tray holding six fiercely pink frosted drinks and a single pitcher of water.

No server, Gamora noted. Interesting. The Collector normally reveled in having people at his beck and call.

Groot had the choice of the zengrita or the water, and took the latter. The rest of them gracefully accepted their drinks. Gamora and Quill made brief eye contact, and she nodded. She'd refrain from sipping until a few minutes had passed. They needed a backup in case the drinks were spiked.

"Groot?" Quill asked casually. The way he eyed the Collector instead of Groot made it clear he was bringing up the topic, rather than addressing their teammate.

"Groot," the Collector agreed.

"I am Groot." Groot practically sighed the words.

The Collector put aside the serving tray, sat down in a plush seat before the console, and tapped several keys. A holo zapped out from one of the screens in the wall, fizzling until it took shape.

"This is a live feed from the arboretum." He sipped his drink, taking a moment to revel in the taste and ignoring the impatient faces around him. "Ah, there he is now."

The arboretum was a colorful, dense mass of trees and shrubbery with small creatures flitting about in the undergrowth. There, at the corner of the feed, a familiar shape walked a narrow path. He bowed to avoid a low-hanging branch.

"*Groot?*" Rocket said. "Gotta say, this one looks a hell of lot like you, buddy."

Groot stared at the screen, his jaw dropping open. "I am Groot!"

"I am pleased to introduce my most recent addition to the arboretum," the Collector said. "A *Flora colossus.*"

7

WAIT, you have one already?" Quill turned to the Collector. "Why did you—"

"Where is this arboretum?" Drax demanded. He did not care *why* when there were more immediate problems to address. "We will go there. Now."

"Where did you find him?" Gamora asked.

The Collector ignored the frenzy, watching the Groot holo from his high-backed chair. The camera followed the Groot, sometimes zooming out to show his surroundings, sometimes zooming in so close that his face stretched the width of the room.

Drax inspected the projection, trying to find some trick. The *Flora colossus* looked every inch like Groot: the set of his eyes, the deliberate movements, the slowly growing smile as a cloud of bright bugs whirled around him.

"I am Groot," Groot—*their* Groot, standing right beside Drax—said in shock. He reached for his look-alike, his fingers passing straight through the holo screen.

The Collector swirled his drink. "My friends, I'm sure you appreciate my diligence in growing my own *Flora colossus,* rather than taking an existing specimen from its natural habitat on the Branch Worlds' Planet X."

The Collector was pushing it. A lot. He was also, however, finally starting to talk about something other than fish.

"Elaborate," Drax said.

If the other Guardians insisted on hearing the *why* and *how* before leaving for the arboretum, Drax could at least attempt to speed up the explanation.

"He's not just any *Flora colossus,* is he?" Gamora studied the projection. "He's an exact duplicate of our Groot. Just like the one at the Kyln. How? We can regrow Groot after he's been destroyed, but it shouldn't be possible to grow a second one while he's still walking and talking. There's only one Groot at a time."

Or so they had thought.

Drax finished his drink and thunked the empty glass down on the control panel. "Answer my friend's questions."

The Collector smiled. "As Gamora says: Once your Groot is destroyed, he can be regrown. Every shard has the potential to flourish anew. Once a single shard is planted and Groot's consciousness takes root inside it—you must forgive my pun there—the potential of the remaining shards dims. Several weeks ago, I retrieved a large splinter from the site of one of your battles. After some experimentation, I found myself able to revive this shard's potential. When one has lived as long as I have, one picks up various obscure but useful branches of science."

"*Branches?* That another pun?" Rocket said, glaring.

"Ah. Perhaps. Now: Before my specimen made it to adulthood, there was an…incident. My assistant took her leave without informing me and destroyed part of my collection as she went. Another part went missing—my prized *Flora colossus.* Naturally, I have been searching for my assistant since. She appears to have taken the *Flora colossus* in order to grow and sell duplicates. A side effect of my manipulations is that it opened the floodgates: Using branches from the altered specimen, it has become possible to *continue* growing new, identical *Flora colossi.* She has…taken full advantage of that fact."

"So—*all* the *Flora colossi* she's selling are Groot dupes?" Rocket sounded horrified. "How many?"

"I do not know." The Collector tipped his drink toward the holo. "I retrieved this particular specimen from one of her customers I tracked. As delighted as I am to welcome him to my collection—"

"You realized," Quill interrupted, "friends don't clone friends? And then imprison that clone? And then imprison a clone of that clone? And then proudly show off that clone to said friends? You—you have a *terrible* idea of friendship, Tivan! Watch *My Little Pony,* bro. There are some life lessons you need to learn."

"Can we shoot him yet?" Rocket asked.

"Or stab," Drax said.

Quill gulped down his drink and wiped his mouth. "Getting tempted."

Rocket snarled. "This is great. Real great. There are who-knows-how-many Groots to track down, and that number is only gonna grow. Soon, her buyers'll duplicate and sell their Groots, and *those* buyers will do the same, and then we got a real problem of multiplication on our hands."

"This could get out of control," Drax agreed.

"Ah, thankfully, no," the Collector said. "I've examined this specimen. He appears to be—shall we say, sterile? He is not capable of growing other *Flora colossi* like the one I manipulated. In fact, I suspect he would not even be able to regrow himself if too badly damaged. My assistant altered him. She stole my research when she took her leave. Although it is not possible for a brain as…*mortal* as hers to comprehend the process fully, she appears to have found a crude way of once more blocking the shards' potential to grow new Groots. She must have wanted to avoid competing sources of *Flora colossi.*"

"So she can grow as many as she wants…but if one of *her* Groots is destroyed, he's gone for good?" Quill frowned at the projection of the Groot. "He's a dead end. A mayfly."

"That is cruel," Gamora said from beside Drax. He nodded his agreement.

"Your assistant is some kinda scientist?" Rocket scrunched up his face.

"She is a botanist, in fact. Still a student, but an advanced one: She is DiMavi, and they choose their specialties young. Her skill is likely why she decided to take the *Flora colossus.*"

"Enough of this," Gamora said. "What are you after, Tivan?"

"Gamora. Ever the delight." The Collector smiled. "I want to find my assistant and the specimens she sold. For two reasons. One, I was exceedingly proud of my original *Flora colossus*—not only a highly unusual species in this part of the galaxy, but a genetic duplicate of a genuine Guardian of the Galaxy. The existence of further duplicates significantly lowers its value."

"I know shooting him won't *kill* him," Rocket said, one hand on his gun, "but it'll probably hurt, right?"

"Two," the Collector went on after a sideways glance at Rocket, "the more time passes, the weaker this *Flora colossus* becomes. It is not only him, I see."

"I am Groot?" Groot said. The Collector was eying him.

"You shuffle your feet. You only noticed your duplicate in the holo once Rocket did. You drank the entire pitcher of water within seconds, as though your body craved it. Your response time…" He spun the serving tray toward Groot, who fumbled for it. The tray skimmed his fingers, changed course, and clattered into the wall behind him. Groot cringed at the sound. The Collector merely shrugged. "Your response time has been better, no?"

"I am Groot," he said sheepishly.

Drax had his hands on his blades the second the Collector tossed the tray, ready to jump in and defend his friend. Now he relaxed his grip slightly, but he stayed on edge.

The Collector was too confident.

Drax did not like it.

"I had a telepath and mystic feel out the situation. They say my specimen has weakened, both mentally and physically. His life force is slowly, constantly draining out, sometimes in spurts. They felt it scatter to separate points."

"One Groot at a time," Gamora said, echoing her earlier words.

"There's only so much Groot to go around, huh?" Rocket's arms were crossed, his gun forgotten by his side and his glass half-empty on the floor.

"I am Groot?" Groot said, unsure.

Quill frowned. "You're saying every time this assistant grows a new sapling, a little of our Groot drains away?"

"It appears so," the Collector said. "And as these saplings grow, they need more energy, too."

"So they're connected? They share a mind?" Gamora watched Groot. "Did you sense that other Groot somehow…?"

"I am Groot."

"That's a 'no,' I assume?" the Collector asked.

"You assume correctly," Drax said.

"Pity. My mystic thought the same. There is no psionic connection between them, except for the essential life force they share."

"So we've got enough energy to power a single Groot, divvied up between who-knows-how-many bodies," Rocket summarized. "Wow, Collector, you really did a bang-up job here, didn't you?"

"So, hey, I have a funny question." Quill held a thumb to his temple and index finger to his forehead as though trying hard to make sense of something. "You know there's no chance in hell we'll walk away with that Groot stuck in your arboretum. Why are you telling us all this?"

"Ah!" The Collector sat up straighter. "Now we arrive at the interesting part. Would you like another drink?"

"No," Quill said.

"No," Drax and Gamora added.

"Yes," Rocket said. He shrugged. "Least he can do."

The Collector laughed. "How about I do even better, yes? I offer you my help. We want the same thing: to find and stop the seller, and to find the other Groots. You may need my resources or my knowledge of my assistant. I may need your unique skill sets. Shall we work together?"

Quill regarded him for a moment. "Yeah, so, you didn't answer my question. Your Groot isn't staying."

"I propose a trade." The Collector steepled his fingers. "If you help me find my assistant and allow me to deal with her, you may take my specimen. No fighting. No arguing. No tricks. The *Flora colossus* will remain here in the meantime, so that I can be confident of your utmost devotion to our cooperation. As you can see, he is not being harmed."

"An assistant is worth more to you than a *Flora colossus?*" Drax asked.

The Collector's face darkened. "I do not take kindly to betrayal."

That part, Drax believed. It set his mind at ease about working with the Collector—but only marginally.

"So what's your plan?" Rocket asked.

"We set out together. I have a lead on buyers who may know my assistant's location." His mouth curved into an almost-smile. "One of these leads is on a nearby moon—"

"Yeah, hold up?" Quill raised a hand as though requesting a teacher's attention. Once he had everyone's eyes on him, he extended an index finger at the projection. "You said you got that Groot from a buyer, right? It was one your assistant grew, not the one you grew yourself?"

"Yes."

"So, duh, we just ask the Groot where she grew him," Rocket said.

The Collector paused.

"Yeah, feeling dumb yet?"

"In my defense," he said primly, "it really does *sound* like he is simply repeating his name."

Groot sighed. "I am Groot."

"He gets that a lot," Drax translated.

"We do nothing without discussing it with Groot. Both of them." Gamora had barely touched her zengrita. Now, she knocked it back in one go.

The Collector winced. "You're supposed to *nurse* that drink—"

Drax stepped forward. "Take us to him."

8

GAMORA would've been impressed with the arboretum, had she not been so focused on tracking the other Groot.

"Groot!" she called.

The others fanned out and did the same.

"I am *Groot!*" The real Groot's voice didn't reach far. The look on his face seemed partially interested, partially unsure. The trees ranged from narrow saplings to oaks so thick they had to be ancient; the ground from rock to dirt to grass to a bed of leaves. The scent was sharp and fresh, and so unlike either their ship or the cities they tended to visit, that Gamora couldn't help taking a second to close her eyes and breathe in deeply.

Under other circumstances, she imagined this really could be Groot's dream environment—but not without other people. Groot loved companionship too much to be alone for long.

Something rustled through the underbrush. She looked over just in time to see a fluffy banded tail skittering away from them.

"Is that—?" Rocket asked.

"—an Earth raccoon?" Quill looked at the Collector following behind them.

"Groot seems to get along with them," the Collector said dryly. "I thought he might feel more at ease."

Rocket stared at the spot where the raccoon had disappeared. "Cree-eepy. Didya see those stubby little paws?" He cocked his head as if listening, and peered intently through the trees. "Oh! Groot! I see him." Within seconds, he was gone, crashing through the underbrush. Quill followed.

After a moment, Gamora spotted him as well. The other Groot had waded hip-deep into a lake behind the trees, and was taking long, stumbling steps toward the shore. "I am Groot?" he called out. "I am Groot?"

He was calling their names.

Gamora knew she shouldn't be surprised, but the realization that he knew them still knocked her for a loop.

"Are they the same person?" Drax said, puzzled.

"Groot's memories and personality are intact whenever he grows back," she said. "The same seems to apply in this case."

"I am Groot." Their Groot smiled feebly at them, then swerved through the sparse trees to follow Rocket.

"A lovely place, is it not?" The Collector lingered behind with Drax and Gamora. "I had been planning to find other species from his planet to make it feel more like home. I treat my rare specimens well."

"You're right," Gamora said. "It's lovely. For being *sold into captivity.*"

She moved forward without another word. They had given the Collector the benefit of the doubt; he had lost it.

Quill and Rocket were already talking to the other Groot when she approached. With both Groots this close by, she could see the differences. The other Groot was younger—a little smaller, narrower, greener.

"I am Groot," he said, gesturing animatedly. "I am Groot—I am Groot!"

"Are you serious? What a douche." Quill half-turned on Gamora's approach. "Did you catch that? About the guy who bought him as a sapling? At least Groot stuck a branch through the guy's neck the moment the Collector distracted him—that's some comfort."

The Groot bared his teeth. "I. Am. *Groot*."

Gamora cocked her head. Violence was not unlike the Groot they knew, as long as the people deserved it—and it sounded like this man had.

But their Groot was not known for grimly enjoying that violence.

Then again, Groot had never been regrown by someone other than the Guardians before; he'd never woken up as a sapling only to find himself mass-produced and sold against his will. That, she assumed, might change a person.

"I'm sorry," she said. "We didn't know."

"How has the Collector treated you?" Quill asked.

The answer came more curtly now. "I am Groot."

The Collector wouldn't have allowed them to talk to this Groot if he had really been mistreated, so the semi-positive answer didn't come as a surprise.

It wasn't about how the Collector treated him. It was about him trapping Groot in the first place.

"I am Groot," their Groot said quietly.

"Look, we need to find the person behind this," Quill said. "We already know *who*—"

"Her name is Kiya," the Collector said.

"Where did she grow you? Do you know?"

The young Groot nodded and shot a dark look at the Collector. "I am Groot."

"Cool." Quill leaned against a tree. "The way I see it, we have two options. One, we take you with us, blow some stuff up, and try to find the seller ourselves, since I'm pretty sure Tivan here wouldn't want to help us out after that. Two, the five of us cooperate with him to try to find the seller together. Once we do, he says he'll let you go."

"I vote for blowing stuff up," Rocket said.

Drax nodded. "If Groot knows where to find the seller, we do not need the Collector's help. I do not trust him."

"You are all aware that I can hear you?" the Collector asked.

"We truly don't care," Gamora said.

"Friend rights are waived," Quill agreed.

"Consider," the Collector said, "that this girl escaped this station by herself, taking with her a securely guarded specimen from my collection. Do you think that's an easy task?"

"I'm thinking—" Rocket started.

The Collector snapped his fingers.

Two trees nearby slid open, revealing slick machine guns pointed straight at them. A camera bot hovered down from the canopy, announcing, *"Six targets in sight."* Three others zoomed in close and repeated the message. *"Six targets in sight."*

Gamora had a feeling they weren't solely camera bots.

Quill reached for his element gun. "Guys—" He didn't need to say it. They instantly formed a back-to-back circle, weapons out, eyes on the targets.

"No need." Another snap of the Collector's fingers. The bots disappeared back into the canopy. The trees slid closed. Within seconds, the scene was indistinguishable from any regular forest. "Just displaying the most visible elements of my security system. To make a point. Yes?"

"I want your toys so bad," Rocket sulked.

"What point? That getting out of here with Groot won't be as easy as we thought?" Quill asked. "That doesn't intimidate us."

"Are you saying I would threaten my dear friends? Never," he said slickly. "I'm saying that grabbing *her* might not be as easy as you thought— because she made it out of here unscathed. I know Kiya better than any of you. Working together would increase our chances."

Quill was silent.

Gamora studied the forest, searching for the narrow slits where the trees had opened up. That she hadn't spotted them at first unnerved her greatly. She couldn't see the camera bots anymore either, nor could she detect the other security measures the Collector had hinted at.

If they wanted to, they could escape. They'd faced worse.

But it wouldn't be easy.

"I am Groot." The other Groot stepped forward until he was face-to-face with the Collector, who looked up unruffled, his gleaming purple cloak entirely at odds with the green and brown surrounding him.

"Yes?" He sipped the zengrita he'd brought with him, peering up at the Groot through his eyelashes.

"I am Groot. I am Groot."

"A translation, if you please?" the Collector asked.

The Groot turned and stalked off.

"I am Groot?" Their Groot ran after his counterpart. His foot caught on a root and he stumbled, only just catching himself.

"He said 'screw you,'" Rocket informed the Collector, "and gave us the location where your assistant grew him."

"That first part wasn't paraphrased this time," Quill said.

"He chose to stay for now, then? Wise."

"I have a question." Drax had his arms crossed. Their Groot returned, his face in a twisted frown. Two toes had broken off from his stumble. "Would eliminating the duplicates help our companion regain his strength?"

"Drax!" Rocket snarled.

"I am Groot?" Groot asked, startled.

Gamora shook her head. "Drax, we're not solving this problem by killing innocents. Especially when those innocents are our friend."

She'd have been lying, though, if she claimed she hadn't wondered about it herself. It was a straightforward, elegant, logical solution, and it played to her strengths.

Of course she had thought of it. First thing.

She'd then summarily dismissed the notion. It didn't fit the Guardians. It didn't fit *her*—not anymore, no matter how much those first instincts said otherwise.

"We would be helping him." Drax clapped Groot on the back. "We have the true Groot. We must return his life energy to him."

"I am Groot," Groot said hesitantly, and looked at Quill.

"We're not doing this." Gamora's voice was flat. She was not going to argue. "*I* am not doing this."

"Yeah, I'm with Gammy. What's wrong with you, Drax?" Rocket said.

"We would be naive to ignore the option. If you do not think yourselves capable, I will take on the burden."

Rocket glared. "The hell you will—"

"All right, all right," Quill said. "It may not even be relevant. Tivan, *would* it solve the problem?"

"I need to gather more specimens so I can run experiments."

"I'm sure. Come on, would you please stop giving Rocket excuses to shoot you? It'd just be messy for everyone involved."

"Primarily for Rocket, I assure you." The Collector took another sip of his zengrita and smacked his lips. "Ahhhh."

"Yeah, I really don't need more excuses than the ones I've already got," Rocket grumbled.

"From what I can tell, however," the Collector went on, "it would not solve the problem. One Groot unfortunately passed away when I attempted to retrieve him; it made no difference in this Groot's behavior."

"Groot?" Gamora said. "Do you feel different since what happened at the Kyln? Stronger?"

He hesitated, then shook his head.

"So we have a deal, yes?" the Collector asked brightly.

"Do we?" Quill eyed the group.

Rocket shrugged.

"I am Groot."

"I suppose," Gamora said.

"I dislike it," Drax said.

"It looks like we're on board, Tivan."

"*Excellent.* I do love your enthusiasm. I look forward to working together."

"Don't screw with us," Gamora said. "Let's go."

She walked past the Collector toward the exit, searching for the other Groot in the distance. He'd be watching them—she knew that, because she knew their own Groot would, too.

It felt both comforting and disconcerting to think that all these versions of Groot genuinely were the same. Comforting, because it meant Groot was still their friend; nothing so simple as this could destroy him. Disconcerting, because it meant that Groot—his body, his mind, his memories, everything that made him *him*—was scattered, at the mercy of whoever bought him, and growing weaker by the minute.

Gamora had already been worried about one Groot.

Now she had a galaxy of them to worry about.

9

ONE HOUR into the three-hour flight to Pirinida, the planet the Collector's Groot had named, Rocket still hadn't shot the Collector.

He was kinda proud of himself. Talk about discipline.

Shooting the guy wouldn't do them a lick of good, of course, but shooting terrible people was really more about the *feeling,* about the *principle* of the matter.

One thing helped: The Collector might be terrible, but his assistant was worse. Kiya was the one who'd actually grown and sold the Groots.

"Got anything yet?" Rocket asked.

Quill sat with his legs crossed on the dash, the pilot's seat tilted back as he tapped lazily at the holo in front of him. "I found a couple of Kiyas—news, arrest reports, the works; it's a common name—but nope. None of them seem to be her."

"So we still know nothing."

Quill shrugged. "I wasn't expecting to find much. It's not like the Collector would hire a celebrity or ex-criminal. And I use 'hire' loosely—I doubt there was payment or, you know, consent. We'll worry about that once we find her. Gamora's busy prying more info out of the Collector. All we've got now is that the girl is smart enough to work around his security, and that she has both a literal and figurative green thumb. Anything else… well, the fact that the Collector knows Kiya and we don't is the main reason we need him. He won't give up that advantage."

"Yeah, he wants us to help him *real* bad. All that sucking up? *Ooooh, my beloved friends,* blah blah blah."

Quill leaned his head back and turned toward Rocket, his holo forgotten. He blew a floppy lock of hair from his forehead. "Does that worry you?"

"Worry me? Nah. Means he's the one who's worried. He can't handle her by himself."

"What kind of person did he hire as an assistant, that she's so dangerous?"

"Maybe he got bored." Rocket shot Quill a sidelong glance. "No luck on my end, either. Whoever handles the Collector's security knows their stuff."

They'd asked the Collector for footage of Kiya's escape. He'd shown them a couple of seconds—enough to prove she really had broken out with the altered Groot as he'd claimed—but no more. It wasn't surprising that he wouldn't share a step-by-step instruction video showing how to get past his security setup. What *was* surprising was that Rocket had spent the past hour trying to hack into the Collector's systems for the full footage, and he'd barely made any progress.

"So we're going in blind. No big."

Rocket smiled toothily. "Could be a fun challenge."

"There is a challenge?" Drax asked, entering the bridge behind them.

"Coming up in two hours," Rocket said.

"Ah, yes. Very well. We will face it together." Drax sat himself in the gunner's chair, tilting it back the same way Quill had and making a satisfied sound.

"Am I the only one actually working?" Rocket peered past the side of his chair. "Can I get a nap? No one ever asks if I want a nap."

"I do not enjoy it back there. The Collector is…vexing."

"What's happening?" Quill asked.

"He keeps asking questions." Drax propped himself up on his elbows. "My physical appearance. My wife. My daughter. My present motivations. He asked"—his face twisted into a frown—"what I wore on the day I lost my family."

"What you were *wearing?* You're kidding." Rocket gawked. Was that the kind of thing the Collector fantasized about in his off time?

"He just wants something for his collection," Quill said. "'Pants of Drax the Destroyer: worn on the day his life irrevocably changed.' That kind of thing."

"Yes." Pause. "I punched him."

"Seems fair. Uh, he's not breaking the ship or trying to kill anyone right now, is he?"

"The Collector seemed displeased," Drax said. "I couldn't gauge his reaction better. Gamora intervened and suggested I leave."

"Call me next time you punch him, will you?" Rocket said.

"I am glad you are not upset about my earlier proposal, Rocket."

"Eh?" He leaned in, scanning the code on his screen like he might suddenly have an epiphany and waltz right into the Collector's system. "Why would I get upset? I'm not a flarking child."

"You reacted strongly to my suggestion of eliminating the other *Flora colossi.*"

"I ain't upset!"

"I had thought, as Groot is your friend, you would want to—"

"*I ain't upset!* Drop it, will you?" He glared over his shoulder, keeping one hand on the control panel. "Eesh, Drax! It was a stupid idea, is all."

"Yeah, hey, heyyy." Quill raised both hands in some kind of peacemaking symbol. "How about we focus on finding the seller, all right? Even if your idea did work, Drax, Kiya would only grow more Groot saplings—Grootlings?—in the meantime. We're better off going to the source. We'll find the rest of the Groots and figure out how to help our Groot after that."

"Yeah. Yeah, go to the source, that's exactly what I was thinking." Rocket scowled at the code on the screen. Drax would get the message, and if he didn't, Rocket could always spell it out for him. He was really good at clarifying his point. He could use props and everything.

Although—

He spun his chair around. "Hey, you're not gonna talk to Groot about your stupid idea again either, all right? There's no need to, you know, waste his energy. He doesn't wanna hear it."

Drax stood, towering over the two of them in their seats. If he'd meant to be intimidating, it didn't work: Rocket had spent his whole life looking up at people three times his size. The only difference between shooting someone in the face from below or from eye level was the location of the brain-splat. The tall ones never seemed to realize that.

"What?" Rocket said.

"I understand," Drax said.

"Eh?"

"I only meant to help Groot. I do not wish to hurt his feelings."

"Psh." Rocket swiveled his chair back around. He wasn't even sure why he'd said it. Groot had been there when Drax first brought up the idea—it wasn't like he didn't already know. He could look after himself. "Whatever, Drax. Do what you want."

THEY landed out of sight.

"All right." Peter took the lead as they exited the ship, his boots clanging on the extended ramp. "Our scanners placed someone warm-blooded exactly where that other Groot said Kiya had grown him, plus a moving shape that may be a *Flora colossus.*" Just as he was about to step off the ramp and onto the dry ground, he kicked off instead, activating his boot propulsors to hover several feet up.

He surveyed their surroundings. They had landed the ship behind a sandy, cactus-covered hill, the only real shelter in the area—the rest was all sparse trees and cracked ground. Across the empty stretch of land sat the greenhouse they'd zeroed in on. It was far enough from the nearest town that Kiya could grow her *Flora colossi* without prying eyes, but close enough to an automated space elevator to reach a decent transport station and travel the galaxy easily. Smart location—even if the nightlife left a lot to be desired.

"All right. Tivan, Drax, you're with me. We'll knock on the door real polite-like. Gamora, Rocket, Groot, spread out. If we call for backup or she slips past us and tries to run, you know what to do."

Rocket slammed a button on his wrist communicator, prompting the ship behind him to lock up tight, and gave a lazy salute. Groot mimicked the movement.

They set off, Drax and Tivan scrabbling up the hill while Peter flew overhead, flicking his helmet active. A pleasant, second-long tingle flitted across his face as the mask formed and the faintest shade of red slid over his view of the world. He did another check of the greenhouse. The warm-blooded shape was inside, pacing in an agitated fashion. The possible *Flora colossus* lumbered in its wake.

Over comms, he heard the others move into position.

The area around the greenhouse was deserted, aside from a foxlike shape darting over a hill in the distance, and fist-sized sand scorpions scuttling away from Drax and Tivan. Pools of crystal twining between the succulents and rocks formed splashes of fierce white against the ground, reflecting the sun so brightly they hurt to look at. In the distance, gleaming metal spires jutted up high from the horizon. That had to be the town he'd seen on the scans. Pirinida was sparsely populated, and its inhabitants fiercely religious—Peter remembered something about the spires being a sign of worship.

This was definitely not the first place they'd have looked for the greenhouse.

The structure itself almost blended into its environment. A dusky gray-brown building adjoined the greenhouse, which was all panes of bright white glass.

The panes. Huh.

He slowed down so Tivan and Drax, below him, could catch up. "You see that?" he called.

"I see it," Drax said.

"Mm? Ah. That missing pane?" Tivan sounded like he was barely paying attention. He was holding his cape high, trying to walk at a distinguished pace instead of crashing through the landscape like Drax. His attempts were unsuccessful: Prickly succulents snared his clothes, inconvenient rocks meant he had to sidestep more often than not, and cracked ground alternated with soft pools of sand that were easy to sink into.

He had spotted it, at least. One of the greenhouse's floor-to-ceiling panes was gone. The skeleton frame held only a few remaining shards.

"The person inside looks agitated," Peter said. "Maybe they're the one who broke the glass."

A voice exploded from the greenhouse. "That *conniving, untrustworthy, duplicitous krutacker!*"

Mere feet away from the greenhouse, Peter descended to the ground. He landed beside Drax. "Full points if he can spell all those words, too."

"He?" Drax asked.

"That voice. DiMavi women don't sound like that. I should know. I've heard them happy—*seriously* happy. And angry—*seriously* angry—"

"That is definitely not Kiya." The Collector kicked his boots against a nearby rock to get rid of the sand in his soles.

Peter sighed. "That's what I was worried about."

He stepped inside the greenhouse through the broken window pane. A fractured pot on the ground—empty. A table stood in the center, and a counter ran along the walls, covered in dried dirt scattered in clumps. A thin layer of sand had blown inside, untouched except for recent footsteps. Someone had been hurried enough to leave behind smears.

"Who the flark are you?" a voice demanded. A Krylorian male stood in the doorway to the house, fists balled.

"Galaxy, Guardians of the," Peter replied. "You're here for Kiya?"

"You know her?" He stepped forward. "Where'd she go? That krut—"

"Groot!" Drax interrupted.

"Hey, Groot! Bro!" Peter said.

The *Flora colossus* that appeared behind the Krylorian was the size of the Collector's—only slightly younger than their own. A bronze collar sat tightly around his neck. He squinted his eyes at Drax and Peter, then at Tivan. "I am Groot? I am Groot? I am Groot!"

"Oh, shuddup already!" the Krylorian exclaimed. "Now's the time you decide to act lively?" He turned back to Peter. "You bought one of these useless bags of timber, as well, I take it?"

"I am *Groot.*"

"Is that all they say? Ugh, maybe it's just mine. I should've known it was broken. It's such a sham. She showed one lifting a damn cargo ship, and this one can't even lift my shuttle. And it *won't shut up.*"

The Groot snarled. "I—am—"

"Nuh-uh." He held up his arm, which featured a bracelet shaded similarly to the Groot's collar.

"—Groot," he finished, dejected.

"Hold on a minute here," Peter said. "You got a, what is that, a zappy thing?"

"What, you didn't?" He laughed. "How else you gonna control these dumb things? You gotta be able to punish 'em. They misbehave, they get zapped. Here, let me show—"

One second Peter was standing across the room, the table between him and the Krylorian; the next they stood face-to-face, his element gun pressed against the guy's nose. "Yeah, no. Hit that button and you're a block of ice. And then Drax will punch the block of ice. Right, Drax?"

Drax nodded tersely. "Correct."

"This is so *interesting,*" the Collector enthused.

The Krylorian blinked rapidly. "If—if anything happens to me, the tree doesn't just get zapped, it blows up. There's a fail-safe."

"I am Groot," the Groot said, resigned.

"Hmm. Hold on a moment." Peter brought his free hand to the side of his helmet. "Rocket, I'm sending you my feed. Tell me what I'm seeing."

"The pink guy? Your gun?" A few moments of silence. "Hmm. That bracelet is a P7 Sartis. It's the entry-level version to the P9, which—"

"If we decide to grievously injure this individual, will anything happen to this Groot?" Peter didn't want to see a second Groot blow up in front of him—especially if these Groots Kiya had grown couldn't grow back after being destroyed, like the Collector had suggested. Once gone, they stayed gone.

At the question, Rocket whooped out a laugh so sharp Peter almost cringed from the sound. "Ha! No way."

"If we smash up the bracelet or collar, will anything happen to this Groot?"

"Naw, you need a P11 for that, at minimum—nasty piece of work, real hard to circumvent. This one doesn't even have 'splosive capabilities. It just zaps. Groot'll be fine. What kinda fairy tales is he telling you?"

More important, what kind of fairy tales had he told the poor Groot? Demeaning him, zapping him, keeping him obedient with threats of a false fail-safe—

This was how Kiya's buyers were treating the Groots they bought?

"Thanks, Rocket. You're a gem." Peter closed the connection.

The Krylorian had sweat drops forming by his temple, leaving deep pink tracks on his skin.

"What did Rocket say?" Tivan seemed eager to hear.

"Good news!" Peter lowered the element gun from the Krylorian's face. "You're full of crap, and we're taking Groot."

"I am Groot?"

"Oh, but he's probably going to kick your ass first."

"I am *Groot.*"

10

THEY turned the building inside out. Kiya had lived there—that much was clear—but she'd left no clues as to where she'd gone next. The Groot they'd freed from the Krylorian didn't know either: He'd been grown right there, and Kiya had never breathed a word about a backup plan during his youth in the greenhouse.

"Aaaand we're back to zero," Quill said, once they'd returned to the Guardians' ship. He slumped in his chair and gave the kitchen table a petulant kick.

"*That'll* help," Gamora said. She shared his frustration, though. She peered at the two Groots conversing in the corner. If it weren't for their difference in age, it'd be impossible to tell their Groot from the duplicate.

"Well, this new Groot and the Collector's are both at least a couple weeks old," Rocket said. "They left the greenhouse ages ago. Leaves a lotta time for Kiya to move."

"We're gonna need a littler Groot."

"That's what I'm sayin'."

"I was making a ref—never *mind*. You're all heathens." Quill said the last part at a mumble.

The five of them were sitting at the ship's kitchen table not far from the Groots. Drax and Rocket were drinking; the others were either pensive or peeved.

"Are your missions usually this filthy?" the Collector asked, scrubbing the dirt from his cloak.

"They're usually worse." Gamora ran a hand through her hair. "You said you had a lead on other duplicates. Let's return to that plan. Are they younger?"

"Unclear," he said. "I wonder: Is it your usual tactic to split up? Would you say—"

"Can we focus?" Gamora said.

The interest the Collector had shown in the Guardians lately was unusual and unwanted, and couldn't be linked solely to his desire to fill his museum. This went further. The Collector had started his collection ages ago to stave off the inevitable boredom that came with immortality; his interest in the team had to be born of the same ennui. He'd probably latched onto them as an intriguing curiosity, a way to pass the time—since he had so *much* of it—and the result was a zillion questions and creepy looks. The way he watched her now, more intrigued than intimidated, was only one example.

It was enough to make her want a steam shower.

"You're completely right, Gamora. I do not mean to interrupt your strategy session." The Collector tented his fingers and smiled eagerly. "Carry on."

"Quill?" she said, suppressing the urge to groan. "Do *we* have any leads?"

Quill shook his head. "I reached out to our contacts at the Knowhere market. They'll keep an eye out."

"I set up a program to watch any rumblings on the channels," Rocket said. "I got one or two leads, but they were talking about *big* tree creatures. If they're Groots, they're probably too old to lead us to Kiya's new location, but I say let's try 'em."

Gamora nodded. "I checked with my own contacts. One thought she'd seen a *Flora colossus,* but it turned out to be a Cotati."

"This Kiya may not have been at her new location long enough." Drax leaned into the table, both hands wrapped around his drink. "If the Groots grown there are too young to sell, we may not find her for a long time yet."

"We're still gonna go find the bigger ones, right?" Rocket said impatiently. "Not like we got better leads."

Quill looked unconvinced. "Yeah, but if we go after the big ones, Kiya might grow and sell more Groots in the meantime, maybe move again... Groot would only get worse."

After the Groot they'd found had ripped off his collar, he'd walked to the ship alongside them: The trip had taken twice as long as it should have, with uncertainty, imbalance, and weakness threaded through the Groot's every movement.

"So you wanna leave the others?" Rocket said.

"Every few hours, there might be more 'others' being grown! The galaxy could be crawling with them by next week, for all we know."

They continued to go around in circles, reaching nothing except the very end of Gamora's patience.

"I may have a solution," the Collector said finally.

"We're all ears, dude." Quill sounded tired. They'd grabbed naps here and there, but it had been more than a day since they'd gotten any real sleep. He looked up at the Collector with forced interest and a weary smile.

The Collector pulled a communicator from his cloak and placed it on the table. A holo popped out to fill the space between them. He rapidly tapped and swiped the projection until a video feed opened.

"The duplicate in my arboretum is not the only one I've retrieved," he admitted. "In my search for Kiya, I found other—"

"Oh, hey, look who admits to being a big freaking liar!" Quill was suddenly wide awake. He slapped a palm on the table loudly enough to jolt everyone sitting at it. "*Damn,* but that took a while. How much desperation did you want from us? Was there a quota you needed filled?"

"Ha!" Rocket said. "Suck it up, Quill, and hand over those hundred units. I knew he wouldn't crack so easy."

The Collector sat stone-still. "You were baiting me?"

"Consider it a test," Gamora said.

"I see. And did I win, or did I lose?"

"You told us the truth. You win. The truth means you're a terrible creature. You lose." She leaned in. "Open your comms. We'll talk to these other Groots."

"I am Groot." The voice rumbled from the corner of the room. Disturbingly, Gamora couldn't identify who the voice belonged to: their Groot, or his duplicate from Pirinida. Only when she turned did she see it was theirs.

"I know," she told him quietly. She didn't like knowing they'd left those Groots behind at the Collector's museum, either.

The Collector let out an abrupt laugh. "*Ha!*"

"What's so funny?" Rocket said, immediately wary.

"The fact that after billions of years in this universe, you can all still surprise me, dear Rocket."

Rocket turned to Groot, his face a mask of disgust. "Did he just call me *dear?*"

"I am Groot." He pointed a long finger at the holo.

The table fell quiet, staring at the projection. This time, they weren't looking at the arboretum. The Collector had patched them into a massive, white-tiled room. A couple of water troughs and potted shrubs stood to the side. A trio of Groots sat on the dirt floor, talking to each other in voices too low to understand. The middle one had to be about a week old. The Groots were hemmed in by a force field on both sides of the room—that twitching in the air left no doubt about it.

The Collector cleared his voice. "You can talk to them."

"Groot?" Rocket climbed from his chair atop the table. "Groot, buddy? It's us. You remember us, right?"

The three Groots looked around. One pushed to his feet, confused. "I am Groot?"

"They are receiving audio only," the Collector said.

"I can see that," Rocket said, irritated. "Listen, Groot, we're coming for you. All right? Hang in there."

"I am Groot," their Groot said urgently, leaning in behind Rocket. "I am Groot!"

"I am Groot!" Pirinida's Groot added.

"Is it just you three?" Rocket said. "Are you in the big frog museum? We'll set a course."

"No, we will not," the Collector said. "Can we focus on finding my assistant?"

"Oh, shut up, Tivan," Quill said.

The Collector's head snapped up. Gamora tensed at that look—cool, a hint of annoyance, then a false smile. "Star-Lord. Friend. Do not mistake my amusement for acquiescence. As much as I enjoy the ride, I would also *quite* like to find my assistant. Another day in my care will not kill the *Flora colossi.* As a sign of goodwill, I will, naturally, toss these three specimens in with our deal."

Quill chewed over those words—literally, it seemed, from the way he was rotating his jaw. The Groots and Rocket were still talking rapidly.

"Okay," Quill said, shifting his attention to the three holo Groots. "You, in the middle. You're smallest. Can you tell us where…"

11

THEY couldn't trust him.

They had to trust him.

They couldn't trust him.

"Shut uuuup, brain." Peter turned over in bed, shoving his face into his pillow—as if that would help him get the sleep he needed.

They didn't have much choice but to work with the Collector. Every encounter with him was a game. Once he decided to stop playing…

Peter had enough trust in the Guardians to know they could deal with whatever situation came up, but he'd also seen enough of those situations go from minor to galaxy-wrecking that he wasn't eager to piss off an Elder just yet. He'd play it carefully—for now.

The Collector really had passed the test: He hadn't lied about his assistant being his top priority. If he'd wanted, he could've easily let the Guardians continue talking in circles while he kept the Groots he'd already found safely in his collection.

For all Peter knew, he still might try something like that. Peter had hoped Kiya might be holed up near the Collector's museum. That would've given them an excuse to crash by and pick up the Groots on the way, before the Collector tried anything funny. The location they'd gotten from the younger Groot had been in the exact opposite direction, though, near the center of the Turunal system.

Which meant they would simply have to trust that the Collector would hand over the Groots afterward.

Except they clearly couldn't trust him—

And there his brain went again.

He stared at the ceiling. "Maybe I should be counting Groots."

GAMORA did not like this one bit.

"There are too many people."

The six of them stood on a rooftop across from the location the small Groot had given them: a fourth-floor apartment in a busy port city on a tertiary Kree planet inhabited by a bustling mix of Kree, Spartoi, DiMavi, and others. Ships flew overhead every other minute, the roaring in the air masking the chatter from the street.

"So we'll take a different approach." Quill looked down at the street, one foot propped on the rooftop ledge. Night was falling, but the streets were crowded. His helmet's red eyes glowed fiercely in the dark. "We can't allow her to run. She'll get lost in the crowd. Worst-case scenario, bystanders get hurt. So we go in from multiple angles. Spook her, grab her, then go for whatever Groots she's harboring. I count at least three shapes on my scanner."

"You are certain it is her this time?" Drax asked.

"Seems to be the right size, and all scans check out. Let's take a look. Rocket, you and me will go in the back. Gamora, you and Tivan take the window on this side."

Gamora sat crouched on the ledge. She nodded her assent and continued to check the crowd and surrounding rooftops for signs of danger.

"Groot and Drax—I want you inside the building, by the front door. Block her way out, but don't go in until we say so. It's too small a space. Try not to give anyone a heart attack on your way up."

"I am Groot?"

"Jeez, I dunno. Look harmless."

Groot tried a grin, revealing mossy, splintered teeth.

"Yeahhhh, that'll do the trick." Quill kicked off to hover a couple of feet over the roof. Rocket latched onto his leg and clambered up to settle on his back.

"Let's fly," Rocket said.

Groot and Drax went next. They jumped down, slammed onto the ground below, and made it to the apartment building's front door in seconds, the crowd breaking apart before them. A single kick from Drax knocked the door off its hinges.

Gamora walked backward from the ledge, keeping her eyes on the window Quill had indicated. No movement yet.

"I'm interested. How good is your eyesight?" the Collector asked.

She didn't answer. She visualized Drax and Groot bolting up the stairs. One second. Two. Three. Four. They'd be at the apartment door by now. Time for her to make an entrance.

"Move," she told the Collector.

Gamora took a running leap off the roof. Legs bundled up—hair wafting behind her—the crowd beneath gasping—

Mid-flight, she pointed one leg. The tip of her boot shattered the window. Glass flew in all directions as she landed inside the building in a crouch. A split second to absorb the impact. Another split second before she was upright and moving to make room for the Collector. She took in the apartment. Mattress on the floor, no pillow, the sheets a bundle. Hooked knife beside the mattress, within easy reach. Nothing on the walls. Pots strewn all around, some filled with dirt, others empty. One corner—comparatively tidy—featured a miniature lab setup: table, microscope, an assortment of glass-covered trays of dirt, some with tiny plucks of green or brown sprouting from the earth. Another blade nearby. The scent: dust, earth, water, plants, sweat.

The Collector landed beside her, sending a tremor through the floor. He'd taken longer than she'd expected. Scared to take the leap, in case he slipped and hit the pavement four stories below? Doubtful. Taking the time to watch her jump and land, with that same intrigued, delighted look he wore now? More likely.

A crash came from deeper inside the apartment—another window breaking; had to be Quill and Rocket—followed by a scream. Female. Kiya.

Gamora sprinted across the room, hurdling over a tipped-over chair.

"I am Groot! I am Groot!" The voice sounded alarmed. Wondering what was happening. Not their Groot—one of Kiya's.

Down the hallway. Past a bathroom. Past a startled Groot duplicate half her size. Past the front door Drax and Groot had to be waiting behind. Around a corner—

Where the hall opened into a makeshift greenhouse. A fine, opalescent barrier hovered in the doorpost, holding in the humidity. Behind it: movement.

"Who the flark—" That had to be Kiya again. Loud. Angry. Her voice skipped on the *a* in *flark,* betraying shock or fear or both.

Gamora strode through the barrier, which fizzled around her. The cool hall gave way to wet, hot air inside the greenhouse. Quill and Rocket stood covering both windows. A moist tarp hung from the ceiling and walls. Crappy kitchen in one corner. Almost a dozen pots containing Grootlings in various stages. Kiya, halfway between the door and windows, had her back to Gamora. (Firm shape—stout with muscle and fat. DiMavi-curved ears, the angle indicating youth. Short, white hair. Dark green skin. Gun on her hip. Her stance suggested one thing—*threat.* She'd either gotten over her shock quickly, or she knew how to suppress it. Either way, she was ready for a fight.) Two grown Groots stood near Kiya, startled, their eyes on Rocket.

Rocket was aiming his gun square at the girl. "Guess what, lady. You start cloning and selling people, their friends might come help 'em out."

"Listen—" Kiya said.

(Commanding. Not aggressive yet. Gamora adjusted her initial assessment: ready for a fight, yes, but not eager for one.)

"Listen to *this,*" Rocket said. "It's my favorite sound in the galaxy."

"I am Groot!" a handful of Grootlings yelped. "I am Groot!"

"Rock—!" Quill and Gamora began.

He fired.

Kiya was hemmed in by Groots on either side. Dodging forward or back would get her killed. She went low instead, her body whipping backward in a perfect curve. As her face flipped upside down, her eyes caught Gamora's.

And widened.

The blast seared across Kiya's torso, singeing the front of her jacket. Almost absentmindedly, Gamora twisted her body sideways and flung one arm through the barrier behind her, shoving the Collector out of the way.

The blast went past both Kiya and Gamora and slammed into the hallway wall. It left behind a scorch mark the size of Gamora's head.

It took about half a second, all in all.

Quill yelled at Rocket. The Collector said something; he sounded surprised. The Groots were yelling. Gamora didn't listen. She focused on Kiya, who'd snapped upright and whirled on her. Shock flashed across the girl's face.

"It's you," Kiya breathed.

"We're here for our friend," Gamora said. "Don't give us a reason—"

Kiya pulled her gun, aimed, and fired.

Gamora dove sideways and slid past a table. Dodged the first three blasts. A fourth skimmed her arm. She kept low. One leg went out from under the table to swipe at Kiya, who stepped out of the way. Leaning back, Kiya sent another two blasts at Gamora under the table.

Kiya was better than Gamora had expected.

Surprising.

Also annoying.

Gamora heard the familiar sound of Quill's element gun. She shot forward, knowing Kiya would be distracted by the new threat, and flung her into the wall. She pressed a knee into the girl's hand—which felt strange, too tough—forcing her to drop the gun. Spun her. Wrapped an arm around her neck from behind. Gamora moved in close, her nose in the girl's hair, her breath on her neck. As she tightened her grip, her gaze landed on Kiya's shoulder. A scar disappeared under the line of her jacket.

Kiya tried to fight back, hands clawing for Gamora's hair or eyes. Not a bad move, but basic. The strength with which she strained under Gamora's grip, though… Gamora managed to contain her, but it took more effort than it should've. This was a DiMavi teenager, for crying out loud.

"I am Groot!" The duplicate Groot sounded anxious.

Another Groot let out a snarl of frustration. "I am *Groot.*"

"Kiya." The Collector stepped through the barrier. "You have been a challenge to find."

Kiya should've been weakening, having her air cut off for so long. Instead, she went rigid—then bucked and flailed, screaming with breath she didn't have.

This wasn't anger.

This wasn't shock. It wasn't even fear.

This was *terror.*

"Allow me." The Collector lifted one hand, presenting a circular metal patch Gamora recognized as a neural subduer.

"I am Groot—I am Groot—" The tallest of the Groots flung himself at the Collector. His shoulder hit Tivan's chest, knocking him back. Tivan recovered quickly, tossing the attacking Groot aside with a single gesture.

Another Groot ran straight for Kiya and Gamora. "I am *Groot!*" he pleaded. *Let her go?*

"Groot? What're you talking about?" Rocket said.

The younger Groot yanked at Gamora's arm. Her gaze went from the Collector to Kiya.

"Gamora?" The Collector took a threatening step closer. "We have a deal."

They did.

It wouldn't be breaking the deal to gather further intel, though.

Gamora spun Kiya around to face her, easing her grip, and pushed the girl up against the wall. Kiya gasped for breath. Gamora's arm pressed into her neck, loosely enough for Kiya to talk and breathe, but offering no chance of escape.

They were inches apart. Gamora narrowed her eyes, scrutinized the girl's face for any signs of what she was hiding. Because *some*one was hiding *some*thing. The girl's panic, the Groots helping her—this situation didn't feel right.

"You have two seconds to convince me," Gamora said.

Kiya coughed, gasped. She tried to twist out of Gamora's grip. No, wait: she was twisting to keep an eye on the Collector. Her pupils were dilated in fear. "He—he can't lock me up again—"Another deep, rattling breath.

Okay. Two seconds was perhaps not long enough for someone she'd just choked.

Gamora pushed up the girl's sleeve. All along her arm was the line of a scar. A fresh one, still healing, the green skin puckered and uneven. She pulled down the girl's collar. A horizontal scar stretched from shoulder to shoulder across her collarbone. From the exact center, a straight line slashed down her sternum. Gamora couldn't see how far it went.

She grabbed Kiya's hand and squeezed. There was metal in there, synthetics. She had implants.

Made sense: She was stronger and faster than any DiMavi Gamora had ever met.

What _didn't_ make sense was why the Collector would have an augmented assistant. Even more than that—the implants were so fresh, he had to have been the one who augmented her.

Why?

Gamora locked eyes with Kiya.

The girl looked back, her chin defiantly raised even if her breath still came shakily.

Then Gamora saw it.

The set of her nose. The precise shade of her skin, lighter than most DiMavi Gamora knew. The scent of hair dye.

She pressed a thumb brusquely into Kiya's cheek, ignoring her flinch. Cheekbone. Jawbone. Chin. The structure of her skull—and that knob, right there—

It was the same as Gamora's.

Her grip went slack.

Kiya took the opportunity to lash out. Gamora deflected the attack without looking. Stepped back.

"You're not DiMavi," she said breathlessly.

Kiya was Zen-Whoberian.

12

THE DEAL'S off, Collector," Gamora said. "*Drax!*"

"Wait, what?" Peter sputtered. "Gamora, what—"

A crash sounded from down the hall. Peter would have bet money on it: Kiya's front door was now split in half.

Drax stepped into the room, with Groot right behind him.

"I am Groot!" one of Kiya's Groots said, startled. "*I* am Groot?"

"We're taking the girl," Gamora told Peter. "Drax, keep the Collector busy."

The Collector narrowed his eyes. "You are making a big—"

Then Drax was on him.

He couldn't kill the Elder. But he could buy the team time.

And, based on his jubilant laughter, he would enjoy it.

Peter didn't have a d'ast clue what Gamora was up to, but she'd seen something when inspecting the girl. Whatever it was, he had to trust that Gamora knew what she was doing.

"Rocket! Groot! Take the duplicates to the ship!" He wanted them out of Kiya's and the Collector's hands—and moreover, he wanted them out of danger. This was turning into a brawl with an honest-to-god Elder of the Universe; bystanders could get hurt. And these particular bystanders wouldn't be able to regrow if damaged too badly, thanks to Kiya's manipulations. "You guys"—Peter eyed Kiya's adult Groots—"will you help get them out?"

"I am Groot," they said in harmony.

Of course they would.

Gamora and Drax kept the Collector occupied, Drax still laughing. Rocket and Groot—all of them—were rounding up the Grootlings. The Guardians' Groot sprouted extra arms to hold onto the pots of the younger saplings, letting the ones who could survive without earth crawl all over him and hold on tight.

Kiya dashed for the broken window. Peter spun to catch her, wrapping one arm around her waist. "Hi," he said, firing up his boots. "Let's get ouuu—ooow!" He yanked back his hand, flapping it around frantically. "You almost broke my hand!"

She dove out the window.

"Get her!" Gamora shouted, fending off an attack from the Collector.

Peter leapt out after Kiya, landing on the balustrade of a ramshackle balcony. He scanned the cityscape. Several stories below, the street still bustled with nighttime crowds. If Kiya had slipped into the masses, he would never— There! Sprinting across the rooftop of the next building! He saw a flash of white hair before she tugged a hood over her head.

"Kiya, we're not handing you over to him! You have the wrong idea," he called out, shooting off through the air toward her. "I mean…you *had* the right one, but not anymore!"

She veered left and leapt over the side of the rooftop. He sped up just in time to see her bolt into the crowd.

He flew lower. She was running—that made it easier to keep an eye on her. She swerved through the crowd, into an alley, and back onto a public square. He saw his chance. He clicked his element gun loose, leaving it barely hanging on his belt for easy access, then slammed to the ground in front of her. He spread his hands out wide, hoping the bystanders wouldn't see him as a threat. Most of them ran. Others frantically yelled into their communicators. Calling law enforcement? Great—he really needed angry Kree in the middle of this mess.

"Look, we won't hurt you, and we won't hand you over to the Collector." *Apparently.* Gamora had better know what she was doing. "We're the—"

"I *know* who she is!"

Kiya hadn't stopped running. Peter planted himself on the cobblestone street, ready to intercept her. Instead, she sprinted past and effortlessly plucked his element gun from his belt. She swerved toward him and fired.

The gun clicked pointlessly.

She inhaled sharply, pulling the trigger again. *Click-click-click.*

Perfect. She'd fallen for it. Peter used the distraction to crash into her, pulling her down to the ground with him. A chorus of gasps sounded in the crowd as people dashed aside.

Peter snatched back his gun, spun it around, and aimed at her face. "Hey," he said, and pulled the trigger. Brown dirt splashed out. "You have mud on your face. This gun is keyed to my DNA, by the way. I should've mentioned that."

"*Rah!*" She knocked him off, scrabbling to her hands and feet. The mud dripped from her face, and she squinted her eyes shut to keep them clean. She blindly swung a fist out through the air.

From his position sitting on the ground, he took aim and fired a second time. "You've also got ice on your boots."

Kiya dropped to the ground, taking the impact on her shoulder. She rolled onto her back. Wiping the mud from her face with one hand, she used the other to beat at the ice on her legs. It was already cracking.

He fired a third time. "Oops. Got some on your hand, too."

She was still writing on the ground as he crouched closer and hooked his arms under hers. "Let me *go!*" she yelled. "Don't *touch* me!"

"Can you fly? No? Gotta have some touching, then, sorry." He pushed himself to his feet, then activated his boots. He ignored the yells from the crowd below. This didn't look good on the surface, and he didn't have time to correct them. "Got her," he said into his comms as they rose straight up.

"I got the Groots," Rocket replied. "I'll fly the ship over to grab you."

"Get Gamora and Drax away from Tivan first. You two still alive?"

Gamora snorted. "Please, Quill. Have some faith—" A thud. A pained grunt he recognized as hers.

"Get them," he snapped to Rocket.

"On it."

WOW," Gamora drawled, as Quill entered the ship with Kiya tossed over his shoulder. "You've been busy."

Quill deactivated his boots, thudding to the floor. It was just Quill, Gamora, two Grootlings, and Rocket in the cargo bay. Most of the Grootlings they'd recovered from Kiya's apartment were in the crew quarters, getting caught up on the situation, while Drax was tending to the bridge and nursing his wounds. The Collector handed out a hell of a beating when he wanted to.

"How long did it take you to find her?" Rocket stabbed at the control panel in the wall. The doors slid shut, abruptly cutting off the wind soaring through the room. Good. It had been messing up his sense of smell and tangling his fur. "I like the mud and ice. Good look on her."

Bet she wouldn't be able to dodge his blast now. It was damn tempting— but if Gammy wanted the girl alive, Rocket would roll with it.

For now.

"She managed to shoot Gamora. I wasn't taking chances." Quill gently lowered the girl to the ground, then stretched, windmilling his arms and making a satisfied sound.

"It was only a surface wound. Don't insult me." Gamora's eyes were fixed on the girl.

Kiya scrambled away—kind of a funny sight, with that ice still weighing her down—and watched them. Eyes wide, breaths sharp.

Eh, she could sit tight for a bit.

"You missed all the good stuff, Quill!" Rocket said. "Flew the ship right between the buildings—had to tilt it to fit, people were *screaming* in the street, it was hilarious—and then Drax 'n' Gammy jumping right out the window—I caught them perfectly."

"We *jumped* perfectly, Rocket." Gamora sounded toneless. Still studying the girl like she'd never seen a DiMavi before.

"None of you got any appreciation for what I do," he huffed. "Anyway, the Collector tried to follow, but Groot shot him back into the apartment and may or may not have set the place on fire. There, I'm done. It was awesome, and you missed it." He pointed an accusatory finger at Quill.

"Kiya." Gamora leaned forward, arms on her knees. "Are you all right?"

"I am Groot?" The two Grootlings, who barely reached Rocket's shoulders, came running across the cargo bay. One lingered near Gamora, who sat on a rusty staircase leading to a higher platform. The other went straight to Kiya, who was pushing herself into a sitting position. The blocks of ice around her feet and hand were dripping, creating a puddle that ran down the grates.

Her hands were starting to claw at the ice. Her breathing was heavy. She watched Gamora, matching the woman's intensity, but every few seconds her eyes flickered to the rest of the room, taking it in bit by bit.

As if satisfied there weren't any other imminent threats, Kiya's gaze fixed on Gamora.

Gamora stared back.

Rocket narrowed his eyes. "Am I…interrupting something…?"

13

FIVE weeks of surviving on her own and staying out of Tivan's hands.

Five weeks of deciphering Tivan's impossible notes, growing the Groots, finding buyers.

And just as Kiya had finished the final batch of Groots, over a dozen that she could sell off all in one go—

In the space of a few minutes—

All her efforts, destroyed.

Pain and cold shuddered through Kiya's legs. She clawed and beat at the ice, a rhythmic thumping, as she tried to get a handle on the situation.

Cargo bay. A big space, with aged-looking metal all around her. Several places to hide. Three exits. A fourth, if she counted the hatch they'd flown in through, but that seemed securely locked for now. Nearest possible weapon—a pair of magnospatial pliers near the control panel—wasn't within reach. Too risky, especially when she could barely move.

She counted three opponents. The angry, chatty, furry creature— Rocket, Gamora had called him—stood across the room, near the control panel. Didn't seem likely to shoot Kiya again within the next few minutes. She dismissed him for now.

The man who'd iced her stood by her side. Close enough to punch in the throat, if not for the ice. The man was a pink Kree, based on his appearance, though he acted nothing like one. If he was actually Kree—

The thought almost made Kiya want to laugh, a panicky sound already bubbling in her throat. She flung the useless impulse aside.

If he was Kree, then her freedom had been snatched away by the combination of a Kree, Gamora—*Gamora!*—and Tivan himself. A trifecta straight out of her nightmares.

Call me Taneleer, the Collector had chastised her, his voice an echo in her mind. *We are on a first-name basis, are we not?*

She flinched.

The final person in the cargo bay was Gamora.

Kiya could no longer look away. Every few seconds, her heart twitched and skipped a beat, knowing that Gamora was sitting right there on that staircase—a dozen feet away

Watching her.

The ice was starting to crack. Every thud sent another jolt of pain through her legs, but she bit through the pain, thudded harder. She was used to pain. And she needed to get out. Now.

Aside from her three opponents, there was just the pair of week-old Groots. No sign of Tivan. He wasn't on board. If he *were* on the ship, he'd be standing right across from her, welcoming her with open arms and a vicious smile.

So she had only these three to deal with. Four, if she counted the muscly, tattooed one who'd barged into her apartment. He had to be flying the ship.

Four was doable.

If one of those four wasn't *Gamora.*

Knowing that Gamora had turned on Tivan the moment she realized the truth about Kiya was a bright spot, but only barely. Kiya still didn't know what Gamora wanted from her. Only that it could not be good.

The ice wouldn't hold Kiya for much longer.

She needed a plan. At a minimum, it'd involve that control panel Rocket had been operating, the maybe-Kree's propulsor boots, and as many Groots as possible. Where were the other Groots? Her captors had taken her d'ast wares. She *needed* those things—

"Are you all right?" Gamora's pose was casual, unthreatening. The look she gave Kiya, though—it was too intent, too focused. As though she had found a target.

Kiya's free hand still beat relentlessly at the ice. Her skin was turning pale from cold, her knuckles already split.

Gamora was angling for something.

For a fleeting, frightening moment, Kiya actually wished she were back with Tivan. The world outside his museum was too damn big, and too damn much to deal with all by herself.

It was not the first time she'd had that thought. As she did every time, she fought it off, shoved it into a deep, dank corner of her mind.

She had gotten away from him.

She would stay that way.

She focused on the pain in her bones, the cold seeping into her skin, and the textured metal she sat on. They grounded her. Kept her present, instead of letting her fear run off with her.

"Hey, teeny tiny question, Gamora." The maybe-Kree man leaned casually against a steel beam curving along the wall. "We took your word on it and all, but mind telling me why the krutack we just declared war on an Elder of the Universe?"

"Ain't that what we do on Wednesdays?" Rocket wondered aloud.

"Collector ain't gonna be happy we left him on that backwater of a planet. Or, y'know, that the Destroyer and the deadliest woman in the galaxy beat him up. Never trusted that he'd make good on that promise to hand over the other Groots, but I'm *pretty sure* that option's gone out the airlock now."

Kiya freed one heel, the ice falling away.

Rocket's words matched the group's actions in her apartment. That didn't mean she could trust them, though. She slowly considered her options. Too slowly. She couldn't think with Gamora right there, on those stairs only a dozen feet away—Gamora could cross that distance and slice all their throats before any of them realized she'd even moved—

Pain. Cold. Metal.

Focus.

"Rocket, shut it," the maybe-Kree said. He seemed to be the one in charge. Laughable. Gamora had to be humoring him. "After pulling that weapon, you don't get to talk about risking our deal."

Gamora was still studying Kiya.

"Gamora?" the maybe-Kree said.

"You're not an assistant." Gamora's voice was frighteningly level. "You were a specimen in his collection."

Kiya tore her eyes away from Gamora as the ice between her feet cracked. She could move her legs independently, even if she couldn't walk yet. A wave of pain caught her by surprise. She rode it out, let it pass.

Cold sometimes suppressed her pain. Now, it seemed to make it worse.

Kiya shifted her focus to her encased hand. Looking away from Gamora was a foolish move, she knew. *Eyes on your opponent. At all times.*

She couldn't bring herself to do it.

She ducked her head lower, letting loose locks slip into her vision. The dried mud clumps stood out sharply on her stark-white hair.

"He augmented you."

Kiya scratched at the ice, more forcefully now.

"You're Zen-Whoberian."

"Whoa, hang on." Startled, the maybe-Kree pushed himself away from the wall. Kiya's head snapped back up, following every movement. "Zen-Whoberian?"

"As in—?" Rocket drew a finger along his neck and made a choking sound.

Gamora shot him an annoyed look that made Kiya's breath stick in her throat. It didn't seem to faze Rocket one bit. "Yes," Gamora said. "As in nigh extinct."

"Not cool, Rocket," the maybe-Kree said.

"I am Groot." A Groot shoved him.

"You're all so sensitive. Jeez." Rocket rolled his eyes. "Weren't you, like, a little kid when the Zen-Whoberi's massacre happened, Gam?"

The maybe-Kree still stood closest to Kiya. He ran a hand through his hair, leaving it standing on end. "You're really Zen-Whoberian?"

"*Half,*" Kiya said, her voice rough.

It was the first thing she'd said since coming on board. She regretted it instantly. She couldn't buy into the banter, the harmlessness. Tivan had been friendly, too. Until he wasn't.

"How?" Gamora asked.

"Well, Gammy," Rocket said, "when a DiMavi and a Zen-Whoberian have got the hots for each other—"

"You Kree?" Kiya asked abruptly, looking up at the man by her side.

"Me?" He gestured at himself. "Uh—no. Long story. Definitely not Kree. Call me Star-Lord."

Gamora leaned in to Kiya. "Your mother? Father? Are they still alive? Please. Tell me."

"Even mixed," Star-Lord said to Kiya, "you are the only Zen-Whoberian we know of aside from Gamora. No wonder the Collector wants you back so bad."

Kiya's lips tightened. He might be realizing how many units they could get for her.

"What did he do to you?" Gamora asked quietly.

"Listen, Kiya, we won't hurt you. What happened in your apartment earlier, that was…" Star-Lord glanced at Rocket.

"She sold Groot," Rocket spat.

"It won't happen again," Star-Lord said resolutely to Kiya. "And we won't let Tivan take you."

Taneleer. His voice in her mind sounded so amused. So pleased with himself. *Tivan sounds far too impersonal. You can call me Taneleer, and I will call you—*

She shoved him out of her thoughts.

"You were working with him." Kiya tried to keep her voice steady, but it came out thin. "You said you had a deal."

"Past tense," Gamora said.

"Yeah, the whole fight should prove that." Star-Lord jerked a thumb at nothing in particular.

Maybe. Maybe not.

"Well! This has been a *great* talk! What a *sparkling* conversationalist!" Rocket said. "What exactly were you thinking bringing her aboard, Gamora?"

"That she'd be safe."

Kiya smacked her iced hand on a thick bolt in the floor.

Rocket snorted. "She seems real grateful."

"Look, I get that you don't trust us," Star-Lord said. "How about… do you want a shower? Steam, water, whatever you want. You can get the mud and ice off. And then we just want to talk. All right? We answer your questions, you answer ours."

So that was why they'd brought her on board: information. She didn't want to cooperate; she wanted to fling this chunk of ice around her hand at his face, but—

Getting rid of the ice would put her in a better position to fight.

"Okay."

Gamora stood.

Automatically, Kiya tried to snap into a fighting position. The ice pulled her off balance. She ended up on her back. Squirming, vulnerable. She gasped as pain surged through her body and thudded in her bones.

"I am Groot," said the the Groot who was helping her.

If she didn't know any better, Kiya would say it sounded worried.

"I won't hurt you," Gamora said.

Kiya managed to shove herself up into a half-sitting position, recovering her breath, and forced herself to look at Gamora. She'd survived being face-to-face with Gamora in her apartment. She could do this, too.

She would play along until she found out what they wanted.

Gamora took another step forward, then winced. One leg gave way for a moment before she caught herself.

"Whoa, whoa, Gamora." Star-Lord shot forward. "You okay?"

Gamora paused, steadying herself. She looked down at Kiya, her lips pursed. "Quill. You should be the one to take her."

She swiveled and left the cargo bay.

Something inside Kiya unclenched, unknotted. She released a shuddery breath of relief.

"All right. You ready?" Star-Lord—Quill?—asked.

No. Not for any of this, she thought, her eyes fixed on the exit Gamora had left through.

She nodded. "Yes."

14

THE TAP-TAP-TAP of Rocket's claws on the floor gave him away before he said a thing.

"What was that about?" he said, catching up with Gamora in the hall. She didn't slow her pace. "Are you trying to spare the girl's *feewings?* Since when do you care? You know what she did to Groot."

"She's a child, and she's scared of me." Gamora kept her eyes straight ahead.

"No duh. You got a bit of a reputation, Gam, and you did choke her."

"And you shot her, and Quill chased and iced her. That isn't the point."

Rocket squinted up, clearly not getting it. He was too absorbed with everything else—the Collector, the Groots, Kiya—to realize what all this meant. She couldn't blame him.

Gamora had seen a lot of frightened faces in her life, though. She knew the precise difference between fear of her reputation and fear of *her.*

She stopped abruptly, even as it sent a bolt of pain through her back. "Don't you wonder why the Collector had her in his collection?"

"She's Zen-Whoberian. She's rare."

"Why did he cybernetically modify her?"

"Yeah, that *is* kinda… Huh."

Gamora leaned against the wall, her head resting right beside one of Quill's old-fashioned music speakers. The moment of rest was welcome. The Collector had done enough damage that her healing factor was taking its sweet time patching her up. Her vital organs had healed first. Surface cuts and scrapes had faded into clean skin. It was the deeper gashes, the ones that had shredded her skin and fractured her bones—the ones the Collector's weapons had left all across her back and left side—that would take longer to heal.

"Think about the questions the Collector has been asking," Gamora said. She breathed around the pain. In, out. "His fawning over us. Growing *Groot*. Not simply any *Flora colossus*—Groot. And the Earth raccoon in the arboretum."

"Yeah?"

The pain was bad.

Voicing these thoughts aloud was worse.

Gamora didn't let either slow her down.

"He's remaking us."

"Wait, what now?" Then Rocket hissed through his teeth. "Ohhh, flark. You're right."

"He's copying the Guardians of the Galaxy."

He grimaced. "*With Earth raccoons?*"

"Kiya's training and implants. They're meant to augment her, to make her abilities mimic mine. And she doesn't know the rest of the team, but somehow she knows *me* well enough to be terrified. I think…" Gamora leaned her head into the speaker beside her, hating the sound of her next words, hating what they meant. "I think he showed her recordings of me in action. The kind that were made before I joined the Guardians."

When she was working with Thanos.

When she'd been the monster—the weapon—that he'd turned her into after plucking her away from the massacre of her people.

"All right," Rocket said. "So we know what he's doing, and it's creepy as all get out."

She snorted inelegantly. "Yes."

"Doesn't change what she did to Groot, Gamora." He pulled up a corner of his mouth in a twisted smirk. "Her being Zen-Whoberian? Her being some kinda Gamora-lite? Doesn't change *anything*."

Except it really, really did.

PETER jogged through the ship. He'd left the Groot they'd found on Pirinida to guard Kiya by the shower.

"Groot?" he called. His voice sounded harsh against the metal walls of the ship.

A Grootling popped up by his side, the same height as Peter. "I am Groot?"

He would need to get used to that. "The other one. The original?"

"I am Groot." He pointed toward the bridge.

"Thanks. You, uh…" He stared at the Grootling.

Groot had looked like that only two weeks ago. Now they had Groots in all shapes and sizes on the ship, from barely sprouted saplings to adults like their own.

What on earth were they going to *do* with them all?

He'd have to think about that, but not yet. "You guys don't need me right now, do you? You're all—I mean, you're Groot. You have his memories. You know the ship. You know us."

The Grootling enthusiastically nodded. "I am Groot!"

Peter held up his hand for a high-five. "I'm glad we found you, too."

As the Grootling had said, Groot was on the bridge. He sat silently on the floor between Drax, in the pilot's seat, and Gamora, who was slouched in the navigator's chair.

Peter took a second to look past them, through the viewport at the stars ahead. They'd exited the planet's atmosphere not long ago. It was good to be back out in the black. The stars felt like coming home. He loved being planetbound, with both feet on solid ground and a problem to solve, but *this* was what made it all worth it.

The stars around him, and his team beside him.

He didn't normally feel bad breaking the silence. For once, though—seeing the weariness that hung over his teammates like a tattered blanket, knowing the chaos they'd fled—he wanted to sit and join them.

Couldn't. He had a job to do.

"There's my favorite bruisers," he said.

"Star-Lord," Drax acknowledged.

"Where's the girl?" Gamora stretched. Peter could almost hear her spine crack.

"Groot's waiting for her to finish her shower. Other Groot. I mean, the Grootling, the big one... This'll get confusing."

"I am Groot," Groot agreed.

"How're you holding up?" Peter crossed his arms lazily over the backrest of the gunner's seat and peered at Groot.

"I...am Groot?" He weighed his words, then shrugged sheepishly. "I am Groot."

"Can't blame you there." They were all overwhelmed. For Groot, it had to be worse. Much, much worse. "We'll find a way to fix this. You know that, right?"

"I am Groot."

His words said there wasn't any doubt about it, but his tone hid a sliver of uncertainty, a tiny nagging fear beneath the surface.

Groot smiled.

Peter smiled back.

He didn't think either of them bought it.

"Gamora? Drax? You two doing all right, or do you need medical help?"

"We are well."

"We'll heal. Don't worry about us, Quill."

"You two fought an Elder of the Universe to a standstill. Of course I'm gonna worry." He blew out some air. This time, his grin was genuine. "Not half bad."

"I enjoyed the challenge," Drax admitted. "It has been some time since I fought such a worthy opponent. And with such a worthy partner."

"Yeah, but forgive me if I don't do it again any time soon." Gamora kicked the control panel, sending her chair spinning to face Peter. She draped herself languidly over the armrests as though she'd spent the day on the beach, instead of crisscrossing the galaxy and getting her ass thoroughly beat. "Quill," she said. "I have a theory about the Collector and Kiya."

"Spill."

"And I don't think you'll like it."

THAT *is the greatest thing,*" Quill cackled.

"Excuse me?" Gamora had been leading him toward the crew quarters, wanting to talk to him in private before they brought in the others. She abruptly stopped. He nearly bumped into her.

"I mean…" He held up his hands as she turned. A mild panic crept into his eyes. "I mean, *wow,* that's bad, really bad."

She blew a lock of hair from her face, not breaking eye contact.

"*Sooooo* bad," he said.

"'*Greatest thing*'?" she echoed.

"I just meant that we have a fan! A billions-year-old creature is so impressed by us that he's making a Guardians of the Galaxy tribute band."

She screwed up her face in puzzlement.

"He's just…doing it in…bad ways," Quill finished. "What with the kidnapping and invasive surgery and holding people prisoner. Those are bad things. Which we will stop."

"Greatest. Thing."

He slumped. "Do you think he's copying the rest of us, too?"

She whirled back around. "I hope not. Another Quill would be a crime against the universe."

"I deserved that," he mused.

"Probably," Rocket chimed in from overhead. A grate clattered open, and he hoisted himself down from the maintenance pipe. He dangled from the edge for a second, then dropped down and dusted off his suit. "What were we talking about? Never mind, don't wanna know. Listen, I found three trackers the Collector must've left. We're clean now. I triple-checked."

Quill nodded. "Good work. I'll tell Drax to abandon the decoy course."

"So where are we really going?" Gamora asked.

"That depends on the conversation we're about to have with Kiya."

Rocket crossed his arms. "We're not keeping her on the ship, are we?"

"That's going to depend, too." Quill worked his way past Rocket and Gamora, picking up the pace.

"I just think—"

"I know what you think, Rocket," he snapped. "You made that d'ast clear when you tried to blow her in half. You ignored the plan, you were stupidly reckless—you almost shot Gamora!—"

"Almost is a strong word," Gamora said. Rocket had been across the room when he fired his blaster—she'd had *plenty* of time.

"—you endangered our deal with the Collector, who wanted Kiya alive, you shot at a teenage girl who posed no threat to us at the time, and for bonus points, you nearly killed what might've been the second-to-last Zen-Whoberian in the *entire krutacking universe!*"

Rocket sputtered.

"Tip?" Gamora said as she passed him. "Don't respond."

15

KIYA'S white hair hung in wet strings over her face, reaching slightly past her jaw. Water dripped down her skin, leaving dark green tracks. She wore clothes provided by Gamora, which were too long around her wrists and ankles and too tight everywhere else. She wouldn't stop rubbing her previously frozen hand, which still looked a little paler green than the rest of her. One eye was starting to swell—a product of her tussle with Gamora, Peter guessed.

She looked vulnerable, but that didn't weaken her glare.

"Fine," she said, standing outside the shower stall. The team shared a handful of bathrooms adjoining their private quarters, leaving the larger, more industrial bathroom adjoining the cargo bay for guests and post-mission emergencies. (Some of those emergencies involved alien slime.)

They didn't clean this bathroom very often. Hopefully Kiya didn't mind some grubbiness.

Kiya didn't take her eyes off Gamora, even as she addressed Peter. "Ask me your questions."

Peter clapped his hands. The sound bounced off the cold tiles. "So: Were you, or were you not, kidnapped, cybernetically modified, and possibly mildly brainwashed in order to turn you into Gamora two-point-oh as part of the Collector's not-at-all-awesome scheme to make a Guardians tribute team?"

After a long moment, she said: "He also dyed my hair to look like hers." She plucked at her hair. "I cut it and dyed it back when I escaped."

Kiya was choosing her words carefully. In Peter's experience, that meant she was leaving a lot unsaid. Baby steps, though. At least they'd moved past the two-syllable sentences stage.

"Your parents—?" Gamora started.

"I won't answer you." Kiya inhaled sharply, as though she couldn't believe she'd said it.

Gamora's lips tightened, but she kept quiet.

"Aw, harsh," Rocket said.

"I am Groot," added the Grootling who'd guarded Kiya.

"So, uh," Peter said, "which of your parents is Zen-Whoberian?"

"My dad. He happened to be on DiMave when the massacre happened. He decided to stay and pose as DiMavi. Once I was born, so did I. He's dead. No, I don't know any other Zen-Whoberians. Now can I go?" She lifted her chin in challenge.

The room fell silent.

"We don't want to hold you against your will," Peter told Kiya.

She turned to him. He wished she'd kept staring at Gamora. The way Kiya looked at him, he felt she was less *conversing* with him and more *analyzing his weak spots.* He kept his hand casually by his side, his gun within reach.

"You broke into my apartment, turned me into an ice cube, and kidnapped me onto your ship."

"That's—a really good point," he said. "But we don't mean you any harm. Anymore. Now."

"It's not safe to leave," Gamora said.

"Well, we can't hold her."

"She's a child!"

"She stayed out of the Collector's hands this long."

"Yeah, until we started helping him out," Rocket said.

"Do I get a say in this?" Kiya asked.

Peter tossed up his hands. "How about we don't discuss this in the *bathroom?*"

He set out with Gamora, Rocket, Kiya, and the Grootling in tow. If Kiya wouldn't cooperate, he didn't know what he'd do. With the Collector pissed off and Groot screwed up—maybe beyond repair—the last thing Peter needed was a homicidal teenager on his ship. The thought of letting her go made him bristle, though, and it didn't look like Gamora was going to sign off on that idea, either.

Another Zen-Whoberian.

He hadn't thought it was even possible.

The group entered the leisure area—a big circular space, the wall lined with hatches to the crew quarters. "Leisure area" maybe sounded too fancy for what amounted to a spare room they'd decorated with some old couches and a mini-fridge, but it worked for them.

Right now, the leisure area was—gently phrased—a circus.

"I am Groot! I am Groot!" babbled a handful of Grootlings as they chased each other across the couches.

"I am Grooooot!" a Grootling so small he must've just sprouted said in delight, watching the goings-on from the confines of his pot.

"I am Groot?" An almost-grown Grootling leaned over a tray of dirt Peter had seen in Kiya's apartment, poking experimentally at the transparent cover.

"I am Groot—I am *Groot,*" others were saying.

One Grootling nestled into his pot, happily sighing as his roots spread out in the dirt. "I am Groot."

"I am Groot!"

"I am Groot!"

"I am Groot! I am Groot!"

"I am Groot!"

"I have a headache," Gamora said, staring.

"I have a *forest,*" Peter said, "on my *ship.*"

"I have an absolute buttload of friends all of a sudden," Rocket said. "Who knew I was this popular?"

Peter did a headcount. They had the Grootling from Pirinida standing by their side, blinking at the havoc in front of them. The original Groot was on the bridge, so all of these Grootlings were Kiya's. He counted 13, not including those who might still sprout from the trays, or those roaming elsewhere in the ship.

Kiya was still squeezing the hand that'd been frozen, as if rubbing away an ache. "They haven't been this…loud before."

"They haven't been *home* before," Gamora said.

"I am Groot!" A Grootling barely larger than Peter's hand came running at Rocket and promptly tripped over his own feet.

"Aw, buddy. Small buddy. Clumsy buddy." Rocket crouched and helped him up. "You okay?"

"I am Groot!"

"'Course. You're tough."

The Grootling clamped onto Rocket's finger. "I am Groot," he giggled.

Rocket gently lifted the Grootling onto his shoulder. "So how's it going down here?"

"I am Groot. I am *Groot.*"

"All right," Peter said. "We'll stock up at our next stop."

"What are you…?" Kiya scoffed. "You're joking."

Peter raised his eyebrows. "What? If they want fertilizer, they're getting fertilizer."

"Are you saying you understand them?"

"Of course."

"They're *intelligent?*"

So Kiya hadn't known. That changed the situation. In a way, it both helped and hurt her case. "He's our friend."

"It's a he?"

"You've spent *how* much time growing them? And you didn't realize he could talk?" Rocket crossed the room and thumped onto a tattered, plaid couch. Another few Grootlings ran up to him.

"I just thought…well." She crossed her arms, then uncrossed them. She hadn't moved from her spot by the entrance. "If he were speaking another language, my translator implant would've picked up on it. It doesn't translate lower-level communication like animals' speech."

"Hey, there ain't nothing lower-level about Groot's talking."

Kiya examined the Groots, then the team. Finally she said, "If they can talk, prove it. They saw me have breakfast this morning. What did I eat?"

"I am Groot," said the Grootling on Rocket's shoulder.

"He says you're a disgusting liar and you skipped breakfast," Rocket said. He lay back on the couch, arms under his head as a pillow. Two Grootlings snuggled under his tail.

"Paraphrased," Peter said.

"I am Groot."

"Gross," Rocket said. "Last night, you ate a synthetic steak. For some reason."

Kiya sucked in a breath. She stared at the Grootlings in front of them.

Peter watched her closely. With the Guardians, he usually had at least a hunch what was in their heads at any given moment. Even the newly grown Groots scattered around the room were familiar to him. They'd gotten quieter since the group entered, as if unsure what to make of their teammates standing side-by-side with the girl who'd grown and planned to sell them.

But Peter didn't know Kiya. Watching her told him only one thing: That silence of hers was only the surface. A hell of a lot went on underneath.

Peter suddenly felt like he had brought an awfully big wild card on board.

He tried to shake it off. Two Grootlings had stood up for Kiya in her apartment; another had helped her chip off the ice when Peter had brought her into the ship.

She'd been wrong to grow and sell them. She'd been shortsighted not to realize they were sentient.

But he didn't think she'd been cruel.

"I thought they were just plants," she said. "Smart plants, maybe, like pets, but not…"

"Would you have sold them if you'd known?" Peter asked.

"No," she said, fast enough that either she'd already been thinking about it, or she knew what he wanted to hear.

Sometimes Peter really missed having a telepath around.

"Did you notice they're getting weaker?"

"Even if I hadn't, the buyers' complaints would've made it clear. It's why I moved locations." She put a hand on her neck. "I've been looking into why—like maybe I wasn't growing them right for long-term survival, or the modifications I made so they couldn't reproduce further had side effects, or—"

"It's *you,* lady," Rocket piped up from the couch. "You're the one doing it. The more of them you grow, the weaker they get."

Peter explained the situation, carefully watching Kiya's reaction all the while. She was studying the Groots, some of which had resumed conversation, while others had come down to the group to listen in.

Her skin turned a shade or two lighter. Her jaw clenched. She scratched at a long, gray-green incision on her arm. Her mouth moved, but no sound came out.

"So?" Peter pressed.

"So?" She looked stricken, her glare momentarily gone, and he knew he'd reached her.

"Can you fix them? Bring these Groots and any others we find back into one?"

"I could try." She shifted her weight to her other foot. Looked up warily. "If I do, you'll keep me safe from…him?"

"We will," Gamora said.

"Question is, are we safe from *you?*" Rocket asked. He propped himself up on his arms. "How can we trust you? You gonna grab the Grootlings the second you can and bolt? You gonna slit our throats while we sleep?"

"You gonna slit mine?" Kiya eyed the blaster, squeezed between Rocket and the couch backrest.

"Not ruling anything out."

"No," she said finally. "I want to go home. That's all."

"Then what're you growing and selling these Groots for? A shuttle to DiMave ain't that expensive."

Kiya didn't answer.

Rocket's face settled into a scowl. He looked down at the Groots that had joined him on the couch. "None of you bundles of twigs are gonna let her try anything funny, are you?"

"I am Groot?" two Grootlings said, blinking owlishly.

"You do right by us, Kiya, we do right by you," Peter said. "We'll keep you safe from the Collector. And no one"—he pointedly looked at Rocket—"is cutting anyone's throat!"

Rocket harrumphed, but wisely kept quiet.

Kiya chewed her lip, glancing at Gamora for a half second, then back at the Grootlings. Peter might have been mistaken, but he thought he saw her face soften.

"I'll help," she said. "I'll stay."

16

NONE of them had expected the Collector to be pleased about their betrayal.

None of them had expected him to take so long to detail just how displeased he was, either—especially since he must've figured out pretty quickly that they'd dumped his trackers. It took well over half a Kree day before their ship was politely hailed.

Gamora, Rocket, and Quill stood on the bridge as the holo flared up. The Collector's grim, larger-than-life face filled the viewport, a glossy scarf wrapped around his neck.

He looked good. Not tired. Not injured.

Gamora supposed she hadn't expected him to—*she'd* healed perfectly by now, and she wasn't even immortal—but it still irked her. The fight in Kiya's apartment had nearly killed her and Drax. She'd have enjoyed seeing a black eye at the very least.

"Friends," the Collector said.

"Still?" Quill asked. "Hate to say it, but you need to take a hint."

"Even one-sided amity is amity, Peter. I am so glad we have a chance to speak, now that I have found transportation and am on my way home."

"What do you want?" Gamora did not feel like indulging him with chatter this time.

"You're being rather rude."

Quill shrugged. "Yes, well, you did kind of lie to us and betray us, and kidnap and experiment on a teenage girl—and all that jazz."

"I hardly lied. Perhaps…withheld? Regardless. I want the girl. I have invested tremendous resources and energy in her. She is a highlight of my collection."

"I would've thought that was the raccoon."

"If that's s'posed to be me, by the by," Rocket said, "I'm seriously offended. Yeah, that's right. We know about your messed-up little project."

"'Messed-up'? Oh, dear Rocket. Here I thought you would appreciate that I chose to form a tribute—"

"Ha!" Quill said. "Tribute! That's what *I* said—I mean, never mind, carry on, carry on."

"—rather than immortalizing the five of *you* in my collection."

"Oh yes, we lo-ove when innocents are screwed over on our behalf," Quill said. "Love it! It's a hero thing."

"It's our jam," Rocket spat.

Gamora crossed her arms. The others were taking too long to get to the point. Having to look at the Collector's face without the opportunity to beat it in was a chore. He'd found Kiya. He'd found another Zen-Whoberian, and he'd kept her hidden and locked up for months—perhaps longer—

How had he even found her? Did he know of others?

"Is that all?" she asked before her thoughts could stray too far.

"Well, I had thought that allowing your continued freedom would be a sign of my admiration for your work, but…*if* one of you wants to join my collection in Kiya's place, I would accept the trade. Happily."

She raised an eyebrow. "I seem to have hit you on the head too hard."

He laughed in delight. "Hard enough to convince me I could never truly imitate the real thing. But if none of you care to take my offer, I'll simply need to keep at it."

"Is that all?" she repeated.

"After we worked so well together, you would simply—"

"Yes."

"Happily," Quill added.

The Collector pursed his lips.

"I want my Groots back," Rocket said.

"If you're open to further negotiations, you can talk to them when I return."

"Great. Bye-bye now!" Quill made a fist with his hand, abruptly fading the holo to nothing. "Well! That was enlightening."

"He's maaad," Rocket said. "He was playing all nice, but he's *seriously* mad. You ever seen a Shi'ar get a buzzcut? No? I have. Don't ask." He snickered. "No, ask me about it sometime, it was hilarious. My point is, I'd say that's about…a fifth of how angry the Collector is right now."

"I do enjoy it," Gamora admitted.

"So!" Rocket clapped his hands together. "We gonna sneak in, or do a full-on attack? What's the plan?"

"The plan?" Quill said.

"To break into the Collector's. We know he's got at least four Groots."

"Oh, that plan. That plan is on hold."

"'Scuse me?"

Quill jabbed a thumb at the spot where the Collector's face had hovered seconds before. "It's a traaa-aaap. Notice how he mentioned he wasn't back yet—twice? He wants us to think the museum is undefended. I bet he's already home. If he really did want to talk to us en route, he could've reached out sooner. I'm guessing he followed the trackers, realized he lost us, sped back home, realized we weren't there either, and promptly reached out to try to draw us in. We're not falling for it."

"So what if it's a trap? We're the Guardians of the Galaxy. We don't let that kinda junk scare us off. He's got *Groot!*"

"Yes. And he *wants* Kiya," Gamora pointed out. She didn't like the idea of avoiding the Collector, either, but she also didn't want to set course for his museum knowing they had precisely what he wanted.

Quill nodded. "We shouldn't play into his hands. We're going to get his Grootlings, but there are other duplicates out there—Kiya knows who she sold them to—*that* need us just as much. And finding *those* doesn't risk the Collector stealing back the person who's our best shot at bringing Groot back together."

Rocket glared up at the both of them, his hands balled into fists. "Yeah. All right. She'd better pull her weight, though."

"She's already given locations."

"Groots to find, people to shoot," Gamora said.

That seemed to cheer up Rocket slightly. "So, where to?"

"You may enjoy this one."

17

NEW TON-TON'S fourth moon was known colloquially as Ton-Four and officially by about 93 different names, courtesy of New Ton-Ton's 93 major languages and its inhabitants' utter inability to agree or compromise on anything.

The other Guardians hadn't spent much time there—too small, too messy, why bother when a perfectly good Knowhere already existed?—but Rocket always thought Ton-Four had its appeal. The moon had good bars, good fighting pits, good trade, a good amount of law enforcement—meaning: zero—and a good mix of folk that meant sometimes he was only the fourth or fifth weirdest thing in the room.

Rocket hated seeing good things spoiled, and he had a hunch Ton-Four was about to be.

"Perhaps the Grootling was not purchased for a fighting pit," Drax said after the second pit that night came up empty. They'd saved a few fighters who had ended up in the pits against their will, offered to save others only to learn the painful way that they were there very much voluntarily, and seen exactly zero Grootlings.

"Trust me," Rocket said. "Anyone on Ton-Four buys a Groot, it's for a fighting pit."

"I am Groot," Groot agreed.

They had left the Grootlings they'd already retrieved at the ship—too risky with so many to keep an eye on, no matter how much all of them had pleaded—but Kiya had come along. No way were they leaving her behind with a ship to steal and a gaggle of Grootlings to sell.

The six of them stood on the roof of a rundown casino, overlooking the third and final underground fighting ring out in the crappy tail end of the main market.

Literally underground, in this case. One entrance was at the back of a narrow, dusty fabric shop, while another was in a bar down the street. The Guardians could've waltzed right in—either trade a few punches with security or just have Gamora and Drax volunteer to fight—but Quill insisted they wait for the audience to leave. Civilians only got in the way and risked getting hurt.

As impatient as Rocket was to find the Grootling, he understood Quill's thinking. The civilians watching these kinds of fighting rings might be scumbags, but Rocket had dropped enough money in these places himself that he wasn't gonna judge.

"They're trickling out," Quill reported.

From their position on the rooftop, the group had a full view of the fabric shop. The audience exited in small clusters, talking and laughing in the cool morning dark. Not far down the street, behind empty market stalls abandoned for the night, another door opened.

"Entrance number three." Gamora sat on the edge of the rooftop beside Quill, with Drax and Groot on the ground beside them, and Rocket pacing back and forth a few feet away.

Kiya sat farther away, leaning uselessly against a busted solar generator. She wasn't even taking notes on merging the Groots or anything—wasn't she supposed to be pulling her weight? She just sat there, legs drawn up and rubbing her shins, stonily watching the rest of them.

"Boo," Rocket said.

Her eyes shifted to look at him. That was the extent of her response.

"What're you staring at me for?" he asked.

"What are you?" she replied.

"'Scuse me?"

"I've never seen a creature like you before."

"And you'll never see one after me, neither, so take a good look. You ain't the only one-of-a-kind one 'round here." He abruptly swerved, ears pricking upright. "I heard the word 'Groot.'"

"I am Groot?" Still sitting hunched by the ledge, Groot peered over, visibly straining to hear the conversations down on the street.

Rocket bounded his way, leaping from the gravel on the roof onto Groot's back to get a better look.

"I am Groot—!"

The moment Rocket's feet touched down, Groot buckled. He slid sideways, his leg slipping out from under him. Rocket fought to keep his balance, latching onto the rough bark on Groot's shoulders.

"The flark?" he said.

"Groot." Gamora stood instantly by their side. "You all right?"

"I...am Groot." Slowly, he regained his composure and pushed himself back upright.

"That weren't nothing," Rocket snarled. He let himself slip down to the roof again, welcoming steady ground under his feet.

He'd hopped onto Groot's back with even less warning than that plenty of times, and Groot had never so much as blinked at the extra weight.

"I am Groot."

Rocket's eyes narrowed. *Just surprised? Bull.*

He knew what this was—they both knew, they all knew—but none of them said a thing.

"—*Groot*—"

There was that voice again, from down on the ground. After a last half-annoyed, half-worried look at Groot, Rocket clambered onto the ledge and scanned the street for a battle-worn Groot, or people talking about the fight they'd just watched or—

Huh. Or neither.

"Grootling." Rocket pointed. Groups of civilians were slowly heading away from the entrances the Guardians had been watching—some laughing and slapping each other's backs, others so drunk they could barely even walk straight.

Way down the street, illuminated by a nearby holo springing from someone's communicator, they could see the unmistakable shape of a pot and the outline of a Grootling. The Grootling's twig-thin arms moved excitedly about. He couldn't have been more than a week old.

"Doesn't look like much of a fighter," Gamora remarked.

"I sold the one we're looking for weeks ago. He should be grown." Kiya stood and joined the others to peer at the street below. "No chance that's the same Groot. This has to be another duplicate, from a batch I sold a few days back."

"The pot is being held by a child," Drax said. "Or by a very diminutive species I am not familiar with."

"Okay. Rocket, Kiya"—Quill looked at both of them in turn—"let's go grab him."

Kiya looked wary. "I thought you only wanted me here to keep an eye on me."

"And now I want you to talk to those nice people you sold our friend to and help convince them to sell him back. Is that a problem?"

"No," she said after a moment's pause.

"The rest of you, watch for the adult Grootling. If he's not out once we're back, we go in."

"I am Groot?" Groot stood, a plea in his eyes.

"Groot…" Quill shook his head. "We need speed right now. Stay with the others."

"Sorry, buddy," Rocket said.

Quill, Kiya, and Rocket ran across the roof, leapt over an alley, and clambered onto the next rooftop, keeping a close watch on the Grootling below.

"You recognize them?" Quill asked Kiya once they'd caught up with the kid holding the Grootling's pot.

She looked down at the street, squinting. "The father, maybe…"

The kid and their father were part of a bigger group, maybe seven or eight adults laughing and shoving each other. Rocket dismissed them, focusing on the Grootling. Those movements—what was he doing? Shadowboxing?

Rocket's ears twitched, shifting until they were positioned just right to hone in on the group's voices even from all the way down and across the street.

"Yeah! Da, look!" The kid, a girl, carried the pot in one arm, leaving her other arm free to do the same thing as the Grootling: punch wildly in midair. "He's gonna beat 'em *all* when he gets big! Just like the one we saw!"

"—Groot! I am Groot!" The Grootling dodged an imagined blow, then threw a punch of his own, his arm stretching out an inch before snapping back to its regular size.

"Maybe if it gets faster," the dad said.

The kid looked at the pot, puzzled, then took it in both hands and shook it. Dirt spilled over the sides. "Can you be faster?"

"I am—Groo-oo-oot—" The Grootling crouched and held onto the edge of the pot to steady himself.

"Welp," Rocket said, his voice tight with rage, "*that* ain't happening."

He climbed over the side of the roof, scampering down the wall from window ledge to window ledge to the tattered tarp coating of a market stall, and dropped from there to the ground.

"Rocket!" Quill yelled from above. "Don't! Flarking! Shoot! Anyone!"

Across the street, the dad flicked the side of the Grootling's head. "Show us you're worth what I spent on you."

"Fight!" the girl crowed. A couple adults around her laughed. She gave the pot another shake. "Fight!"

Rocket darted across the road on all fours, swerving around another cluster of folks who must've come from the pits. He came to a stop promptly upright in front of the kid. "I'll take *that*," he snapped, and reached for the pot.

"Ah! Ah!" She hugged the pot close, stumbling to get away from Rocket. His claws raked empty air. "Da! What *is* it?"

"I am Groot!" The Grootling furiously punched in Rocket's direction, as though trying to reach. "I am Groot!"

The others in the group had dashed aside in surprise. Only the dad stepped in. "What the…" He raised his leg to kick Rocket.

Without thinking, Rocket leapt and threw his claws into the father's leg. He felt the man moving under his grip, trying to wrench free. He clutched tighter with front and hind legs both. Sank his teeth in. He heard the guy's pants tear, felt the skin break, and tasted slick salty blood.

The man screamed. "Off! Get it *off!*"

A low growl rumbled in Rocket's throat. He bit deeper—one last satisfying chomp. He could've stayed there all day, hearing the guy scream like he was getting murdered, but there was still the Grootling to worry about. And the other people in the street, too. He heard voices, loud and angry. He was kinda surprised they hadn't jumped in yet. This was Ton-Four: a third of the people would be drunk, a third would be armed, and a third would be dangerous.

And those groups overlapped an awful lot.

Rocket let go, spat out a mouthful of nauseating purple-red blood, and bounded away. Back on the ground, he spun toward the girl.

"Now," he snarled, "give me that—oh, hey guys."

Quill stood with the Grootling's pot under one arm and his element gun in his free hand. Kiya stood behind him, whirling slowly to keep an eye on the bystanders. Most had backed away. A few lingered, looking tough, but none were brave enough to step forward just yet.

The little girl stood by her dad in the center of the clearing, shaking, her face wet.

"Rocket? Bit excessive, don't you think?" Quill asked. His arm snapped out. He pointed his element gun at the dad without looking, keeping his gaze fixed on the girl. "Don't move a damn muscle." He shifted the gun left, toward two civilians who'd stepped out of the crowd. "Or you, back there—don't you move either. Don't think I don't see you."

"What's the problem? You only said I couldn't shoot 'em." Rocket spat another glob onto the ground, then wiped his mouth, leaving gross smears on his fur. "You taste *disgusting,*" he told the man.

"I want my Groot!" the girl sobbed. She reached up with grasping seven-fingered hands. "Give me my Groot!"

"So you can shake him some more? He ain't a toy," Rocket growled.

Quill sank into a crouch before the girl. "This little Groot is a friend of ours, okay? We're taking him home. Making him fight doesn't make him happy."

"I! Am! Groot!" The Grootling punctuated each word with a punch. One landed on Quill's upper arm. The impact didn't even crease the leather of his jacket.

It would have been cute, if not for what he'd said. Rocket frowned at the little Grootling. What'd he mean, *Yes it does?* That wasn't Groot. Groot wanted to drink from fountains and travel the universe and talk to shrubs and tickle kids with vines and save lives and guard galaxies and stuff. *Those* were the kind of loser hobbies that made Groot happy.

He was just confused, Rocket decided.

"I want my Groot," the girl repeated.

"Leave my kid alone," the dad finally said. He stumbled forward, holding his bleeding leg.

"*Now* you're worried about her?" Quill looked the dad up and down, keeping his element gun pointed steadily. "But you'll take her to midnight fighting pits on *Ton-Four* and let her torture Groot? You're a terrible father. Did you know that? I mean, holy crap, dude, I am the galaxy's leading authority on terrible fathers, and you rank pretty high! That's not a compliment!"

"Star-Lord." Drax's voice buzzed through their earpieces. "Another Grootling is being led out."

"Terrible! Father!" A shake of Quill's gun emphasized the words.

"On our way," Rocket told Drax. He clambered up the side of Quill's leg and crouched down on his shoulder. It wasn't as comfortable as Groot's— for one thing, Groot was bigger, and for another, Groot was *Groot*—but it would do for now.

Still holding the Grootling's pot, Quill rose into the air, his boots spraying white-hot energy onto the pavement. Rocket held on tight.

"Kiya?" Quill said. "Run back to the others. Rocket and I will be just overhead." The hidden meaning of his words went unspoken: *If you try to run, we'll be on you in a second.*

Rocket had a mental addition of his own: *And Rocket's got a big damn gun he's itching to use, so don't test him.*

Kiya nodded brusquely and took off.

Quill saluted the girl's dad, then shot off toward the other Guardians.

"Give my Groot back!" the dad hollered after them.

"Look after your d'ast kid!" Quill yelled back.

Looking down from Quill's shoulders, Rocket kept an eye on Kiya. She snaked through the still-confused crowd, ducking under an outstretched arm and weaving around three men trying to block her path. She was fast, Rocket grudgingly admitted. Not as elegant as Gamora, and not as much of a bulwark as Drax, but somewhere in between—compact, practical, no frills.

Then she stumbled. Twice. She caught herself both times, but there'd been nothing on the ground—the way she'd stumbled looked more like her knees had given out on her.

At least she was doing as told. Rocket tore his attention away. Groot came first. He saw theirs up ahead, balancing on the edge of the roof. The new Grootling was below, across the street, just exiting the fabric shop. He bowed deep to fit through the door. In front of him walked two men; another two followed behind.

They had the Grootling in chains. Red strands of energy held his arms against his torso and gave his feet barely enough room to shuffle. The men around him each held a strand of the cords. Other men followed behind, but Rocket was too focused on the Grootling to do a headcount.

One arm ended in splinters at the elbow.

His entire right leg and part of his torso were scorched black.

Deep gouges marred his bark all over.

He shuffled along, hunched, silent, and tense.

"Ship here yet?" called one of the men transporting him.

"They said they would be... Aw, they late again?"

"I am Groot." On the roof, Groot stared down, unmoving, at his duplicate. "I am Groot?"

"Hey, Quill." Rocket hunched close to Quill's ear. "*Now* can I shoot people?"

"Yes. *Please.*"

"Aw, yeah."

18

IF PETER hadn't known Rocket so long, having the raccoon pull out a massive blaster right next to his head might've made him a bit nervous.

As it was, he just made sure to keep his flight steady, allowing Rocket to aim properly.

Blam—

One of the men holding the battered Grootling went down. The energy cord he'd been holding whipped through the air, then dropped uselessly to the ground.

"You gotta get mufflers on those guns, dude," Peter told Rocket. "I think my ear is bleeding."

Peter dropped to the ground just as Kiya arrived. He passed the pot to her, waited for Rocket to leap from his shoulders, and shot back into the air to survey the situation.

Clusters of drunk civilians in the street were scrambling to disperse after Rocket's blast. Near the fabric shop, the three remaining handlers were holding the Grootling captive. They reached for their weapons. Rocket shot at one of them and missed.

More people streamed out from the fabric shop. Bulky. Threatening.

All kinds of genders and species. Based on their matching clothing and the identical communicators by their ears, Peter ID'd them as hired security from the pits. They were already starting to circle the group, weapons drawn.

And on the Guardians' side:

A pissed-off Rocket. Drax and Gamora were just leaping down from the casino rooftop. As for the others—

"Kiya, keep that Grootling in the pot safe. That's your one job," he called into his communicator. "Groot—stay put on the roof."

If these people were forcing the Grootling to fight in the pits, they needed some way to control him. Whatever weapon they had, Peter didn't want the real Groot falling prey to it.

"Drax, Gamora—take on the security guards. Rocket, I'll distract the handlers. Try to get our friend free."

"On it," Rocket said—

—AND SKITTERED across the road, staying low.

Between Rocket's size and the midnight dark, he was easy to miss—even more so with Gamora and Drax leaving behind a trail of bleeding security guards. Quill flew overhead, simultaneously distracting the Grootlings' handlers from noticing Rocket and drawing their fire skyward, reducing the risk to bystanders.

Rocket reached his goal. He scrambled up the Grootling's side, a dark shadow, and grabbed a blade from his belt. He started to saw through the cords binding the Grootling—who was making low, confused noises but not fighting back. Even the whirlwind all around them—bullets, energy blasts, and hot-and-cold bursts from Quill's blaster—didn't seem to aggravate or frighten him.

"I gotcha, buddy," Rocket muttered.

One cord dropped and fizzled into nothing. On to the next.

He kept one eye on the handlers, only a few feet away. Two of them had noticed him, but they weren't a threat—Quill had already disarmed them. One gun lay in a half-molten heap on the ground, while another was stuck to the outside wall of the fabric shop, encased in ice.

The third handler was still armed, though. He turned toward Rocket, who bolted upright.

"Get offa my..."

The handler decided to fire rather than finish his sentence.

Rocket yelped. He leapt out of the way, his hind legs kicking off against the Grootling to shove him away from the blast, as well.

Too late: The blast slammed into the Grootling. It tore off more of his missing arm and clipped his side, but he only staggered. "I am Groot?" he said, his voice low and angry. He didn't even *attempt* to move on his attacker.

What had they done to this Groot? He seemed to be sleepwalking.

Rocket was veering out of the way of further gunfire, when—

"I—am *Groooo-ooot!*"

That wasn't the Grootling.

That was their *own* Groot—

—LEAPING down from the roof.

Drax slammed a security guard out of the way, spinning toward his friend just in time to watch him land in the street.

The sound of splintering wood cracked through the air.

Groot had landed on the pavement in the center of the road. He crumpled, not moving for several long moments. The remaining bystanders backed away in terror.

Drax watched, worried. A fall from a two-story building should not have injured Groot so severely.

Kiya stood a few feet away, between Drax and Groot. She clutched the pot with the small Grootling to her chest. "Is he…"

Groot stirred. He pushed himself up and looked himself over. "I am… Groot?" His legs were barely recognizable. They had splintered and cracked on impact with the ground. One foot pointed the wrong way; half of his ankle was torn open.

"He is alive," Drax informed Kiya.

"Another Groot?" one of the handlers yelled. "We gotta grab him! We'll be *rich!*"

Groot's head snapped up. He stood shakily and tottered forward on broken feet. "I am Groo-oot!" He stumbled his way toward the third handler—who was still firing at Rocket—and smacked him aside.

"Yes!" Drax crowed. Nothing so simple as a *fall* could break his friends—

—BUT A gun might. Too late, Peter saw the weapon.

One of the Grootling's handlers—one he'd already disarmed—pulled out a damn *spare,* pointed it at Groot, and pulled the trigger. Peter aimed his own gun and shot a ball of fire—too late.

Farther down the street, Groot hurtled forward. His movements were so uncoordinated, he seemed drunk.

The zap from the handler's gun struck Groot in the chest.

He shook off the hit and lurched forward. Another zap, fired within a second of the first, sent splinters flying. He dropped to one knee, swaying.

Before the shooter could take aim a third time, the fire from Peter's element gun reached him. He ducked aside, screaming.

Rocket was just facing off against the third handler. There was only one other left standing—disarmed, and without a spare weapon, or he'd have pulled it by now.

"Drax, free the Grootling," Peter said. "Gamora? Status?"

"Sending the final guards scattering," she reported. "Some of them got *interesting* ideas about teaming up on me."

Peter almost felt sorry for them.

He had a team to look after, though. Groot sat in the middle of the street, trying to stand up. Kiya was helping him, but every time, his damaged legs gave out. His torso cracked with each haphazard movement.

A pair of bystanders was sneaking up on Groot and Kiya. The idea of grabbing two vulnerable *Flora colossi*—one injured, the other young—had to be too good to pass up. Peter sent down a warning shot of hail.

"Anyone else?" he called down—

—BUT THE Grootling did not respond.

He had still not even attempted to fight. He watched Rocket's battle with the handler, tense and confused but unmoving.

Drax decided to worry about that after they were back at the ship. He stepped in close and tore the bonds around the Grootling's torso clean off. Then he crouched to rip the cord from his legs. "Come with us. We will hold off anyone who—"

"Groot!"

Drax looked over his shoulder at the source of the call. It was one of the handlers—sprawled on the street a couple feet away, his clothes charred, a burn on his face.

"We are taking our friend," Drax said. "This is not negotiable."

The guy laughed, the sound wild and shrill. He was not even looking at Drax. He stared at the Grootling. "Listen: *I. Am. Grooter.*"

At the three words, the Grootling stiffened. His back straightened. Rage slid over his features like a curtain being drawn. A guttural yell rose from his throat—and then he lashed out, swiping at Drax with an overgrown hand.

Drax leapt sideways and landed in a crouch, avoiding the claw by a hair's breadth.

"Groot?" he said. "Have I provoked you somehow?"

"Great," Gamora said, rushing up to Drax's side. She snapped into a fighting stance, peering up at the Grootling. "Brainwashing. That's just what we needed."

"We did not need brainwashing at all, Gamora," Drax corrected her.

Quill had been hovering protectively near Kiya and Groot. Now he flew toward the Grootling, firing his element gun. "Sorry about this, buddy. You'll thank us when you're all un-brainwashed and stuff." The Grootling's legs froze to a clump.

"I am *Groot!*" The ice cracked, then shattered. Enraged, the Grootling dashed at the nearest foe: Drax.

Drax raised his arm to shield himself. The tips of the Grootling's fingers cracked off on impact, but he kept moving. He roared again.

"Why can't anything ever be simple?" Quill mused. "Drax, keep the dupe busy, wear him out. He'll be short on energy like the others. Rocket, help Drax. Create a distraction, talk the Grootling through the brainwashing—anything. Gamora, Kiya, get our Groot and the little Grootling out of here. Too many people seem to want one of their very own after seeing the Grootling perform in the pits." Quill paused and opened another comms channel. "Hey, Grootlings on the ship—can you fly it to our location? In one piece, preferably?"

Keep the brainwashed Grootling busy. Drax could do that.

"Meanwhile," Quill continued, "I'll keep the bystanders at a distance. Are they placing *bets?*"

"Ton-Four, man," Rocket said. "Ton-Four."

Drax dodged another two of the Grootling's blows. He stepped out of the way of a third—or tried to. The Grootling's claws raked his chest, leaving nasty scratches.

The problem was this: Drax was unused to dodging. Dodging was a terrible tactic in a fight. Charging forward and crushing skulls was more effective. Twisting necks. Tearing off limbs. Ripping out spines.

There were *many* good tactics in a fight, and none of them involved this vexing "stay out of reach" approach. It took every bit of his self-control not to strike back when attacked.

The only thing that held him back was the fact that his attacker's face was his friend's face, also.

Drax was beginning to feel conflicted—

—THIS fight could get nasty. Rocket came to a sliding stop beside Drax.

"Groot!" He flashed a toothy smile up at the Grootling. Absolutely zero percent of the smile was sincere—he didn't even *recognize* the Groot's face, it was so angry. "Heyyyy, buddy. What's gotten into you? Grew too many leaves in the brainpan?"

"I am Groot," the Grootling cried out.

"*Destroy?* That's all you have to say for yourself? That's *Drax's* jam."

Drax nodded briskly in agreement.

"Hate to be cliché," Rocket said, shooting forward on all fours and skittering onto the Grootling's back, "but this ain't you, Groot. See that sad sap in the street, leaning on Gamora's shoulders? *That's* you."

The Grootling twisted. He reached back with his one battered arm, but Rocket zipped out of reach too fast, propping himself up on the Grootling's opposite shoulder.

"Do you even recognize us? Hel-*lo?* This voice ring any bells?"

"I am Groot!" The Grootling spun ferociously, still trying to grab Rocket. "I—am—Groot!" He hunched over, body tight and tense. Branches sprouted from his back. One smacked into Rocket's hip; another struck his face. He went flying and landed in a heap several feet away.

"Was that necessary?" Rocket shouted. He climbed upright—too late. Pressure on his tail. The Grootling had him pinned down with a leg that was still partially iced from Quill's element gun. Rocket tried to scramble away, his nails scratching uselessly at the pavement.

The Grootling lifted his other leg, ready to stomp down hard.

"Oh nonono—" Rocket gave up on trying to escape. He threw himself flat on his back, jerked the blaster from his belt, and pointed it straight up. "Don't make me do this, buddy—"

—THE GROOTLING'S foot came down.

Drax crashed into him. The two of them tumbled toward the fabric shop. Pavement and bark scratched at Drax's skin. The branches on the Grootling's back broke off with a clean *crack*. Drax tried to keep the Grootling pinned, straddling his torso and forcing down his arms.

"You are supposed to be weakened," Drax said.

"I am Groot!"

By Drax's side, Rocket clambered to his feet and protectively held his tail. "Yeah, brainwashing'll do that to ya." He spat on the ground. "Always comes with stupid strength. He ain't at full power, though. We'd be toast if he was."

"I would not be toast." Drax leaned into the Grootling, straining—although his opponent seemed to be weakening. "I do not wish to hurt you, Groot."

"I am Groot!"

"The feeling ain't mutual," Rocket translated, unnecessarily.

Drax glared down at the Grootling. He had always wondered about fighting a foe as versatile as Groot—but not once had he actually wanted to do so. Groot did not tend to inspire enmity or aggression.

A vine twined out and curled around Drax's torso. He braced himself. The Grootling pulled, trying to drag him off, but it felt like a half-hearted attempt.

Exhaustion dampened the fury in the Grootling's eyes. The energy drain all the Groots experienced, the damage from his fights in the pit, the struggle with Drax and Rocket—all this had clearly left him tired.

"I am...Groot." He grew thorns to twist into Drax's skin, but they did not even pierce the outer layer. The attempt only drained him further.

"Star-Lord?" Drax said, climbing off the Grootling. "He is ready."

Quill approached, stopping to hover above the Grootling. A single blast with his element gun was enough to freeze the Grootling into immobility.

Drax had not expected any of this to be simple, but he *had* always expected the mission to end in victory. That was how this worked: They would defeat their enemies, rescue those who needed rescuing, and— satisfied with their inevitable victory—return to the ship for a drink.

He would still take that drink.

But with the original Groot in pieces and this Grootling a twisted imitation of their friend, this did not come close to feeling like a victory.

19

THE PROBLEM with getting Groot out of danger was twofold: His size made him unwieldy, and he didn't cooperate. He kept pushing Gamora away and turning back toward the street where the others were fighting.

"I am Groo-oot." He reached toward the Grootling.

"Trust Drax and Rocket to handle it." Gamora redirected him forward.

Groot half-leaned on her shoulder, half-walked on his own, a crooked imbalanced gait that had his weight thumping down on Gamora with every step. His injuries were growing over—his feet reshaping, his cracked torso straightening—but it was a slow process. At this rate, it could take well over an hour before he fully recovered.

He shouldn't have been this badly injured in the first place.

"We're being followed," Kiya said. She trailed Gamora and Groot at a distance, holding the pot with the younger Grootling close as the four of them hustled down the alley. It was the first time Kiya and Gamora had even been close to alone, with no other Guardians around that Kiya could communicate with. The girl was tense—Gamora could almost taste it on the air—but she'd obeyed Quill's order to follow without a word of argument.

Maybe she was wary of turning the Guardians against her.

Maybe she wanted to escape the bystanders who were itching to steal the Grootling.

Or maybe she was realizing that Gamora wasn't her enemy.

That possibility felt unlikely—foolish, as though Gamora had let her hopes get away from her. (She was not sure, precisely, what she was hoping for, or even when she had started doing so.)

But the truth was, Kiya could have fled from the Guardians just now. Easily. The team had been distracted, and with the buildings, the market stalls, and the bystanders, there'd been plenty of ways to hide and escape. Kiya would've seen all the hiding spots and exits.

And yet, here they were, running through an alley together. Kiya was even speaking to her unprompted.

Perhaps Gamora's hope was not so foolish after all.

She stopped and turned. A handful of silhouettes came jogging at them. Blades flashed in their hands.

"Only three?" Gamora stepped past Kiya to face them. "You're not even trying."

"I am Groot!"

"You're in no shape to fight," she told him. "Stay back."

"I am Groot."

"I know you want to help—"

"I am Groot?" the Grootling in Kiya's arms piped up.

"Give me that pot!" one of the men yelled. He walked with a limp, his pants torn and blood-covered, but it barely slowed him down.

"You get the pot!" another man said. "We'll get the big one!"

Sometimes, Gamora wondered where mediocre people found this kind of confidence.

"That's the father—the guy who bought this little one from me," Kiya said.

Gamora glanced over her shoulder. "He won't get him back." Kiya had spread her stance and lowered her core, readying herself for a fight even with her arms full. Her eyes flicked between Gamora and the men coming toward them.

"Keep the girl intact!" one guy shouted. "Bigger reward that way!"

Reward?

Gamora narrowed her eyes. The first guy who'd shouted was reaching inside his pocket. From the shape of it, not for a knife. Something worse.

"Back!"

Gamora spun around, flinging Kiya down and covering the girl with her own body.

Kiya hissed at the movement even before she hit the pavement. A split second later, the grenade thunked down.

A bang—small, too small—

sssssssssssstttttt—

Light drained away. It spiraled into the explosion point and vanished with a blip, leaving the alley pitch dark.

A darkbomb.

Interesting choice.

Pathetic choice.

Pointless choice.

"Cowards," Gamora said.

The darkness didn't matter. She could hear them. *There.* She went low, easily tackling the nearest attacker. His face smacked against the wall. She heard a crunch. (Not a skull. She'd recognize the sound of a crunched skull. Goggles, maybe, to help them see in the dark.)

The next man went down with a punch. *I don't even need to bring out my sword for this,* Gamora thought.

The third—where? She listened, filtering out the noise from the street, the rustle of Groot's movements, the groaning of the men she'd taken down, Kiya making a pained sound as her feet shifted—

Ah.

"You want this so bad?" Kiya yelled. "*Take* it!"

Something cracked—still not a skull—and a body too heavy to be Kiya's slumped to the ground, surrounded by a rain of something both hard and soft. Shards of the Grootling's pot, if Gamora had to guess, and the dirt inside.

"I am Groot," the Grootling said miserably.

"You hit him with the pot?" Gamora asked.

A pause. "Yes."

"Little Groot? You okay?"

"He can survive without a pot for a while at this age."

"I am Groot," the Grootling said, sullen but seemingly healthy.

"And you? Groot?"

"I am Groot."

Good. Everyone was in one piece. Gamora brought up her arm, dragging a holo from her communicator and rapidly entering search queries. Within seconds, she found what she was looking for. Letters glowed bright in the dark of the alley, revealing an ad promising a reward for Kiya's safe return to the Collector.

Her lips tightened. She flicked off the holo, plunging them back into the dark.

This would complicate things.

"I am Groot?" Groot asked.

The Grootling snickered. "I am Groot. I am Grooooot."

"What are they saying?" Kiya asked.

"Groot asked whether we're all right. The Grootling said it's an insult to ask me that after a lousy two opponents. He's not wrong, but I'll let it slide."

She paused. Kiya answering Gamora's questions—even asking one of her own—was more than she'd expected. Gamora shouldn't be pushing her luck. Still, she had to know: "Kiya. *Are* you all right? Are you injured?"

"No."

"You were in pain when you moved."

"It's nothing."

Gamora walked back to where she'd left Groot. "I know what I heard."

Kiya didn't answer.

"There is no point in lying to me."

"You're not my—" Kiya started, but cut herself off. For a moment, she stood silently. When she continued, her voice was rushed but hostile, as if she couldn't stop herself from talking but hated doing so at the same time. "It's the enhancements. All right? Their implementation is a long process. Months. Years. I escaped before Tivan"—she paused after that name, inhaling sharply—"could finish."

Kiya put her hand to the wall (the soft sound of skin on stone) and shuffled over (quiet treads on the pavement).

"Dangerous," Gamora mused. Incomplete implants meant Kiya could have strength enhancements without the durability to support them, or speed without the flexibility. Incorrectly healed implants might not be properly integrated with her existing or remaining bone, musculature, joints, tendons… "We can find a way to complete the process."

"Complete?" Kiya scoffed. "If I wanted the enhancements complete, I'd look up that ad you just saw and hand myself in. I want this stuff *out of my body.*"

Gamora shook her head, glad that Kiya couldn't see her. You could replace bone with metal. Reversing the process was more complicated.

"Why do you think I was selling the Groots?" Kiya's words were quieter, more strained. "It *hurts.* All the time. I needed units for a qualified cybernetic surgeon."

Gamora absorbed the words, walking along in silence.

Semi-silence. She heard footsteps behind them, bumbling about in the dark.

"I have an idea," she said. "But let me dispatch the people tailing us, first."

20

THE FORCE FIELD hissed across the open hatch. Only when it had hit each corner of the hatch, locking the brainwashed, still-iced Grootling safely in Groot's quarters, did Peter dare loosen his grip on his element gun.

"Well, that was fun," Rocket drawled.

"I disagree," Drax said.

The five Guardians and Kiya stood scattered across the leisure area, facing the force field. The other Grootlings had been temporarily moved into the rest of the ship while the team conferred.

"So," Peter said. "Telepath?"

Rocket nodded. "Cosmo or Moondragon could sort out the brainwashing, no big."

"Telepaths typically have a hard time with Groot," Gamora pointed out. "His mind has an unusual structure."

"I am Groot." Groot—the original—stood at the back of the group, tall and quiet. His body was only just growing back into its proper shape. His tone was distracted. He was so tightly focused on his own quarters and the Grootling inside, Peter wouldn't have been surprised if he'd forgotten about the rest of the team.

Gamora and Kiya stood on opposite ends of the room, their arms crossed, poses wary and expectant; Rocket stayed near the brainwashed Grootling, either to keep an eye on him or show support.

"He seems well." Drax stood behind the central couch, propping his fists on the backrest and leaning in. The force field separating the Grootling from the Guardians was barely visible; just a tremble in the air across the open hatch when you looked at it from the right angle.

The Grootling looked back, silent.

He hadn't cooperated as they'd carried him into the ship and locked him in Groot's quarters, but he hadn't fought either. They'd hoped that being in Groot's—*his*—quarters, which he had to have memories of, might help bring him back to himself. He hadn't so much as glanced at the rest of his quarters past the hatch, though. He'd stayed right by the opening, making no attempts to remove the remaining ice on his legs. He'd muttered a few words that translated to nonsense. As time passed, he'd shrunk in on himself, exhaustion overtaking him.

"Sure, as long as no one says…" *I am Grooter,* Peter thought. The code words. "…you-know-what. We don't know what else might set him off." He turned toward the Grootling. "I'm sorry. We'll do what we can."

"I am Groot," Groot added, his words a promise.

That promise nagged at Peter. This was uncharted territory. He was winging it even more than usual—and with his friends at stake, it didn't feel nearly as comfortable as he was used to.

"I am Groot?" Groot asked.

The Grootling didn't respond.

Peter waited a few moments, hoping the Grootling might change his mind about answering their questions. As it was, they didn't dare let him loose in the ship.

Groot finally sat on the couch. His body creaked with the movement.

"We can try again later," Peter said. "For now, well, we fought him when he'd just come off a night of pit fighting. I don't want to see how much damage he can do once he's recovered."

"Even a weakened Groot poses a danger," Drax agreed. As he leaned over the couch from behind, his face was right beside Groot's, but Groot didn't look up or even acknowledge his words. Groot sat perfectly still, his eyes fixed on the Grootling.

"Groot," Drax continued, "I do not think you should accompany us on our next mission. It is too dangerous."

"You joking?" Rocket scooted onto the couch to stand on one armrest.

Peter and Gamora met each other's eyes. Kiya was nodding her agreement.

Groot did nothing for another second, two—and then it seemed to sink in. He sprang upright, a branch cracking from his leg. "I am Groot? I am Groot!"

"Your legs splintered when you simply leapt from the building," Drax said. "We do not wish to see you harmed further."

"You can't just bench him, man," Rocket said. "If we're benching anyone, it's Kiya. She's got a fricking reward on her head! Anyone who recognizes her could bring the Collector down on us."

Groot turned to Peter, pleading.

"Whoa, look, I don't know." He raised his hands. "We're not benching you. But you do have to consider it. You're not exactly in top shape."

The bark on Groot's shoulders crackled and shifted, as if new branches were about to sprout. They didn't. Peter hoped that meant Groot was holding back his anger and panic—and not that he simply didn't have the strength to grow more branches so abruptly.

"I am Groot." His face twisted in despair. "I—am Groot?" He staggered out of the room.

"I'm coming, buddy." Rocket bounded after him.

"I am Groot?" The brainwashed Grootling raised one hand to the force field.

Peter glanced back. He couldn't make much sense of the Grootling's words—they were slurred, making them hard to translate. But the fact that he was reacting had to be a good sign.

Kiya looked from the exit to the remaining members of the team. "He seems upset."

"I believe he is," Drax agreed.

"Wouldn't he rather be safe?" Kiya asked. "Given how slowly he's recovering, getting injured again seems like a bad idea. Why does he want to come along on missions so bad?"

"Same reason the Grootlings keep begging to come along," Gamora said.

"Groot is..." Peter waffled for a moment. Kiya had only just come aboard the ship, and even if she hadn't meant to, she was directly responsible for a whole lot of their current problems. Groot might not appreciate them talking to her about him. As affectionate as the Grootlings seemed toward her, the same hadn't counted for the real Groot.

If it helped Kiya to better understand the situation she'd caused, though—and moreover, if it sparked anything in the brainwashed Grootling, still watching them through the hatch—it was worth it.

"How much do you know about *Flora colossi?*" he asked.

Kiya watched Peter as though the question were a trap. "Physiologically, I picked up a lot these past weeks. Practically or culturally, not much."

"They're not all like Groot. Yes, they're smart, and yes, they're strong, but they're also cold. They look down on anyone different. To them, mammals are good for nothing but grunt work and experimentation. Groot didn't agree. He stood up against them to help mistreated mammals, and, well, he's not exactly popular on his homeworld now."

Gamora stepped in. "He defied his entire species and gave up his home, simply because he cared so much. What the Guardians of the Galaxy do? Traveling the universe, meeting new people, helping those who need it? Groot loves it. He *loves* getting to be this person—getting to be himself."

"Except now…" Peter looked at the Grootling, then at the tray of sproutlings in one corner and an abandoned pot of dirt a sapling must have used earlier. "I think he's worried that that 'self' might not be set in stone anymore."

"He does not want to suspend his role on the team," Drax said. "He feels strongly about this."

"He's scared," Gamora said. "He's scared he's losing everything that made—makes—him *him*."

The room fell silent.

Kiya worried at her lower lip. Hesitation played across her face, even as the rest of her stood as springboard-tense as ever. When she realized the others were waiting for her to respond, she drew her face back to normal. "I'll—" she said, blinking. "I'll find the Grootlings that've been helping me test some theories. About merging them."

It seemed, for a moment, she might say more.

Then she walked out, almost tripping over her own feet. She shot back a look at the Grootling stuck behind the force field. Peter could have sworn he saw a flash of guilt on her face.

It left the four of them behind: Drax, Gamora, Peter, and the trapped Grootling.

"You remember what I just told Kiya about the *Flora colossi*, don't you?" he asked the Grootling.

The Grootling nodded. His expression was unsure—Peter wasn't convinced that he'd followed the whole story—but it was a start.

"I'm sorry about this, man. I am. I'll reach out to the telepaths we know. In the meantime, let's just…recover. Are you okay staying in his—your?—quarters for now? We'll come talk to you."

The Grootling sank to the floor on the other side of the force field, wrapping his arms around his legs. He observed the leisure room as if settling in for the long haul.

"We'll let you rest," Peter said. "The other Grootlings could come back in here later. You'd have some company."

The Grootling nodded again, not making eye contact.

The moment they left the room, Peter let out an uneasy breath. "I need a burger," he groaned. "Even a crappy Zelarian knock-off."

"That sounds disgusting," Drax said. "I will join you. Let us see if Groot will, too."

"Gamora?"

"No," she said. "I need to find Rocket."

21

IS THIS necessary?" Rocket asked.

"Yes." Gamora stalked down the hall of the ship with Rocket in tow. He hustled to keep up. Why did people always forget his legs weren't exactly lengthy? There was a *reason* he hitched a ride with Groot so often.

This time, Groot was hitching along with Rocket. To be more specific, two Grootlings he'd picked up in the cargo bay sat on Rocket's shoulders. The weirdly violent little one they'd found today was trying to rile up the other one, who was sitting on Rocket's other shoulder, making occasional worried noises. Their twig-thin legs and hands gripped Rocket's fur and the straps of his shirt as Rocket bounced after Gamora.

"Oy! I like my fur where it is, you two!" he said after the 10th time one yanked out a couple of strands by accident. "But Gammy, why are you asking *me* to help? Far as I'm concerned, Kiya can take a nice long spacewalk with no suit on. Enjoy the sights, do some stargazing, get all that fresh vacuum up in her lungs. Or, hey, I could hand her over to the Collector and get back a pleasant amount of units in the process. I don't flarking *care* about her implants."

"You should care, because you know what it's like to be treated like a lab rat," she said sharply. "I'm asking you because you're the smartest person on this team with the most tech experience."

"Aaaand?"

"No. That's all the flattery you get."

"All right, fine, I'll take it," he grumbled. "You don't have to do this, you know. You don't have to help her."

"I do."

"It ain't your fault."

"I am Groot," the quieter Grootling agreed.

"Is that what you think?" Gamora glanced down at Rocket. For a second, he thought she was angry, but her face skewed closer to amused. "You think I'm doing this out of guilt? That I feel responsible for what the Collector did to her?"

"You don't?"

She stopped in front of the med-bay door, one hand on the handle. "Rocket. I'm responsible for too many things in this universe that I've actually done to take on guilt for what I *haven't* done. The Collector is responsible. I won't absolve him of that."

So it wasn't guilt, and it definitely wasn't business as usual.

Rocket grimaced. It was the whole Zen-Whoberian, last-of-their-kind thing, wasn't it? She was getting all *attached.*

Gamora slid open the door.

Kiya sat cross-legged in a chair. On the counter in front of her sat another Grootling, his legs dangling over the side. Kiya was inspecting his shoulder.

"I am Groot," he greeted them.

Kiya sat abruptly upright, then relaxed—marginally—when she saw Rocket and Gamora. Why that would make her relax, Rocket didn't understand—out of everyone on this ship, he figured they'd be the least welcome. Rocket was the one who'd argued against her presence at every point, and Gamora was her personal bogeyman.

Maybe Kiya was just skittish.

She wasn't the only one.

Gamora's reaction was so subtle, Rocket probably wouldn't have noticed if he hadn't known her so long. He saw the tiny widening of her eyes as she spotted Kiya, and the way she studied her for a few long seconds, as if she was re-familiarizing herself with Kiya's face. It gave him the heebie-jeebies.

Yeah. This was definitely about the Zen-Whoberian thing.

Rocket didn't like it. And not just because Gamora's obsession with the girl was the number one reason Kiya was even on board, which made it the number one reason they weren't going after the Groots in the Collector's grasp, which—

She's fixing Groot, he told himself. He glanced at the Grootlings on his shoulders. *Try and remember that part.*

It was better than acknowledging other nagging thoughts. Rocket would never get to stare at anyone the way Gamora got to stare at Kiya.

"Any progress?" Rocket tried to sound sour, rather than murderous.

"Not sure."

He waited for more, but Kiya was silent. "Thassit?" he continued. "That's what we're feeding you three meals a day for? All right—the Kiya experiment is over. We tried. To hell with this."

Kiya looked down. She breathed deeply in and out, as if she were either steeling herself or trying to convince herself of something. "I'm gathering information for now. That's how this *works.* What I have so far is...*Flora colossi* can easily absorb other plant matter. Absorbing other *Flora colossi* seems to be different. In this case, at least. They get close—their torsos sometimes fuse together, or their bark shifts and overlaps—but each time, they break apart again before they can merge completely. We need more."

No kidding.

"I have some avenues to explore. I've been asking different combinations of Groots to try to merge and taking notes. I'm watching how far they get, how smoothly it seems to go, and studying each individual Groot involved"—she tilted her head at the Grootling sitting on the counter—"to determine if there's a pattern. I suspect there are physiological factors, maybe related to their current weakness. I'm also studying pieces of bark from when they're melded for those few seconds, seeing whether the Grootlings actually combine on a cellular level or just grow around each other, what happens with them while they try to merge, whether they're affected afterward..." She shrugged. "So, like I said: Not sure whether I've made any progress. *Yet.*"

Rocket stared at her, eyes narrowed. "Hrm."

Maybe their food wasn't *entirely* going to waste on her.

"I am Groot?" one Grootling gulped near Rocket's ear. He guessed that one hadn't had the pleasure of being part of her little science experience yet.

"What might happen if the Grootlings try to merge," Gamora said, "and one of those Grootlings is...damaged?"

It was the first time she'd spoken since entering the room. It'd taken her *that* long to get over her mesmerized staring. Or maybe she just hadn't been sure what to say, which was a weird thought with Gamora of all people. Since Kiya flinched whenever Gamora so much as opened her mouth, though, Rocket kinda understood why Gam might be choosing her words carefully.

He didn't like seeing his teammate get all weird about this girl. With everything going on with Groot, Rocket had plenty of weirdness to deal with already.

"I wish I knew," Kiya said, not quite looking at Gamora.

"I am Groot." The Grootling Kiya was working on wrapped his hands around the edge of the countertop, leaning in slightly. "I am Groot."

Rocket grimaced. "I know, buddy."

"What did he say?" Kiya asked.

Gamora answered, "He's worried about the Grootling we found at the pits today. He'd thought the other Groots were like him. A duplicate, but with the same memories, the same personality. He thought they would all cooperate."

"Even if they retain their memories, being raised like that one"—Kiya tilted her head toward the aggressive Grootling on Rocket's shoulder—"and made to fight in the pits will still mess you up. I noticed it in the greenhouse, too. They're easily influenced when young. Probably even more so, now that they're weakening."

And whose fault is that, huh? Rocket bit his tongue. "Yeah, well, you're gonna fix it. It's the only reason you're *here*."

"I'm trying." She turned brusquely toward the Grootling.

"You'd better. I ain't keeping you safe for nothing."

"You're keeping me safe, now?" Kiya sounded skeptical.

"Damn right. Me and Quill, we were talking about sending the Collector false tips. We can mask our signals, say we spotted you on this moon or that planet, and send him scrambling all over the galaxy. It'd drown out whatever real tips he gets. Also, it'd be hilarious. 'Course, if you don't want us to…"

"No!" she said. "No. That…sounds good."

"Thought so." He hopped onto a chair, rummaged through a drawer, and held up a scanner. "Next order of business."

"I brought Rocket to run a scan of your implants, see what he can learn about them," Gamora explained. "He's smarter than he looks."

"And I look like a krutacking genius, so that's sayin' something. Let's get started."

Kiya looked struck. "What? Right now?"

He leapt nimbly to the ground. "I seem like the type you can make an appointment for? Pick a fight with Gamora if you don't like it."

She sat anchored to her chair. She looked to Gamora as if for help, then immediately turned away. "Do I need to…?"

"Get naked? Lie down? Do whatever gets you going, lady. I'll just be scanning your leg here." He took hold of her calf, grumbling. She hissed, hauling it back instantly. She'd hoisted both legs onto her chair and wrapped her arms around her knees before she even seemed to realize what she was doing. She looked down at him, startled, her breathing suddenly sharp and fast.

"Rocket!" Gamora said. "Slow down."

"Eesh. She come with a manual?"

"Slow. Down. Kiya, do you want someone else here for this? Do you want him to stop?"

She pressed her lips together, as if she were running through the options. After a couple of seconds, she shook her head. "No. I can do this." She let the leg dangle down again.

Rocket pulled it closer with one hand, holding the scanner with the other. She was all shaky. That wasn't gonna help the readings. He gripped her tighter to hold her still, running the scanner from thigh to ankle, then slowly over her foot. Then he did the same from the other side of her leg.

"Kiya…?" Gamora said.

"I *said* it's fine!" The moment Rocket let go, she pulled her leg back up. "You need more?"

He fiddled with the scanner until a holo popped up, showing a nearly transparent version of Kiya's leg with sharp, thin metal running through nearly every part—a mess of threads and rods and knobs, most of them wrapped with fine sheets of what he suspected was gnitium, or maybe gnitium-reinforced anjar. Curiosity gnawed at him, but he shoved it aside. "All right, got it. I'll do the rest later if I need it." He zapped the holo off and jammed the scanner into his pocket. "Groot, I'm going to check on brainwashed evil-you."

"I am Groot," he said.

"What? I thought it was hilarious."

With a cackle, he was out the door.

22

SO...HE said what Rocket said wasn't funny?" Kiya ventured, looking from the Grootling to Gamora. She only held eye contact for a second, then turned away again, leaving Gamora looking at the back of her head.

Gamora tried to take this as a positive: If Kiya could turn her back to Gamora, she was less frightened than when she'd come on board.

"Correct."

"How do you know? I only hear 'I am Groot.'"

"Tone, emphasis, pronunciation, how he breathes around the words. It's a language like any other."

"I am Groot." The Grootling nodded at Gamora over Kiya's shoulder.

Gamora hesitated. "I'm sorry if Rocket was—"

"I can take it. They did worse to me back at the Collector's."

"Who's 'they'?"

Kiya shrugged gruffly. She was still facing the Grootling rather than Gamora, but had abandoned her inspection. It wasn't hard to tell where her focus lay. Her entire demeanor screamed it: alert, wary, cautious. "Collector. Associates."

Gamora didn't know how to say her next words—few people had ever said them to her. She knew it was the correct thing to do, though. Rocket was right, and so was Gamora herself: What had happened to Kiya was not Gamora's responsibility.

What happened to Kiya next, though—

Gamora couldn't help but feel that was different.

She stepped nearer to the counter, careful to keep her distance but wanting to catch at least a glimpse of Kiya's face. "If you want to talk about it..." The words felt cold on her tongue.

Kiya tensed up.

"Not to me, if you don't want to," Gamora added, already knowing that was the case—and feeling so abruptly twisted about it that it startled her—"but to any of us. We might understand better than you think."

"Do you?" Kiya asked stonily.

Gamora took a moment to find the precise words. "I know what it's like to be turned into a weapon," she said slowly. "Peter knows what it's like to see your mother die in front of you—because of what he is, what his father is—and get sucked into a world you didn't even know existed. Rocket knows what it's like to be turned into something you're not, without your consent. Drax knows what it's like to lose a family. Groot knows what it's like to be alone and far, far from the only home you've ever known."

We're all broken, she wanted to say.

We're a family nonetheless.

You could be, too.

She didn't say it.

The way Kiya sat—hunched over and still, and with bottled-up anger and fear Gamora couldn't help but recognize—told her enough. Kiya didn't want to talk. Maybe she couldn't talk, not yet.

There was something else Gamora could do better, anyway.

"And I can teach you, if it would help. If you want to feel safer."

"'Scuse me?" Kiya tilted her body slightly, but still didn't face Gamora.

"You're a good fighter. You can be better. I can help you fight despite the pain. Around it. Because of it." She tried a smile, a narrow one.

"No."

The smile, narrow as it was, disappeared.

"He called me by your name, you know," Kiya said.

Gamora closed her eyes for a moment. She was not surprised: The extent of Taneleer Tivan's cruelty could no longer surprise her.

She still hated to hear the words.

"I *don't*"—Kiya's words were clipped—"want to be you."

"I didn't—"

"Ever."

I don't want you to be me, either, Gamora thought. *Ever.*

Gamora wouldn't wish that on anyone. It wasn't what she'd meant—

So why had she made the offer?

"I want to go home," Kiya said. She pulled one leg onto her chair and rubbed her knuckles into her shin, as if trying to massage away the pain. "I want to *stop* fighting."

The churn of disappointment Gamora felt told her precisely why she'd made the offer, which answer Gamora had hoped for.

And it wasn't going to happen.

Kiya wouldn't be part of the Guardians' world. She wouldn't stay.

Gamora had met what might be the sole other Zen-Whoberian in the universe, and it was a traumatized girl who didn't understand why Groot might want to keep going on missions, who didn't want to fight, who wanted to go home and grow her plants and leave this part of the world behind for good and never think the name *Gamora* again.

She had to push out the words: "All right."

"I am Groot," the Grootling said apologetically. He looked torn between staying put and coming to Gamora's side. Gamora shook her head: Kiya's work with him was too important for him to leave now.

"Good luck with your research." Gamora stepped back and quietly slid the door shut behind her.

THE GIRL had been busy since her escape from the Collector.

Over the next days, they found another three Groots, along with the remains of a fourth. There were still others out there. Some, Kiya had jotted down in a list she updated whenever she remembered a buyer or location; others would be harder to track, like the handful she'd sold in open markets or to anonymous buyers, but they had leads on even those. They intercepted transmissions, overheard gossip, put out the word. Their list of locations grew quickly.

It wasn't going fast enough for Rocket's taste—for any of their tastes—but this situation was never going to be resolved in a matter of hours.

The telepaths they knew were either impossible to track or wouldn't be available for days. The for-rent ones they tried on various planets were too green to even recognize the brainwashed Groot's thought processes, let alone stick their psionic fingers inside without risking damage.

"We can try"—Rocket made a disgusted face—"Earth. It's a trash-fire planet, but it's infested with telepaths."

It was on their list of options, but that list was growing longer and more nebulous, and they didn't know what other surprises the Grootlings crawling around the galaxy might hold. Retrieving them took priority.

While they were retrieving them, though, the team could still handle other issues. They spoke to the brainwashed Grootling as much as they could, and sent false tips to the Collector whenever they found a moment—sometimes a dozen tips at once, sometimes nothing for hours.

And there was, of course, the issue of Kiya herself.

"Any progress on those implants?" Gamora leaned against the kitchen counter, watching Rocket and Drax eat. Groot sat by her side, with a smaller Grootling on the edge between them. Two more Grootlings sat cross-legged on the kitchen table.

"Eh." Rocket chowed down on the oddly shaped fruits they'd bought on a nearby moon. They were chewy, with a juicy, meaty taste, which was a lot easier to enjoy when Gamora wasn't yapping at his head. "Not really."

"Meaning you haven't looked yet, or meaning you don't know?"

He tried to weather Gamora's stare, but after a few moments, he admitted, "I dunno. Look, it's a big universe, I got a lot on my plate. I can't recognize *every* bit of tech out there."

"Yet you often claim that you do." Drax raised his eyebrows at him from across the table. The two Grootlings on the table did the same, giggling quietly.

"What? I never said that."

"You said those precise words yesterday, when we retrieved that Grootling at the circus after he escaped and contacted us—"

"Never said it." Rocket tore off another chunk of fruit. "Look," he said while chewing, "it's good tech, I can tell you that. Advanced. Not only predicts her movements, and reallocates energy and shifts elasticity based on those predictions, but the way the cybernetics integrate and interface with her remaining biological functions is some of the smoothest work I've seen. I'm almost jealous—I don't see why she wants it torn out so bad."

"I am Groot," one Grootling on the table said, disapproving.

Rocket had dubbed that one "Yellow." He didn't want to give the Groots *actual* names—they had a name already—but Kiya's research required labeling them in her notes. He'd helped her once or twice with the tech side of her research, or with translating the Groots; he'd ended up naming them after colors instead of numbers like Kiya had proposed.

"What's the problem?" Rocket said. "I don't know who put the implants in, and I can't get them out, but that don't mean I can't admire them."

"I am Groot," Indigo—the other Grootling on the table—said. "I am Groot."

"Oh, please, the implantation process can't have been that bad. The incisions looked clean, the integrations solid, and the Collector would've knocked Kiya out for the surgeries. He's a fanatic, not a sadist."

"I am Groot."

"I am Groot."

Their own Groot, standing by Gamora, watched the conversation on the table uncertainly. "I am Groot?"

"Yeah, that's what I'd like to know." Rocket leaned into the nearest Grootling—Indigo. "What do you mean, Kiya talked to you about the surgeries? I thought she didn't think any of you were, y'know, smart?"

Indigo clambered upright to answer, looking self-conscious in a way Rocket wasn't used to from the original Groot. Maybe this was another case of the Grootling being raised differently, like the fighting one at the market. As far as he knew, though, all three of the little Grootlings in the room had been taken directly from Kiya's apartment, and they looked the same age. They couldn't be *that* different from each other.

Still chewing on the fruit, Rocket listened to Indigo's explanation.

All right, that made sense: When Kiya got lonely with no one to talk to after her escape, she'd talked to the plants she grew, even without realizing they were sentient. It was kind of pathetic, but Rocket understood.

And see, according to Indigo, the Collector *had* made sure Kiya was knocked out for the surgeries. It was a *little* messed up that the Collector hadn't warned her beforehand when new surgeries were about to happen, but Rocket had heard of worse.

All right, yeah, if the Collector anesthetized her while she slept and carted her out for surgery, he could see how that'd make her nervous about going to sleep.

And if the Collector had mixed anesthetics into her dinner so she couldn't stay awake and alert at night, that was a jerk move.

And yeah, all right, fine, Rocket understood it might be traumatizing to wake up in the morning and find new scars stretched along your skin and not know what part of your body had been changed or how, but—

"All I said was the tech was good. Sheesh." He slumped back, arms crossed. He knew Groot cared about this kind of stuff, and that the Grootlings had gotten weirdly attached to the girl—he didn't know why, and probably neither did Groot. But he didn't need a fricking sensitivity lecture.

The other Grootling on the table, Yellow, had stayed quiet, sitting and listening. Now he said hesitantly, "I am Groot?"

"Oh?" Drax replied. "It seems like a memorable story."

"Perhaps you weren't there when Kiya talked about it," Gamora suggested.

"I am Groot," Indigo said, confused.

"You are certain this other Grootling was indeed present at the time?" Drax asked Indigo. "You all bear a strong resemblance. It may have been another."

"I am Groot." Orange—that was the Grootling sitting on the kitchen counter in between Gamora and Groot—bobbed his head, backing up Indigo's claim about Yellow.

"I am Groot," Yellow said, looking embarrassed at having to deny remembering a second time.

"Aww, flark," Rocket groaned. He had a hunch where this was going.

"You two, you're sure he was there when Kiya talked about this? And you, you're sure you don't remember?"

"I am Groot!"

"I am Groot."

"I am Groot. I am Groot?"

The fruit abandoned, Rocket stood upright on his chair. He faced Groot, his Groot, leaning against the kitchen counter. "Groot, you notice any missing memories?"

This was the point where Groot should have shaken his head or shrugged sheepishly. Instead, he looked scared.

"Guessing that's a yes. All right, all of you sap-brains, hands up if you remember this one: You and me, scamming the fighting pits on Kara-ae. I mean, participating. Legally. I mean... Aw, Quill ain't here anyway."

Three out of four pairs of hands went up.

"And this one: saving that herd of weird cow things because you felt bad about leaving 'em as food for Fin Fang Foom."

Four hands.

"Rescuing the galaxy from all of time and space collapsing around an intergalactic, interdimensional rift of terrors?"

Two hands.

"I figured that one would be memorable." Rocket wrinkled his nose.

The Grootlings looked at each other, stricken. Groot seemed to shrink in on himself.

Looked like it wasn't just the Grootlings' bodies that were chipping away. It was the rest of them, too.

KIYA'S slow progress, and the Grootlings' continued deterioration, worried Drax. The girl kept herself isolated, sitting out the missions to work long hours in the med lab. Bit by bit, she deciphered patterns in her observations of the Grootlings.

The first correlation she reported was *age.* Grootlings of around the same age seemed to get further along in the process, on average, before rejecting the merge.

Kiya's other findings were more nebulous: similarity of *demeanor.* Or perhaps it was *mood,* or something else entirely—but when she tried to merge a cheery Grootling with, say, the violent little one they had retrieved near the fighting pits, their bark didn't so much as twitch. She had more luck combining similar Grootlings.

Bits and pieces of progress was not enough. Drax did not want notes, or theories, or disturbing attempts at fusions that went nowhere.

He wanted his friend fixed.

The clearest conclusion of Kiya's research was that the barriers keeping the Grootlings separate could be more mental than physical. That, perhaps, the core problem lay in the presence of multiple, incompatible consciousnesses bumping into each other.

So how could they circumvent that?

Grudgingly, Kiya and Rocket put their heads together and stopped by the Knowhere market for supplies. They managed to pick up two dozen custom sensors that could measure the Grootlings' brain activity more accurately than what they'd been using.

"This will read their minds?" Drax asked on a late-night visit to the med bay, frowning at the screens Rocket had set up to keep track of their readings.

Rocket was fixated on one of those screens, so it was up to Kiya to answer. She shook her head. "Just energy. Activity. Whatever you want to call it. It's the only thing we *can* measure." She took a second to attach a new sensor to the Grootling sitting on the counter, pinning it gently onto the bark. "Groot's physical makeup is so odd, we're not even 100 percent sure whether these readings correlate to neurological activity, his physiological state, or both. We can't translate what the sensors pick up, only measure it. Look…" She pointed at one screen, which showed the sensors' readings from across the ship. "This is the original Groot. See the waves? They're calm. He may be asleep. But these two, these are younger Grootlings. They're energetic. They're probably running in circles around the couch again."

"Yeah, but they're the only ones." Rocket sat perched on one of the chairs, flipping through dozens of readings in a matter of seconds. "Yesterday, when they were swinging from those vines in the engine room, there were at least five of 'em, and the readings were way different. Now it's just the two. And all day long, they've been slowing down."

"You sure?" Kiya tested the Grootling's sensor with a light pull. It stayed put.

"'Course I'm sure!" he said. "Averages and peaks for all the Grootlings we're measuring are down since yesterday. You think I don't know how to read these things? You think I can't tell how my best friend is doing?"

Kiya shot him an annoyed glare, but didn't push. "Well, it makes sense. Even if we're not planting any new ones, the Grootlings are using up more energy as they grow bigger."

"The young Grootlings still have a lot of growing left to do. And there are many of them." Drax did not like how worried he sounded. He preferred his voice to fluctuate between "simmering anger" and "Thanos-inspired rage."

"Exactly."

"That is not good."

"Nooope," Rocket said.

"It's really not," Kiya said.

"I am Groot."

She smiled crookedly at the Grootling in front of her. "Heh. I know, right?"

"Hey!" Rocket shot upright in his chair. "Don't do that. Don't freaking *fake* it."

"I was only—"

"You don't know what he's saying. Don't pretend you do."

Kiya pressed her lips together. Then sighed. "Gotcha," she said, turning away from him.

Rocket kept grumbling, only so low that neither Kiya, Drax, nor the Grootling could hear.

"I am going to leave," Drax announced.

"I am Groot," the Grootling said.

23

EVEN in the low light of the ship's nighttime mode, Peter could see the chaos in what had been the leisure room.

The couch was flipped over. A few feet away, a pile of Grootlings lay curled up in a sleepy heap.

Two Grootlings had climbed into the water jug and were trying to dunk each other. One splashed out when he saw Peter, tumbled onto the table, then thunked down to the floor.

"Shhh," Peter said, crouching to help him up. "Don't wake up the others."

"I am Groot," the Grootling whispered confidentially. He stretched, splashing drops everywhere. "I am"—yawn—"Groooot."

The brainwashed Grootling sat off to the side, still in the entrance to Groot's quarters. The hatch was open; it looked as if he could walk right out. The force field keeping him contained was barely visible even under full lighting—now, in the dark, it might as well not have been there.

Peter had offered to let the Grootling free yesterday. They'd been able to have a handful of peaceful conversations. The Grootling had refused, though. He felt the Guardians would be safer with him trapped behind the field—even *he* didn't know for sure what might trigger him.

The thought that the Grootling trusted himself so little nagged at Peter, but he had to admit that part of him felt grateful. One less thing to worry about.

Another Grootling—nearly an adult—and the original Groot sat dozing beside the force field, branches slowly growing in their sleep. Rocket lounged in that Grootling's lap, curled up so that the tip of his tail just barely brushed his face. His hand twitched. Peter was almost sure he was trying to pull a trigger.

He watched them for a moment, a pale shadow in the dark, wearing only a T-shirt and shorts.

The brainwashed Grootling leaned into the force field. "I am Groot?" he whispered.

Oh, good. He was talking. He'd been up and down: Sometimes engaging in hesitant communication, sometimes withdrawing as if he wanted to disappear into the walls.

"No, nothing's wrong." Peter kept his voice low, but the two Groots by his feet woke up anyway.

"Mrrrr?" Rocket lifted his head at the movement. He looked around, blurry-eyed, then snapped awake and scrambled to his feet when he spotted Peter. "Quill. The hell are you doing, scaring me like that? I could've shot you. I know I got a gun here...somewhere..."

"I am Groot." Groot helpfully dug Rocket's blaster out from under him.

"I couldn't sleep," Peter said. Rocket didn't seem to have that problem—he'd looked downright comfy in the Grootling's lap—but even Peter wasn't enough of a jackass to point that out, under the circumstances. "Wanted to check on whether Kiya had heard from her DiMavi buyer yet."

"Her what now?" Rocket rubbed sleep from his eyes, then took the blaster from Groot.

Peter sank to the floor, cross-legged, and yawned despite himself. "She sold a genetically modified version of Groot to another DiMavi, but doesn't know where to find him."

Groot sat upright. The web of branches growing across his skin retreated slowly. "I am Groot?"

"Genetically modified as in poison spores." Peter grimaced. "We really need to get a hold of this one."

"Poison spores, huh?" Rocket looked up at Groot. "Wow. That one's got to be a real badass."

"I am Groot."

"I mean, you're *sort* of a badass—"

"I am *Groot.*" He gave Rocket a playful shove.

"I can shoot you, you overgrown houseplant," he said, then turned to Peter. "Once we get this one, can we drop by the Collector's or what?"

"Not yet."

"Oh, come on. It's been ages." He propped the blaster on the floor and leaned on it. "This about Kiya again?"

Peter wasn't yawning anymore. "The Collector wants her, he practically invited us over, it's—"

"I know it's a trap! So what? Since when do you care about plans, Quill? Now that Groot's life is at stake, you're suddenly playing it safe?"

"I don't want to risk it. The Collector is an Elder with a grudge, and I already—" He cut himself off and looked away. He let air hiss through his teeth.

He didn't want to say it. Not with Groot here. But Groot already knew, didn't he?

"Groot had been weakening for days—weeks—before we found out about the Grootlings, and I didn't see it. I didn't do anything."

"I am Groot," a timid Grootling behind him said.

"No, it's not okay. We messed up. We need to fix it. But I don't want to walk into a trap and risk even more of the team because I'm too stupid to stop and consider the facts."

Rocket rolled his eyes. "Wow. This was all it took for you to stop being such a dumbass?"

"Since when do you *not* care about plans?" Peter refused to let himself be intimidated by Rocket.

He also wouldn't dismiss him.

He leaned forward, elbows propped onto the insides of his knees. "Give me a solid idea that doesn't involve blowing open his museum and walking inside, and I'll listen. Tell me the Collector's plan for us so we can circumvent it, and I'll listen. You're the tactician here, Rocket. You're the one who keeps us safe."

"Maybe I don't care about keeping *her* safe."

"We know, Rocket. You've told us. A lot. And it's getting old."

"Soooo sorry I'm boring you." His ears flattened.

"I am Groot," Groot said quietly.

"What do you want us to do? Just drop Kiya off at the Collector's with a bow on top, maybe a note that says, *Have fun cutting her open and traumatizing her more; love, G.o.t.G.?*"

As confrontational as Peter's words were, he kept his voice calm. He wanted to know the answer. He really did.

"Oh, boo hoo, trauma. I got trauma, you got trauma, the dirt between my toes has trauma. Kiya's alive and she's got Gammy as her personal fairy godmother—she could do a lot worse."

"I am Groot," Groot said, disapproving. That he was the only Groot uncomfortable around Kiya apparently didn't mean he liked Rocket talking about her that way.

"Stay outta this," Rocket snapped. "You're too nice for your own good, you know that? Quill, c'mon. We save a lot of people. We don't tend to adopt 'em after that. Did you count the Groots in the room?"

Peter cocked his head. "They aren't all here?"

"Nope! Y'know why? 'Cause *she's* got, like, three standing guard in her room. Every night. The Groots don't talk about it, but I see. She messes up his life and thinks she gets to use him as a bodyguard—like those knives she stole from the kitchen and keeps by her bed aren't enough." Rocket gestured animatedly with his one hand, the other still propping him up on the upright blaster. "She hides in our ship, makes us go up against a fricking Elder, and still barely talks to us? We're the ones trying to help her! I've been sending Tivan fake tips constantly! Apparently Kiya is a busy lady—didya know she got spotted on Knowhere last night? And Kree-Lar, Kree-Pama, *and* all their moons? She should be grateful."

"She was kidnapped. For a year." Peter scratched at his bare leg. "I think she *wants* to connect—I think she's lonely—but come on, Rocket, you know it isn't that simple. She went from a normal life on DiMave of all places, one of the quietest planets around, to being part of the Collector's museum, to"—he spread his hands to indicate the ship—"this. Look at us: We're loud and scary and different, part of a big terrifying universe, and all she wants is to go home. I can't blame her for being prickly. For being scared. She's associating us with him."

"So that makes it okay to protect her while we leave those Groots with the Collector? I know you wanna help her. We're the Guardians. But part of being the Guardians means we don't dump our own."

"She *is* one of our own. She's Gamora's family."

"Family? Oh, please! They're the same species, is all. And you know what?" He leaned in, the gun teetering precariously under his weight.

He prodded a sharp finger into Peter's shirt. "Family you know is more important than the family you don't."

"She's all Gamora has. Gam thought she was alone so long—Rocket, you understand that. I know you do. And we *have* Groot. We have the real one right here—"

"Oh, is *that* it?" He stood abruptly upright, letting the blaster clatter to the floor.

By now, the Grootlings in the room had either woken up or stopped their playing. They watched, quiet and wide-eyed.

"They're just expendable?" Rocket continued.

"That's not what—"

"There is no 'real' Groot, Quill. We grew him from a shard." He motioned at Groot, then across the room at the flipped-over couch. A Grootling slept on the backrest—the oldest one they'd found with Kiya, the one she'd stolen from the Collector when she escaped. "Collector grew that one from a shard, too. How're the two of them any different? They ain't. All these others? Grown from twigs, the same way we do it every time something happens to him. *All* of 'em are Groot. And you—and Drax—you just think, 'Oh, well, if we don't find them, at least we got the real one'? 'If one of 'em dies, at least they won't be growing and sucking more energy away from the rest'? You wouldn't let it slide if you had little Peter Quill clones running around, would you? Getting brainwashed—and fighting—*agh.*" He made a frustrated sound. "You'd run out and save them all. Trap or no trap. Collector or no Collector."

"Rocket…"

The way Rocket stood there in the dark, wearing only his shorts, his hair on end and his tail lashing—he looked so *small.* It sure didn't stop him. He looked up with a fierceness that might've scared Peter if he hadn't known Rocket so well.

"We can't lose 'em, Quill, not even one. Any of them might have a memory all the others have lost by now. And it's more than memories! They're different. We got shy ones and loud ones and nervous ones and...it's getting easy to tell them apart, too easy. A Grootling that was raised at Kiya's laughed when another one fell and got hurt—laughed! That ain't like Groot! And it didn't have nothing to do with how a buyer treated him. He's losing parts of himself. Strength and memories and bravery and his stupid niceness and who knows what else. We need all that if we wanna put him together the way he was. And we'd need to keep 'em all safe even if none of that was true, 'cause they're still Groot, okay?" He was getting more fired up as he talked. "But none of you see that. And I notice you weren't in no rush to save them"—he wrinkled his face—"them creepy raccoon things from the Collector, either. Why is that? Huh? If you care so bad about our kin?" He scoffed. "Forget it. I know why. None of you smooth-skinned, average-sized krutackers take us seriously."

"That's not true. We're trying everything—"

"I said, forget it!"

Peter looked away, his jaw set. A half-dozen Grootlings stared back at him.

Grootlings.

That was what he was calling them, but—Rocket was right. There wasn't a difference. Every one of them was their Groot, raised in other circumstances. That was all.

And he was letting them rot with Tivan. The exact same fate he was trying to save Kiya from.

"You asked what I want?" Rocket said. "What I want is to know that, push comes to shove, this team ain't putting *her* above *them*." He nodded at the roomful of Groots.

"You're asking me to choose."

"*Yes,* I'm asking you to choose, and I'm asking you to choose *right.*"

Peter rolled his eyes. "Oh, if that's all."

"Yup."

Despite everything, he snorted with laughter. "And you're having this conversation with me instead of Gamora because you know she'd kill you."

"She'd use my fur as a pillow, man." Despite his anger, his mouth half-twitched.

It wasn't a smile. Rocket would never admit to it being a smile.

Peter didn't need him to admit it.

"You see her with that girl?" Rocket picked up the gun and slung it over his shoulder, using it to scratch his back. "Eesh. She's obsessed. I ain't getting between them if I can help it."

"You've gotten between them every single day."

"Well, can't help it, most of the time."

"I am Groot."

"Fine, I don't *wanna* help it," Rocket said.

"I am Groot," two Grootlings across the room said, snickering.

"Look." Peter leaned back on his arms. He looked around the room. "We take you seriously, Groot. We wouldn't be doing any of this if we didn't. You're part of the team. You're part of the family. Even if there's a hundred of you and I have to buy a bigger ship. I'd love that. I could make another *Jaws* reference none of you would get. Even then you'd *still* be part of the family."

"I am Groot."

"I am Groo-oot."

"*Duh?*" Peter echoed. "*Duh, we know?* Is that what I get for being heartfelt?"

"I am Groot."

"Yeah, it's gross, Quill," Rocket said. "Caring. Who needs it."

"Not us." Peter clambered to his feet. "Definitely not us."

24

DIMAVE was the greenest planet Gamora had ever seen.

The skies turned a soft green-yellow as the Guardians dipped into the
atmosphere. The oceans rolled out beneath them, reflecting that same shade.
The land was the deeper green of lush forest and wild fields, with stretches
of brown and gray making up the cities.

"I've never actually *been* to this part of the continent." Kiya was glued
to the bridge viewports, watching the town below loom into view, her eyes
apprehensive but her posture eager. "But I tracked our contact to this bar. I
met the buyer, Baran, when he placed the order for the poison-spore Groot.
Once the Grootling was grown, I sent a transmission to this bartender, and
she told Baran to come find me on Knowhere." She frowned, her reflection
in the glass mimicking the movement. "If the bar turns up empty, I don't
know where to look next. His first name is all we have, and it's too common
to be useful."

Drax stood beside her. Three Grootlings sat across his shoulders, eager
to be part of the mission for as long as they could.

"DiMave looks just like I remember," Rocket said, wrinkling his nose
at the sight. "Boring as flark."

He wasn't wrong. Still: Boring might be precisely what Kiya needed. Gamora idly wondered whether there might be some appeal to boredom that she had never considered.

"Port coordinates and approval to land just came through. We're here." Quill leaned over the dash, flicking a few switches to initiate the landing. "The town of Anayin, northeast quadrant of the OnoMave continent. Welcome."

Kiya looked pained.

"I think you botched that pronunciation," Gamora informed him.

"Butchered it," Kiya snorted. Then she looked at Gamora, startled, as if she hadn't realized who she was responding to. She looked instantly away again.

"Welcome home," Quill said.

Kiya didn't respond.

LOOKS closed." Quill craned his neck to read the bar signage.

"It is morning," Drax said.

"So?" Rocket gestured at the group. "*We're* here, aren't we?"

"We're not customers," Gamora said.

"What are you talking about? Trust me, I am definitely a customer. It's a *bar,* Gamora."

She tried the front door. To her surprise, it swung open. She took a moment to allow her eyes to adjust to the dark as she entered. The bar was precisely what one would expect of a shoddy dive in a dubious port-city neighborhood—dank, small—except emptier. The walls were a mix of wood paneling and floor-to-ceiling draperies that might've looked nice if not for the layers of dust and grease. Three DiMavi sat in a shadowy corner at the back, looking wary but not aggressive. Gamora noted three exits: the front door, another one near the DiMavi, and one behind the counter.

On the walls, blaster marks had been inexpertly painted over. Fourteen, at first glance. At least eight separate shootings, based on the spread and the age of the repairs.

The bartender was crouched behind the counter, visible only because the spikes running along his back poked up over the edge.

"Oh, good, that makes six," Rocket muttered from the back of the group.

Kiya and Groot gave him unsure looks. Gamora had a good idea what he meant, though.

"Sixth non-DiMavi species I've seen here, not counting us," Rocket said, exaggerating his irritated tone. "None of you noticed? This place is a port city! And they're *all* green! It's creepy."

They *had* gotten a lot of stares on their way here, even though they'd tried not to attract attention. They couldn't do much about Rocket and Groot standing out—those two often did—but it'd been surprising how people had stared even at Drax and Quill. Gamora had tucked her hair away, which helped her blend in with the DiMavi from a distance, but that wouldn't work up close. The DiMavi people were more isolated than she'd thought, to spend so much time staring at unknown species.

On the plus side, they hardly gave Kiya a second look. The Guardians had been unsure whether to bring her, given the reward on her head. The potential benefits of having a local with them—one who'd been in touch with the bartender before—had won out, especially when Kiya assured them that by DiMavi standards, she didn't stand out in a crowd.

"Can I help you?" the bartender said. He placed four hands—the arms split off at the elbow—on the counter, leaning in with an appraising look.

"We're looking for the owner, Annay," Kiya said.

"She's in the back. I'll get her."

"And I want a tuma-beer!" Rocket called out as the bartender disappeared through a door.

"I am Groot," Groot added.

"And water for my friend! Think he heard us? He heard us, right? Maybe I'll grab the drink myself—"

Quill raised an eyebrow.

"Fine, I'll wait. You're the worst, though." He hopped onto a bar stool, letting his tail swish behind him. "But it's weird, right? For a port city? I'm not the only one who thinks it's weird?"

"It's weird," Gamora confirmed.

Kiya cocked her head. "I'd think you were used to it." When Gamora didn't reply, she went on, sounding hesitant. "My dad, he always said Zen-Whoberi was the same—not many visitors or strangers. Except for the spring feasts."

Gamora stood very still for a moment.

Zen-Whoberi.

Quill was waiting for her reaction, she knew; so was Groot. The others didn't get the significance. Neither did Kiya, judging from the tone of her voice.

"Spring feasts?" Quill said, saving Gamora from having to ask the question herself.

"Yeah. It's when they invited children from every country and from nearby allied planets, and threw a festival in their honor. I mean, I don't know the details, it was supposed to be some sort of religious, cultural exchange…" Kiya made an annoyed face. "It's not important."

It is.

Keep talking—it is *important—*

Rocket shrugged. "Just 'cause DiMavi aren't the only isolationist losers don't make it any less creepy. I mean, jeez, I might've seen six species, but only one or two people from each. Except Kree, but having a bunch of Kree on a Pama-galaxy planet ain't a surprise."

Gamora tried to relax. Tried not to think about spring feasts.

"Actually, the Kree are the only ones that *are* surprising." Kiya leaned with her back against the counter, her gaze continually flicking between the DiMavi at the corner table and the street past the grubby windows. Her arms were crossed, but Gamora caught the tightness in her seemingly casual stance. "Where I'm from—a few hours away—they haven't been welcome since the Maraud."

"Yeah, I have no clue what that is," Rocket remarked.

"I guess it's not a big deal to anyone outside the planet." Her crossed arms tightened further, like she was grabbing onto herself. "The Maraud happened four years ago. A group of Kree took over eight villages and went after a major city, too. They had advanced weapons. And hostages. The government tried to defend the city, but couldn't do much about the other towns. The occupation lasted months. A lot of people died. Like my dad." She watched Gamora during those last few words, as if gauging her reaction.

Gamora didn't know *how* to react.

She had known there were no other Zen-Whoberians. Whether they had died in the massacre when she was a child, or more recently, at the hands of the Kree—like Kiya's father—shouldn't matter.

They were gone either way, and they had taken the spring feasts with them.

"I'm sorry," Quill said. "And this was sanctioned by the Kree government?"

"No." She bit her lower lip for a moment, then explained, "They ignored that it even happened. Before I...*left,* several DiMavi organizations were petitioning the Kree Empire to denounce the Maraud. At the very least, to acknowledge it. Just now, on the way here, we passed posters—I saw something about a ceremony to celebrate 200 years of peace between the DiMavi and Kree people. The Kree must have finally given in."

A DiMavi woman came in through the same door the bartender

had just used, probably from the back room. Short hair, like Kiya's, with wide shoulders, wide hips, a round bust and belly. A firmness to her motions. A certainty.

Dangerous, if she wanted to be. Gamora could tell that much.

The woman—Annay, Gamora assumed—took in the group before speaking again. If she was intimidated, she didn't show it. She plucked a bottle of tuma-beer and an empty pitcher from below the counter and placed them before Groot and Rocket. As she filled the pitcher with water, she spoke, sounding friendly but wary. "I don't know what's cuter, little one. That you think the Kree Empire would ever acknowledge what happened, or that you think our government would actually show a spine and refuse the ceremony on principle." She shoved the pitcher at Groot. "Guardians of the Galaxy?"

"That's us." Quill leaned over the counter, putting on the flirty face Gamora had seen a thousand times before. "Would you mind helping us out with something?"

"Depends. Are you ordering?"

"I'll take a second one." Rocket held up a finger. He was already gulping down the first.

She slid another bottle at Rocket. "Anything more?"

If it would make her cooperate, Gamora would happily volunteer. "I'll take one."

Drax nodded. "Yes."

"Water?" Kiya said reluctantly.

"Give me something local," Quill said. "Whatever you recommend. I'm sure you have great taste."

"You bet." Her mouth twitched into something resembling a smile.

"So, we were wondering—" Quill started.

"Nope. Pay first." She gave Gamora and Drax their beers, then grabbed a bottle from the top shelf. "I have too much experience with threatening groups of people coming to ask questions and somehow never paying."

"Threatening? Us?"

"Your luscious locks don't fool me. I can tell when someone knows their way around a gun." She slid him a pitch-black drink in a square glass. "Pay up, Earth boy."

"Half." He held up a finger for emphasis, then placed his hand on the counter. "*Half* from Earth. Are you, ah, into luscious locks?"

She regarded him for a moment. One corner of her lips curled up. "Depends on how this little chat plays out." She took his hand to scan the chip, holding on perhaps a second or two longer than she needed to. "See? Much easier this way. So, ask your business."

"You and I have been in touch before," Kiya said. "I'm looking for Baran."

Where Annay's demeanor had relaxed over the past minutes, she now shifted into a guarded posture. "You're the tree girl, aren't you?"

"I'm…the tree girl."

"I'd suspected." Annay peered up at Groot.

"I am Groot."

"That's nice."

He held up the water pitcher as if to toast her. "I am Groot."

"You mentioned that," she said, more wary than annoyed.

"Where's Baran?" Kiya said.

"Not here."

"But you know where to find him. I need to see him. About the—tree."

Kiya didn't seem intimidated. Gamora wasn't sure whether it was because she had the entire Guardians team behind her, or because she had been dealing with buyers—not all of them friendly—for weeks. Either way,

Gamora felt a strange sense of pride in the girl.

Misplaced pride. Misguided.

It was not Gamora's place to feel proud. They shared DNA and a ship, and that was all. And soon—sooner than Gamora liked—they would no longer even have the ship in common. Kiya would return home eventually.

Gamora took a gulp of her beer to banish the thought, and welcomed the sharp, bitter taste.

The source of Kiya's confidence could be as simple as that: She was *home*. Even if she'd never been in this city before, she could still see people who looked like her, read store signs and posters in familiar script, walk past homes that resembled her own, speak with Annay without translator chips filtering every word…

Gamora didn't know what a connection like that—with a people, with a place—felt like. She wondered whether it felt similar to sitting three feet from a girl with Gamora's skin and Gamora's nose, and with the words *spring feasts* on her lips.

"What do you want Baran for?" Annay wiped down the counter.

"To talk to him." Kiya wasn't budging.

"And you need a team of"—she tugged her head toward the Guardians—"them for that?"

"Look," Kiya said, annoyed, "he bought a weapon from me, and we need to talk to him about it." She didn't get further.

Before she could continue, Rocket suddenly stood upright on his barstool. His ears swiveled, like he was trying to pick up on a certain sound. "Quill? Take a look over there." He nodded at the back wall.

"Those guys in the corner?" Gamora asked, one hand on her sword, already considering a dozen ways a confrontation could unfold.

"No. Outside. Something doesn't sound right." Rocket grimaced.

"Here I was, thinking we could just enjoy our drinks for once. Do we get vacations? I want a vacation."

"Let's see what's up." Quill activated his helmet, prompting an intrigued look from Annay, and focused on the back wall.

The shift in Quill's posture over the next couple of seconds told Gamora enough. His scans could not show anything good.

"Ah, Annay?" Quill said. "Is there a spaceport in the alley behind your bar, by any chance?"

"Something happening I should know about?"

"Only a ship. Hovering. In the alleyway." He deactivated his helmet just long enough to throw back the last of his disturbingly colored drink and grin at Annay. "Nothing alarming at all."

Drax got to his feet, abandoning his half-empty bottle on the counter. "I am somewhat alarmed," he told Gamora.

"You two. Let's go." Quill crossed the bar, pointing at Drax and Gamora. "Rocket, Groot, stay with Kiya."

"Yeah, you should go see what's up," Rocket said, his second tuma-beer at his lips. "Groot and I've got this covered." He snatched up Drax's abandoned bottle and made a shooing motion.

Annay looked at the back door, seemingly conflicted between following and staying. She opted for the latter. "This is why I make people pay first," she informed Groot.

Gamora bolted through the door in the back wall, right behind Quill. Through a narrow hall, past a bathroom door, then outside into a trash heap of a garden.

She scraped to a halt.

A large shuttle hovered above the alleyway. The remnants of blue-gray teleportation energy glittered around the hull. The shuttle was disc-shaped, with a cockpit jutting out from the front like an arrow. That cockpit was cracking open, the roof lifting up to reveal the pilot.

He sat leisurely in a seat massive enough to be called a throne, overlooking the street with equal parts cruelty and fondness.

"Good morning," the Collector said. "I am looking for a girl."

25

APPARENTLY, Drax had been right to be alarmed.

He glared up at the shuttle, considering ways to reach it. It would likely involve his blades and some minor property damage to the apartments across the street.

Quill was already taking flight to get a better view of the situation, the eyes in his helmet blazing red. "You're looking for a girl?" he said. "I have— oh, Tivan, I have so many responses to that, I can't even choose."

"That's okay," Gamora called up from beside Drax. "None of them would be funny."

Through the windows of the run-down apartments that faced the back of the bar, Drax saw frightened and curious faces looking out. Only a handful of civilians were left in the alley itself, all scrambling away.

The shuttle hung above them like a cloud, backlit against the bright green sky. It cast a shadow that covered half the alley.

Quill was hovering up high, facing the Collector in the air from several dozen feet away. "Rocket, we need you out here." Quill kept his voice too low for the Collector to hear, but the communicators still picked up on it. "Groot, evacuate the civilians from the bar. Can you get Kiya out unseen?"

"Annay seems like she'd have escape routes," Gamora added, at the same volume.

"Guardians?" the Collector said. The shuttle magnified his voice, projecting it throughout the alleyway. "I would hate to sour our friendship."

"*Ha,*" Drax scoffed. He stalked down the street, unsheathing his daggers as he went. When he reached the front of the shuttle, he raised his voice and looked up. "Collector!"

The Collector looked down with interest. "Yes?"

"If you do not leave, we will tear off your limbs."

"As I recall, you tried that. I welcome a rematch to further observe your technique, but a simpler option would be to hand over the girl and send me on my way. No? None of you are interested?" The Collector sounded exasperated. "Very well. We'll do this the difficult way."

"Oh, good," Rocket said as he exited the bar. The door slammed shut behind him. "Difficult way's only just starting. I didn't miss nothing important yet."

A high hiss filled the street, and a side panel of the Collector's shuttle slid open. Lean, metallic bodies leapt onto the street three at a time. *Thud—thud—thud—*

"*Robots?*" Gamora said, disbelieving.

"Robots," Drax confirmed.

"Those are Zemende-K3s," Rocket said. "Second build, I think. Careful. They go boom."

"Oh, crap," Quill said.

Gamora unsheathed her sword. Rocket had his blaster in one hand, a laser pistol in the other.

More robots were leaping from the shuttle. "Find the girl I showed you," the Collector said. "Bring her to me—unharmed."

The robots were tall—as tall as Drax—and their smooth, featureless faces glimmered golden in the morning sunlight. Nine. Twelve. Fifteen.

They shot forward toward the bar. Drax blocked their path, daggers flashing.

Eighteen. Twenty-one.

They could fly, too. Half of them took to the air, bypassing Drax with ease, while the other half stormed toward the Guardians on foot. Drax caught one in mid-run, jabbing his dagger into its belly and slicing up to the robot's skull, exposing its innards. He kicked the twitching body aside. A fraction of a second later, the bot exploded, taking out a chunk of the pavement and blowing scorching air at Drax.

"Told ya." Rocket stood near the bar exit, picking off approaching bots from a distance. "They go boom."

"The explosives appeared to be in the shoulder," Drax noted. "We can take precautions."

"Nah, they're all over the body. Makes it unpredictable." Rocket skittered across the backyard. "Ain't it great? Pow!"

"*So*—great—" Gamora said through gritted teeth.

Quill shot down two airborne bots with globs of ice. Gamora caught another in flight and sliced it in half with a neat diagonal cut from neck to hip, then took on the next bot before the first one had even hit the ground.

And above the fray, the Collector sat in his shuttle—fingers tented, his expression delighted.

"Our—" Drax slammed two bots' heads together. They went down in a shower of sparks. "—friendship—" He tore off a bot's head and flung it up at the Collector out of spite. "*—is soured!*"

Destroying the robots was one thing. Keeping them away from the bar was another matter. Within seconds, the street had turned into a battlefield:

the four Guardians fighting, fallen bots littering the ground, and intact ones trying single-mindedly to reach the building. Even the ones the Guardians tore apart rapidly rewired themselves and got up again.

"Groot, Kiya?" Quill called over comms. "An update?"

"I am Groot!"

"The guests are safely out, but Annay's not cooperating," Kiya said, her voice rushed. "We're still inside the bar. It's *him*, isn't it?"

"Yes. I'm sorry." Quill paused. "Drax—help them get to safety."

Drax nodded once, brusquely.

"Quill, I can get Kiya out." Gamora slashed through another bot, then dropkicked it away before it had the chance to detonate.

"No. I need you here." Quill grunted as he flung a half-broken robot into another. Both bots plummeted to the ground. "Working on a plan."

"Are we gonna love or hate this plan?" Rocket asked.

"Depends on how you feel about bringing down Tivan's shuttle."

The robots were backing Drax steadily closer to the bar entrance. He turned and sprinted across the backyard, smacking away assailants as he went. Partway through the yard, a hand attached to half a torso grasped his legs. Its fingers skimmed his calf for a fraction of a second before a laser struck the arm in the elbow. The severed arm slid across the ground, out of reach.

Then it exploded.

"You're welcome." Rocket stood on a low ledge separating the backyard from the alley. He kissed the muzzle of his laser gun. "Forget anything I said about a vacation. *This* is what I call relaxing."

"Thank you, Rocket!" Drax stalked toward the door.

Rocket called after him, "If the barlady still ain't cooperating, I hear bribery's real effective."

"Go nuts," Quill chimed in, wind rushing in the background.

Drax was not the only one entering the bar. Before he could kick the door shut behind him, three bots were already following. Their blank faces betrayed nothing as they fought to get through the narrow entrance to the hall.

Destroying them would do little—others would take their place.

Drax decided on another course of action.

He grabbed one by the arm, pulled it inside, and flung it at the hallway ceiling. The ceiling cracked. The bot dropped down instantly. Drax hurled it at the ceiling again, again—

"Explode," he instructed. "Now."

He grabbed a second bot by the leg and flung them up in unison—

He heard a click.

He grinned, then leapt back.

Not quite fast enough.

The dual explosions knocked him flat on his back and scorched off his eyelashes. Something pierced his leg. He gasped for breath and tasted dirt on the air.

The dust hung heavy. The ceiling had collapsed in front of him, taking part of the wall with it. Rubble blocked the hallway.

Good.

The robots would get past the debris, but it would slow them down, and they would be easy for the other Guardians to pick off in the meantime. He had bought himself at least 30 uninterrupted seconds.

He stood up, ignoring the jab of pain in his leg—some of the fallen debris had cut through—and exited the hall. The door to the bar proper had been knocked from its hinges. Kiya and Groot stood facing Annay, several feet away.

"What the d'ast just happened?" Annay said. She held a massive shotgun in her hands, and was using the counter as a barrier between herself and the Guardians.

"I collapsed your hallway," Drax said, enthused.

"Oh, great. That's great." She tugged her head toward the front door. "Out."

"We must leave unseen."

"I am Groot," Groot confirmed.

"That's nice! Do it somewhere else. Out!"

The three of them could easily stop a single person with a shotgun. Quill did not enjoy it when they attacked civilians, however. And they still needed information from Annay about Baran and his Grootling.

"Ma'am," Kiya said, "someone's trying to kidnap me. He's"—her voice hitched—"he's *right outside.* Please."

"We will pay you," Drax said. "Afterward."

Annay hesitated.

"We don't have much time. They'll be inside soon." The pleading note had faded from Kiya's voice. Her stance shifted. *Good,* Drax thought. *She is willing to fight.*

"*They* are exploding robots," he said helpfully.

From the back entrance came the sound of shifting rubble, metal on metal, and more detonations.

The bots were already clearing the hall of debris.

Annay lowered the gun. "Fifteen thousand units. At least."

"Agreed." Drax extended his hand to shake on the deal.

She ignored his hand and turned briskly. The four of them ran for the door behind the counter. Inside, they sped through a cramped kitchen, into a storage room. Annay went for the back wall without stopping and ran straight though a projection of stacked crates. When she clapped, the holos fizzled out, leaving the room half as full as it had appeared.

She traced a pattern on the wall. The ground slid open, revealing a circular chute and a ladder. Drax peered down. Only blackness.

"Follow the tunnel. Two lefts, then a right. Keep going straight. Once you see a"—she made a sound Drax couldn't identify—"paint a"—another sound. "You'll exit near the spaceport."

Drax's universal translator hadn't been able to interpret the sounds correctly, but Kiya understood. She nodded, leaping down without bothering with the ladder.

"I am Groot!" Groot said, urging Annay to follow. Two vines whipped out and turned her to face the chute.

"You should come." Drax heard glass shatter from inside the bar. More bots, he realized, had flown across the building to enter via the front windows. "The robots are too close now."

"You want me to leave my bar?" Another explosion sounded. Annay cringed. "Actually, yeah, that's a good plan." She climbed into the hole, swinging down the ladder's rungs two at a time. "But you're paying for all of this!" she bellowed, her voice echoing up the chute.

Drax paused, standing inches away from the opening.

If he was correct, the robots were right outside the door, in the bar proper. If they entered the back room too soon, they could spot the escape route and follow—and in a confined space like the tunnel, it would be harder to avoid damage from the explosions. Drax could stay. Hold off the bots and give the others a head start.

"I am Groot?" Groot had the same strategy as Drax in mind.

"No. Go."

"I am Groot!" He wrapped vines around Drax and deposited him halfway down the chute. "I! Am! Groot!"

Groot retracted his vines, sending them snaking back up through the chute. The opening promptly closed above Drax, shutting him off from the bar—and his teammate.

Drax glared up. He considered climbing the rungs, smashing through the hatch, and helping Groot keep the robots at bay.

It would be a foolish move.

For Groot to stay behind was equally foolish. In his present state, he was not strong enough to hold off the bots.

"Where's Groot?" Kiya's voice bounced up through the chute.

"Guarding." Drax set his jaw, and followed her and Annay down.

26

"GAM! THEY'RE already inside!"

"One sec."

Gamora followed Rocket into the building through an opening in the debris. She landed smoothly inside the remains of the hallway, and immediately whirled to stab her sword back through the opening.

Her sword plunged into the skull of the bot attempting to follow them inside. She yanked it back a second before the bot exploded.

The explosion tore more rubble from the ceiling. Not much—but enough to cover up the opening in the debris and give her a few seconds without having to worry about her back.

"They're inside?" Gamora stalked through the back hall. Quill, Rocket, and Gamora herself had taken out all the robots that had been clearing the rubble blocking the busted hallway.

Rocket—standing in the doorway to the bar itself—was trying to hold off another group of bots. His blaster was working overtime.

Past him, Gamora counted five active robots and another two on the ground, twitching. Apparently they'd entered from the front—but not through the door. The barroom was open to the outside, with the windows in shatters on the ground.

"Rocket. Let me." She strode past him, trusting that he'd pull back his blaster in time. "Block off the back entrance for real. I want the street side to be the only one way in and out."

She decapitated the first bot. The flat of her blade flung its head into a second bot.

"I got just the thing." Rocket was already bounding back toward the hall, rummaging through his utility belt.

He would enjoy his part of Quill's plan.

Good.

She was rather enjoying her part, too.

GROOT?" Rocket called through his comms. "Gimme an update."

Rocket walked back into the intact—ish—part of the bar, shaking dust from his tail. The explosion he'd just set off had permanently closed off the hallway, finishing what Drax had started. In the main barroom, the blast had knocked a couple of chunks from the ceiling, torn a large crack into one wall, and sent several bottles crashing to the ground—*aw, what a waste.* The place was still standing, at least. He'd have plenty of time to work in peace.

Rocket knew a thing or two about blowing up buildings. He could do it with surgeon-like precision.

Having cleared the barroom for him, Gamora had moved outside, leaving behind a carpet of sparking, twitching metal body parts. He spotted her through the broken windows, a green blur on the street fighting off any bot that approached the bar. Quill hovered above, assisting her.

"Groot? Hel-lo?" Still nothing. Rocket shifted channels as he walked around the bar studying the robot corpses.

Nah, that one won't work for my purposes, he thought. The next one: *Wow, Gamora really did a number on you, didn't she?*

"Drax?" he asked, crouching by one particularly promising robot body. "You have Groot with you, right?"

Drax had checked in a couple minutes ago, reporting that he was on his way to the spaceport via a hidden tunnel. Maybe the tunnel was blocking his comms, or something—*Yeah, that's it*—

"Rocket. Groot is not with me."

"What?"

"He stayed in the bar to hold off our assailants."

Rocket shot upright.

Drax went on, "I knew you would be unable to reach him in time to assist. I…did not wish to distract you."

"We're gonna have words, you and I," Rocket growled. "Back room?"

"Yes."

Gamora would've checked the back room for bots—unless the door was locked, which would suggest the robots had never made it in.

He tried the door. Yup. Locked.

Could be a good sign. Could be a bad sign. Time to find out.

One explosion later, the door had a hole in it the size of Rocket himself. He crouched, peering through. Right away, he saw why the door hadn't opened. It wasn't because it had been locked. A heavy industrial rack from the narrow kitchen had been yanked away from the wall. It had crashed against the edge of the kitchen counter, a few feet across the room. The rack still leaned against the counter, positioned diagonally against the doorframe. The weight had held the door firmly shut.

A vine was curled around one metal beam.

Rocket climbed through the hole in the door, wiggled a path through the metal rack, and landed on the other side.

The vine formed a trail through the kitchen, into a storage room that was packed with boxes, steel racks, unused chairs, and a messy desk. Rocket assumed the three robot bodies he counted inside the room were new additions.

The vine ended abruptly. Another torn-off vine lay farther down. And strewn all around the room:

Splinters.

Rocket unleashed a string of curses.

A voice came in over comms. Quill's. "Any progress on the—"

"Groot's gone," Rocket snapped. "He's splinters in the back room. That d'ast idiot stayed here to hold of the bots and then—" And then, as his last act before falling to the bots' explosions, he'd yanked down the metal rack in the kitchen to block the door and keep more bots from following the other Guardians down the tunnel.

Rocket continued his string of curses.

"Rocket—" Gamora said.

"I *know*. We got a robot army to annihilate. I'm on it."

"I'm sorry, Rocket," Quill said.

Rocket tuned them out.

The first thing Rocket did was stick five decent-size chunks of Groot into a pouch on his belt. Not the charred pieces—he only took the good, healthy wood, the ones that could grow a brand-new Groot without any problems.

Maybe some problems, he thought. Given how slowly the Grootlings grew nowadays, Rocket couldn't tell whether there was enough energy to grow another Groot from scratch.

The string of curses got a third installment.

The next thing he did was check the robot bodies. None of them suited his purposes—too banged up. As much as he hated to think it, the damage was probably more from the bots' own explosives than from the weakened Groot.

Rocket did a final scan of the room. Earlier, he'd asked Groot to do something for him. Just maybe, Groot had pulled it off...there!

He bolted across the room, crouched to sift through charred bot pieces and splinters, and picked up Annay's communicator. A little busted, but it seemed to work.

Groot might not have been able to put up much of a fight against the bots, but he'd still picked Annay's pocket like a pro.

"Owe you one."

Rocket picked up an extra splinter, just to be on the safe side, and wiggled his way back through the broken door into the main barroom.

He had a job to do, and a guinea pig robot corpse to find.

27

THE COLLECTOR'S shuttle had slowly risen into the sky. Now it hung above the building housing the bar, giving him a view of both the street before the bar and the alley at its back. Whether Tivan had taken his distance to stay clear of the fighting or to scan the streets for Kiya, Peter couldn't tell—and he didn't have an awful lot of time to wonder about it.

He soared past the shuttle to chase down a stubborn bot. "Hope you're taking notes for your d'ast *tribute band!*" he yelled.

With so many airborne bots out here, all Peter could *do* to the Collector was yell. He would do as much of it as he could—in between picking off robots from above or engaging them in fights up in the air. Sometimes, Peter had to dive to the street and stop bots before they came too close to curious onlookers and civilians trying to evacuate nearby buildings. At least the bots weren't actively going after the civilians.

The street below Peter looked like a flarking battlefield. The back of Annay's bar had partially collapsed, damaging neighboring buildings in the process. Robots crept over the rubble like overeager ants.

Rocket, still inside the bar, was out of the fray for now. It was up to Peter and Gamora to take care of the remaining bots.

Gamora did the bulk of the work. She was a sword-wielding whirlwind guarding the bar's blown-open windows against encroaching bots, sometimes playing offense out on the street, sometimes leaping inside the bar when a bot sneaked past her.

When Peter asked Gamora to cover someone's back, she took it seriously.

"How far are you now?" he yelled at Rocket over comms.

"Oi! This stuff takes delicacy. *You* try hacking a robot that might explode at any moment."

"That's what I have you for." Peter shut one eye to help his aim, dousing an approaching robot in flame. "Now how far are you?"

"Close," he said. "Ish."

"Location?"

"Behind the counter. Aw, come on—the mirror just got shot up. I think there's glass in my beer. Gamora, do you *mind?*"

Peter wondered whether there was any point in asking Rocket not to drink mid-robot-attack or while working with high-tech, explosive machinery, but discarded the notion. Between sifting through his friend's remains and sticking his nose into a bomb just 'cause his boss asked nicely, Rocket deserved a beer.

"Glass in your beer or your blood splattered on the ceiling," Gamora said, her voice cool through the communicator. Noises followed—unidentifiable, but Peter suspected they involved a robot meeting its untimely end at Gamora's hands. "It's your choice."

A pattern on the ground caught Peter's eye. "Guys, something's up."

The robots were fanning out.

Instead of focusing their efforts on the bar—the last place they had seen Kiya—several robots moved onto the street. They passed the last few terrified DiMavi still on the street, ignoring them in favor of zeroing in on the windows of neighboring buildings. Each robot took a different building. In unison, they smashed the windows and climbed inside with quick, efficient movements.

It took a second to dawn on Peter: The Collector must've given them new orders, in case Kiya had sneaked into a nearby home or business and was lying low.

Then Peter spotted shuttles gliding toward the street from opposite directions.

"We have law enforcement, guys," Peter said. The shuttles' markings were ubiquitous across planets. "And the bots are doing house-to-house searches now. Rocket, you'd better hurry. Gamora, if there's no more bots coming into the bar and Rocket's safe, we need to evacuate those buildings—get the civilians out. Now let me try and make some friends."

He jetted down to the ground just as a shuttle landed, raising his hands in a gesture of peace. "Star-Lord, Guardians of the Galaxy," he called out. "Uh, first time on DiMave. Hi. Sorry about this. We're trying to fix this mess. Here's the situation…"

HE SHOULDN'T have done that," Kiya said after several minutes of silence.

Drax looked up, expecting her to elaborate.

A dim orange glow lit the tunnels. Although the chute leading down from the bar had been brand new, the walls down here were old and crumbling, with the occasional rusted-through pipe running along them.

Kiya walked at the front of the group. She looked sideways, a muscle in her face twitching. "He really shouldn't…"

"Well, if those were actually exploding robots back there, I'm grateful," Annay said from a couple feet behind Kiya. "But I'm sorry about your friend."

"He will regrow," Drax said. He brought up the rear.

Kiya shook her head. "Forget it."

She looked small. It was not simply her frame—most people looked small to Drax, and Kiya was larger than most teenagers Drax had met. It was the way she held herself: Kiya seemed to have all of Gamora's reflexes, all her efficient, tightly wrapped violence, yet none of Gamora's confidence or elegance. So she walked stiffly, her movements alert, looking like she would rather have been anywhere but here. Both hands were jammed into the pockets of her jacket.

Drax had not spoken to Kiya much since her arrival. He saw no point. She was not a threat, and she kept to herself on the ship. Even now, she walked apart, her eyes on the goal ahead.

This was not a problem to Drax. He did the same.

"Annay," Kiya asked, "what are these tunnels for? Why does your bar connect to them?"

They had told Annay the truth about Kiya being a target of the Collector's, but Annay had kept quiet rather than return the honesty. She also had not answered any of Drax's repeated questions about Baran.

"Your bar attracts unusual clientele," Drax said. "Political activists? Terrorists? Organized crime?"

Annay looked at him over her shoulder. "I just provide the drinks. What people choose to discuss over those drinks isn't my business."

"That sounds like a yes," Kiya said.

Drax slowed, putting distance between himself and the other two, and looked over the hallway behind them. There was no sign of the robots. If Drax was correct about the kind of clientele Annay's bar attracted—as he appeared to be—they might escape unseen. The tunnel would be lined to block basic scans.

"Would someone mind telling me why this 'Collector' is so eager to kidnap a DiMavi girl that he sends an exploding robot army and she requires intergalactic heroes as her babysitters?" Annay asked. "There must be a story there."

"We are not babysitters." Drax shot a flat look at her back. "Babysitters get paid."

"Do you know DiKirrin?" Kiya asked.

"Yeah." Annay made a thoughtful sound, as if trying to recall something. "Few years ago, it was one of the occupied towns in the Maraud. Last year, it was attacked again. A small group, in and out. Some of my customers looked into it in case they were Kree. Two people died, and a girl was taken. That was you?"

"The Collector was behind it. The people who died were my mother and neighbor, who came to help."

"Hm." She considered that information. "Sorry for what happened."

"Yeah." Kiya looked stubbornly ahead.

"The village spent a lot of time looking for you. I know that much."

"Did they?" She slowed slightly.

"Of course. They lost enough people in the Maraud. They were torn up over losing more."

Kiya looked aside, skeptical.

"If they knew you were alive…"

"Don't tell them."

"You don't want to go back?"

"I can't."

"Once this Collector guy is—"

"I *can't*," Kiya said without turning.

The three of them fell silent. The only sound in the tunnels was their footsteps, out of sync and bouncing off the walls, all the louder without speech to mask it. Drax used the moment to listen for noises behind them. Nothing.

"You have said you wanted to return home," he said.

"I do."

He raised an eyebrow. Kiya seemed inconsistent.

"It's not safe," she finally said. "My parents were always honest about where my dad came from, and that I couldn't tell anyone. So I didn't. We weren't sure what might happen—Zen-Whoberians weren't being actively pursued, but maybe no one thought there were any left to go after." She snorted. "Except for Gamora. And Gamora is a bedtime horror story. No one *would* go after her."

"People have tried," Drax said. "They are now dead."

"Wait, wait, Zen-Whoberian? You're half Zen-Whoberian?" Annay caught up to Kiya and studied her from the side, as though the traits would suddenly leap out at her.

"Stop that." Kiya looked away. "Gamora stares at me that way, too. It's creepy."

"I never realized Zen-Whoberians and DiMavi could mix."

"Neither did my parents, until I showed up. Apparently Zen-Whoberians have a hard time procreating outside their own species. *Our* species?" Drax could not see her face from his position, but he could practically hear her tight smile. "So my dad and I dyed our hair. He hid his marks with makeup and gained weight. We blended in. No one suspected anything—why would they? Then, when the Kree came, he tried to defend our home. They killed him. My mom and I couldn't even follow the Zen-Whoberian death customs he would've wanted, or people would've found out about me. So he died a DiMavi.

"I ended up… A year and a half ago, I got a girlfriend. I talked to her. I *told* her." Kiya went quiet. She cleared her throat. "She was the only person I ever told. And after that—after being safe my whole life—suddenly the Collector showed up, killed my mom, and took me. I don't know how else he could've known. So my parents shouldn't have trusted me, I shouldn't have trusted my girlfriend, and because of that, my mom is dead and I spent a year in Tivan's hands.

"And just now, he knew where we were so fast, within the hour…either someone saw the reward, or he had people on lookout at the ports. People know how much he wants me, now. DiKirrin doesn't have any money; it won't take much for them to sell me out.

"So, no. I can't go home."

Drax was still watching the tunnel behind them, but had listened to Kiya's story equally carefully. She seemed to be finished. He rolled her words over in his mind and came to one conclusion.

"That seems reasonable," he said.

Annay looked aghast. "That's an *awful* thing to say—how can you—"

Kiya laughed a sharp, sudden laugh. "No. It *is* reasonable, isn't it? I gave it a lot of thought."

"It's not your fault," Annay said. "What happened to you or your mother. Okay? It's not your fault."

Kiya shrugged. She had finally slowed down—maybe to talk, maybe because she was lost in thought. "It is, though."

"It's that Collector's fault."

"We can share the blame. There's plenty."

"Do you want revenge?" Drax asked. "He took your family. I know what that is like."

"You do?" She looked away thoughtfully. "Do you want revenge?"

"Yes," he said.

She considered that for a moment.

"Strongly," he added.

"Heh."

"Very strongly."

"I don't know if I want revenge," she said. "Mostly, I just want her back."

Drax nodded.

He understood that, too.

"We're here," Annay said. "I don't know where your ship is parked, but this hatch opens on a loading area behind the main spaceport."

She walked past them to open it, leaving Drax and Kiya behind her. The girl glanced up at him. She offered a slight, wary smile.

Drax found he did not mind the girl. Kiya was a fierce fighter who had known loss. He could understand those qualities, both in himself and in his friends.

He rested a hand on her shoulder. "If you decide to avenge your family, you should let me know. We will have much to discuss."

28

ROCKET was so. freaking. close. He only needed a couple more moments of concentration—which wasn't easy in the middle of a destroyed bar, with explosions still resounding in the street. "Quill!" he said through comms, not looking up from where he sat crouched over the disabled robot. "What'd I tell you? Easy on the detonations!"

"It's not me! It's the blasted soldiers. We're ejecting the robots from the buildings. I *said* to keep them intact as much as possible, but..." Panicky screaming came through the earpiece—evacuees, Rocket guessed—followed by Quill's voice trying to calm them down.

"Yeah, yeah, just do what you can," Rocket said.

"How close are you?"

"Less'n a minute. You got a visual on the Collector?"

"Yeah," Quill said. More screaming. Unidentified noises. Possibly a wall being blown out. Rocket was missing all the fun. "The Collector's shuttle is a few blocks away. He just turned sharply for the port. Drax, check in."

"We have the ship," Drax said. "The Collector had people guarding it."

"He's on his way to you." Quill sounded tense. "Those goons must've tipped him off you were there before you—"

"Murderized 'em," Rocket cut in helpfully. "They didn't get the Groots, right? How are the little buggers?"

"Annoying."

"Kiya?" Gamora asked.

"Intact."

"The bartender?" Quill asked.

"Demanding."

"Yeah, yeah, I'll transfer those units to her when I'm done saving lives. Did you tell her how trustworthy I am? It's okay to exaggerate."

"*Quill.*" Gamora's voice was flat.

"Yeah, yeah. Drax, get that ship straight here."

"I am already underway."

"Rocket?"

"Would be doing better if you weren't all yapping in my ear!"

He triple-checked the connectors, then leaned back to survey his work. The hacked bot lay splayed open before him—a beautiful, homicidal, immobile, blinking mess of his own making. "You have sight of any bots, Quill?"

"Yep."

"Tell me, what're they doing right..." He fiddled with his makeshift controller and spoke the words "stand still" into the microphone. "Now?"

"They froze up."

"Fly," he said into the mic. "And now?"

"Flying!"

"Looks like I got it. What're you supposed to say?"

"You're the greatest." Quill didn't even sound annoyed at admitting it. Rocket wasn't sure whether that made it more or less fun. "Wait for my signal."

"Aye." Rocket bared his teeth in a wide smile that only the bot could see. "Thanks for your services, sucker," he told it. He clambered onto the counter, took a drink of his beer, and surveyed the bar. All that was left inside was debris, robot husks, and Rocket himself.

He pulled out Annay's communicator. His program had juuust about cracked her security.

"What do I even need a team for?" he asked aloud. "I got this *covered.*"

"Rocket!" Quill bellowed over comms. "Keep your finger on the trigger and get your tail out here! Drax is incoming, and Tivan is right behind him."

Rocket hopped off the counter, regretfully leaving his beer behind, and climbed out of the bar through the busted windows.

He ran to the center of the now nearly abandoned street, swerving around robot remains and craters left behind by the exploding bots. The buildings on each side of the street showed similar damage: cracks in the walls, scorch marks from the explosions. Some buildings were missing walls entirely—Rocket had a perfect view of two grungy offices, open to the world like a kid's dollhouse.

Gamora and Quill must've had a field day out here.

Farther down the street, law enforcement was cordoning off the area, and soldiers were barging into office buildings and stores with weapons raised. They couldn't cover the whole street at once, though: There were still bots going about their business. They would leave buildings they'd finished searching, march down to the next building over, and methodically crack the glass and climb inside to continue their hunt for Kiya.

Up in the air—there, Rocket recognized the shape of the Guardians' ship against the fierce green-yellow sky. Drax was flying it Rocket's way: fast, soaring low over the city. They would be here in seconds.

Behind the ship was a second shape, too small to make out in detail yet. That had to be the Collector's shuttle.

Rocket turned, checking the sky behind him. Ah, his ride was here. Rocket held up one hand in a hitchhiker's thumb.

Quill swooped down, grabbed Rocket's outstretched hand, and snatched him up into the air. Gamora dangled from Quill's other hand.

"Do your thing, Rocket," Quill shouted over the wind rushing past them. "Drax, incoming! Open the door, will you? I can't deal with this kinda weight for long!"

Rocket's tail whooshed and whipped in the gusts of wind as they flew up higher, on a swift trajectory toward the Guardians' ship. He brought his makeshift controller to his mouth. "Hey, rust buckets," he yelled. "Go outside. See that shuttle coming our way, the one you that brought you here?"

Rocket watched the ground below for the results, eager to see his labor pay off.

Within seconds, robots began to exit the homes, climbing through broken windows or walking through open front doors to gather in the street. The robots already outside slowed their movements, not responding even when soldiers began to surround them.

As one, the bots looked up. Rocket even thought a couple of damaged bots on the ground were twisting to do the same, though he was too far up to tell for sure.

The Collector's shuttle was approaching the street fast.

The Collector might be immortal.

But his shuttle wasn't.

"Bring it down," Rocket said.

PETER had barely made it on board the ship before his communicator buzzed with an incoming request.

Rocket was rushing to close the hatch behind them, while Gamora ran up the rusty stairs toward the bridge. Peter followed at a slower pace, deactivating his helmet as he accepted the transmission. He wasn't particularly surprised to see a holo of a heated DiMavi in uniform pop up—it was the captain he had just met on the ground. Peter had managed to coordinate rescue efforts with the captain's forces, but it wasn't exactly a truce.

"We still have business," the captain said curtly.

"Look, we had a fun time. It doesn't have to be anything serious." Peter sidestepped a Grootling and headed up the stairs after Gamora.

"You can't bring this kind of destruction onto our planet and take off without any consequences!"

"You know, you'd be surprised."

"You wrecked an entire city block, then flew off."

"A third of a city block!" he protested. "Half at most! And only 'cause we were trying to help. The Collector sent in *robots*—it wasn't our fault. Robots just happen sometimes. Look, the bar got hit hardest, and we're already in talks with the owner to reimburse her." Peter turned and sat on the top step, overlooking the cargo bay.

Across from him, Rocket sat against the now-closed hatch, studying a communicator in his lap. A Grootling watched with interest.

Huh. Peter had expected Rocket to be on the bridge already, wanting to see the fireworks as the bots attacked the Collector's shuttle. It was only a temporary victory—the Collector would simply find another ship to attach his teleportation device to—but it was sweet nonetheless.

Peter was kind of sad to be missing out, himself. Hopefully Drax would record it.

But he didn't want the Guardians to get chased off or blacklisted from yet another planet.

"Look," Peter told the DiMavi captain, "I think we can figure this out..."

29

DIPLOMACY is the woooorst," Quill said, stepping into the bridge.

This should be fun, Gamora thought. She spun the navigator's seat around just in time to catch the moment when Quill realized they had a guest on the ship.

Annay leaned one arm on the backrest of the pilot's seat Drax occupied. "'Sup."

Quill stood in the entryway, blinking at her. "You're on my ship."

Annay watched him, amused.

"Drax forgot to tell us something," Gamora said.

"I—" Quill did a check of the rest of the bridge as though expecting to find further surprises, but it was empty aside from Drax, Gamora, Annay, and himself.

"Is this is how you welcome girls here?" Annay asked. "I was just getting my hopes up."

"Why the flark are you on my ship?"

"We said we would pay her." Drax leaned sideways to look at Quill over his shoulder. "Also, she would not leave."

"Give me my units," Annay said, "drop me off, and maybe I'll give you another chance at offering me a *proper* welcome. Fifteen thousand units for helping your buddies escape, and another ninety thousand for the damage to my bar." She nodded her head at the viewport. "And hurry. You're about to leave the atmosphere."

On that note…Gamora briefly turned back, entering a few commands to pump up the shields and artificial gravity. Drax had the rest covered. She turned back to Quill and Annay.

"I didn't mean we'd pay *now!*" Quill was saying. "I meant we'd come back later! After this mess!"

"You don't seem too busy now." Annay looked him over from head to toe. Her gaze lingered.

"Do we have a destination?" Drax asked.

"We absolutely do not. Improvise." Quill stepped deeper into the bridge toward Annay. He hooked his thumbs into his belt loops, looking indignant. "I am captain of this ship"—a familiar laugh sounded from down the hallway behind him, but Gamora didn't think Quill heard—"and leader of this team. I have a galaxy to guard. I'm busy. Like…*super* busy."

"Captain?" Rocket cackled again as he entered the bridge, with Kiya on his heels. "That's a laugh. Hey, Gam, let me take over."

Gamora vacated the navigator's seat without protesting. She stood and crossed her arms over the backrest of the gunner's seat instead, watching Quill and Annay impassively. Kiya was doing the same thing from the doorway.

On the one hand, Gamora was ready to declare the conversation over and flash her sword at anyone who disagreed. On the other, Annay *might* still have information about Baran, the man who had bought the Grootling from Kiya. Gamora had started to doubt that, but she could let the situation play out. Every now and then, Quill knew what he was doing.

"Look," Annay went on, "just pay me now and drop me off—aaaand you just went into hyperspace, okay, so drop me at a halfway decent station on the way to wherever you're going, instead. I'll get my own transport home. You'll never have to see me again."

"You're suddenly making this sound less appealing." Quill seemed unable to help himself. "Maybe I should keep those units."

"You know, for a guy who just robbed me of my livelihood, you're pretty confident."

"I hear that a lot."

"It's not a compliment," Gamora sighed.

"Mmm." Annay regarded him. Quill's belt-loop pose happened to pull his shirt tight enough to outline his abs, which Gamora knew was not an accident. "It just might be," Annay decided. "I'll let you know. Pay me, drop me off—"

"Busy," he interjected in a singsong voice.

"—and I'll tell you where to find Baran."

"I also don't have access to over a hundred thousand units right this second." Quill cocked his head, letting a lock of hair flop over his forehead. (Not an accident.) "Tell us anyway?"

"No need." Rocket leaned into the control panel, his tail lashing. "Drax, focus, will you? Work the thrusters. You're gonna strand us before we ever get to Vadin."

This was new information.

"*Vadin?*" Kiya echoed, softly enough that Gamora wouldn't have noticed it if she hadn't been keeping an eye on her.

Gamora sharply turned to Rocket. "The Kree planet? Why?"

"To find our buyer. Baran Amav-Am, special security advisor currently assisting the DiMavi delegation on Vadin. Keep up, guys. I can't do *all* the work around here." He twisted in his seat and tossed something at Annay—a communicator. It sailed toward her in a neat arc. "Thanks for letting me borrow that."

"I wondered where that had gone." Annay held up the communicator. A couple of lights still glowed, but it was covered with scorch marks and had a big crack running along the side. "Another seven thousand units for a new communicator," she said, annoyed.

"Yeah," Quill said. "That's fair."

"What? It was like that when I found it." Rocket turned back to the dash. "For the record, you should get better encryption on your next com. Any tech genius with software that's been outlawed in 12 galaxies can just slap a homebrew on it to circumvent your security, root through your address book, find someone's full name, run it through public databases, come across their government profile, contact their place of work, and scam the nice secretary into giving up their boss's location. Big security risk. It's like you're rolling out the welcome mat."

Annay glared.

"Guys? I have something." Kiya stepped into the bridge properly, coming to a stop beside Quill. Her shoulders were tense, her gaze shifting rapidly between all the faces suddenly looking at her. "I saw that name—Vadin—earlier today. It was mentioned on those posters advertising the 200-year peace ceremony between DiMave and the Kree Empire. The event is being held there. If Baran is assisting the DiMavi delegation like you said, that has to be why he's on the planet. And"—she hesitated—"did you say Baran's family name is Amav-Am?"

"Does that mean anything to you?" Quill asked.

"It might be a coincidence. But it's a local name. Local to where I'm from."

"Meaning, local to where the Maraud took place," Gamora said, catching on. She gave herself a second to mentally run through the information, then pushed herself upright from the gunner's seat she'd been leaning on. "Meaning, he'll have a grudge against the Kree. Might even have lost family to them. We have trouble."

"You think he's using Groot...?" Rocket said. He reached across the dash, reeling in the thrusters.

Quill was thinking the same thing. "He must've bought the poison Groot for a purpose. If that purpose were sanctioned by his government, he wouldn't have had to hide it by going through sketchy contacts. No offense, Annay."

She considered that. "I'll admit to sketchiness."

Gamora nodded. "And for Baran to buy a weaponized Groot weeks before that ceremony..." To make certain they were all on the same page, she asked, "We're thinking terrorism?"

"I didn't think he'd do anything like that," Kiya said. A hint of yellow crept into her face. She stepped back toward the doorway. "I didn't even know he was with the government. He said he wanted the Groot for protection. For defensive purposes."

"When's the ceremony?" Gamora asked.

Kiya frowned, as if trying to recall the poster.

Annay offered, "It's hosted in the Vadin capital, sometime between six and nine hours from now. I'm not sure about the Vadin-DiMave time conversion. What? You all think Baran bought that tree thing to sabotage the ceremony?" She sounded skeptical.

"That's news to you?" Rocket slid off his seat and crossed the bridge.

"I knew he was on Vadin for the ceremony. I don't know about any plans."

Rocket scoffed, half-turning in the entryway. "You have a fricking escape tunnel, and you're saying your hands are clean and you don't know what your buddies are up to? Baran might not be happy about that ceremony, but you didn't seem thrilled 'bout it in the bar, either."

"Find me a DiMavi who *is*," Kiya said flatly.

"I do not see the value in such a search," Drax remarked from the pilot's seat.

"Forget it." Rocket yanked a wooden shard from his utility belt and held it up to Kiya's face. "If you'll ex-*cuse* me, I got a dead friend to plant."

With that, he stalked off.

Kiya closed her eyes for a second. A dozen emotions crossed her face and instantly vanished again. "I should...I should help with that," she said finally. She slipped out after him.

The urge to follow her felt like an itch Gamora couldn't scratch, but she stayed put. They needed to figure out this Annay situation.

"You didn't answer Rocket's question," Gamora told her.

"I don't know what you *want* from me." Annay held up her hands, as if in self-defense. "You burst into my life, break everything in sight, demand my help, and you're upset because I didn't immediately tell total flarking strangers exactly where to find a customer of mine? Come on. If you must know, the previous owner put in that tunnel. Of course I know my customers are shady as hell. Of course I know they're not using the tunnel for cupcake deliveries. I just don't ask what they *do* use it for. Plausible deniability. I get tipped damn well and it keeps me out of trouble. Getting involved in that kind of business any further is a good way to end up dead or incarcerated." She paused. "Also, it's...bad, and hurts people, and stuff."

Gamora glanced at Quill.

He gave a shrug that said: *I buy it.*

"Are we dropping her off?" Gamora asked.

"We're sure as hell not going back to DiMave. Annay, we can drop you off at a space station on the way and pay for your trip home. We'll find you about those units when this is over. Best we can do."

"Oh, sure. 'I'll call you.'" She pushed away from the pilot's seat, closing the distance between her and Quill. "I've heard that before."

Quill examined her face from up close, not backing down. "If I say I'll call, I call."

"You're so very *busy,* though."

"I make time," he said lightly, "given the right circumstances."

Annay tilted her head toward him, seemingly intrigued. "I do like a guy who keeps his word."

Quill leaned in. His breath stirred the hair by her temple. "I—"

"I will not hesitate to drop off *both* of you at the nearest station if you keep this up." Gamora strode to the front of the bridge and dropped back into the navigator's seat beside Drax, but kept the chair facing toward Quill and Annay. She didn't particularly want a free show—she just held the idle hope that her presence would dissuade them.

Annay pressed the tips of her fingers to Quill's chest, putting an extra inch or so of space between them. "If you're not paying me, I'm staying on board. I'll keep out of your way—although that part *is* negotiable—but I'm not going anywhere until I have my money."

"That still seems like a decision the ship's very important captain should have a say in," Quill suggested. He stepped away, reluctance in his every move, and raised his hands in surrender. "All right. We'll reach Vadin in a few hours. Do what you want, but stay in sight. Drax—can you show her around the ship?"

"There are small talking trees everywhere," Gamora said. "Don't freak out."

"Not a problem," Annay said.

Wistfully, Quill watched Annay follow Drax out of the bridge. Once they were gone, Gamora kicked the vacated pilot's seat to face Quill. "Really, Quill?"

"What?" He dropped into the chair and spun it around. "We've had guests before."

"We have bigger priorities than your libido. We can drop her off at the station. She'll live."

"Thought about it." He tapped the dash, then spread his hands. A holographic galaxy flickered into existence between his palms. Two planets were lit up brightly: DiMave and Vadin, not far apart. With practiced ease, he plotted out a course. "Thing is," he said as he worked, "Annay knows her alcohol. I appreciate that in a woman. That black stuff she poured out for me at her bar? Seriously—"

"Quill."

He laughed. "Look, dropping her off will only delay us. Besides, we do owe her, and we can use her. Kiya doesn't know about recent Kree–DiMavi relations. Annay does. Plus, she doesn't have a reward on her head, and she's an adult. She might prove handy if we need a DiMavi on our side to go the diplomatic route."

"If that's still an option." They'd been on DiMave for less than an hour and left behind a smoking pile of debris. They had ignored Kree borders, interfered with Kree prisoners, and fought a Kree ship. And now they were planning to visit a Kree planet in the middle of a politically sensitive ceremony to confront a DiMavi terrorist-slash-government-advisor who planned on using their friend as a biological weapon.

Gamora did not feel optimistic about diplomacy at this point.

She did, at least, feel better about Quill's decision to let Annay stay on board. He'd had enough sense to send Drax on the tour instead of volunteering himself—a sign that he was still using his brain.

"This should do the trick." Quill clapped his hands, and the map fizzled out. "I need to check on Groot. Can you keep an eye on things here? Watch for a tail. Just in case."

"We'll have one, sooner or later." Gamora stretched as she spoke. "We know the Collector will keep chasing us as long as we have Kiya. We're easy to track."

"We're not very low-profile," he agreed.

"Kiya might be safer somewhere else."

"Groot needs her."

"We can park her and the Grootlings somewhere under the radar. I think we can trust her to continue her research."

"Is that what you want?"

"No," she admitted. The thought of the Grootlings out of reach and easy prey for whoever wanted to grab one—the thought of Kiya left without back-up if the Collector *did* somehow find her—made Gamora uneasy. She wanted them close, even if it meant more risk. "But it may be the best solution."

She should want that, she knew. She should want what was safest for them, and not what was most comfortable for her.

"For now, she stays. With that reward of the Collector's, I don't want to risk it."

She nodded, not showing her quiet relief.

"I don't know about what happens after," he continued, answering her unasked question. "We need to figure out how to remove Kiya's implants and keep her safe from the Collector. We need to find all the Groots and put them back together. We need to stop the Collector from continuing his Guardians two-point-oh project, and figure out how far he's gotten.

We know he has the raccoons—has he worked on them yet? Does he have a mini-Drax and mini-Star-Lord? Is he trying to copy other teammates we've fought alongside? I don't know, Gamora. For now, I'm focusing on what we do know."

"One," she said, "you are dying to know about that mini-Star-Lord."

"No comment."

"Two, no one expects you to have all the answers."

"But you do expect me to make the decisions." He smiled wryly.

"We let you believe that. For the most part, we simply do what we want."

"Thanks. Real helpful." He shook his head, suppressing a laugh, and stepped away from the pilot's seat.

"Peter…" Gamora rested a hand on his arm as he passed. "We let you make the decisions because we have faith that you make the right ones. None of us trust ourselves. Not fully. That's why we need to trust each other."

He slowed mid-step and watched her pensively. "I'm not sure what this team would do without you, you know?"

"There'd be no team left," she told him. "Go see Groot. I have the ship."

30

PETER peered inside the med bay.

Kiya sat facing the opposite wall, her legs drawn up on her chair, her shoulders slouched. Several mounted screens surrounded her workspace. Dirt lay scattered on the counter, and a little farther away stood a single pot with two Grootlings, both covered in sensors.

Peter paused, setting his jaw. Did the Grootlings know what had happened to the original Groot yet? Would it matter to them? He couldn't tell. One was stretching, while the other looked at Kiya in concern. She had one pant leg hiked up, revealing a stretch of green skin, and was running her hand up and down the leg in a way that seemed intentional rather than absentminded.

"I thought you and Rocket were planting Groot?" Peter asked.

She jolted and turned toward him. She pulled down the pant leg, hiding the pale green scars that ran vertically along the skin, and let her legs slip off the seat. "Rocket left. I pissed him off."

"What happened?" Kiya and Rocket wouldn't ever be friends, but Peter had thought they'd come to a grudging understanding.

"He wanted to plant the splinters he found at the bar. I had...suggestions."

"And he didn't appreciate the feedback."

"He did *not*." Kiya grimaced.

"That's Rocket for you." Peter ran a hand through his hair. "It's...Rocket doesn't have many friends outside this ship. And in our small group, the one person he's closest to in the whole galaxy is pretty much unkillable. When it turned out that friend might be more killable than anyone thought..." The Grootlings seemed to visibly shrink at the words. "He's taking it hard."

"I am Groot," one Grootling said, sympathetic.

Kiya blew out a breath. She dragged the Grootlings' pot closer, focusing on them as she spoke. "Rocket said I was being a know-it-all krutacker, and that Groot shouldn't even be in this state to start with." A dissatisfied frown grew on her face. "He's right. I messed up Groot's life. In return, he tried to help me escape Tivan—and got himself blown up for it."

"I am Groot." The second Grootling winced.

"And that's Groot for you. You're getting to know the team pretty well." Peter stepped into the room and dropped onto the examination bed at its center. "Groot has gotten himself blown up for a lot of reasons over the years. I'm not surprised he did it for you. He knows he can grow back, and he knows you're harder to replace."

He leaned back, resting his hands on the flimsy mattress. The bed creaked under his weight.

"You're saying it's not a big deal?"

"He doesn't talk about the regrowing process much, but I asked him once." Peter peered at the Grootlings. They nodded in unison, inviting him to go on. "It hurts, it's traumatizing, and it means spending hours or days—however long it takes for us to plant him—without any sort of consciousness. And that's *if* we plant him. If we can't obtain a splinter, or if something goes wrong, he's gone for good. He doesn't do it lightly."

Kiya nodded. She didn't seem to be taking Groot's sacrifice lightly, either. If she had, Peter would've felt a lot more conflicted about her presence on board.

It should have felt strange for Peter to talk about this—about losing Groot within an hour of it actually happening; about regrowing Groot with two versions of him in the same room, and more than a dozen elsewhere on the ship.

Strange was what the Guardians *did,* though. All Peter felt as he spoke was a lump of worry in his chest.

Kiya busied herself checking the sensors on the Grootlings. They squirmed under her grasp, giggling when she reached a ticklish spot. "I am Groooot!"

Peter got the distinct impression she didn't know how to respond.

"It might be an even bigger deal now," she said finally, hunkering over the Grootlings' pot. "The last Grootlings I planted grew slowly. A few didn't sprout at all. I think that the more they need to share the energy, the harder it is to grow a full Groot from just a splinter. Groot knows this. I told him before we landed on DiMave."

And he'd stayed behind anyway.

Peter had known Groot too long to be surprised. He still closed his eyes for a moment, simultaneously cursing him for his stupidity, thanking him for his kindness, and pleading for him to poke his leafy face out of the earth as soon as he could.

Kiya was still facing away, adjusting a loosely attached sensor. "Even if he grows, planting him the regular way would be a slow process. It might take days to know whether it's working."

If he grows. Peter hated the words. *If.* This couldn't be happening. Not to *Groot,* of all people.

"I suggested an alternative to Rocket," Kiya continued.

Peter would take any glimmer of hope he could get. "Tell me."

Kiya kept playing with the sensor even after reattaching it, as if trying to figure out where to start. "I'm making progress," she said after a minute. "You know my theory: that the main problem keeping the Grootlings apart is that each has its own consciousness. So I wondered: If the obstacle is having two dueling consciousnesses, what about when there's only *one* consciousness present?

"A while ago, you found the remains of a destroyed Grootling. I asked one of the other Grootlings to try to merge with those splinters to see what would happen. Turns out: nothing. It was just dead wood."

For a moment, Peter's hopes had flared. Now they dimmed. This wouldn't be a solution.

"I tried something else around the same time. I asked a Grootling to try to absorb a sproutling too young to have developed conscious thought—it had only just popped up from the dirt, hadn't even developed limbs yet. The merge *seemed* to work. I just couldn't tell whether it was superficial, or whether there were deeper consequences—until now. I checked the logs when I came on board. While we were on DiMave, that merged Grootling's energy levels started climbing in a way I haven't seen in any of the others. I think it worked. Properly." She turned to Peter and watched him with gleaming eyes, biting her lip. She seemed to be trying to hide her excitement.

Both Grootlings seemed interested, hopeful. Their reaction reminded Peter of the Groot he knew. He was glad to see it, but he couldn't share in their optimism yet. "An energy surge? Is it possible that when Groot was destroyed in that back room, his energy went—?"

"I wondered the same thing, but the energy surge happened before… that happened. It must be the merge. It succeeded. And here's my thinking:

Maybe we *can* have one of the Grootlings merge with Groot's splinters. His situation is different."

Peter sat up straighter. "Oh?"

"The way all this started…Tivan had recovered one of Groot's shards, right? He activated the potential to grow a second Groot from that shard, even with another Groot already in existence. That trait was carried forward. Any splinters or branches originating from that altered Grootling could grow their own new Grootlings. That's how I grew mine. But in my Grootlings, I shut off the process Tivan had activated. I couldn't have my buyers growing their own supply. I wanted to control the market." She smiled wryly, seeming to realize how callous she sounded. "I couldn't figure out 99 percent of Tivan's notes—most are in some kind of four-dimensional Elder language, I don't know—but between the one or two snippets I did understand, and studying the Grootlings' cells myself, I managed to sabotage Tivan's alterations. It's not elegant. More like sticking a branch into spokes of a wheel. It shut off the Grootlings' ability to generate others, but also the ability to regenerate themselves. Once they're destroyed, they're straight-up gone. But *your* Groot…"

"He still has the potential to regenerate."

"Exactly. The splinters Rocket recovered from that back room aren't dead—they can still grow into Groot, like every other time he's been destroyed. They just might not have enough energy for it. If they still have the potential, though, it might mean they *can* be absorbed. That way, Groot wouldn't need to grow a whole new body when energy is so scarce—he could combine with an already existing one. Memories and all."

As Kiya finished, she seemed to withdraw onto her chair. Whenever she got to talking about her research, she appeared to shed her self-consciousness, that wall she'd drawn up around herself. Peter only realized it afterward—when she stopped talking and that wall slammed back down.

She peered at the exit. "Rocket didn't want to hear it."

"I'll talk to him."

"Yeah?" She managed a half-smile.

If this increased their chances—if it got their friend back sooner—it was worth risking a grouchy Rocket. They could always try to plant Groot afterward. Peter wanted to go up and find Rocket right away, but he stayed on the bed, considering the Grootlings behind Kiya.

"What are you doing with those guys?"

"I am Groot." One Grootling patted his sensors, as if making sure they were properly attached.

She hesitated, then slowly slid off her chair. "Taking more readings?" She circled the room, flicking on the monitors and projectors scattered throughout. She was so engaged in the work that Peter could almost believe she wasn't intentionally keeping several feet of distance between them. "Look. The energy patterns the sensors pick up help us see how similar— how compatible—the Groots might be. These two Grootlings are the most similar. See, over here and here…"

She indicated several side-by-side charts. Peter hopped off the bed and examined them closely. The two Grootlings' readings didn't line up exactly, but they followed the same pattern. Dips and hills of similar intensity at the same times; similar colors in similar locations on color maps. Peter couldn't understand the maps for the life of him, but they matched up convincingly.

"Even these two aren't similar enough to merge successfully," she continued. "They come closer than the rest, though. Most of the Grootlings are far more different from one another. They're all Groot, with their unique experiences on top of that. They have the same starting point, but they—"

"Branched off," Peter supplied helpfully.

"I am Groot," the Grootlings snickered.

"—they *diverged* the moment you and Tivan each grew one, then diverged further when I grew mine." She seemed to be trying her hardest not to smile at the pun. "Add the missing memories and personality traits, and it could be that their minds are too dissimilar to fuse together."

Peter nodded as she pointed at another chart—this one a table of scribbled notes and numbers.

"I am Groot?" The Grootlings watched in fascination.

"Every time after they try to merge, they're tired. Not physically—mentally. Like they were fighting to merge, to fit together and override those differences. If there aren't as many differences to fight, if we can somehow get their minds to line up, we might actually see a successful merge."

Of all the Guardians' screwups lately, the decision to take Kiya on board to work on Groot hadn't been the worst. She was young, but DiMavi chose their interests and specialties so early in life that it hardly made a difference. She was good at what she did—and whether out of guilt, responsibility, or sheer academic interest, she was *absorbed* in it as well.

Now he just needed her efforts to pay off. Even without new Grootlings being grown, Peter had the nagging feeling that the longer they waited, the worse this problem would get. The Grootlings required more energy as they grew. The ones still out there could be in trouble. And if Kiya was right, then with every passing day the Grootlings diverged further, making it harder to bring them together.

And none of that even touched on the Collector.

Peter rubbed a hand on his cheek. "Could a telepath align the Grootlings' minds?"

"Could be. Right now, I'm thinking: If you can't tackle an obstacle in your path, you have three options. One—you remove the obstacle. That means finding a way to smooth over the Grootlings' differences and sync up their minds. Two—you work around the obstacle. That's what I'm investigating with the sproutling and shard experiments. Or three—you go *through* the obstacle. You become strong enough to tackle it. The Grootlings are wiped out after trying to fuse with a Grootling who's too different; maybe if one or both are stronger, they could keep trying longer, and work around or override those differences."

"So you're saying that they need to merge to become stronger, but they might need to become stronger to merge."

"It's a theory." She grimaced. "Science is fun?"

"I am Groot," one Grootling chimed in.

"It's still progress," Peter said. "We can tell the other Grootlings."

We can tell Groot, he thought, and winced. He wanted his friend back.

And the truth was, he wanted his teammate back, too. They'd lost their heaviest hitter, and it showed. With Tivan chasing them, Peter wanted the Guardians at full capacity.

"I am Groot."

"Kiya?" Peter leaned back against the counter, crossed his arms, and peered down at her. She was scrutinizing the charts. "You did good. Thank you."

"Oh." She tore her eyes away from the screens. "I mean, I'm still not sure—"

"I need to get ready. We're about two hours from Vadin."

"Okay."

Two hours to prepare for Vadin and Baran, to convince Rocket to let Kiya try her approach with Groot's shards, to check on the Grootlings, to check in with his team after the mess on DiMave, and to talk to Annay. He could show her some impressive parts of the ship that Drax might've missed.

Kiya could help him with at least the first item.

"We need to talk about the Groot you grew. The odds are good he'll be brainwashed—we may need to fight him." Peter hated the thought. But not as much as he would hate fighting Groot unprepared. "Tell me what we need to know about the poison."

31

ROCKET?" Drax stared at the open hovercar in front of them. He squinted to keep the sweat out of his eyes. "Your contacts are terrible."

"My buddy generously drops off a car for us, and you complain? You wanna walk?" Rocket spread his arms to indicate the scorching Vadin desert around them and gave Drax a *well?* kind of look.

Tough as Drax was, Rocket figured even he'd pass on walking in this heat, on this landscape. Vadin's equatorial zone was all rock, scorching sun, and Kree too stubborn to leave for the more sensible climates on the planet's poles. *Great* place to stick a capital city.

It would've been easier to land in the city itself, but after the incident on Levet, Quill had wanted to avoid announcing the Guardians' presence and attracting the attention of the Kree authorities. So instead, they'd landed the camouflaged ship in this empty stretch of desert a few miles outside of the city.

Rocket's contact, a Kree named Dab-Norr, was the only one who'd been able to hook them up with decent transportation on short notice. "Any of you even *know* people on this planet?" he went on. "Didn't think so. But do I ever hear a 'thank you, Rocket'—naw, didn't think so."

"Thank you for arranging this piece of junk, Rocket," Quill said. He ran a hand across his sweaty forehead—Rocket shuddered; hairless skin was *so* gross—and checked out the vehicle, from its scratched metal and dented doors to the half-rusted thrusters protruding from the bottom.

"That's all I ask." Rocket climbed up the side of the car and hauled himself over. A dust cloud sprayed up as he landed in the driver's seat. Gamora climbed into the back seat, followed by Annay and Kiya.

The car really was a piece of junk, but it'd get them into town unnoticed. Blending in was easier without Groot, but that didn't so much put Rocket at ease as frustrate him—in fact, it made him want to blow up random crap even more than usual. The Grootlings had asked to come along a hundred times, but Quill had resolutely told them no. They were too weak, and the team couldn't risk losing more of them. The Grootlings wouldn't come back if they were shattered.

Of course, it was possible that none of the team would come back from a ride in this rusty gearbin, either.

Rocket rubbed his hands. The controls looked outdated, but easy enough to figure out. There was even a rudimentary AI on board, if he recognized the model correctly, so it was probably just a matter of getting the system going and...

"Voice authorization?" a voice chirped.

"Rocket."

"I'm not familiar with that name. Try again?"

"Rocket," he repeated. "Dab-Norr said he prepped the system for me."

"I'm not familiar with that name. Try again? You have one attempt left."

"One attempt before what, exactly?" Quill asked from the passenger seat.

"I got this, Quill." Rocket glared at the control panel and spat out the next words: "*Mangy rodent.*"

"Authorization accepted."

"I'm gonna murder Dab-Norr," Rocket announced. "Let's move."

They rose a few feet above the rocky landscape and floated forward, fast and silent. Clumps of dry desert grass wafted beneath them; gusts of sand billowed in their wake. At the horizon ahead, they could see the shimmery outline of the city; in every other direction they saw only empty desert.

The rush of wind brought welcome relief from the burning sun. The car had no climate control, dubious safety measures, and kinda twitchy controls, but to Dab-Norr's credit, it was actually a pretty smooth ride. Vadin's eponymous capital wasn't far, anyway.

"There *is* a roof to this thing, right?" Quill asked.

"Who would want one?" Annay said from the back seat. Her hair was a tangled mess of white, and she looked absolutely delighted about it.

"Inside the city, bring up the roof," Quill instructed. "Even without Groot, we're too recognizable."

"Are you trying to kill us, Quill?" Gamora asked. "This heat is almost worse than Levet's. Speaking of killing us—what are we actually up against?"

The team had been so busy on the short flight to Vadin—researching the ceremony and Baran, discussing Groot, sending the Collector more bogus tips about Kiya's location—that they hadn't gotten together for a proper briefing. They had just shared bits and pieces of info over comms or when passing each other in the halls.

Quill twisted around in the front passenger seat and propped his arms up on the headrest. The wind tugged at that ridiculous hair of his, but he didn't seem bothered. "Good question. Truth is, we don't know what kind of spores we'll be dealing with."

"What do you mean, you don't know?" Rocket said, yelling over the wind.

Quill was silent for a moment. Rocket got the impression Quill and

Kiya might be exchanging meaningful looks, but he was too busy steering them around a clunky rock formation to check.

"Kiya spliced the Grootling with a weaponized form of the tirrinit tree from one of Kree-Pama's moons," Quill said eventually. "On landing, the spores send out a…signal?…to disrupt or damage nearby nerve endings. The spores were designed to take effect even through protective gear."

"Sounds nasty," Annay said.

"*Is* nasty," Rocket said. "I've dealt with weaponized tirrinit before. Only a Badoon-level intellect would play with that stuff."

"Baran said he wanted it for defensive purposes," Kiya snapped. "And it doesn't *have* to be lethal. It depends on the nutrients the tirrinit absorbs from the soil. The spores might only make you itch for a few minutes."

"They might also permanently numb your skin, cause agonizing pain for hours, or straight-up kill you," Quill added. "And if Baran wants revenge on the Kree, I don't think he'll feed the Grootling the friendly, itchy kind of nutrients."

"There is nothing friendly about itching," Drax said. "It is deeply irritating."

Rocket chanced a look over his shoulder to give Drax an *are you kidding me?* face, only to find Quill and Annay nodding in grudging agreement.

"I don't know what kind of spores Baran would go for," Kiya said. "I didn't even know he worked with our government. I thought he was maybe local law enforcement. He wanted the DiMavi villages to be able to defend themselves in a way the Kree—or anyone else—wouldn't see coming and couldn't easily block."

"What was he like?"

"He seemed—I don't know—determined. To the point."

"That's about right," Annay said. "Baran doesn't visit the bar often. I think he does favors for my more politically inclined customers. Lost reports, delayed raids, a heads-up here and there. You didn't hear that from me, for the record. I don't make a habit of sharing my customers' business with super heroes. Anyway, couple months ago, Baran got rid of some troublemakers in the bar for me. So, when he asked, I agreed to take a message from Kiya. Which I'm beginning to regret, now that I've lost my bar, communicator, and pride, and somehow ended up in a Kree desert of all places."

"Funny how that goes," Quill said.

"There may be one upside." She looked up at him, squinting at the sun. "To be determined."

Rocket groaned, partly at her words, partly at Quill's appreciative grin.

"What kind of attack would he launch?" Gamora asked.

Annay only shrugged.

Based on Kiya's silence, Rocket guessed she didn't know, either.

Well, that was *real* helpful. It made him all the more worried about what kind of state they'd find the poison Grootling in.

Scattered farms started to dot the landscape, along with the campus of a military academy. The city was close. "Bringing up the roof," Rocket announced. "Someone get me a route to the embassy, will you?"

THE DIMAVI embassy on Vadin was on the city's outskirts, in the middle of a bustling neighborhood filled with hotels and ports. As they approached, Peter peered down the side of the car to take in the area.

Vadin was an old city, and it showed. Ancient Kree buildings and aged footpaths sat side-by-side with towering skyscrapers and six layers of road decks that crisscrossed the space between buildings. Most of the newer buildings had main entrances at least half a dozen floors up, providing easier access from the raised skyways—the city's surface was so cramped and neglected that ground-level traffic was at a minimum.

"The embassy is over there." Annay indicated indicated a square, robust building that stood out against the curved Kree architecture around it. It was only a couple stories high, with the entrance stubbornly on the ground floor. Peter guessed the DiMavi weren't fans of the Kree approach to civil engineering. Most people he saw in the area—whether on the surface below or on the raised walkways that connected the taller buildings—were Kree, but DiMavi were a close runner-up, and more so the closer they came to the embassy. They had to be in town for tonight's ceremony.

As Rocket steered their car off the fastdeck and onto the slower lanes below, Peter got a better view of the embassy down on the city's surface. A modest courtyard lay in front of the building's entrance, and there was no fence or wall to separate the area from the public street, which would— theoretically—give it a welcoming impression. At the moment, though, red do-not-cross lines glowed on the ground, and wary groups of DiMavi guards secured the building and the courtyard perimeter.

"Are the DiMavi particularly paranoid, or is something up?" Gamora pressed close to the window on her side.

Annay sounded worried. "Something's up."

"Rocket, stay on this lane," Peter said warily.

Rocket had started to steer them toward the surface streets, but immediately course-corrected. They zoomed past the embassy, leaving it safely behind them.

Peter had hoped to be able to slide up to the embassy and inquire casually about Baran at the front desk. He doubted they would even *reach* the front desk now, and he didn't want to take chances if the DiMavi were on high alert. Annay had complained about her government being buddy-buddy with the Kree; anyone who recognized the Guardians might turn them in.

"Can you check—?" Peter started.

"—local news and transmissions for information on a recent DiMavi-related incident," Drax said, his face obscured by the holo hovering over his communicator. "Yes. I am working on it."

The ceremony wasn't until tonight. The odds that this was Baran-related were slim—and from what they knew of him, Baran was unlikely to target DiMavi.

Something still felt off.

"Traffic accident," Drax said. "The locals seem to be exasperated with their DiMavi guests' driving skills."

"Oh, come on!" Annay gestured at the tangled mess of roadways outside the windows. "Who designs roads like this?"

"Actually, those higher lanes look fun." Peter turned around in his seat, propping one arm on the headrest, to face the green crew in the back seat—Drax studying the holo over his communicator, Gamora glancing over at his findings, Kiya keeping to herself, and Annay still looking indignant about the Kree road system. "Can you rent motorcycles on Vadin...?" Peter mused.

Annay sounded skeptical. "You're kidding."

"Star-Lord has few self-preservation instincts," Drax said, not looking away from the holo. "This usually does not surprise people."

"I suppose it doesn't." Annay met Peter's eyes. He raised his eyebrows at her, half-expectant, half-challenging, and couldn't help but notice that she was fighting to contain a smile.

"I'd invite you to join me," he told her, "but those DiMavi driving skills, I just don't know..."

Drax went on, "Another traffic accident. Another traffic accident. Another—"

"Please stop mentioning the traffic accidents," Gamora said.

"You're on," Annay mouthed at Peter.

He winked before looking to Drax, who had paused in his work. He seemed to have found something more interesting than traffic accidents.

Drax offered, "Nine people were injured in a surface-level park two hours ago, including several DiMavi. Reports do not go into details."

"Any rumors?" Peter ran a hand through his hair. He could be worrying over nothing, but in the middle of a possible political disaster, he wanted to be sure.

"Apparently, a DiMavi diplomat may have been among the victims. This would explain the increased security at the embassy. And—ah."

"Now that's interesting." Gamora was leaning into Drax, reading along on his communicator.

"Care to share with the group?" Rocket asked.

"Witnesses are talking about a monster," Gamora said. She locked eyes with Peter in the front seat.

"A tree monster," Peter finished.

Found them, he thought.

32

THE HOSPITAL was ancient by Kree standards, which wasn't exactly surprising to Rocket. Vadin was full of old crap. It was, apparently, the planet's main draw: Vadin was one of the first planets in the Kree Empire and had enough culture to fill up a z-chip and make it dance a traditional fenin waltz—in other words, just enough history and art to put Rocket right to sleep.

At least the welcome bots hovering by the ceiling had been built in the past decade. One buzzed up to the three visitors—Quill, Kiya, and Rocket—as soon as they entered the main lobby.

"Good morning!" chirped the perfectly round, metallic ball hovering in midair before Quill. "What's your purpose today? May we assist?"

"We're visiting family," Quill said.

"Do you need any help locating the room?"

Rocket scanned the lobby. Scuffed floors, walls cracked and pale with age. Clean, though, and the security system was halfway decent, with 3-D recorders and gen-seven force field barriers at strategic locations. A flesh-and-blood receptionist farther down seemed too busy to notice them. Security guards? He kept an eye on them, but they didn't seem on edge.

Other visitors talked to the welcome bots or went straight for the elevators, while nurse droids guided patients toward the inner courtyard for fresh air.

This would be no problem at all.

"We know her room number," Quill told the bot. "Where are your intensive-care and emergency wards?"

"Those are not accessible to visitors."

"Oh! You misunderstand. We don't want to *go* there! We need to know so we can avoid them. Since we're just visitors. Obviously."

The ball-bot spun twice, as if thinking. "Great!" it said then, its voice light. "We at Centravada Hospital appreciate your thoughtfulness. Allow me to show you a projection of the hospital. The off-limits wards are indicated in red."

The emergency room was on the ground floor, south wing. Intensive care was two stories above, east wing. Rocket memorized the floor plan in one look.

"Thanks! You're a champ. I'll leave something in the donation box on the way out." Quill walked past the bot, a hand up in thanks, with Kiya and Rocket close behind him.

"I got a question." Annay's voice came through Rocket's comms. "Am I getting paid for this?"

She'd been asked to check the streets—maybe hook up with local contacts—for a sign of Baran. People would talk to a DiMavi more easily than they'd talk to the rest of the Guardians.

"*We* don't get paid for this," Gamora informed her. She and Drax were out looking for eyewitnesses—especially ones with information on where Baran and his Grootling had disappeared to—in case the victims in the hospital weren't in any shape to speak.

"You're a member of the team, though," Annay said. "I just got drafted."

"Do you have anything better to do than help our friend and prevent an attack on innocent lives?" Quill asked, his tone casual.

"Fine, fine," she sighed. "But if I save the day, I expect a *thorough* thank you."

"I can arrange that." He turned to Rocket, still looking amused. "Rocket, try to access security footage. See where they took the victims. Kiya, check the emergency ward. Get a glimpse of the situation, see if you can spot the victims—or any suspicious extra security. Anyone asks what you're doing, act worried and say you're waiting to hear about your brother. Cooperate and leave. Me, I'll check out intensive care."

Quill went for the elevators, and Kiya and Rocket headed into another hallway together—he'd seen a good spot on the map, a stairwell just past the ER that looked like it'd be quiet enough to do his job undisturbed. Rocket tended to get looks. He wasn't eager to get those looks while he was trying to sneak into their security system.

He didn't talk to the girl. She didn't talk to him. They parted ways without words. Looked like they'd come to an understanding.

Rocket still wasn't thrilled that Kiya was accompanying them—it seemed like a good way to risk the Collector mucking things up again. She was right that most Kree couldn't tell her from any other DiMavi teenager, though, and the Guardians needed an extra set of hands given the time crunch. Besides, he'd sent the Collector a burst of false Kiya sightings just before landing, including some with forged snapshots of her at various locations. Hopefully that would throw off Tivan for a while.

As he moved, Rocket kept a subtle eye on the cameras. Motion-activated. Wired. That was a plus, mostly. Wireless would've meant he could do this from outside the building, but now that he was already in, it was just a matter of hijacking the signal. It might not even be secured.

He slipped into the stairway, paused to scratch his knee where his fur had gotten bunched up, and peered up at the cameras.

He could do this the careful way: avoid the cameras, freeze the image so no one suspected a thing, and set up his connection to the system without a care in the world.

He could also do it the effective way, which would give him the access he needed—and the info he was looking for—a hell of a lot quicker. He'd just have to cross his fingers and hope the feeds weren't actively monitored.

He chose option two.

Rocket scrabbled up the wall and pinned himself up high, humming cheerfully. He glanced at the ceiling to estimate its thickness, then adjusted the power level of the gun clipped to his waist and pressed the muzzle against the ceiling.

"Boom." The gun sent a soft pulse into the structure. The approach was quiet, so no one could overhear, and gentle, so he could crack the ceiling without bringing it down. He plucked away layers of synthic and rubber to reveal the wires.

Ha. Wires! This hospital was adorable.

Now, he only needed to—

Footsteps. He heard them a split second before the door opened.

"…saying is, whoever is behind the attack, it better not get blamed on…" The voice trailed off.

Rocket looked down from his position on the ceiling. Two Kree guards stood in the doorway, staring up at him in puzzlement.

"Really?" Rocket said. "*Really?* You had to choose now to use the stairs? You couldn't wait one minute?"

"What are you—"

"Oh, well. Wanna hear my favorite sound? Listen close." He grabbed the gun. It wasn't his blaster of choice, but it'd do the trick.

"Rocket!" Quill's voice came in so loud over his earpiece that Rocket cringed. "Don't! Shoot! Innocent! Hospital! Guards!"

He still had the line open? Oops.

The guards already had their guns aimed at him. They clearly weren't obeying Quill's rules. "Come down from—"

He didn't let them finish. He dropped to the floor, landing in a crouch. A half-second to aim, and: *BLAM.*

At this setting, the gunblast would only feel like a punch to the face. He hoped it was a painful punch, though. Crap-timing bastards deserved worse.

He aimed the gun up at the exposed wires and sent out an electrical blast strong enough to fry the entire camera system. Assuming security was on the way, he didn't want to help them out with pretty pictures of him. If their system was particularly poor, the blast might even be enough to take out the rest of the security measures.

Time to go. He bolted on all fours between the guards, through the open door, and into the hall.

"Status?" Quill asked.

"Status: whoopsie," Rocket snarled. His nails tapped down the hall, echoed by footsteps farther away. The guards seemed to take getting shot at as a personal offense.

"Where are you at?"

"Being chased back the way I came. They're—yep, they're calling for backup."

"I'm on my way to you."

Kiya interrupted, "You seem a little busy—"

"Ya *think?*"

"—but I found where they're keeping the patients."

"Scratch that," Quill said. "Kiya, I'm on my way to *you*. Give me directions. Rocket, lead the guards away. Keep them distracted. And no killing."

"You wanna tell *them* that?" he yelled. Energy crackled past his ear and struck the ground just in front of him. His tail lashed frantically as he ran. He fired over his shoulder, the setting now cranked up significantly above "punch to the face."

"Broken bones are okay," Quill said.

"Trust me," Rocket said. "Already on it."

33

VADIN seemed to like its parks—the surface level was littered with them. Some were only narrow strips, while others stretched across dozens of city blocks, twining around buildings and replacing what must once have been streets.

The park where the incident had taken place was on the average side: about ten blocks long, running beside a quiet surface road. Between the skyways overhead and buildings across the street, only the occasional sunbeam made its way to the ground, painting fiercely bright splotches across the artificially lit grass and streets.

Gamora and Drax had found the correct park, but the reports had not indicated where in the park the incident had taken place.

That didn't stop the gossip.

"I wasn't around, but it happened over there," a DiMavi parent said, attempting to wrangle two children from a pond while pointing across the park. "Past the hill, way over by the edge of the park. You can't miss it."

Gamora nodded *thanks,* then stalked off across the grass toward Drax, who'd stayed at a distance so as to not frighten the children. Typically, his attempts to sound unthreatening still came out pretty damn threatening.

They walked on, checking the area for any sign of a struggle, although

Gamora doubted they would find anything. If something had gone down here, there wouldn't have been families with children around so soon afterward.

If they found anything, it would be at the other side of the park, where the DiMavi had indicated.

As she walked, Gamora glanced over her shoulder. The DiMavi children weren't cooperating with their parents' attempts to get them out of the pond and onto the grass, turning it into a game that largely involved splashing pond water around.

Gamora wished they would leave. Skip the ceremony, go straight home. Even if Baran's attack wasn't aimed at DiMavi citizens, there could be casualties. Civilians always got caught up in the Guardians' messes. People like these kids and their parents—people like Kiya—hadn't signed up for that.

They hadn't signed up for anything but living their lives.

What was that like? No responsibility, no danger, no atonement— simply doing what you wanted, when you wanted? The thought had always filled her with distaste, on the few occasions when it occurred in the first place. She'd rarely had cause to wonder.

Now, she didn't know how she felt about it.

"You are staring, Gamora," Drax said.

"Do you ever want to go back?" she asked. They started to climb the hill the DiMavi had indicated.

"It is too soon. We have only been in the park for ten minutes."

"You had a normal life once. A family. Do you ever think about going back to a life like that?"

"That life is gone."

She paused to find her words. She shouldn't have been talking about this, she knew—not now, and not with Drax. "You know what it's like. You weren't always the Destroyer."

"As long as Thanos lives, that is all I can be."

She could press on—*what if*—but there would be no point. If Drax ever thought about a life beyond Thanos, he didn't show it, and wouldn't tell them.

Gamora also didn't know what she'd tell him if he turned the question back on her. There was no Zen-Whoberi with its spring feasts to return to, no "normal" to hope for, and no family to find—

Or so she had thought.

Kiya wants nothing to do with you, she told herself.

Gamora knew the girl existed, now. She knew she wasn't *alone.* That should be enough. Gamora would help Kiya to safety and then move on with the life she had been leading before.

That was what the rage in her heart said, what her sword arm yearned for, what the guilt pulsing in her every memory pushed her toward.

But now, for the first time, the blood in her veins had a say in the matter, too, and it said: *What if?*

She breathed in, trying to let the thoughts slide off her. She should not be asking pointless questions. She had a job to do.

"There." She pointed. "They've cordoned it off." They stood atop the hill, traffic roaring on the skyways above, and looked down at a small creek that wound its way around the field and floating flower beds before them. At strategic positions, bright-red poles stuck up from the ground, with hovering lines of energy stretching between them to section off the area where the Grootling had attacked. The energy grid covered a corner of the park and part of the street beyond.

Gamora noticed only two things out of the ordinary. One, parts of the lawn near the edge of the park were disturbed, with clumps of grass piled up beside unearthed dirt. And two, bots were systematically sweeping the area, some the size of her fist and others so small she could only spot them when they moved.

Kiya and Quill had said the Grootling's spores took effect on impact, and it had been hours since the attack. If anyone else had been affected by stray spores since then, the authorities would've been far more thorough in cordoning off this zone and keeping people safely at bay.

That was one positive, at least. The Grootling was only dangerous in the moment.

They didn't cross into the zone—no reason to, yet. They stuck close by the barrier, investigating the surrounding area, although Gamora didn't expect to discover anything new.

When they reached the edge of the park, Drax eyed the torn-up lawn. "Those marks are from the Grootling's feet."

"Hey, does that look… Those people are interviewing that woman across the street. Let's go." She crossed the street toward the trio of Kree. With the street cordoned off, there was no traffic.

Two men—their shoulders adorned with patches from a local branch of a Kree news show—were interviewing an excitable-sounding woman. A camera bot hovered in between them. The closer Gamora and Drax came, the better they could make out their words.

"Got away *just* in time!" the woman was saying. "That thing *almost* got me!"

"And you said it was a tree?"

This was bad.

"It was! It was! Not like a Cotati, no, different—" She stopped talking as she noticed Gamora's brisk approach. "'Scuse me?"

"Stop recording," Gamora said.

One of the men shook his head, looking at his partner askance. "I *told* you we shouldn't ignore a media blackout—

"We're reporting the news!" he said, indignant. "We're within our full rights to—"

Drax reached for the camera bot and crushed it in his hand as easily as snapping a twig. The bot fell to the ground. It bleeped once before powering down.

"You'll need to pay for that," the first guy said.

"This is *censorship*—"

"You knew about the blackout," Gamora said. "These are the consequences. If you publicize the footage you've already recorded, there will be more consequences."

"But you aren't with the Association of—"

"We are."

"We are not," Drax said.

Gamora elbowed his side.

He amended, "We are the Guardians—"

"—of media," Gamora finished. "Please leave. We need to question your subject to determine the level of your infraction."

They narrowed their eyes, but didn't argue further. They picked up the crumpled bot and walked to their nearby shuttle.

"Blackout?" blurted out the woman they'd been interviewing. "What blackout?"

"This is a politically sensitive incident. We'd like certain details to stay under wraps." The fewer media outlets reporting the truth about the Grootling, the lower the odds of the Collector picking up on it. He knew they were after the Grootlings; he knew Kiya was with them; he might even connect the dots between their presence on DiMave and the ceremony tonight. The last thing they wanted was to lead him here. Having Kiya in the open, with that reward on her head, was dangerous enough.

"I'm not in trouble, am I?" the woman asked.

"Not at all," Gamora said. "Tell us what you told them."

"And what you *planned* to tell them." Drax crossed his arms. "Speak."

34

KIYA had hidden herself in an unused room across the hall. Peter found her easily. The alarms blaring through the emergency ward kept doctors and patients away from the hallways, and he looked enough like a patient or plainclothes employee that the few guards he'd seen hadn't paid him any mind except to bark at him to clear the area. More to the point, he *didn't* look like an angry anthropomorphic raccoon.

"Not sure how much time we have," Peter told Kiya. "Let's go."

"There are security measures on the door. I saw a doctor enter through some kind of fizzling barrier."

"Fan-tastic." At this point he might as well blast a hole through the wall, although that probably wouldn't put the Grootlings' victims inside at ease.

He and Kiya crossed the empty hall to the door, and he took a second to examine the mechanism above the frame—

Footsteps were pounding their way. Guards came running from the left.

And from the right, screaming. Rocket rounded the corner, running against the wall and leaping back onto the floor to land on all fours. He bounded forward, shooting blindly behind him. Three guards were on his tail. Blasts ricocheted off the walls.

"Oh," Kiya said.

"Incoming!" Rocket yelled.

Peter unclipped his element gun and pointed it absently at the ground to his left. One…two… When the guards were close enough, he fired. A mud slick splashed onto the floor, and they went sliding.

"Hey, Rocket!" he bellowed down the hall. *"Do you not understand what 'lead the guards away' means?"*

"Wouldya shoot them already? They singed my tail, I'm deaf in one ear, and I'm two seconds away from tossing a bomb!"

"Fine, fine. Kiya, can you disarm those guys?" He aimed a thumb at the mud-covered guards. She was on them in two seconds, jamming a knee into one guard's back to keep him down. Mud squelched underneath him. The other guard was trying to aim his weapon: Kiya grabbed it, redirected it toward the wall, then slammed it to the floor with enough force that Peter suspected she'd cracked a bone or two in the guy's hand.

Peter lifted his gun and took aim at the other guards, who were still running.

Ffzzzt. One guard went down, her arm encased in a block of ice.

Ffzzzt. Missed that one. The next shot did the trick.

That left just the one guard on Rocket's side of the hall, the two Kiya was disarming behind Peter, and—

Something tore through Peter's shoulder from behind. He screamed. His grip on the element gun slipped, and it bounced to the floor. Reaching for his shoulder, he swiveled out of the way and dropped low. A half-dozen more guards were running down the hall on the left-hand side.

"We don't want to fight!" Peter yelled.

That didn't seem to work.

Kiya bolted toward the newcomers, leaving the other two guards crumpled in the mud. She flung a stolen energy-gun clip at one guard's face and hurled the gun itself at another. By the time they went down, she was already pouncing on a third guard.

That gave Peter a short breather. He glanced at the wound on his shoulder. It was a clean cut, but a wide one, leaking blood all over the place. He hissed through his teeth. The pain was sharp, the wound deep.

One of the guards Kiya had disarmed was back on his feet. He charged at Kiya from behind.

Peter tried to reach for his gun, then yelped, letting it clatter back to the floor. That cut must've gone deep into muscle, to hurt this bad. No time to grab his gun again now. Instead, he bolted forward, wrapping his good arm around the guard's waist and bringing him down. A quick choke: The man was out. Peter snatched up his fallen blaster, trying to bite past the pain.

Peter had meant to keep this mission clean and simple. He really had. But somehow, it had devolved into this: Kiya in hand-to-hand combat with four guards at once, with several more already unconscious by her feet; Peter attempting to ice people with the element blaster in his wrong hand, missing half his shots; Rocket climbing up on one guard's shoulders and using the leverage to kick another one in the face with his hind legs.

They were winning—the day hospital security beat them was the day he retired the Guardians—but more guards would arrive soon.

"Kiya! Your left!" Peter bellowed.

She pivoted, elbowing the approaching guard in the face.

A sound fizzled behind him. Instead of the guard Peter expected, a door opened—the one leading to the hospital room holding the Grootling's victims. A blue-skinned Kree stood in the doorway, blinking at the chaos.

"What are you doing?! Keep that door—" someone yelled from inside.

"Kiya?" the Kree asked.

Well, that was intriguing.

More important: The door was open.

Peter reached out and grabbed hold of Rocket's tail. He yanked Rocket away from the guard he was assaulting and shoved him inside the room. Turned. Headbutted an approaching guard, stepped between Kiya and her targets, and pushed her toward the room, as well. She got the hint: She shoved past the Kree and immediately spun to defend the doorway.

"Hey," she said to the Kree. "I know you."

"Out of the way," a guard yelled, gun raised, trying to get off a shot at Kiya or Rocket.

Peter was about to ice the guard and crash into the room himself, when the Kree in the doorway raised his hands. "Whoa. Whoa! Hold on. Give me one—"

"Out of the *way!*" the guard yelled.

"Excuse me?" The Kree looked more annoyed than threatened, even with several guns pointed at or past him. "Which one of you is in charge? You? Okay." He flicked a holo card to the guard; it stopped in midair, hovering between them. "I'm telling you to *hold on.* I need to talk to the girl."

The guard pointed her gun at Rocket. "We caught that one trying to disable security."

"Whaaaat?" Rocket said. "Me? Naw! Big misunderstanding."

"And those two"—she glared at Kiya and Peter in turn—"shot at us."

"That's nice," the Kree said. "Read the card and shut up."

Reluctantly, she plucked it from the air. After a moment, she nodded. She didn't look pleased about it, though. "I apologize, sir. Can we have the other two?"

"Nope," Kiya said. "They're with me."

The Kree shrugged. "You heard her."

"Can we have them when you're done?"

"Maybe. Depends on how this goes. Feel free to guard the room if that makes you feel better." He made a shooing gesture, then looked at Peter. "In or out?"

"In." Peter stuck his tongue out at the guards. "Hi. So who are you, exactly? Can we take a look at that card?"

"Kai-Lenn, right?" Kiya said.

"Ka-Lenn," the man corrected her as he closed the door.

Peter did a check of the room, clamping one hand over his injured shoulder. Ten beds. Privacy sheets hovered between them, blocking them off into neat sections. Only a few sheets were transparent, revealing sleeping or half-awake Kree and DiMavi, the front of their beds displaying readings of their vitals. Two beds were empty.

Across from them, by the windows, stood a single doctor. Her hands gripped the back of a chair as though she was considering using it as a defensive weapon against the group. Peter nodded at her in a way he hoped was reassuring.

Ten beds, two of them empty. Reports had mentioned nine victims. One of them either hadn't made it, or was elsewhere in the hospital.

"Ka-Lenn is one of my buyers," Kiya said. "His Groot was the last one on my list, after Baran's."

Peter turned back just in time to see Ka-Lenn's gaze flit over to the doctor, as if checking her reaction to Kiya's words.

So Ka-Lenn didn't want anyone to know he'd bought a Groot. *Noted.*

"And he's also...owner of this hospital?" Peter guessed. "A part-time Kree Accuser? Local teen idol? How'd you get them off our back?"

"Doesn't take much to outrank a *hospital security guard,*" Ka-Lenn replied.

Military? No, he didn't have the formal demeanor. Government—Peter was betting government. Between the arrogance, expensive clothes, and access to a secure hospital room, it all fit.

Ka-Lenn turned back to Kiya. "I apparently should be grateful I never pissed you off." He eyed her rumpled clothing. Kiya's implant scars were on full display through a torn pant leg and on her exposed arms, making it clear where her strength came from. "How are those treating you?"

"Is that really the issue here?" she asked, not hiding her impatience.

Kiya was trembling, Peter realized suddenly. A shudder in her legs, an inconsistency to her breathing. It could be the pain from her implants—but it felt like something more.

He'd known she could fight.

He'd known she was willing to fight.

It was easy to forget she wasn't used to it. Not the real thing, outside of whatever training the Collector had put her through.

"You okay?" Peter asked.

She nodded once, tightly.

He could push—but if she was trying to hold it together, he didn't want to undermine that. The least he could do was take her at her word.

Peter took his hand off his shoulder and grimaced, both at the pain and at the blood coating his palm. He shot a pointed look at Rocket, who'd hopped onto an empty bed and was humming as he checked his blaster. "Lead. The. Guards. Away. It's four words, man."

"They blocked the exits, all right?" Rocket grumbled. "Trapped me in the ward. Didn't even know you were that close."

"Let me look at that," the doctor said, recovering from her shock. She nodded at Peter's injury.

"To the point," Ka-Lenn told Kiya. "I heard your name and voice in the hallway. I know I'm not the only one you sold the *merchandise* to. And we know that similar merchandise caused all this. Did you have anything to do with it?"

"I grew it," she admitted. She kept her voice low so the doctor couldn't overhear their conversation, but she'd opened a comms line to Rocket and Peter so they could listen in. "But I didn't have anything to do with the attack. We're here to fix things. What are you doing here? Aren't you from Kree-Lar?"

"I'm in town for the ceremony. I heard about an attack by a tree monster. As you can imagine, as a fresh tree-monster owner, that piqued my interest. I thought I'd take a look and ask this helpful doctor what she's learned so far."

Kiya had mentioned a buyer from Kree-Lar before. He apparently worked with weaponry of all kinds—from pyrotechnical to biological, magical to robotic—and she'd reached out after seeing him trade with the Collector, assuming he'd want to analyze a Groot up close. She hadn't mentioned that this buyer was, apparently, in an influential enough position that he could waltz into a secure hospital room in the middle of a potential diplomatic disaster just to sate his curiosity.

"So, you got a Groot?" Rocket stood upright on the empty bed. "How about you give him to us?"

Ka-Lenn glared at him.

"Please keep your voices down," the doctor hissed. She tended to Peter, numbing and closing up the wound. "These patients need their rest."

Speaking of the patients... As much as Peter wanted to ask about Ka-Lenn's Grootling, Baran's took priority. He stepped toward the beds, then paused, hearing Gamora's sharp voice in his earpiece.

"You have something?" He held up his good hand, indicating for Ka-Lenn and the doctor to be silent so he, Kiya, and Rocket could hear their comms.

"Nothing on Baran," Gamora said, "but we know more about the park attack—I think it wasn't one. It sounds like an accident."

An accident.

Peter considered that for a second. An accident could be good or bad. If the poison Grootling was a loose cannon, it might make him easier to find.

On the other hand, the one thing worse than a poison Grootling controlled by a terrorist might be a poison Grootling controlled by no one at all. He'd be harder to predict.

"Our witness saw the Grootling escape from a private shuttle mid-flight—a shuttle flying on the surface level, which is apparently suspicious in and of itself. They had been passing by the park. The breakout startled another driver and caused a crash. The shuttle turned around and landed in the park. Several people ran from the shuttle to try to contain the Grootling. Our witness says they seemed panicky. It doesn't sound planned."

The Grootling might have tried to escape his handlers mid-transport. Maybe he wasn't brainwashed—or he'd been fighting it? And where had they been transporting him to?

"What was the species of the people in the shuttle?" Peter asked.

"Our witness couldn't tell—they had distortion holos around them."

"Because normal, non-shady people wear distortion holos all the time," Rocket said.

"When the Grootling was confronted, he seemed to send glitter into the air. She was...very descriptive about the glitter. Must have been the poison spores. It affected several people in the park, and some of the people from the Grootling's shuttle who'd gone after him. They all dropped and started screaming. Others—wearing the same holos—shepherded the Grootling back inside the shuttle. They bolted before any help arrived on-scene."

"And you said some of the people from the shuttle got poisoned, too?" Peter asked. If any of Baran's crew were out of commission, it'd throw off Baran's plans.

"At least one got carried into the shuttle, along with the Grootling. Our witness lost track of the others."

"Got it. Let us know if you find more."

"Any luck on your end?"

He glanced over the patients. "I'll let you know."

35

PETER checked in with Annay over comms to see where she was with regards to finding Baran. He couldn't help mentioning the accident at the park. The people who crashed the shuttle had been DiMavi, after all.

"There is nothing wrong with our driving skills," Annay laughed.

"I'm open to being convinced," Peter said. "Motorcycles, Vadin roads, a drink of your choice after—plan? Plan. Let me know if that contact you're chasing works out. Ciao."

"Oh, you're done?" Ka-Lenn raised his eyebrows. "How nice."

Peter was tempted to flip him the bird. So he did.

"Sit still," the doctor demanded, still tending to Peter's shoulder.

Ka-Lenn flashed Peter the smallest smile. "If you want the specimen I bought, you can purchase it back at the same price. No problem. I have it stored on Kree-Lar. For now—Kiya, what can you tell us about this poison?"

The doctor looked up sharply and gestured around at the hospital beds. "I don't care how you know or what you did," she told Kiya. "Just tell us what you can. We need to help these people."

Kiya nodded—at first hesitantly, then firmly. "Okay. The poison is derived from—"

"The tirrinit tree, yes. We discovered that much."

"It's a weaponized form. What kinds of symptoms are the patients showing?"

The doctor joined Kiya over a nearby unconscious patient, the doctor outlining symptoms while Kiya ran through the different effects of the poison. Ka-Lenn stood nearby, listening without interrupting.

Kiya still looked messy from the fight: a cut on her face, her hair a mess, her pant leg torn, her shirt crooked. She seemed to be trembling less, at least. If she knew how she looked, or knew she was being watched, she was too engrossed in the patient to care. Her teeth pressed into her lower lip in worry or guilt.

Peter made eye contact with Rocket, then tilted his head toward the beds across the room. They peered past the privacy screens. Most of the patients were kept in induced comas, as the doctor explained. The pain had been too intense.

Peter counted two Kree, both blue-skinned, and two DiMavi—one of whom seemed awake. A fourth patient—also DiMavi—seemed awake. If you could call it that. He was writhing in his sheets, slowly, as though fighting through sludge. His eyes were open, but Peter couldn't tell whether he could see anything.

Peter crouched by the bed. "Hi?"

For a long moment, the man didn't seem to be able to see Peter. Then their eyes met. DiMavi pupils were normally nearly the size of their eyes, but this man's were pinprick-tiny. He wheezed. "Attack? Was it…?"

"It was an accident." Peter hoped he wasn't entirely off the mark.

"Not…targeted?"

"We don't think so."

"Embassy. Embassy should know. Tell…" He breathed deeply, seeming to steel himself. "Tell them."

"You work with them?"

He made a rattling noise that sounded like a yes.

Knowing this victim was a government official of some kind made Peter reconsider whether the attack really had been an accident. On the other hand, there were so *many* DiMavi officials in town currently, it could have been a coincidence.

Based on Gamora's discovery, Peter had doubted the victims could provide much information. They hadn't been targeted, and wouldn't have seen anything if Baran and his team were wearing distortion holos. They were still the Guardians' best lead, though. And if this guy was with the embassy, he might be able to help in another way.

Rocket stood behind Peter. He seemed thoroughly grossed out—he'd never liked hospitals. "You know a guy named Baran?"

The man closed his eyes, squirming. He didn't answer.

The victims weren't dead; Peter told himself that was a good thing. Baran might not be aiming for lethal.

Looking at someone in pain like this, though, it was hard to see the positive.

From the next bed, a voice croaked. "Hey. Hey. I need..."

Peter stood, swiping away the privacy screen. It turned transparent. A DiMavi woman lay in the bed, her sheets half kicked away, her light-gray hospital clothes wet with sweat. "Show me," she said, gasping.

Same pinprick eyes.

Same pain.

"Hey! I never said you could talk to my patients." The doctor crossed the room, glaring at Peter and Rocket. "I need to sedate them. They shouldn't be awake. DiMavi physiology paired with this toxin...it's unpredictable." She turned a worried eye on the patients.

"Show me!" The woman in the bed clawed at the mattress. She was trying to lift her hand, stretching it toward the other DiMavi. No, past him. "I want to see...others..."

"*Others?*" Peter asked, looking up. "Other patients?"

Ka-Lenn swiped his hands over the privacy screens between the other beds. They faded into nothingness to reveal unconscious Kree.

"Yes," she rasped.

"Shh, shh," the doctor said, bowing over the panel on the wall. "It'll pass soon."

"Wait." Kiya joined her by the side of the bed. "Wait one moment..." She bowed and inspected the mottled green skin of the patient's hands. "The Grootling releases a certain sap—I had these same stains. This woman worked with the Grootling up close. Look: Some marks are faded, some are fresh. These aren't all from today."

The woman must've been part of Baran's crew transporting the Grootling. If she'd been left behind by the rest of the team in the chaos, she could have discarded her distortion holo and blended in with the other victims.

Rocket leapt onto the bed and stood by her side with a snarl on his face. "Where is Baran? What's the plan? Where's the Groot?"

"Was today an accident?" Peter added.

"Was trying...find the words...Baran..." Her eyes lost focus. She stretched her arm, making an unclear noise.

"Where is he?" Rocket repeated.

"She said she wanted to see other patients," Peter said. "Why?"

"I'm sedating her," the doctor snapped. "She's in pain."

"We need to ask her—"

Too late. She'd already adjusted the settings. A new, dark liquid coursed through the IV. "And get off my patient's bed," she said, glaring at Rocket.

"Heh," the woman in the bed mumbled. She was still looking at the other patients. "Heh. Works on them. Blue...blue kru..."

Her eyes drifted shut. The outstretched arm slumped down.

"Can you wake her?" Peter said.

"No. And I wouldn't if I could. Withholding pain management is akin to torture." Briskly, the doctor walked to the other DiMavi's bed.

"Baran?" the man slurred. "Why...Baran?"

"He's behind this," Peter said, talking fast. "He'll do worse. He'll attack the ceremony tonight. Where is he?"

"No...no. That would...war."

"I don't think he cares if he starts a war," Kiya said. "He wants revenge. We need to find him and stop him."

For the first time, the doctor seemed to hesitate.

"That...d'ast..." The patient turned his head away, taking a moment to breathe. The pain shuddered through his body. His next words were deliberate, louder, as if he wanted to make sure the Guardians would understand. "Right before the park. Baran's assistant called. Urgent... wanted to move up...inspecting Kree security. For ceremony." A pause. "What time? Now?"

"We just passed midday," Ka-Lenn replied.

"Inspection now," the man mumbled.

So Baran had moved up his plans. "Where?" Peter asked urgently.

The man turned away again. Pressed his face into the pillow. His breathing came fast.

"I can't watch this," the doctor said. "I need to—"

"Don't even think about it. 'Less you wanna end up in one of them empty beds." Rocket blocked her way to the panel.

She didn't flinch. "I have a duty—"

"Porovi Hall," the DiMavi slurred. "Porovi. Porovi Hall. Porovi…"

"Rocket, let the doctor pass," Peter said.

She adjusted the dosage. The man's eyes closed; the tension seeped away from his body, letting him sink into the mattress.

For a moment, the five of them were silent.

"I need to check on my other patients." The doctor backed away.

Peter pinned her down with a look. "You can't tell anyone what you just heard."

"If there's an attack, our military needs to know. They'll stop it in its tracks."

Rocket shrugged. "Kree Empire ain't half bad at what they do. They could help."

"No. The attack would be bad enough—but this could blow up way beyond that." Peter indicated the unconscious man in their midst. "He was right."

Peter had hoped to keep this situation straightforward: Get in, stop Baran, grab the Grootling, and get out without the Kree noticing a thing. If Baran had moved up his plans, that would be a lot harder. Peter knew the Kree well enough to know this situation was a damn powder keg.

"Don't tell anyone," Peter stressed. "If the Kree know a DiMavi is using a *peace* ceremony as an opportunity for an attack… The Kree are too proud. They'll retaliate."

Kiya had her arms crossed, her muscles tense. "DiMave couldn't fight a handful of Kree criminals. We definitely can't fight the entire Kree Empire."

"Yeah, your planet's kinda wimpy," Rocket said.

"They'll retaliate," she said, echoing Peter. "Declare war. Annex us."

"No, they won't," Peter said, "because we're going to stop the attack, and we're going to do it before the Kree ever find out there was an attempt. Okay?"

She nodded tightly. "Yeah."

"Okay?" Peter repeated, this time facing the doctor. "Do Kree doctors take an oath? 'Do no harm,' or something?"

"It's more of a contract—"

"Point is the same. You help people. You don't want to be responsible for a war."

"If there's an attack, I can't just let it happen—"

"You're not letting it happen. Do you know who we are?"

She nodded.

"Then you know we'll stop it."

She held his eyes for a long moment, then looked to Kiya, and then to the DiMavi patients. A long sigh escaped her. "All right."

He nodded his gratitude. "You and Kiya, check out the other patients together. Make sure any who might've been working with Baran and the Grootling are kept unconscious—so they can't tell doctors what's happening, and so they can't hurt anyone else. And *you*." Peter turned to Ka-Lenn. "Let me make this clear: I know you're high up on the food chain. I know you work with weapons. I know you'd probably profit off a war. But if you tell any of your people about Baran's plans? Or that DiMavi are behind today's incident in the park? *We'll* tell them about your trades with the Collector."

It was a gamble, but the alarmed look on Ka-Lenn's face told Peter he was right on the money. Ka-Lenn's trades weren't sanctioned by the Kree government. "Low," he said. "Real low."

"All is fair in love and war prevention. I do appreciate the save in the hallway, though. So where's Porovi Hall?"

"Downtown. It's part of Vadin's primary military and government complex. Today's ceremony will be held in the central courtyard." Ka-Lenn looked over Peter, Rocket, and Kiya. "You'll leave the planet once you find Baran and his Groot?"

"Sure. We'll head straight to Kree-Lar to have a drink and do Groot business."

Ka-Lenn tightened his lips. "I have access to Porovi. I'll get you in. It'll be faster. Which means you'll be *gone* faster."

"Sweet," Peter said, all brightness. "Let's go."

36

GAMORA could not quite tell whether Ka-Lenn was a threat, but at least he seemed honest about his priorities.

Ka-Lenn didn't object to being forced to ride along with Quill in their crappy hovercar so Quill could keep an eye on him.

He didn't object to Gamora searching him for communications equipment so he couldn't contact his fellow Kree.

He didn't even object to the group taking his own hovercar along so they'd have an extra getaway vehicle.

What he *did* object to was Rocket climbing in the driver's seat of that car.

"One: Is that *safe?*" Ka-Lenn asked in horror. Rocket was so small the vehicle practically dwarfed him.

"Safe is overrated," Rocket called back, starting up the engine. Drax entered the car and sat down beside him.

"Two," Ka-Lenn told Rocket, "one dent, and you pay up."

"Like we don't have enough debtors following us," Gamora said.

It was a nice ride, though: sleek paint job, extra lines of maneuverable thrusters along the bottom for maximum flexibility, programmable solid-holo roof and windows. Too bad it only had room for two.

"Three: After all this, I'll need to ask about your…unique…physiology."

Rocket gave him a look that was part disgust, part incredulity. A moment later, the windows zapped up, stealing him from sight.

"Is that a no?" Ka-Lenn turned to Gamora, one eyebrow raised. "Is it entirely genetic? There must be a cybernetic component, no? I'd love to take a closer look."

"You can ask him." Gamora planted herself in the passenger seat beside Quill in the main car. "But please hold your questions until we're done with you. You're no good to us as a corpse."

"Very well." He thumped into the back seat, beside Kiya and behind Gamora, and let out a breath. "What about *you?* I've always been fascinated by your—"

"No."

"I only want—"

"One more word, and I will consider ways your corpse *could* be useful to us." She said it absently, watching as the other car rose and slid smoothly into traffic on a fastdeck above them. "Kiya, if he asks any more questions about your implants"—like he'd been doing the past several minutes—"do as you please."

Their car rose up from the ground, hovering unsteadily before Quill got it under control. Within moments, they were on the deck. Gamora brought her hand to her ear to establish a private comms line.

"Annay?" she said.

"Good. I was just about to call. I have a location for Baran."

"We know. Porovi Hall. We're on our way."

"Oh," Annay said, disappointed. "Good to know I went to all this trouble for no reason. Am I off the hook?"

"Go back to the embassy. Find a high-level individual and tell them what's happening. If they can delay the ceremony without suspicion, tell them to do it." If the Guardians could trust anyone to be on their side now, it was the DiMavi: They would be just as eager to stop Baran from attacking the peace ceremony, and just as eager to resolve the situation without the Kree finding out.

"I'll see what I can do. Hey, is Peter—"

Gamora killed the connection.

Porovi Hall was only minutes away. Gamora hoped to let those minutes pass in silence, mulling over the situation and considering ways to subdue the poison Grootling without giving him enough time to release his spores.

They might need to take him out permanently.

She kept coming back to that, and she hated it.

Ka-Lenn leaned forward, propping his elbows on her and Quill's seats. "You have to leave Kiya."

"Excuse me?" Gamora said.

Sitting beside Ka-Lenn, Kiya kept silent, but her position shifted, turning tense. She was paying attention.

"Between the ceremony and the incident in the park, security is up. I can make up a convincing story to get to get the four of you inside; people know who you are. They don't know *her,* and she's a DiMavi child to boot. And if they scan her, the Collector's reward might come up."

Kiya's lips tightened, but she didn't object.

"Hate to say it, but…" Quill glanced sideways at Gamora.

Ka-Lenn had a point. Kiya would invite questions the Guardians didn't have the time to answer and suspicions they wouldn't have the time to assuage. She could be an asset, but at this stage, it might not outweigh the risk.

"I can go back to the Grootlings," Kiya said.

Quill took a moment to run through his options. Gamora knew that face—he'd made his decision. "Rocket?" he said. "Fly up from traffic for a sec. We need you and Kiya to swap cars."

The two cars rose to hover side by side, above the traffic and the rooftops below. Gamora turned in her seat, watching as Drax took the wheel and slid into the driver's seat. Rocket leapt across the empty space between the cars to land almost in Ka-Lenn's lap. Rocket skittered away in disgust, pulling his tail close to his body. A moment later, Kiya nimbly jumped across and landed inside the other car.

"Drax, get her to the ship," Quill instructed.

Good. Kiya wouldn't have to travel alone—nor would she have to endure Rocket spending the entire ride to the ship complaining about babysitting her and missing the action. And as reluctant as the Grootlings had been to sit out this mission, Kiya seemed fine with it. Gamora didn't mind, either. Kiya would be safer on the ship.

Jumping into danger was the Guardians' job. Not Kiya's.

Drax didn't waste words on agreement. The car swerved and tore off toward the ship, haphazardly merging into another fastdeck.

"Tell me he's at least a decent driver." Ka-Lenn watched the car go, his face pained.

"You know?" Quill said, taking off at high speed. "I have no idea."

Rocket stood up on the back seat and dusted himself off. "So, if I got this right, the plan is to get into Porovi Hall, find Baran and his Groot, and get out." He looked at Ka-Lenn. "Who would be giving Baran the security walkthrough? Get in touch. He's gotta be kept busy till we arrive."

Gamora tossed Ka-Lenn the communicator she'd taken from him earlier.

Ka-Lenn fiddled with it, then called a name. There was a moment of silence. He repeated the name once, then again.

Gamora turned. "Nothing?"

"Something is wrong." He looked at the communicator, his lips pursed. "I talked to him earlier today."

"And we're supposed to believe you?" Rocket snatched the communicator, studying it up close.

Gamora's eyes met Quill's. Ka-Lenn could be lying, but if he was going to the effort of bringing them to Porovi, this seemed like a strange time to start deceiving them.

And if he wasn't lying…if something was blocking communication with Ka-Lenn's contact, or even all of Porovi Hall…

"They're speeding up their plans," Quill said. "Between Baran urging for the security inspection to be moved up and this…"

Gamora pursed her lips, thinking. "They must've been transporting the Grootling when he escaped in the park. Maybe already taking him to Porovi Hall."

"But the ceremony isn't for hours." Ka-Lenn cocked his head. "Except for the Ono Circle, of course."

"*Of course,*" Quill echoed. "What in the krutack is the Ono Circle?"

"It's a ritual in a prominent DiMavi religion—a group prayer often performed in advance of events like tonight's. We offered to host it in the basement of Addil Hall since the place could easily fit a few hundred DiMavi."

"Are there many Kree at the Circle?"

"Aside from security personnel, maybe two diplomats. No one high-ranking."

Not a good target for Baran, then. Still, Gamora didn't like having that many civilians on site.

"I'm going to take a wild guess and say we're in the right neighborhood." Rocket stood with his hands on the side of the car, wind rustling his fur.

The area ahead seemed like a clearing in the woods. One moment, the

Guardians were stuck in the crush of traffic on the middle deck of five levels of skyway, buildings towering on all sides. The next moment, the buildings fell away, and most of the road decks above and below them veered aside to make a wide half-circle detour around the nearly empty space ahead. Only a handful of raised roads entered the area directly, headed toward the complex at the very center of the clearing.

The complex was made up of gleaming silver-glass buildings standing in a half-circle around a wide courtyard, which was part park and part sparkling-clean pavement. A few transparent walkways connected the buildings to each other at various levels. With so few skyways and no other buildings around, the area seemed easier to secure than the frantic mess of downtown. The Kree could see anyone approaching.

Gamora scanned the courtyard as they passed by—a handful of Kree and bots working together to set up a podium and fences; a group of DiMavi walking into the central building—then looked at the buildings and skyways ahead.

"Look," she said. "One deck up, left and ahead of us."

"They have Accusers as guards now?" Quill said, blinking in surprise.

The Accuser hovered several feet above the deck of a neighboring road, keeping a close eye on the skyways and courtyard both. His armor was impossible to miss: the bulk, the flexibility, the sheer *power*.

"This is unusual," Ka-Lenn said.

"It's an impressive demotion," Quill said. "One moment, you're a badass judge-jury-executioner type tracking enemies of the Kree Empire; the next, you're babysitting a prayer circle."

"Embarrassing," Rocket said.

Gamora had fought against Accusers. Gamora had fought alongside Accusers. Gamora had, one time, slept with an Accuser. She knew them well enough to know: "I don't think this Accuser is acting as a guard, Quill."

As they watched, the Accuser let two vehicles ahead of the Guardians through without more than a cursory glance. He was looking—waiting—for something or someone in particular.

"I'm getting that," Quill said.

Could be the Kree had learned about the threat against them.

Could be Guardians-related.

Gamora would put her money on the latter.

The Accuser spotted them. A split second later, he leapt down toward the Guardians' car. He didn't land straightaway—for a moment he hovered nearby, studying them. Then he crashed down, directly ahead, blocking their path.

Quill jerked the steering wheel. The car spun 90 degrees and came to a halt mere inches from the Accuser.

He didn't flinch.

"Hi, you." Quill raised a hand in greeting. "Are you here because of the mess at the hospital? Sorry about that. Wow, you work *fast*. But isn't it kind of overkill to send an Accuser over that little tussle?"

There wasn't the slightest chance this was about the hospital instead of Levet. Quill sounded like he didn't really believe it himself.

"Guardians of the Galaxy." The Accuser looked them over, perhaps wondering where the rest of the team was.

Gamora's hand went to her sword. They didn't have time for this.

"Let me guess," Rocket said. "We stand—what was the word? C'mon, say it. You know you're itching to say it. Aaa…*aaaaaaa*…"

The Accuser narrowed his eyes.

"You stand accused."

37

KIYA did not talk too much. Drax liked that in a person—it was one reason he got along so well with Gamora.

Peter Quill talked too much.

Rocket talked too much.

Groot talked too much.

(Although right now, Drax thought Groot talked rather too little.)

Kiya, however, sat silently beside Drax as he drove, occasionally peering sideways. She seemed to be observing him. Mulling something over, perhaps.

He was content to spend the rest of the trip to the ship in silence, but he suspected the Accuser who landed on the ground before them when they entered the desert outskirts had a different idea.

Kiya let out a warning shout.

Drax considered evading the Accuser. He decided against it. Anyone who decided to land in front of a moving vehicle did not have good intentions—and could likely take a hit from said vehicle, anyway.

The Accuser held out her Universal Weapon, pointing the hammer end at the front of the car. Drax stretched out a hand toward Kiya beside him, bracing her against the seat.

They hit.

The Accuser didn't move a hair.

The car crumpled around the hammer, easy as the crack of a skull. Kiya and Drax hurtled forward—but only barely. A rush of artificial gravity shoved them back into place, while a puff of near-solid air cushioned them from impact.

The passenger cabin stayed in shape—more or less—although the windshield had cracked. Illegible data stuttered across its broken surface, half the symbols missing.

"Kiya?" Drax still gripped her shoulder.

"I'm all right, I'm all right," she said, though her breathing was shallow.

"Impact detected," the car AI finally bleeped. "Running vital scans. Vital scans complete. No sign of injury."

"Is that a...? That's a Kree Accuser." Kiya stared at the figure before them. "That seems bad."

The Accuser stood at the center of a cloud of sand dust. She pulled her weapon free from the crumpled wreck of the hood with a sickening metal crunch. "Drax the Destroyer: You stand accused."

"This is vexing," Drax announced. He attempted to open the door. It did not cooperate. He kicked it open instead, then climbed out, stalking toward the Accuser.

"You stand accused of crimes against the Kree Empire." The Accuser did not flinch at Drax's approach.

Impressive.

Unusual.

And extremely unwise.

"The Guardians of the Galaxy knowingly interfered with the Kree penal system and committed violence against members of our esteemed military.

For this, you shall stand trial."

"I am busy," Drax told her. "Try me later."

"You will accompany me now so that you may stand trial as a group."

"No."

The Accuser's grip on her weapon tightened.

As a group.

This could mean the Accusers planned to round up the other Guardians next. It could also mean they already had.

Drax considered calling Quill. The status of the team would not change Drax's own situation this minute, however. And Drax knew the team's priorities: to stop Baran, to prevent casualties, to avert a war, to protect Kiya, and to restore Groot. Cooperating with the Accuser would accomplish none of those goals.

It would only slow them down.

Decision made. Drax rushed the Accuser, daggers in hand.

(He hoped the Kree would not take this too badly.)

The Accuser raised her weapon, leaving behind a sheen in the air where it passed.

His daggers bounced against the energy shield. He spun, trying again. The shield trembled, but held.

"You will not win this," the Accuser said.

"I am the Destroyer." He lowered his body, throwing himself into the shield. It splintered into nothingness. He slammed into her, knocking her off her feet. "I destroy," he declared.

They were almost on the ground when she swept her hammer up again. It flared. A wave of energy hit Drax in the chest, flinging him back. The force of the blow knocked the air from him and sent him scraping over the desert ground.

The Accuser caught herself mid-fall, not touching the ground. She maneuvered upright and, within moments, rose high in the air. "Stop this. I am armed and armored. You are neither."

He was already on his feet again. He flashed his blades by his side, one in each hand.

"Those…don't qualify as being armed," the Accuser said.

"We shall see."

"Let us go," Kiya shouted. Drax had not noticed her leave the car. "He *said* he'd cooperate later."

Drax was already sprinting forward. "I said that she could try me," he corrected her.

"I don't think that's actually helpful to point out!" Kiya yelled back.

Drax leapt up, wrapping his arms around the Accuser's legs. He yanked her down, grinning fiercely, and smashed her to the cracked-dry ground.

The Accuser twisted her Universal Weapon into place. This time, Drax was prepared. He knew when to expect the blast, and how to use it to his advantage. The Accuser was correct that his knives would not pierce her armor in head-on combat.

They had other uses, however.

Drax stuck his knives into the creases of the Accuser's armor along her sides, between layered segments. The blades couldn't crack through and hurt her, but he only needed them jammed tight. He clung to the handles, braced himself—

The blast knocked him away, sending his head spinning. He landed on hot, sun-drenched ground, so far away it took him a moment to find the others. There: Kiya, running toward him. There: the Accuser. The sun outlined an irregular silhouette, dipping harshly into her sides, precisely where he'd stuck his blades behind segments of her armor. The force of her blow had been enough to yank off pieces of her armor with it—just as he'd planned.

"Ha!" he cried.

The blast had also peeled off half the skin on Drax's shoulder. That part was inconvenient.

"Drax! Are you all right?" Kiya ran up beside him. "Can we outrun her?"

"I do not run," he scoffed. "Unless it is *toward* my opponents. Then I run extremely fast."

Kiya tossed his arm over her shoulder, helping him to his feet. "What about the car?"

"Who are you, young one?" The Accuser came floating their way. Almost absently, she raised her hammer, creating another energy shield to ward off any surprise attack. "You aren't in my system. But given who you're associating with, I have reason to bring you in for scrutiny. As for you…" She turned to Drax and gestured at the damaged armor on her sides. "This? This will not bring me down."

"I agree," he said. "That will come after I take your hammer."

Drax bolted forward. Behind him, Kiya said something, but he was too far away to hear. He collided with the Accuser again, then again, taking and doling out blows, laughing wildly, knocked away and blocked and slashing and spinning around and coming back for more.

She was tough. He had expected no less from an Accuser; he would have been disappointed otherwise. It did not matter, though. He did not need—or even want—to kill her. Simply to disable her long enough for them to get away.

"Wait!" Kiya yelled.

Drax and the Accuser were face-to-face on the ground. His arm was stretched out, holding her weapon hand in place, the hammer an inch away in the dirt. The Accuser held up her free arm, pressing her elbow into his throat to prevent him from bearing down on her further.

Kiya ran at them. "I talked to the other Guardians—an Accuser came at them, too. Drax, *communicate with your colleagues,* will you?"

Drax turned to look at her. Then back at the Accuser beneath him.

"Drax?" Quill said in his ear. "Drax, stop fighting. We've reached an understanding."

"You have encountered an Accuser, as well?"

"Yeah, but we're good. Ka-Lenn informed him about our, you know, agreement. Where Ka-Lenn hired the Guardians to help with security for tonight's event."

"I know about no such—"

"*Oh my god stop talking,*" Quill groaned.

"Drax, just pretend," Gamora said.

"Our…agreement," he repeated dubiously.

The Accuser, still on the ground under him, was speaking into her armor—presumably with the Accuser the other Guardians had met.

"Look, as long as we formally apologize to the Elder Council for our interference at Levet, they'll let us help Ka-Lenn for the ceremony, and we'll figure out our, uh, trial after."

"We have nothing to apologize for."

Quill heaved a sigh for reasons Drax could not determine. "Just let the Accuser follow along as you drop off Kiya. Then come down here together, okay? We'll do all the talking, apology-wise."

The Accuser finished her conversation at the same time as Drax. They stared at each other.

"This does not mean you win," Drax told her.

"It doesn't mean *you* win, either, Destroyer."

"Hm." He released her arm and climbed to his feet. "I was close, however. We can determine the winner another day."

"I am Sor-Vall the Accuser, and I do not fight over petty reasons or pride. I fight for the glory of the Kree Empire." She picked up her weapon, used it to push herself upright. "Also, you were not remotely close."

THE CAR still worked.

They rode along in silence, the Accuser following in the air behind them. Drax felt somewhat uncomfortable leading her straight to the location where he would soon leave Kiya and the Grootlings by themselves. The Collector would pay well for that information, but Drax knew he could trust the Accuser not to sell them out. One could say a lot about the flaws of the Kree Empire, but their Accusers were honorable to a fault.

"You're not in pain?" Kiya asked.

"Some."

"You don't look it." She watched him thoughtfully from the passenger seat. "In those tunnels on DiMave, you said you lost your family. You're a father, aren't you?"

Drax did not answer immediately. "Yes."

"I thought so."

"Why?" His eyes narrowed.

"When we were about to collide with the Accuser," she said, "you put your arm in front of me. My parents used to do that. It's a...very *dad* thing to do."

"I see."

She was silent for a moment. "A daughter?"

"Yes."

Fortunately, she did not ask further. The story of his family was complicated, and he did not see why it was relevant. It was clearly unrelated to their present situation or interactions.

"That fight was impressive to watch," she said. "I didn't realize anyone could go toe-to-toe with an Accuser. And you took on Tivan, too."

"Gamora and I did that together."

"I can fight, but I couldn't take on an Accuser." She peered up at the Accuser flying overhead, as though wondering whether her words would reach so far. "I couldn't help you just now. I need to be better. I need to defend myself. Will you teach me?"

"No." He peered sideways. "Ask Gamora."

Gamora was a better teacher than Drax, adept in more fighting styles than he knew existed. And she would be happy to teach Kiya—he knew that without needing to ask. Whether Kiya would be happy to be taught by Gamora was a different matter. He expected a horrified reaction, a knee-jerk *no,* but instead Kiya sat in silence for the rest of the ride.

When they reached the ship, she started to exit the car. Then, with one foot already out the door, she turned to face him. All at once, her next words rushed out: "I—thank you, Drax."

He stared at her, expressionless. "Thank me for what?"

"For not pushing. Letting me be." She looked determined. "The others all want something from me, good or bad. I get why. But it's nice to just *be.*"

"I see." Perhaps Kiya did talk more than he liked.

Or perhaps she just said things he did not know how to respond to.

"*Destroyer,*" the Accuser called impatiently from above.

"I must leave," he informed Kiya.

Kiya stepped out of the car and leaned into the window. Her voice was all urgency. "Good luck with those Accusers, and with finding Baran.

Thank you for—trying to solve the problem I caused."

"We do not need luck," he said. "We are extremely skilled."

"I've noticed that." She stepped back, the Guardians' ship looming behind her.

Drax nodded at Kiya. Then he tore off with the car, the Accuser following from the sky, leaving Kiya and the ship behind them.

38

I DON'T know if I can save your asses a *third* time," Ka-Lenn said, standing in the massive courtyard outside the complex, "so try not to cause any intergalactic incidents when you apologize to the Council for Levet. Please."

"Psh! Us?" Quill said. "We'll be fiiine."

"We cause intergalactic incidents over breakfast," Gamora told him.

"Yeah, and it's always a blast, so I'm not seeing the problem," Rocket said. "Have fun with that junk apology, guys." He wasn't exactly crushed about the group splitting up: As far as Rocket was concerned, that apology sounded boring as flark. The other Guardians were always saying Rocket wasn't "diplomatic" enough to go near government officials, anyway.

The Accusers had demanded a formal apology before letting the Guardians roam the complex freely with Ka-Lenn. At first, they'd demanded that the entire team be present. But with Drax still away, Groot out of commission, and Ka-Lenn insisting he needed Rocket *right now* to look at an urgent-yet-routine security matter, they'd eventually agreed that only Quill and Gamora would accompany the Accuser to the Vadin Supreme Elder Council. Ka-Lenn had reassured the Accuser that he would contact him if necessary.

"This way." Ka-Lenn led Rocket through the open courtyard, past people preparing for the ceremony and a handful of privates on guard. The guards' eyes went to the massive gun dangling from Rocket's hip, then to Ka-Lenn walking by his side.

"Yeah, that's right," Rocket told them. "I'm entering your precious building. Any of you got a problem with that?"

None of this felt right without Groot. It hadn't felt right at the hospital, having to actually *run* from guards instead of letting Groot smack them down, and it didn't feel right here. The guards only looked disgruntled instead of staring at Groot in abject, delightful terror.

Rocket missed that terror.

Although maybe if he pulled that blaster on them, he could still cause a little bit of—

"You're really not helping." Ka-Lenn looked pained.

"Why? What's the problem?" Rocket said.

He didn't answer.

"That's real enlightening." At least he could ditch Ka-Lenn once the guy got him security clearance. Rocket followed him to a building with the words *Porovi Hall* stretched out in tall, sober Kree lettering over its curved walls.

"I hope you all appreciate what I'm risking to help you."

"Not really," Rocket said. "So what do you do, anyway?" He watched as Ka-Lenn swiped his fingers by the door, stood still for a full-body scan confirming his identity, and demanded full guest clearance from the building AI, allowing Rocket access with guns and all. "You seem like a big deal."

"I'm on the Supreme Science Council." The door slid open, and the two of them walked inside.

"You guys sure like your supremacy, don't you?"

"We do. It's everyone else who seems to have a problem with it."

Rocket snickered. Kree were the worst.

He studied the building as they passed through, focusing on security. There was a lot of equipment, but he couldn't tell whether any of it was working. Even the most advanced security systems usually emanated noise, whether from the movement of a scanner or a high-pitched hum most species couldn't hear. He'd picked it up on the system outside. In here? Nothing.

Ka-Lenn tried to call his contact inside again. Just like when he'd tried in the car: No use. A second person in the building did answer, saying they hadn't seen either Ka-Lenn's contact or Baran; a third person, in the security hub, also didn't answer.

"Well, that ain't worrying at all," Rocket remarked.

They picked up their pace, half-running toward the central security hub. "If something's wrong, the alarm should've gone off," Ka-Lenn said. "I'll check with central comms to see if anyone is in contact with security."

"And tip them off? Don't even think about it. Besides, odds are Baran's crew got into your communication system, as well. It really ain't that hard."

"I would like to see you try." He slid open the door to the hub.

"That a challenge? 'Cause if you got time after this, I could—aw, man, corpses."

Rocket made a face as they stood in the doorway to the security hub. Four Kree—one blue, three pink—lay slumped against the left wall, looking pretty spectacularly dead. Their bodies were covered with scorch marks and what appeared to be stab wounds—this definitely wasn't the Grootling's doing. It looked like Baran's people weren't afraid to get their own hands dirty.

Gross, Rocket thought. Murder was way less fun when you weren't the one responsible.

The rest of the room looked empty: a long stretch of terminals on one side, several desks placed in a circular pattern, and a central screen featuring dozens of security-camera feeds—

Or it was supposed to show those feeds, anyway. Rocket had broken into enough of these places to recognize the setup. Usually the screens only showed that blank, transparent fizzle *after* he was done—not before.

"Yeah, whatever they're doing, it's in full swing." So much for Quill's hopes of getting to Baran early. Rocket brought a hand to his ear. "Hey, Quill? You free to talk?"

"Give me one minute—our Accuser friend is escorting us to a waiting room. He's about to formally request an audience with the Council."

"Naw, no need, just listen. Can *I* talk?" You never knew when people were listening in.

"Go for it."

"Sweet. So, hey, we got dead folks."

"*Really?*" Quill kept his voice amicable, but it wasn't hard to detect the sudden tension.

"Yeah, four dead Kree in the security hub. Baran's in motion. If you have to, scratch that apology—we've got priorities."

"Gotcha. Have fun."

"Always." Rocket hopped into one of the seats in front of the terminals. "Ka-Lenn, get me into the system, will you?" Asking someone else to log him into the system the boring way spoiled some of the fun—but then again, bossing around a high-ranking Kree wasn't half bad.

Ka-Lenn was kneeling by the Kree—checking for vital signs, Rocket guessed. Cute, that kind of optimism. Once he'd confirmed the bodies to be dead, Ka-Lenn rose and joined Rocket at the terminals, tapped rapidly at the keypad, and made a few swipes at the screen to confirm.

"Good. You wanna do a sweep of the room?" Rocket made a vague gesture at the rest of the security hub—there were plenty of terminals and desks for Ka-Lenn to check while Rocket did his job.

Ka-Lenn looked unimpressed, but didn't object. He knew he was better off helping the Guardians. "Drax's encounter with the other Accuser," he said, slowly making his way across the room. "How much do you know about what happened?"

"What now?"

"What was the Accuser's response to Kiya? Did she get a...good look at the girl?"

"Why're you asking?"

"There's a reward. The Accuser could sell her out to the Collector."

"You ever *met* an Accuser?" Rocket wasn't exactly the trusting type, but worrying about Accusers selling out semi-innocent teen girls seemed pointless.

"I only want to make sure she's safe."

That sounded real likely.

Rocket scratched at his chin, digging his fingers nice and deep into the fur, as he worked the terminal. First priority: restore the camera feeds. If he could spot Baran—or the Grootling—that'd make their job easy.

Problem was, he was dealing with DiMavi, who were obnoxiously good at what they did. It wasn't as easy as flipping a switch back on. He couldn't even *find* the cameras in the system. They'd hidden the references to the point that—

"Actually, hold on." Rocket stood abruptly upright in the chair. In a split second, he had his blaster pointed at Ka-Lenn halfway across the room.

Ka-Lenn had been glancing under a desk. He looked up, unblinking, looking somewhere between surprised and offended. "Excuse me?"

"Why do you care, huh? About the girl?"

"Is that a bad thing?"

"Well, you seem more concerned about risking your job than kicking off a war, so you don't strike me as a fuzzy 'all life is sacred' type." He narrowed his eyes. "Heyyy. Quill?"

"I can talk freely now," Quill said. "Do you have an eye on the Addil Hall basement yet—anything suspicious near that prayer thing? What've you got?"

"I got a rat, is what I got. Ka-Lenn seems awful worried about Kiya."

"Go on."

"Spe-*ci*-fically, he's worried about that Accuser selling her out. I bet it's 'cause he doesn't want competition for the reward. And the way he convinced you to send Kiya back—I'm thinking he wants her away from us to make it easier for the Collector to grab her. We already know they're buddies."

"This is completely—" Ka-Lenn began.

"I'm talking here," Rocket said, wagging his gun at him. "Don't be rude, man."

"I didn't expect you to be so worried about Kiya, Rocket," Gamora said in his ear.

"You forget she ain't alone on that ship?" The Collector wouldn't pass up an opportunity to grab the Grootlings, if he had a chance. "So? Can I shoot this guy or what? Ehhh, I'm gonna shoot him." He held the trigger, letting the gun charge up.

"Wait, what did he say?" Quill sounded thoughtful. "Exactly?"

Rocket repeated the words impatiently.

"You're right. It's suspicious." He took a few moments to talk it over with Gamora. "I hate to do this, but…"

Rocket grinned. "But I won't?"

39

NOW, KA-LENN, I want you to listen *real* close…" Rocket said.

A moment later, he shut off the connection.

Good. Peter didn't need to listen to the rest. Rocket was enjoying this way too much.

"I didn't like this situation to start with," Gamora said, staring at the courtyard through a massive curved window. "It just got worse."

"Worried about Kiya?"

She turned to meet Peter's eyes. She didn't need to answer, and he didn't need to reassure her. Gamora knew as well as he did that Kiya had the Grootlings, the ship, and her own skills; the Guardians could do nothing for her beyond that. The best move they could make was to prevent her fellow DiMavi from making a colossal mistake and dooming her planet to the fury of the Kree.

"Why are you here?" a voice behind them said.

Peter turned away from the window. Down the hallway stood the Accuser, his whisper-silent cloak wrapped around him.

"You were meant to wait where I left you." He looked—Peter hated to use the word—accusatory.

"We were..." Looking for a terrorist and his botanical weapon, and checking whether Drax had arrived yet. "Admiring the view?"

"The Vadin Supreme Elder Council will see you soon."

"Perfect."

"You will wait in the assigned location until then."

"And that'll take how long?" Peter kept his voice light despite his impatience. If Rocket was right and Baran's group was already killing Kree, then they couldn't afford to sit and wait. The collateral damage would pile up as Baran and his Grootling drew ever closer to their final target. Also, with every minute, the risk increased that the Kree would find out that DiMavi were responsible for today's events.

"However long it takes until the Vadin Supreme Elder Council will see you."

"Ka-Lenn hired us for a reason," Gamora said. "We only mean to help. For your own safety."

"We cannot let..." The Accuser paused, tilting his head as if listening.

The elevator doors opened behind him. A swarm of bots spilled into the hall—their dark metal bodies buzzing, an array of red-white lights flickering across their surfaces. Security bots: Kree, as far as Peter could tell from the dish-like design. He counted four.

The Accuser turned.

"Enemy detected!" the bots declared. "Enemy detected!"

They fired.

The Accuser raised his weapon in an arc, leaving a protective sheen in its wake. The blasts pinged off harmlessly, but the bots were already zooming through the hall, some crawling on a dozen legs thin as fingers, others flying close to the ceiling. They fired again, again, from different angles. The Accuser blocked some of the shots. Others got through, charring the metal of his armor.

"Stop. This." He braced himself and held the hammer high. A bolt shot out. The nearest bot slammed against the ceiling, its metal dented, then clanged to the ground.

Peter ran forward, pulling out his element gun. A blast of fire damaged the nearest bot, which dangled crookedly in midair, lights blinking. Gamora shot forward, kicking it out of the air and smashing it into the wall. It collapsed to the ground.

"Enemy detected," another bot bleeped. It turned toward Gamora and Peter just as the Accuser took it down. For the final bot, he didn't bother with an energy blast: His hammer smashed it flat into the floor, sending sparks shooting up.

For a moment, the Accuser and Peter simply looked at each other.

"Malfunction?" Peter said. "Technology is so fickle, am I right—".

"What is happening?" The Accuser's voice was tense. It took a moment for Peter to realize he was talking over comms. "I'm dealing with rogue bots. Addil Hall, C3. Check security. We're under attack. Is anyone reading me?"

"We can help," Peter said.

The Accuser had to know they weren't behind this. For all of the violent disagreements between the Kree and the Guardians of the Galaxy over the years, they had maintained a tenuous understanding. No assassination, no political attacks. The Guardians weren't their enemies.

But that didn't mean the Kree necessarily wanted them meddling in internal affairs.

"Wait until I find you. Return to the waiting room." The Accuser nodded goodbye and left, his cape flowing behind him.

When the Accuser was gone, Peter looked to Gamora. "Baran."

"Baran," she confirmed.

Peter narrowed his eyes, thinking. If the DiMavi still meant to target the peace ceremony, they wouldn't make themselves known now, hours in advance. That would only give the Kree time to stop them.

If Baran meant to target the Ono Circle prayer instead… Peter couldn't rule out the DiMavi attacking their own, but why? What else was down *here,* especially?

"The Elder Council," Gamora and Peter said in unison.

If Baran couldn't set his Grootling loose on the ceremony later, the Council—now—was his next best target.

"Rocket, where's the Elder Council located?"

"Don't you mean the *Supreme* Elder Council, Quill?" He snickered. "Scanners and cameras are still down, but I have maps of the compounds. Let me see…you're on the third level of Addil Hall? The Council has personal quarters on the ninth and tenth levels, and they convene on the eighth."

"Sabotage the elevators. Slow down anyone trying to reach them. Looks like they took a page from our book at DiMave—security bots are turning on the Kree. And us."

"Security bots? In Addil Hall?" Rocket said. "The security system ain't even active—I don't have anything in the system that shows—aw, man, I can't decide whether to love or hate these guys. All right, I'm getting on it. What're they trying to do, anyhow?"

"Up the victim count?" Peter said.

"Or clear a path," Gamora suggested. They ran down the hall, toward the stairway. "The Grootling must be weakened like the others—too easily taken out. They can't risk confrontation before the big finale."

Either way: They had to stop the bots.

And they still had to find Baran.

40

DRAX accessed the complex via a road deck connecting directly to a small visitor parking area on Addil Hall's fourth floor, filled with a handful of colorful personal shuttles, cars, and air scooters. He stepped out, letting the car park itself behind him, and followed the Accuser on foot.

She was trying to reach someone on her comms. "Location?" she asked, one hand on her ear. "I have the Guardian Drax with me. Location?"

Her face settled into a frown. She walked on.

"Friends?" Drax asked the other Guardians over his own communicator. "We have arrived."

"About time," Rocket said. "We have work to do. Ditch the Accuser."

"Violently?" he asked.

The Accuser looked over her shoulder without slowing down. "Violently *what?*"

"I heard that!" Quill said. "Do not answer her, Drax! And don't attack her—jeez, it'll take too long, and you'll get hurt. We need you in one piece."

"Get hurt? Ha!"

"Just don't. Okay?"

The Accuser raised an eyebrow at Drax, then opened the door connecting the parking area to the rest of the fourth floor. She took two steps into the hallway, then paused, turning left toward the sound of footsteps. A screen projection slid down from her headpiece over her face, either running scans or displaying information or both. He joined her in the hall.

Two blue-skinned Kree privates were running their way.

"Identify yourself," the Accuser called. "I don't see you in my system. I'm not even…" She shifted her stance, her entire body tense, and raised her hammer as a warning. "Who are you?"

The air in front of the first private shifted. The effect reminded Drax incongruously of snow: white flecks, flickering where the light caught them, tumbled from the private through the hall toward the Accuser and Drax.

Flickering.

Sparkling.

Just like the spores the witness in the park had described.

Drax grabbed the Accuser's shoulder and tried to pull her back. She shoved his arm away. Her hammer flashed at the Kree. The last thing Drax saw before tumbling back into the parking area was the flash clipping the shoulder of the front Kree—but the blast did not damage him the way it would have hurt a normal person. Instead, he flickered, like a holo malfunctioning. Another form became visible for a split second.

"Groot." Drax stared at the doorway, stunned.

The Accuser's blast did not stop the spores. They clung to her body, her armor. "What *is* this—" she said.

The Kree private—no, the *Grootling,* his holo now back in place— ran closer. The second soldier sprinted to catch up. The Accuser lifted her weapon again, then let out a scream and bent over double.

"What—"

She tried to aim her weapon at the Grootling and the other soldier as they passed by, but lost her footing and thudded into the wall. The holo-soldiers ran past, down the hall.

"What is happening?" she asked, panting.

"You have been poisoned."

"Is this what happened—the park—"

"Yes," Drax told her. Then: "Star-Lord, I spotted the Grootling. He and…someone else are disguised as Kree privates via holos. The second person could be his handler. I will follow."

Drax shoved past the Accuser, who was scrabbling against the wall, as if trying to keep herself upright.

"Wait!" Quill said. "Don't pursue! You can't fight him."

"I can fight anything."

"You can't punch poison spores, Drax, and you don't have any long-range weapons. Go to the basement. I don't think it's a target, but Baran reprogrammed the security system to turn on us, and there are hundreds of civilians down there."

Drax watched the Grootling turn the corner at the end of the hall, following the other soldier. Drax's nostrils flared. He was letting an enemy escape.

He was letting a *friend* escape.

Disgusted, he tore his eyes away and crouched by the Accuser's side. She was panting, looking up with wild, uncomprehending eyes.

"Your armor may slow down the spores," he told her. "Call for medical assistance."

"Done. Already done. I am"—wheeze—"I am a professional."

"Yes." He thumped her shoulder. "How do I reach the basement?"

THOSE DiMavi bastards had killed the security bots' network connectivity. Rocket tried via the network, then sent out offline signals in five different protocols—nothing. In, out, didn't matter. Baran's crew had cut any possibility of contact. Rocket could see just how they'd done it, too—the traces of their actions lingered in the security system. If he'd had a bot in front of him, he could have reprogrammed it right back.

Even then, though, the bot wouldn't be able to *talk* to the others, because the DiMavi had *made that impossible.*

Worse, Rocket had spent too much time trying to undo the damage. He'd wasted just as much time trying to get the cameras back.

He could try one more thing, though. The DiMavi had managed to scramble most of the communication signals, but the devices themselves were still functioning. If he could pick up on their signals, he could place their locations within the building. Then at least he'd have a map of who was where.

The door opened.

"…distraction across town, it might clear up the halls," one voice said. "Not that the Accusers worked so well as a distraction."

Another voice made a sound of agreement. "It's risky, especially with—"

"With the Guardians of the Galaxy in town?" Rocket clambered onto the desk, whipping out his blaster.

Across the room, the two DiMavi came to a dead halt. Their hands snapped to pull their guns—but they didn't shoot.

Maybe they'd seen his blaster. Maybe they wanted to have a halfway civilized chat. Either way, he could work with this.

Rocket padded across the desk, alternating his aim between the two of them. "Did you two flark up the system here? I'd be impressed if I wasn't so pissed. I coulda been out there! Shooting people! Instead, I'm stuck doing the boring work while the others get to play whack-the-bot. You mind dropping those guns and giving me a hand with—hey!"

He ducked away as they fired. He fired back, clipping one in the shoulder. He cussed and hurled himself low. Right on time. The terminal by his side shattered, sending shards of metal and plastic flying in the air.

"Come on!" he shouted. "You either shoot or you don't! You don't change your mind halfway through!"

On the bright side, his work had just gotten a lot less boring.

He dashed forward. Another terminal blew up. "I still needed those!" He poked his head out. One of the DiMavi was only a few feet away.

Easy target. The DiMavi left a nice splash on the desk.

The other one—hmm. Odds were, he was hiding.

"If you changed your mind about trying to kill me..." Rocket called out.

Shots rang out above and behind him. One passed so close to his tail it snagged a few hairs.

"Guess not."

Rocket leapt off the desk onto one of the chairs, sending it rolling along the floor. He ducked low, searching from underneath the desk. Nothing— nothing—*there.*

"Wanna hear my favorite sound in the world?" He took aim and fired.

It was a nice sound, indeed.

The chair came to a stop past the end of the terminals, near the entrance the DiMavi had used. He could see the splayed-out legs of the one he'd just shot.

And, right next to them, a set of feet poking out from under a desk.

Huh. He hadn't shot anyone *there.*

He cocked his head, hopped off the chair, and headed over. He kept his gun handy, just in case the two he'd shot got stubborn about being dead. No one gave so much as a twitch. He reached out for the unidentified feet, prodding them with the fun end of the blaster, and—ah! Movement. Slight, but there was life in there. A stretch of green skin showed between the boot and pant leg. This wasn't another Kree guard.

Rocket peered under the desk. Another DiMavi lay there, tied to a desk leg. This one was a lot less blown up than the one by Rocket's side. He let out a soft moan; his eyes fluttered, then fell back shut.

"Oy." Another prod with the blaster, this time in the guy's belly. "Wake up. I got questions."

"Mmmhh." The DiMavi tried to open his eyes. One was swollen shut.

"Lemme guess." Rocket crouched. "You didn't play nicely with your terrorist friends?"

He mumbled something. Coughed. "Mmmwhat?"

"How'd you end up here?"

Finally the man's eyes opened properly. He looked around, dazed.

"I don't have all day," Rocket said, exasperated. "You're in the security hub of Porovi Hall in Vadin, blah blah blah. Answer my flarking questions."

The man's gaze settled on the dead body a few feet away. That startled him awake. He lurched, but his arms were still tied to the desk leg behind him.

"Oh, come on! It's just a body. It ain't even smelly yet."

"Is that…that's Mani. That's Mani. Mani is dead."

"Yeah, yeah, that's nice—"

"That's my *assistant*. That's Mani. What happened, what—"

"Why do I now know more about this dead bastard than I know about you? Answer. My. Questions." Rocket narrowed his eyes suddenly. This guy looked familiar. He'd cut his hair, and the black eye had thrown Rocket off—but this was definitely the same face Rocket had seen in a government profile on his communicator just a couple of hours ago.

"How'd you end up under this table, Baran?"

"I was here for a security inspection. Because of the ceremony tonight. Oh no—is it already happening? What time is it?"

"Not yet happening! Keep talking."

"The inspection. Mani said it had to be moved up. We got here, everything was normal, and suddenly my team, they...I don't know what happened. They started shooting the Kree. They knocked me out. They turned on me. Oh, no. Oh, no."

"And the Groot?"

"The...Groot?" He was trying to climb into a sitting position without touching any of Mani's blood, which seemed to Rocket like a lot of hassle for no good reason. "What does that have to do with anything?"

Rocket let out an annoyed sigh. "I don't get people like you. Who's got the gun? Who just killed two guys? Yeah, that'd be me. And who's tied up sitting under a table like a big dumb loser? Yeah, that's you. Now, outta those two, which one gets to ask the questions? Come on, tell me about the flarking Groot."

For a few obnoxious seconds, Baran only stared at him. Then, slowly, the words came. "A couple of weeks ago, I bought a *Flora colossus*. Groot, as you say. I wanted to see if it was suitable for defense, if we could employ it to protect the more vulnerable towns... But it disappeared last week. It ran away or got stolen, I don't know. I've been looking for it, but I had to prepare for the event here, so..."

"Any idea who stole it?"

He looked up helplessly. "What's happening? Can you untie me?"

"Untie you?" Rocket spat on the ground. "Baran, you're lucky I ain't planning to shoot you. If you stay nice and quiet, you might even live through this. That's probably more than the Groot you misplaced gets to do."

"I didn't..."

Rocket twitched his gun. It was enough for Baran to smarten up and start talking.

Once Baran was finished, Rocket climbed to his feet. "Good. Keep that up—I got a few friends to update."

41

DRAX'S encounter meant Gamora and Quill could place the Grootling's location:

Right below them.

And if Rocket was correct about the layout of this building, the Grootling would come up via the nearest stairwell, and be forced to exit here into the building proper.

Good.

It would've been better, though, if Gamora and Quill had been able to make time to calmly set a trap instead of having to fight off these d'ast bots. Gamora kicked aside a bot she'd left in shambles, then stood alert. She heard something from the stairwell. Footsteps, thundering closer.

"Quill?" she said.

He turned, the eyes of his helmet glowing red as he studied the wall. "Two shapes," he reported. "The scans aren't clear, but the first could be Groot."

Gamora could think of approximately 14 ways to take out anyone exiting the stairwell into the hallway. All of those ways, however, involved being close enough to get hit by the spores.

She had to fight every instinct in order to keep her distance. Her jaw twitched in annoyance as she joined Quill down the hall.

"Close now," he said, voice low, his element gun up and ready.

The door cracked open.

Then—before anyone exited—

A shot grazed her hip.

Gamora jolted aside instinctively. One leg snapped out, kicking Quill away. A shot burned through the air where his head had been seconds before.

Gamora turned and saw two attacking bots hurtling toward them from behind. She had her sword at the ready. She blocked further shots, deflecting them into the walls before diving forward and slashing one bot in half. Quill took the other one, engulfing it in a gout of flame even as he scrambled away.

Poor timing. By the time they turned back, two Kree privates were running their way. Gamora had been warned by Drax about the holos; now that she knew, it was easy to tell. The edges of their bodies flickered, and the shadows didn't quite line up right.

"Spores!" the Kree at the back commanded.

(That voice—)

The Kree in front—the disguised Grootling—spread his arms and puffed out his chest. She recognized the style of movement even if she didn't recognize the outer layer of Kree projected on top.

"Groot, don't!" Gamora shouted. "It's *us*!"

The holo twitched. Quill fired his element gun. It came too late: Flickering spores spurted into the air before the Grootling. Quill's shot cut an empty streak through the cloud whirling toward them, but it couldn't stop all the spores. A moment later, ice encased the Grootling's upper leg.

They had a fraction of a second before the spores would hit. No time to run. A blast of air from Quill's gun wouldn't help, this close—its range was too narrow. Too many spores would still get through. Even straight-up killing the Grootling, a thought that Gamora loathed, wouldn't help now.

"Get low." Quill drew her into a crouch against the wall. He fired his gun a second time. This time, it wasn't at the Groot. The air shifted—solidified—twisted. The wall of ice curved in front of them and overhead, forming a shield. Gamora and Quill ducked under it as the first spores bounced off harmlessly.

The Grootling crossed the hall until he stood right before them, his Kree image misshapen through the ice. Gamora watched him, unmoving, her hand around her sword and ready to strike. Beside her, Quill clutched his gun the same way. It was set to worse than ice, she knew.

If the Grootling broke the barrier to strike again, they would strike, too. They had no choice.

But she couldn't tell who would be faster—and attacking the Groot might make him instinctively unleash more spores.

The Grootling tilted his head, and reached to press two disguised Kree fingers to the surface of the ice. Recognizing Quill and Gamora? Testing the barrier? Then he twitched, drawing the hand back.

"Leave them," the second Kree-holo told Groot.

Again—that *voice.*

Rocket had told them that Baran wasn't the Grootling's handler, so who—

Beside her, Quill sat up straight. "Annay?"

"Well." Annay came to a halt in front of the ice. "This is awkward."

Gamora was still considering ways to take out the both of them without risking another spore attack. Another part of her mind was busy putting it all together:

Baran really *had* meant to use the Grootling defensively.

Annay, however, must have seen the Grootling's potential. She'd told someone else about it, or maybe she'd even organized the ceremony attack herself, from afar. As for how she'd gone from working at her bar this morning to steering the Grootling through the halls now, Gamora couldn't say—

Unless—of course. When Annay had first come on board the Guardians' ship, she'd been eager to return home. There had been no reason for her to worry: The Guardians knew nothing. But when the Guardians had discovered the attack on the ceremony and set course for Vadin, Annay had abruptly decided to stay on board. She'd been worried about the Guardians interfering with the attack.

"Sorry, Peter," Annay said. "You really do have nice hair."

"I am so disappointed right now," he said, staring blankly.

"I'd hoped my distractions would mean we didn't have to do this, you and me. We still don't. This isn't any of your business, Guardians. It's between us and the Kree. You weren't there to help us when they attacked us; you shouldn't be here to stop us now."

"We didn't know then," Gamora said. "We do know now."

"Convenient. Still not your business."

"You're kind of using our friend as a weapon, though," Quill pointed out.

"Fair point."

"I am Groot."

His voice was so mangled, Gamora couldn't make out what he was saying—but it was undoubtedly his voice coming from that incongruously smooth, incongruously *Kree* body. She wished she could look up at him and see the familiar bark of his face.

But it would not help her get through to him.

"Look, this day didn't turn out like I'd planned, either," Annay said.

"I would've preferred to be throwing violent drunks out of my bar at this point—that's my favorite part of the day. Maybe keeping an eye on the channels for news of an attack on Vadin. It's much safer arranging these things from a distance."

Plausible deniability, Gamora thought.

"But when you figured out the attack, I tagged along to delay you, and gave my crew a heads-up to speed things along before you could interfere. They rushed it, messed up transporting the Groot, and then they were too scared of him to even get close. They wanted to send him up here on his own with only long-term commands. I stepped in, and here we are. You guys want to save lives? You want to bring justice? Find those Kree that attacked our home. They're still out there. Because our government? Or this government?" She tugged her head toward the ceiling. "They sure have no intentions of doing it."

"We'll put that on our to-do list," Quill said. "There's still the issue of you trying to straight-up murder people right now."

She blew out a wistful sigh. "Don't get in our way. Groot? Move along."

He turned, dragging his feet along without complaint.

"Groot!" Quill called after him. "*Fight it!*"

Before, Annay had kept her distance from the Grootling—probably to avoid the spores. Now, she walked closely by his side, keeping him as a shield between her and the two Guardians.

"Your taste in women…" Gamora started.

"Don't," Quill said, then let out a defeated sigh. "I know."

THE GUARDIANS of the Galaxy had handled worse problems before Kiya came along, and they would handle worse after she was gone.

Kiya was perfectly aware of that.

But those other problems hadn't been and wouldn't be caused by *her*. After seeing the victims at the hospital, it was impossible not to imagine the same agony on the faces of the Guardians, or any Kree or DiMavi visiting the ceremony.

She was taking readings from a Grootling, his legs crossed on the counter across from her. "Those people at the hospital will be fine, right?"

"I am Groot."

She jabbered nervously at him. "I know the Kree are proud, and I know they're still hurting and angry over what happened to the planet Hala while I was with the Collector, but they wouldn't actually start a *war* over this. They know DiMave isn't a threat. They know we couldn't survive a war. They wouldn't."

"I am Groot?"

"I swear, I thought Baran would only use the Groot defensively."

"I am Groot."

"Those people at the hospital…"

"I am Groot."

"Is it working yet? Do you feel any different…?"

"I am Groot."

Kiya ran a hand through her hair, examining the Grootling before her. He'd absorbed the original Groot's shard into himself easily; that was progress. But whether that meant he was actually *combining* with Groot, absorbing his memories and experiences…

She couldn't tell yet.

She'd done all she could here. She needed to go back to focusing on how to sync up the Grootlings' minds enough for them to merge.

"All right," she said, thinking out loud. "What if I try—"

"I am Groot!" An adult Grootling came running into the med bay, sounding panicked. "I am Groot! I am—" The yelling seemed to exhaust him, and his voice skipped on itself. "—*Groot!*"

"What? What's happening?"

He grabbed her, pulled her up out of her chair, and dragged her through the ship. "I am Groot!" He didn't slow down until they were on the bridge, his legs buckling from the sudden exertion. He looked at her intently, then pointed at a screen on the dashboard.

She took a hesitant step closer. Several feeds showed the area around the ship—the nearby rocky outcrop, the dry, cracked desert ground. One screen showed movement. The hull of a private shuttle amidst the sand and stone, and the confident stride of a man walking away from it.

"Oh," she whispered. The cold prick of goosebumps ran across her back.

She recognized that shuttle, and she recognized that man.

The Collector had found her.

42

THE CLOSER Drax came to the ground floor, the more the halls buzzed with activity. Kree soldiers went door-to-door, escorted away office workers, and fought off aggressive security bots. A captain gave instructions in a booming, amplified voice.

The Kree had started an evacuation.

A few soldiers tried to stop Drax. He swatted them aside, more or less gently. Most were wise enough to ignore him.

He stepped over a deceased employee. The holes in her chest suggested an encounter with a security bot.

Drax stopped abruptly in the lobby. The Kree weren't just evacuating their own: Dozens of DiMavi were crowded together on one side of the room. All civilians, by the looks of it. At least 10 or 12 security bots hovered overhead, firing rapid shots that lit up the air in yellow amid the sea of green skin.

There was a distracting amount of screaming.

The DiMavi huddled for safety against the walls. Some pushed toward the open stairwell to return to the basement, which other DiMavi were still trying to escape from—they spilled into the lobby, escorted up by Kree soldiers.

Armed soldiers scattered around the lobby. Most pressed close to the DiMavi civilians, weapons raised as they tried to hold off the bots.

Drax broke into a run. He leapt up, plucked a security bot from the air, then brought it down on another bot—hard—smashing the both of them to the floor with a hearty, satisfied laugh.

Two down.

Many more to go.

The group dashed away from him, then swarmed back together, kept in line by the bots. One bot fired at a Kree soldier; several shots hit his arm. Others landed in the crowd behind him. Two DiMavi screamed, their gray-pink blood spraying the air.

The bot had not aimed for them, though. Drax knew that much. Its aim had been narrow, focused only on the Kree soldier instead of the easier targets behind him.

Drax studied the room, zeroing in on the other bots and their targets.

"Run!" one Kree—a lieutenant—called to the group of DiMavi. "Go for the exit!"

Three Kree privates led away some of the DiMavi. The group instantly fell under assault, pushed back by the bots.

Drax had seen enough. The bots only targeted the Kree—never the DiMavi civilians.

He stepped forward, striking a security bot firing at him. "Kree!" he bellowed, coming ever closer to the group. "Move away from the civilians!"

They seemed unwilling to listen.

The lieutenant aimed her weapon at Drax. "Step away."

"*You* are attracting the bots," Drax said.

Annay's team, he realized, had reprogrammed the bots to avoid attacking DiMavi like themselves. If the bots targeted only the Kree and other species working in the building, the attackers could move through the halls freely. That precaution might keep these other DiMavi safe.

As long as they kept their distance from the real targets.

"Step! Away!" the lieutenant said. "We will not abandon our charges!"

Drax had talked enough. He would not talk further while innocents were caught in the crossfire.

He charged at the group. The DiMavi screamed. The Kree soldiers shifted their focus from the security bots to him. A shot scraped his cheek—

Drax roared. Grabbed one Kree private by the arm and tossed her back, sending her sliding across the floor. Pushed through the DiMavi crowd. Took hold of another Kree. Flung him over the heads of the DiMavi, halfway across the lobby.

The remaining Kree fought their way through the DiMavi to reach him.

The bad: The security bots all congregated on the same spot—Drax and the Kree.

The good: The DiMavi were no longer hemmed in by their Kree guards. They dispersed, jostling to get away from Drax and the wildly firing security bots.

"The exit." Drax's voice boomed above the noise. He pointed over the crowd. "They will not follow!"

Not all of the DiMavi listened. Some stayed fearfully near the guards Drax had flung aside. Others tried to fight their way down to the basement.

Some ran, though.

"Look," Drax told the soldiers around him. Not a single DiMavi was being targeted by the bots.

The Kree paid no attention; they were too busy looking at him. They circled him, staying at a safe distance. At least half a dozen pointed their weapons at him, while the outer ring tried to fend off the bots. Red and white lights along the bots' sides flickered aggressively as they fired another round of shots.

"On the floor!" one Kree yelled at Drax. "On the floor, now!"

Drax crossed his arms. He looked down at the soldier.

"On the floor…please?"

"Stand down!" the lieutenant called from outside the circle, watching the DiMavi run and scatter to safety. "He's right. Keep your distance from the civilians! Focus on the bots and draw them away!"

The soldier lowered his gun, visibly relieved. "You're the Destroyer, aren't you?"

"Yes." Drax uncrossed his arms, swinging them loose. He had his eyes set on the nearest bots. "So let us destroy."

THE GROOTLING and Annay had gotten ahead of Peter and Gamora.

The best way to catch them by surprise was to reverse that situation.

Peter shot up straight through the air, a mere two feet outside the building. The sun glittered against the glass and beat down on his body, but he barely felt it with Gamora's arms around his neck and the wind rushing past him. Far below, people started to spill from the buildings onto the courtyard—some running in a panic, others merely confused.

Rocket had said the Elder Council convened on the eighth floor. Peter counted the floors as they rose, slowing when he reached the eighth. His helmet ran a scan: Seven people sat clustered near each other in a large, otherwise empty room. That had to be the Council members. Outside the room, a dozen others stood guard.

"Rocket, are there any Kree on their way up?"

"I locked the doors and slammed down some force fields," he said. "They're already working on breaking 'em down, but you're good for now."

"Sweet. Bring up those two elevators."

The thrusters on Peter's boots dwindled, firing just enough to keep him in the air. He turned away from the window to give Gamora room.

She dropped one arm from his neck, his thrusters compensating for her weight, and drew her sword. "Thank you."

A moment later, glass shattered and spilled over the floor inside. Gamora leapt away from Peter, landing in a crouch.

Peter touched down by her side.

A dozen angry Kree soldiers pointed a dozen fierce weapons at them.

"Guardians," one soldier barked, stepping forward. The wind gusting through the broken window tugged at her tightly bound hair. "I am Captain Mari-Kee. You're interfering with a sensitive operation. Leave."

"We're *helping* with a sensitive operation, actually." Peter held up his hands to show he meant no harm, even as he analyzed the situation. "We know more about the threat than you do." He hoped so, anyway. If the Kree had found out that DiMavi citizens were behind this…

"We know enough." The captain shot a glance at the stairwell doors. If the Grootling and Annay made it up here, it would be through that entrance.

Down the hall, more Kree soldiers were stationed in front of the doors to the Council's conference room. A few defeated security bots by the far wall—along with an unmoving, blood-covered Kree body—showed that Mari-Kee's people had already dealt with the other threats roaming the building.

"What's your plan?" Peter asked.

Captain Mari-Kee studied Peter and Gamora, then nodded as though coming to a conclusion. "We stay at a distance to avoid the poison and shoot on sight."

"*Flora colossi* are resilient," Peter said. "To take him out, you'll need to completely destroy him—and he might release the spores in the process."

The hallway outside the Elder Council's conference room was spacious, both tall and wide, but it was still a confined space. If the spores reached farther than the Kree expected, they would have nowhere to run.

"Then so be it. The threat would be neutralized."

Peter groaned. He should've seen that coming. The Kree and their blasted hierarchy—they'd do anything for their leaders. "We have an alternate plan that'll actually keep you alive. Help us evacuate the Council—"

"Out of the question."

"I have a plan! A good plan! A totally thought-out plan!" He managed to swallow the words *for once*. "Come on—"

"We're not letting outsiders near the Elder Council at a time like this, and we're not moving them until the situation is secured," Captain Mari-Kee stated.

"We don't have time to argue this. There's a plan B."

She shot another glance at the doors. "Hurry up."

"Plan B…"

Peter smiled sunnily.

"…is we evacuate them *without* your help."

43

THIS is fine. I'm calm. I can do this."

Kiya was not calm, and she could not do this.

How had the Collector found her? Even if someone had tipped him off she was on Vadin, the ship was well hidden. The only people who knew its location were the Guardians, Annay, and the Accuser who'd followed Drax and Kiya out into the desert.

The Collector had *found* her. He'd *found* her. This time he wouldn't let her escape; this time there wasn't any Star-Lord to spearhead a getaway—

"I am Groot? I am Groot!"

The voice dragged her back. She'd been staring at the screen showing the Collector, his clothes a garish purple against the desaturated landscape. Her eyes were wide, her breath barely there. She forced air back into her lungs.

"We need to fly away." She didn't feel steady, but at least she sounded it. "We can escape."

She studied the control panel. There was an autopilot, she knew—the Guardians had used it often enough in the few days she'd been with them. She just didn't know how to activate it. The only ships she'd ever flown were private rental shuttles. Those were designed as straightforwardly as possible and worked on voice commands half the time.

Fear crept into Kiya's voice. "Can you fly it?"

She looked at the Grootling beside her. He was trying to figure out the control panel as well. She'd seen the same look on the other Grootlings as they tried to recover faded memories.

This was up to her.

Decision made, she sat down in the pilot's seat. What did Star-Lord normally do now? He would flick some switches (which of the seven?) and give Rocket a command (not possible now) and then grab that throttle—

Lights flashed to her right. "I haven't even done anything yet!"

"I am Groot?" The Grootling leaned in and hit a button.

The Collector's voice rang through the bridge: "Do I not get a friendly welcome?"

That *voice*.

Kiya sat rooted to her chair.

She'd escaped him, she told herself. She'd wrecked his museum, taken his specimen, and made him look like a fool. Yet that voice still pinned her down, still made panic burn her eyes.

"Anyone aboard?" The voice came from all around.

At least there wasn't an accompanying holo. She didn't think she could stand to see his face. She stretched over and smacked the same button the Grootling had. The connection was cut.

"Where was I, where was I," she murmured as she took the throttle into her hands, pretending her eyes didn't leak and her heart wasn't thudding into her ribcage.

Then—

The ship shook.

"Aack!"

Kiya was slammed forward, almost knocked from the chair. The throttle dug painfully into her belly. Next to her, the Grootling had caught himself on the navigator's seat and clung to it for balance. The ship shook a second time.

"I am Groot!"

Several screens flickered on—some built-in, some holo. Her head darted from left to right, taking them in one at a time.

That screen: graphs.

That screen: numbers. The phrase *Hull Integrity: 29%* wasn't a good sign.

That screen: a 3-D image of the ship. Parts of it were lit up in orange; others glowed red.

That screen: the same camera feeds as before. She fixated on the one showing the Collector's shuttle outside, catching a glimpse of Tivan's face in the pilot's seat through the front viewport. He'd climbed back into his ship.

Two massive cannons on each side of the shuttle glowed bright.

Oh crap—

She wildly sought out the switch she'd seen Rocket use for announcements. "Hold on!" she yelled at the Grootlings throughout the ship, a second before the next blast hit.

The orange parts of the 3-D image turned a fierce red. The numbers on the other screen dropped. *Hull Integrity: 0%.*

On the camera feed, the Collector calmly exited his shuttle again. He adjusted his cloak and strode toward the Guardians' ship.

Kiya stared at the screens, frozen. Via the interior camera feed, she saw the inside of the Guardians' cargo bay, with a gaping hole revealing the ground past it. The Collector had blasted it right open. The impact had left sand and smoke in the air, thick clouds that obscured the view outside.

Tivan could simply walk in. And she couldn't do a thing to stop him.

She wanted to hide.

She jolted away from the control panel. He was inside. Too late to flee. She needed to hide. She needed to—

There had to be other exits. Could she make a run for it? Could she slip past him and escape through the hole he'd blown in the ship? She could take the Collector's shuttle. She could be gone before he even realized she was there.

Or she could lock the bridge tight, hide right here under the control panel, and pray for him to leave.

"I am Groot." The Grootling leaned in, his face next to hers. He smiled. How? Why? The Collector was inside the ship—he was on his way—

The Grootling took her hands. One by one, he placed them back on the throttle. Then he patted them. "I am Groot."

He turned and ran off the bridge.

She stared at the throttle, not comprehending for a too-long second.

When it did hit her, it was obvious. Fly away. Get out of this damn desert and find help in the city. That was another option. She nodded at no one in particular and considered the controls in front of her, every joystick and switch and button and screen.

She tried not to watch the camera feeds. Some of the Grootlings were pulling the larger duplicates toward the cargo bay.

They were buying her time. She had to use it.

One slider said AUTO. When she tried to move it down, it wouldn't give.

She tried to envision the times she'd seen Star-Lord or the others put this ship into motion.

Sliders on the left, all the way up. These switches. Pull the throttle. Lights flickered on across the dash. Just like that, the ship came to life.

Alarm lights bathed the bridge in flashes of red, warning her of the damage the ship had suffered. A nervous look over her shoulder revealed only an empty bridge.

Don't think about Tivan.

Don't think about the Grootlings.

She stole a look at the camera feeds. The two oldest Grootlings faced the Collector. He'd made it inside, lingering halfway up a metal staircase and looking up at the Grootlings with interest. She couldn't hear them clearly over the audio feed, but she could make out enough to recognize Tivan's amicable voice and the Grootlings' warning tone.

Back on the dash. Back to the AUTO slider. Focus. This time—yes!—it gave. She left it on the first setting for a moment; when that didn't do anything, the next; finally, the third. Several more lights flicked on.

The ship started to move.

"Location?" a mechanical voice asked.

She thought for a moment. She could only think of a single place to find help she trusted, and where the Collector might hesitate to make trouble.

"Porovi Hall," she told the ship.

It bleeped in acknowledgment. Kiya felt a rush of joy.

It didn't last. They were moving, lifting away from the ground agonizingly slowly, but the Collector was still in the ship, and now—now she had to deal with that.

The fear surged. She closed her eyes. The flashing alarm lights burned through her eyelids, impossible to ignore. She felt the same urge to run, hide—but she'd just given up her only hope of escaping, and hiding wouldn't make him go away.

She needed to see him. She needed to know where he was, because unless she knew, she would always think he was right behind her.

Kiya opened her eyes. She hunted through the screen controls, experimenting until she managed to change the camera feed to display the leisure area. She saw several smaller Grootlings in hiding. Another two were running out the door. The med bay was empty; the bridge showed only Kiya herself, bathed in flashing lights; and the cargo bay—oh no, the cargo bay. Her stomach roiled at the sight of it. The hole was so big the entire team could've fit through with room to spare.

There was no sign of life. Only the cargo bay, the blasted-in doors, and of the planet dropping farther away.

The next screen revealed the Collector standing by the kitchen counter. He steadied himself with one hand, the other raised to defend himself from three Grootlings lashing out with sharp, pointed fingers. They'd torn his clothes, but didn't seem to be able to touch the rest of him. The Collector looked more inconvenienced than frightened.

(She was responsible for that. Groot should've been able to do more damage than this.)

The Collector swiped one arm, swatting the Grootlings aside with ease.

Their voices were louder now.

"I am Groot!"

"Ga-mo-ra…" Tivan sing-songed.

Kiya's skin went cold.

Two more Grootlings rushed at him from off-screen. He stopped a small one in midair. Instead of tossing him back, Tivan held him up. He asked a question, too soft to hear. His face tightened in annoyance. He grabbed hold of one arm, then tore.

A gasp escaped her. Kiya watched the screen numbly as the Collector tossed away the arm—and the Grootling—like trash.

He turned toward the next Grootling.

She couldn't watch this.

"Ga-*mo*-ra…"

A thought in her mind: *If I lock myself in the bridge, we'll reach the Guardians before he can find me—they can keep him busy—*

The pit of fear in her stomach told her it was a good idea. That it was the only idea. She could hide until it was over and…

And then?

She thought of the Grootling's hands on hers just now, and of the last sight she'd caught of Groot at Annay's bar before he'd sealed off the hatch.

She jerked away from her chair.

She couldn't escape, or hide, or go back home. There was no safety for her anymore. Instead, she had this: the Collector coming after her, and the people whose lives had been ruined fighting for her. She couldn't sit by.

She had to fight.

The Collector had taught her to fight, and now she would turn that training back on him.

She was halfway down the bridge when two Grootlings staggered in. "Good," she said. "Can one of you watch the bridge?"

"I am Groot!"

"Tell the Grootlings fighting Tivan to drive him back toward the cargo bay." Her best hope of escaping this was to get him off the ship. Her best hope of getting him off the ship was tossing him out of that gaping hole in the cargo bay. And her best hope of tossing him out—

She had a pretty good idea of how to pull that off.

"And you…" Kiya turned to the other Grootling. Despite the fear clenching her gut, she found herself smiling grimly.

She didn't want to face Tivan again. She would be happy to never, ever set foot on the same planet as him.

But if they had to come face-to-face once more, at least there was a way to enjoy it.

"I am Groot?"

"Show me where Rocket keeps his bombs."

44

CAPTAIN Mari-Kee was fast on the uptake: She realized what Peter meant in a split second.

He knew that split second was plenty for Gamora. The captain hit the ground with a smack. Gamora leapt over her, diving low. A sweep of her leg brought down another two soldiers.

"Again: We're here to help." Peter fired his element gun, freezing a soldier trying to attack Gamora from behind. "If you don't want to fight us, toss down your weapon and get into that elevator."

Right on cue, the doors slid open to reveal two empty elevators.

He encased another soldier in ice. Gamora would've taken her out easily, but Peter liked to be useful.

Within moments, the hallway was clear. They dragged the unconscious and frozen Kree into the first elevator. Two other soldiers went willingly, not wanting to end up frozen solid—Peter hoped they wouldn't get in trouble over cooperating, but knowing the Kree military, they probably would.

"Sorry, dude." Peter patted a half-frozen private on the shoulder. "It's still better than getting hit by those spores."

The elevator doors slid shut.

"Rocket, send them down a floor or two, but keep those doors closed," Gamora said over comms. "We need to get into the Council's conference room. Any help?"

"Done!"

Peter turned toward the conference-room doors. The physical locks clicked open, followed by an almost imperceptible *fzzzt* as Rocket overrode the force field. With the rest of the security measures already deactivated, getting in would be simple.

Rocket went on, "Hey, is anyone doing murder yet? No? Hm. Keep me in the loop."

"I'll evacuate," Gamora said to Peter, wrenching the doors apart.

He gave a lazy salute. By flying up the outside of the building, they'd gotten well ahead of Annay and the Grootling—but they'd used up most of their lead time.

Inside the chamber, Gamora began speaking in a firm voice to the Council members. Peter tuned her out, watching the stairwell with a sideways eye as he moved back toward the broken window. The wind threatened to suck him out, but he grabbed hold of the ledge and leaned down to peer at the ground far below. Clean: Everyone was being evacuated via the main exit, congregating in the courtyard farther left. Using his foot and the wind setting on his element gun, he swept the glass outside, sending it spinning through the air. He switched the element gun to fire, painting strategic scorch spots on the wall. He dragged the broken security bots down the hall near the opening—then did the same with the deceased Kree body.

No movement in the stairwell yet.

Finally, Gamora escorted out the Council members. "Into the elevator," she told them. "Go. Rocket, the conference-room doors are closed. Lock them again."

Another *fzzt* sounded by the room's entrance. The force field was back up. The locks clicked shut a moment later.

One Council member walked at the tail end of the group, her stride stiff and her head held up proudly despite one rapidly swelling eye. "How," she asked, her voice deliberate, "can we trust that—"

"Because if I wanted to kill you, I'd have done it when you pulled that weapon on me," Gamora said, "and if I wanted to kidnap you, I wouldn't ask nicely."

She herded the rest of them into the second elevator, ignoring their demands. The moment the last member's cape flowed inside, she said, "Rocket, get them all down. Don't open the elevator doors until the security bots are taken care of."

"But what if—" one Council member asked. The doors popped closed, cutting off his voice.

"You're welcome!" Peter called after them. Standing by his side, Gamora looked determined, exasperated, and invigorated all at once. "You look like you're having fun."

One corner of her lips curled up. "Ask me when Groot and Kiya are safe."

"Will do. Let's go."

He wrapped an arm around her waist and kicked off the floor, his boot thrusters propelling them back outside through the broken window. He maneuvered along the outside wall to the side of the window, out of sight of the hallway, and began to hover in place. Far below, the evacuation proceeded across the courtyard. Office employees, injured soldiers, DiMavi civilians, workers who had been setting up the ceremony stage in advance of the evening's events... Shuttles were arriving to get them out, but there was hardly anywhere to land, and those shuttles weren't set up to transport hundreds at once.

Peter tried to tune out the noise and the wind soaring around their ears. He turned toward the outer wall, listening for anything going on inside the building.

There. The click of a door.

Footsteps.

Peter ran a scan with his helmet, revealing the same readings as before—two figures, their holos skewing his view of them. It had to be Annay and the Grootling.

"They're here," he whispered to Rocket over comms. From the look of Annay's silhouette, she was checking out the empty hallway—the scorch marks, the missing window pane, the broken bots nearby, the deceased Kree—and hopefully coming to the conclusion he wanted her to come to: that the glass had been shattered outward, and that the guards had either fled or fallen in the scuffle with the bots.

Annay's silhouette approached the conference-room doors. She reached out, presumably testing for a force field. Then she crouched down, pulling something from a bag or pocket and placing it on the ground.

"We have bomb action, Rocket."

"Why am I missing this?" he complained. "I mean, I *am* tracking down the last of Annay's crew, so I'm getting to shoot people, but bombs! It ain't the same. Can I run over? It's only four or five floors up."

Peter's helmet ran scan after scan, frantically trying to identify the bomb. He'd be in trouble if the explosive was homemade, but even then, the timer mechanism—

His display flashed with information. Got it. "Two seconds left!"

One.

Two.

Peter imagined the same *fzzt* as before as the force field fizzled out, and—

BLAM!

The doors blasted open. Dust filled the hall, obscuring his sensors for a moment before they filtered it out.

Annay was holding an arm to her eyes, shielding herself from the dust. "Have at it," she told the Grootling.

The Grootling walked toward the conference room. He took firm steps, but the rest of him seemed hunched, as though he was trying to make himself smaller. Every now and then he shifted his head left and right—checking his surroundings? A side effect from the brainwashing?

Once he was inside the conference room, Peter yelled, "Now!"

"Field's back up," Rocket buzzed in Peter's ear. "Did it work? Is he trapped? Hmm. Turning off the force field before the blast protected its circuitry somewhat, but it's still down to 61 percent power."

That wasn't good. Peter had only anticipated a 20 percent loss—oh, of course. It must've already been damaged by the security bots.

"Hey," Rocket went on, "I'm about to murder a DiMavi who was sending bots after Kree interns. Wanna listen in?"

"No," Peter and Gamora said in unison.

"Aw, fine." He paused. "Try and go easy on Groot?"

Peter didn't answer. In part because he was a tiny bit busy at the moment. In part because he couldn't make that promise.

He and Gamora surged inside the building.

"Hi again." Peter pulled his element gun before he even had his feet on the floor. He froze Annay instantly, trapping her gun arm by her side, then landed.

Annay tried to pull her arm free. The hologram of her false Kree face twisted. "I hate you guys," she said. "A lot. I was *so*—oh, forget it. Groot! Bash through the force field!"

Past the transparent force field and blown-open doors, they could see the other Kree—the Grootling in disguise—in the conference room, walking through a cloud of dust. He made a sad figure, hunched and alone. He was looking around the room as though trying to find something or someone, or trying to remember what he was meant to do.

The moment Annay shouted her order, he turned and stormed the force field.

"I am Groot!"

Thud. The noise felt out of place, incongruous with the small Kree holo.

"I *am* Groot!"

Thud.

The Grootling scrambled back and shook his head, an abrupt tug left, right, as if he had to shake off stars from the impact.

Then he was back in motion. "I am Groot!

Thud.

The force field started to fizzle. It couldn't take much more. If they wanted to take the Grootling out without risk to bystanders, they had to do it now.

"You've lost," Gamora told Annay. "Even if he escapes, the Council is long gone."

"The other Kree aren't," Annay said.

A scan of the stairwell confirmed it: Whatever measures Rocket had taken to slow down the Kree military, they'd broken through. Several were headed to this floor; they'd be here in moments.

"And you know what the great thing about the Kree is?" Annay reached for her neck with her unfrozen hand, flicking something away. The holo promptly blinked off. There she stood, 100 percent herself again: green and strong, her white hair a sweaty, tangled mess over a grimly amused face.

Peter really had liked that face.

Not so much anymore.

"It doesn't matter whether I kill the Council," Annay said. "It would have been nice. But a DiMavi even getting this far—"

"It'd still start a war," Gamora said.

"You're catching on. If our cowardly government won't fight back against the Kree—well, now the Kree won't give them a choice."

"Thousands will die," Peter said in disbelief. "Tens of thousands! DiMavi, too!"

This had never been about justice, he realized. It wasn't even about revenge. It was about bloodlust.

"At least they'll die in a fight that needs fighting." Annay looked over her shoulder. "Hey! Kree!" she bellowed. "The people responsible—"

In the space of a breath, Gamora stood behind her. She clamped one hand to Annay's mouth to shut her up, wrapped another around her neck to choke her out, and waited impassively as she slumped to the floor.

Peter glanced down at Annay's unconscious body, still partly encased in ice. Shutting up Annay now wouldn't prevent the Kree from finding, apprehending, and eventually interrogating her. If they wanted to keep this mess under wraps, they needed to get her out of the building.

"I am Groot!"

Thud.

"Yeah, I haven't forgotten about you," Peter muttered, thinking through his options. With the Kree racing up the stairwell, and the force field weakening with each impact, he had zero time. The Grootling would break through within a minute.

D'ast. Peter's totally thought-out plan maybe wasn't so thought-out after all.

Unless—

He glanced at the broken window they'd entered through.

Gamora raised an eyebrow, catching on. "You sure?"

"*I am Groot!*"

The Grootling's pace had been inconsistent, sometimes hitting the force field several times in the space of a few seconds, other times pausing as though he needed to gather his strength. He'd even stumbled once, the same way the other weakened Grootlings did.

What *had* been consistent was the fury in his voice. He wouldn't hesitate to attack. In an enclosed space like this, with a hallway soon to be full of Kree, his spores would cause a massacre.

"I'm sure," Peter said.

"And her?" Gamora looked at Annay slumped by her feet.

"Yup."

"Risky. Let's do it."

"Rocket?" Peter said over comms. "We're onto plan D."

"Yeah, sure, Quill. What the frick is plan D?"

He grimaced. "Defenestration."

45

I AM GROOT!"

Thud.

Gamora dropped Annay's unconscious body near the window, then walked back, dusting off her hands.

Peter activated his boots. He flew up as high as the hallway would allow and hovered over the conference-room doors, just above the force field. He kept his back to the wall, staying out of the Grootling's sight.

"I am Groot!"

Thud.

By now, the Grootling had to be rushing back, preparing for his next assault on the force field. Peter heard his footsteps, the scrape of wood on the floor.

Peter didn't want to do this. He really didn't.

But the Grootling's cries of rage—that wasn't like Groot.

The way he mindlessly bashed the field—that wasn't like Groot.

The way he'd killed people…

That *really* wasn't Groot.

Peter breathed deep, then nodded at Gamora. She watched the Grootling, ready to give the word to Rocket the second he was close enough to—

"Go!"

fzzt

The Grootling lunged into the hallway. Without the force field to stop him, he overshot the doorway. He made a confused sound and windmilled another few feet, trying to slide to a stop.

Peter didn't give him the time.

He swooped down toward the Grootling's back, slung one arm around him, and held on tight, taking advantage of the Grootling's momentum to pull them both forward. He screwed his eyes shut and averted his head. He pumped his boots as fast as they'd go, shoving the Grootling farther, feeling the prickle of the holo and the raw bark against his face.

Please don't fire off spores please don't fire off spores please don't—

They reached the broken window.

I'm sorry, Groot, he wanted to say, but that'd be nowhere near enough. The Grootling would never survive a fall from this height. Not in his weakened state.

Peter let go of the Grootling, and abruptly turned back upright in midair. He hovered just inside the hallway, the Grootling two feet in front of him.

"I am—" The Grootling teetered over the edge, trying to catch his balance.

Peter readied himself to deliver the final kick. He found himself saying it anyway: "I'm *sorry.*"

"—Groot—"

The Grootling fell before Peter even reached him.

For just a second there, he'd stopped trying to catch his balance. He had allowed himself to drop.

And even though the Grootling's words had been too twisted and slurred to translate, Peter knew one thing—

Those last three words hadn't sounded enraged. They had sounded almost like his friend.

Groot? Peter thought.

From deeper into the hallway, a sudden *slam* sounded. Muted voices. The Kree were right behind the door, about to break it down and spill into the hall.

"Quill—" Gamora warned.

He shook off his confusion. Then he grabbed Annay under her arms, pulled her with him outside, and burst straight up.

Toward the roof.

GAMORA dropped to her knees and threw up her hands in surrender a fraction of a moment before the Kree broke into the hallway.

Immediately, four Kree soldiers surrounded her, weapons pointed at her head.

"That's *Gamora,*" one breathed.

Another four soldiers promptly joined the first four.

Gamora kept her head dipped so as to seem harmless. She counted the soldiers by the sound of their footsteps and the glimpses she could see of their shoes. Twelve in total.

She could take all them down in…25 seconds, she thought. Probably less, given how jittery they already were.

But she kept herself still. The bulk of the job was done: Annay was no longer a threat, and the poison Grootling had been eliminated. There was no reason to antagonize the Kree any further. The Guardians could afford to be diplomatic and attempt to salvage a semi-friendly relationship.

Even if it meant Gamora needed to kneel in a puddle of water left behind from the ice Quill's gun had scattered around the hall.

"Captain—Captain Ol-Varr..." the soldier continued, trying to keep her voice even. "What are your orders?"

"May I speak?" Gamora said. She still did not look up. In her experience, people considered her less of a threat when she wasn't looking at them.

Some of the Kree had fanned out. She heard footsteps behind her, in the conference room. Others investigated the hallway. One Kree took decisive steps toward her. Captain Ol-Varr, no doubt.

"The Supreme Elder Council?" he asked.

"Alive. They're in the elevator, currently on the..."

"Ground floor," Rocket said into her ear.

"Ground floor. I helped the Council get to safety before one of the hostiles infiltrating the building could reach them. I'm on your side."

"Are you? There were supposed to be soldiers up here already. Instead, there's a dead private in the hall."

Only one, Gamora thought. *If it'd been me, there'd be a carpet of them.*

Her voice was neutral as she answered. "The reprogrammed security bots were responsible for that body. Ask Captain Mari-Kee; he's one of hers. She'll confirm. She and the other soldiers are in the second elevator. Unharmed." Mostly.

"Hm."

"May I stand?"

"Couldn't stop you if I wanted to, could I?"

She would've shrugged, but the motion might set off the nervous soldiers around her.

"Sure. Stand." Captain Ol-Varr sighed. "You're saying they were after the Council? Who is *they?* And where are they now?"

"The *who* is a *Flora colossus.* He's the same species as my teammate, Groot, although they are unrelated. A holo disguised this *Flora colossus* as a Kree private." Slowly, Gamora rose to her feet, raising her hands high to keep the soldiers semi-comfortable. "I don't know who he was working for or with. He was responsible for the incident at the park today. He could shoot out poison spores. He was the main threat, so we focused on him instead of possible accomplices."

It was a half-truth. But identifying the attacker as an offshoot of one of the Guardians' own members—well, that wouldn't help anything.

"Okay, that's the who," Captain Ol-Varr said. "And the *where?*"

Gamora pointed at the window with one raised hand. A small gesture. It was enough for a soldier to her right to suck in a breath and tighten his grip on his weapon.

He didn't shoot. He'd been close, though. Gamora glanced at him sideways and raised one eyebrow.

"You're saying you tossed this creature outside?" Captain Ol-Varr looked between her and the window.

"Yes. You should be able to see his body on the ground. He may still be wearing the holo."

"That's funny. Because I just looked down there, and I didn't see any body. No blood, either. Not even splinters."

Gamora looked up sharply. She'd seen the Grootling go over the edge. If he wasn't down there…

She decided to give up coddling Ol-Varr's twitchy little soldiers. She shot up from the floor and kicked off from the wall. A moment later she stood at the edge of the hall, looking down through the open window.

Behind her, two shots went off. They hit the wall or floor, judging from the sound of their impact. Captain Ol-Varr barked a reprimand.

Amateurs.

She studied the ground, wind tugging at her hair.

No holo-Kree body.

No Grootling splinters.

"Guys?" Gamora said, one hand raised to her earpiece. "We have a problem."

46

THREE glass-tube walkways connected Porovi Hall, where Rocket had been working from, and Addil Hall, where Drax had helped evacuating the DiMavi prayer group from the basement and where Gamora and Quill had taken care of Annay.

Right now, the one connecting the buildings' fifth floors was most important. Rocket stood just inside Porovi Hall, looking down the fifth-floor walkway toward the other building.

"That ain't good."

In the center of the walkway, the ceiling had shattered, leaving it wide open to the air. Glass glittering in the sun lay scattered across the transparent floor.

Something had crashed through.

Some*one* had crashed through.

Rocket crept down the walkway toward the gap in the ceiling. Wind soared inside and ruffled his fur. He looked up toward Addil Hall, squinting against the sun. Up there: One window was missing. That had to be where the Elder Council had been located.

By now, Gamora would've been able to shake off the Kree attempting to interrogate her. Quill was zipping through the air between the buildings, running every scan he could to find the Grootling. He'd just come from the roof, where he'd cuffed and secured the still-unconscious Annay. They needed to keep her out of sight from the Kree until the Guardians could pick her up.

If the Grootling had fallen straight down from that missing window, he'd have smashed into a thousand pieces on the surface below. Somehow he must have directed the fall instead. Maybe used his vines to shove himself away from the building, toward the walkway.

Rocket's boots crunched on broken glass. He kicked it aside, sifting through it. He found nothing more than two snapped-off branches and a few pieces of bark. The fall had damaged the Grootling, but he'd gotten right back up again. He could've escaped into either one of the buildings. Heck, he could even have climbed back up through the hole in the walkway and somehow made it to the ground.

They'd lost him.

They'd lost him even worse than before, in fact. Now they had no idea where he might be headed.

"Great job, Quill," Rocket growled. "Fan-*tas*-tic."

"Yeahhhh, my bad," Quill said. "Now let's go find him."

GAMORA sped through the hallways of Addil Hall. If the Grootling was inside, he was likely still in disguise. That meant he could easily blend in with the Kree soldiers occupying the building.

Gamora had seen the Grootling sacrifice himself, before Quill could kick him out the window. But even if the Grootling had temporarily broken through the brainwashing, it clearly hadn't stuck. Otherwise, he wouldn't be trying so damn hard to stay out of the Guardians' sight.

"Has anyone been in touch with Kiya or the other Grootlings?" Quill asked, his voice clipped through the comms system.

"Why?" Gamora didn't slow down. She yanked open doors, searching office after office.

"Because I'm outside and seeing our ship approach the courtyard, and the rest of us are accounted for. Hang on, let me—Kiya?"

After a few moments, her voice came through, sounding hesitant. "Is this a bad time to talk?"

"Very," Rocket said instantly.

"I am Groot!" a voice chirruped on Kiya's end.

Other Grootlings on the ship agreed: "I am Groot! I am Groot."

"We have lost the poison Grootling," Drax said. "We do not know his location, what he is doing, or which commands he may still be following. In addition, the evacuations are nearly complete and the security system nearly defeated, which will allow the Kree military to focus fully on hampering our efforts."

"Yeah, we're doing *great,*" Rocket said.

"However, none of it prevents us from talking," Drax finished.

"What's going on, Kiya?" Gamora asked.

"I'm near Porovi," she said, her words rushed. "I'm flying the ship. The Collector came and I didn't know what else do to do and—"

"The Collector?" Rocket said. "What? How? How'd he find you?"

"Are you okay?" Gamora asked.

"Are the Groots okay?" Rocket went on.

"I am Groot," a Grootling answered assuringly.

"Is the Collector following you?" Drax asked.

"No, I threw him from the ship when we were right inside city limits, but—"

"You *what?* Awesome," Quill said. "I need you to stay close. Keep an eye on the courtyard. If you see the Grootling, let us know immediately. He might still have a Kree holo on, but if not... Rocket, tell her how to hover the ship in place. We may need a sudden escape."

They went silent, switching to a private channel. Gamora was glad: She didn't need to hear Rocket giving the girl a none-too-patient blow-by-blow on how to switch from autopilot to manual without crashing into the crowd. She was already struggling to direct her mind away from the thought of the Collector coming for Kiya. How had he found her? Maybe Ka-Lenn *had* managed to contact the Collector, but he couldn't have known the ship's location.

Annay had known, though.

And she would've wanted them distracted.

Gamora's jaw tightened. She needed to focus. "Quill. I don't think the Grootling is inside Addil Hall."

"I cannot find the Grootling in Porovi Hall, either." Drax sounded displeased.

"The Kree are keeping a close eye on everyone passing through. They would've noticed if a lone private unable to speak in full sentences came by."

"He's probably out here." Quill said. "In this mess he'd blend in easily. Oh—crap. Be riiight back."

Gamora cocked her head. That probably wasn't good. She cut short her search of a massive staff kitchen and ran toward the windows. There: The Guardians' ship was hovering above the podium, across the courtyard.

And there: another ship—smaller, sleeker, likely uncrewed—chasing after Quill. He was horizontal, his boots firing at full force, his eyes flaring red. He bent in midair to send a flare of flame at the ship behind him, then swerved underneath the nearest skyway, off to the side of the courtyard.

"The Kree are slow on the uptake today," Gamora grumbled. "Haven't they realized yet that we're trying to save their asses?"

"Focus on finding the Grootling!" Quill called. "I can manage!"

One problem with that command: Quill's helmet and its array of scanners was the best tool they had to find the Grootling. Gamora took a second to analyze Quill's and the ship's trajectories: He was moving in circles to try to lose his tail, but she had a hunch where he was headed.

Gamora bolted back into the hallway. She was on the fifth floor, near the transparent walkway that the Grootling had crashed into. She ran to the walkway's center, shards of glass cracking under her boots, the sky open above her.

As she'd thought: Quill was staying near the skyways and buildings, where his maneuverability might be an asset. He shot past like a bullet, offering a salute as he went.

Gamora leapt.

The Kree guard ship—she recognized the type; uncrewed and remote-controlled—flashed past. As soon as she landed on its hull, she began to lose her footing. She pinned down her sword, cleaving the metal to hold herself in place. Wind came at her full force. The ship turned sharply to follow Quill, heading back toward the courtyard. She took a moment to look down. The courtyard was crammed full, but still more people were being evacuated from the buildings. Some left in groups, huddling close together. Some left on their own, clutching bleeding body parts as they ran.

(Those lasers firing at Quill were bothersome. She crawled upside down along the bottom of the ship and took the weapons out with fast, decisive slashes of her sword.)

The crowd was a colorful array of blue Kree, pink Kree, green DiMavi, and a handful of other species. Several heads craned to look up at the ships.

Other people shoved each other, pushing across the courtyard toward what looked like designated shuttle landing sites. Two shuttles sat there now, but they were small—barely able to hold 40 people apiece. At this rate, the courtyard was filling up faster than it was emptying out.

(Whoever was directing the ship had become aware of her presence. Abandoning the pursuit of Quill, the ship zig-zagged wildly, spinning overhead once, twice—trying to throw her off. Kids' stuff.)

Kree military were herding people into position, directing them to either side of the courtyard—separating the civilians, Gamora noted. It was as if they'd drawn a line from the ceremonial stage down through the courtyard, keeping the civilians on one side, and using the other side to give the remaining military enough space to regroup and to treat the wounded.

(Gamora stalked forward along the ship's hull, ignoring the various weak spots. She didn't want to bring the ship down over all these people—only direct it away.)

Across the courtyard, a sudden movement among the civilians caught her eye. A flash of a striped tail, a gun swinging by the figure's side. Rocket leapt from head to head, occasionally pausing and standing straight up to study the crowd, then scampering away again.

(It was time to end this. Uncrewed ships still typically had manual-override controls inside. Gamora planted herself right on top of the ship and thrust her sword down, working to open a hole.)

Drax had made it to the courtyard. He was storming his way through the crowd, head whipping from left to right, searching for the Grootling.

"Thanks for the distraction, Gamora." Quill hovered above the crowd, the red eyes of his helmet scanning the military personnel. "I can only scan three soldiers at a time—and they keep *moving around*. By the way, Kiya, was my ship always like that?"

"Um. You mean the hole?" she said.

"I mean the hole."

"…It was there before."

"Huh," he said. "Must've missed it."

Gamora slipped into the Kree shuttle through the opening she'd carved, landing on the floor with a thud. She'd been right: manual-override controls, right in front of her. Her hands raced over the dashboard, flicked the holos that came up, and tore back the thruster. Within moments, she had control of the shuttle. She set it to hover in midair not far from the Guardians' ship and clambered back out, striding across the hull.

As she drew nearer to the Guardians' ship, she saw what Quill had been talking about. The Collector must've blown a hole through their cargo bay doors to get to Kiya. Four—no, five—Grootlings crouched low in the opening, holding onto each other to keep from falling out as they scanned the ground—presumably for a sign of the poison Grootling.

"Kiya blew a hole in the ship?" Rocket said. "Typical." Gamora spotted him in the crowd below. He was speeding up, bouncing from skull to skull and leaving behind a trail of cringing civilians. "Hey. Hey! Near the stage. That Kree's movements look familiar."

"Scanning him now," Quill said.

The Kree soldier Rocket had indicated moved strangely, the way someone much taller might, or someone severely injured. He seemed confused— looking around him, sometimes hesitating, then rushing forward again. He climbed onto the stage, ignoring commands from the military officials clustered on the other side.

If Annay had given the Grootling a preprogrammed command—and she must have, for him to strike out on his own like this—Gamora would put money on it being "take out the highest-ranking Kree you can."

This qualified.

"I see him." She breathed deep. "Take the shot."

She hated to say the words. If the Grootling had been shaking off the brainwashing, maybe they could talk to him and get through—

But not fast enough to stop him from hurting people.

"Groot!" Rocket dashed toward the Grootling, running across the heads of the crowd. "Groot!"

The disguised Grootling stood on stage, facing the military side. He spread his arms.

Quill aimed and fired. A blast of ice slammed into the Grootling's chest. It knocked him back, off balance. The holo around him flickered rapidly, alternating between Kree soldier and battered Grootling.

Then the holo fizzled out completely, leaving only the Grootling.

He stretched again, looking dazed, arms wide—

The lieutenants were climbing onstage, running over to tackle him—

"They're in the way!" Quill yelled, flying down like a spear. "I can't— *Rocket, get away!*"

Rocket abruptly stopped a few feet away from the stage.

The Grootling had gotten turned around. He faced the civilian crowd now, roaring, his voice splintering. He didn't even seem to see Rocket.

"Groot?" Rocket shrank back.

"Don't!" Kiya said, her voice shrill over comms. "I can't stop them!"

Them?

Gamora's head snapped up. There, in the open cargo bay of the Guardians' ship. Where she'd counted five Grootlings before, now they filled the entire opening. Adults, saplings, and every stage in between. The smaller Grootlings clung to the older ones' legs to steady themselves against the wind. The Groots peered past the edge of the ship to the scene on the ground.

They looked determined.

Gamora knew what that determination meant, that tension in their legs. Their fixation on the stage right beneath them. They were going to jump.

She wanted to shout at them to stop, the way Kiya was doing.

They couldn't survive a drop like this.

They would lose themselves.

But if they *didn't* jump—if they walked away when they could help— they would lose themselves anyway. They wouldn't be Groot.

They wouldn't be a Guardian.

Groot couldn't give that up so easily. Gamora understood that with a sudden sharpness. She wouldn't have been able to give it up, either.

The Grootling on stage knocked the approaching Kree lieutenants aside. "I am Groot! I am *Groot!*"

The air in front of him shattered into glittering spores.

Just a few feet away, perched atop a DiMavi's shoulders, Rocket froze.

Nowhere to hide, no time to run—

"Rocket!" Gamora screamed.

And the Grootlings in the cargo bay leapt.

47

THE GROOTS could block the spores.

Their duplicate stood on the stage below them. The spores spun toward the crowd and Rocket, irreversible and unstoppable. Their friends were scattered around the courtyard, down in the crowds and up in the air, too far to help.

But the Groots were close—so close they could jump. If enough of them landed on that stage, if they spread out fast and gathered every scrap of energy they had left—maybe they could catch and block enough of the spores to make a difference.

The Groots had changed, these past weeks and days. Shards of memories had slipped into nothingness. Traits and habits had faded. Bit by bit, each of them had twisted, shifted further away from who they had been and from the others around them.

They hadn't felt apart. They hadn't felt separated.

They had felt like themselves, only *less*.

But even with everything that had changed, three things had stayed the same:

Their desire to help.

Their love of people.

Rocket.

They leapt.

As they fell—air rushing past them, screams and gasps below, gripping each other's shoulders and hands tight—for the first time in weeks, they felt—

They felt a little bit *more* again.

Rocket was down there. They could see him as they fell. He was a small statue of fear, his ears pressed flat to the sides of his head, eyes wide and fixed on the Groot on stage. His mouth moved in a quiet, frightened question: *Groot?*

The spores glittered and spun and shone, a snowstorm in miniature.

The civilians in the crowd didn't realize the danger. As the spores whirled their way, they watched with a mixture of uncertainty and curiosity. DiMavi and Kree, adults and children, each of them alive and bright and beautiful.

Rocket did realize the danger. Every inch of him showed it.

The Groots realized, too. As they fell, they feared and loved, all at once, all the same, their minds surging closer and aligning for just this moment.

And the hands they held slid into one. They slipped into each other, grew toward each other, legs twisting into one and arms stretching into one and minds spinning into one—

—*flashes of the fighting pits—the greenhouse on Pirinida—the Collector's smile—sitting on the kitchen counter beside Gamora—Kiya's hands—*

—*vines around Drax in the back room of the bar, depositing him in the chute—*

All of it whirled together.

They might not have *felt* apart—but Groot realized, now, that he had been. He'd been more apart than ever, apart and alone and separate, and nothing, nothing like the way he felt now:

more

and

whole

and

strong

and

him

Groot landed on the very edge of the stage on two massive feet, bending his legs to absorb the blow.

"I!"

He stood straight, tossed his head back.

"Am!"

He spread his arms, stretched them wide, grew them thick.

"Groot!"

Twigs sprang to life across his body. They grew along his shoulders, raced across the length of his arms; they sprouted from his sides and chest; they twined out from his legs. He was a forest. He was a wall. He was a shield. Each twig sprouted another, coiled farther, forked off into more, burst into wild, curled leaves.

The spores settled on him gently, harmlessly. They nestled in the cracks of his bark. They lingered in the leaves. They sank into him and faded into nothing.

The air no longer glittered.

Across from him, the other Groot stood. He was so small—or perhaps Groot himself was now so large. He'd grown; he was twice his normal size, perhaps bigger. He couldn't tell, he just knew he felt *alive*—

"I am Groot," the other Groot said, defiant, unsure. Confused.

"I am Groot," Groot returned. He stepped forward. He crouched, letting their eyes meet.

"I am Groot—"

He embraced the other Groot, pulling him in tight.

"I...am..."

The other Groot's voice was muffled. Groot's bark grew into his. Twigs wrapped around him, braiding together and drawing him in close, close, closer.

Groot felt an initial spark of resistance, as though he were being pushed away. Their minds had strayed apart. He reached out further, and embraced those differences, too.

They sank into each other.

"Buddy?" a small voice behind him said.

Groot turned.

Rocket climbed onto the stage. His ears were pointed upright again, but his tail dipped low, and his eyes were wary.

"It's really you? It's all of you?"

Groot crouched. Slowly, the branches he'd grown across his body drew back in, shrinking down and smoothing over.

He flicked Rocket's nose.

"We are Groot."

48

PETER shot straight up, past the walls of Addil Hall toward its roof.

As he went, he watched the courtyard below. The Kree were continuing the evacuation, even with the biggest danger passed. He listened in on Gamora, who was on the stage trying to convince the generals to let the Guardians take Groot with them. The Kree insisted he stay to be quarantined and interrogated.

Groot made the decision for them.

He nodded at the generals, smiling. He took hold of Gamora with one oversized hand and Drax with the other—Rocket had already settled in on his shoulder—and stretched his arms high enough to reach the Guardians' ship still floating overhead.

It seemed to take no effort at all. Even when Peter saw small flashes of red and orange bouncing off Groot—the Kree were shooting at his legs—he shrugged it off.

"Rocket?" Peter said through his communicator. "I want to talk to Captain Mari-Kee or Captain Ol-Varr once I'm on board. Find a way to get hold of them."

Groot might be unfazed, but Peter would still prefer the Guardians to take their leave without being chased by laser beams and energy blasts—let alone a warship.

The team would stick around Vadin for at least another day, and there was plenty of time to sit down and talk through the Guardians' role in what happened. They had saved the Elder Council and attempted to cooperate with the captains, and everyone in that courtyard had seen the Groot from the ship defending against the attacker. Those things should buy the team some good will.

For now, the Kree needed to focus on the panicky civilians in their courtyard. The Guardians had a couple of things to take care of.

Like Annay, to start with.

Peter deactivated his helmet and slowed as he reached the roof. Annay sat right where he'd left her, cuffed to one of the transmitter masts that stretched up from the building. She'd woken up.

She watched him, her head resting back against the mast. He'd left her in the shade. It turned her skin dark and her eyes shimmery.

"Hey, you," she drawled.

"'Sup." He landed a couple of feet in front of her.

"Still up for renting those motorcycles?"

He walked over, crouched by her side, and started to uncuff her. The wind was fierce up here—tugging at their clothes, tangling their hair, thinning their voices.

Annay's head turned, her eyes on Peter's even as he kept his averted. "I'm guessing you saved the day," she said. It wasn't quite a question.

"It's kind of what we do." A moment before releasing the cuffs, he paused. "You know fighting me now would just be embarrassing for you, don't you?"

"Don't worry, Earth boy. I've got more sense than that."

He considered her for a moment. The white hair, the round face and sharp eyes. She looked tired in a way he wouldn't have been able to picture earlier that day. "Yeah. You did seem sensible."

"I should've stuck with the hands-off approach." She sighed. "Are you handing me over to my government?"

"Your favorite people. Looks like we're visiting the embassy after all." He unclicked the cuffs.

She scrabbled to her feet and offered him a wry smile. "You gonna come see me in prison, at least?"

A massive shape rose up from Peter's left. The Guardians' ship was approaching. Peter caught a glimpse of the bridge—Rocket grinning wildly in the pilot's seat, and behind him, the unmistakeable shape of Groot leaning in to peer through the viewport.

Peter held up a hand in greeting.

So did Groot.

Drax, in the navigator's seat, thumped Groot on the back and exclaimed something Peter couldn't hear.

As the ship rose to hover overhead, Peter looked back at Annay to answer her question. "Yeah…murder? Actually a big turn-off." He stepped closer, grabbing her tightly around the waist.

He paused. "So—don't read anything into this part."

He kicked off from the ground, straight up toward his ship.

If only this meant the Guardians were done for the day.

THE SHIP was a flarking mess.

They left the DiMavi embassy behind, flying their busted ship out of the city to find somewhere they wouldn't be disturbed for a while.

The desert seemed like a good place.

Space seemed like a better place, Rocket thought, but the gaping hole in the cargo bay kinda prevented that. And they had to stay on Vadin for a while longer anyway, to clean up their mess. Rocket would still have preferred the novelty of having their spaceship actually be spaceworthy—especially with the Collector out there. It was always possible the Kree would change their minds and come after them, too.

Either way, it was time to go get Kiya.

Rocket stomped around the ship, eventually finding her in the med bay, where—for the first time—she didn't have any Grootlings in front of her to study. She sat cross-legged on one of the seats, pondering the wall.

He entered the room, watching her warily. "What're you doing?"

"Thinking." She looked up. "How's Groot?"

"He's fine." Groot was better than fine, in truth—he was strong and alive and remembered every single event the Guardians asked him about. Ever since he'd boarded the ship, he'd been watching the rest of the team with the broadest, stupidest, most embarrassing smile on his face.

Rocket had kinda liked seeing that smile.

Kiya frowned. "We're slowing down. Are we landing?"

"'Course we're landing! We gotta assess the damage, don't we? You blew a hole in the ship."

"The Collector did that," she said. "The bomb I set off to blast him outside only left that *little* crater in the floor."

She looked nervously in the direction of the bridge. Rocket had a hunch why she was suddenly so anxious about landing. She was worried about the Collector coming after them. Wherever Kiya had dropped Tivan, he'd probably found a way back to his ship by now.

It almost made Rocket feel bad for her.

Almost.

"I don't care who did it, but it's done, so we're stuck on Vadin, all right? How're we going to get into space?" Rocket crossed his arms. "We ain't. That's how. Unless we wanna all get sucked into a vacuum and die horrifically. Do you want that? Didn't think so."

She glared at him. "Fine. We're landing. I get it." She dropped her hands in her lap and took a breath. "He shouldn't have been able to absorb the poison Grootling."

"Say what now?"

"The rest of the Groots—they saw their duplicate seconds away from murdering their best friend and a crowd of civilians. If they all felt an emotion strongly enough—the exact same thing at the exact same time—it might've been enough for them to sync up and merge while falling."

"But after that? The merged Groot and the poison Grootling? I bet that whatever they were feeling at the time, it didn't line up. My theory—"

There she went again, with the *theories*.

"—Groot is stronger. The Grootlings needed their minds aligned perfectly because they were too weakened to cope with any mental resistance. Groot, at full strength, doesn't have that problem.

"Which is a good thing, because I'd been wondering how to elicit an emotion strong enough to eventually sync him up with the remaining Grootlings—Ka-Lenn's and the ones Tivan still has. Maybe someone could've pulled a gun on you. Damsel Rocket in distress seemed to do the trick before."

Oh, he really did not like this girl.

Which made the next part a little more fun.

"Yeah, great, nice theory." He half-turned in the doorway and gestured for her to come with. "I'm gonna check out that big flarking hole in the ship, and you just volunteered to be my assistant. C'mon."

For a moment he thought she might argue or make another smartass comment—but a flicker of fear crossed her face, and she climbed to her feet to follow him. Probably figured that getting the ship up and running again soon would be in her best interest.

After they landed in the desert, safely away from civilization, Rocket kept Kiya busy for a while. He made her stand outside in the evening wind, which whisked dirt around their feet and blew a fine layer of sand into the open cargo bay. He had her take notes and hold up big metal plates, allowing Rocket to crawl underneath and check out the damage.

Then Quill's voice sounded through the ship's comms.

"We have incoming."

Kiya started. "Kree?" she said, but she didn't sound like she believed it.

"We picked up a burst of teleportation energy."

No elaboration needed.

"Get inside," Quill said. "We'll shake him off."

Rocket shook his head. "We had to shut down the whole ship to run these inspections safely. By the time we get her moving, we won't be able to shake him."

"What's your bright idea then?" Quill sounded frustrated. "Camouflage the ship with leaves and hope he won't notice us?"

Rocket's eyes met Kiya's. "I'll take her with me on foot," he said. "Let the Collector chase you away from here, then tell him she ain't on the ship. Let him run a scan. He'll lose interest. We'll meet up you-know-where."

Quill was silent. Then: "Kiya?"

Rocket jogged outside, giving her an impatient look. She was sweating, leaving little trails of deep green on her dust-covered face. If she didn't cooperate, there were alternative options—one of them dangled by his side. It'd be easier for everyone if she just came along nicely.

"All right," she said. "Let's go."

He ran away from the ship, keeping low. They'd landed in a different part of the desert this time—more rocky and uneven, with knobby trees and prickly bushes growing low to the ground.

Behind Rocket, Kiya's footsteps crunched on dead leaves and dried grass. Then she screeched to a halt. "He's already—"

Oh, so she'd noticed the shuttle. It was parked closer than Rocket had expected.

Time to play.

He scooted to the side, getting some distance from Kiya before she could get any funny ideas about putting that training of hers to use. He pointed his blaster at her. With his other hand, he fumbled for his communicator. He'd hooked it up to the ship earlier. One tap, and doors all over the Guardians' ship firmly locked, from the bridge to their quarters to the emergency hatches.

Kiya stood petrified. She stared at the Collector's shuttle.

The Collector himself stepped onto the charred earth. He still wore his fur coat, despite the heat.

"Got a clean cape, Tivan?" Rocket called out. "How many spares you have on board? 'Cause I saw the footage of her blowing you out that hole, and that looked real painful."

"What's past is past," the Collector said. His eyes were on Kiya. "I won't hold it against you."

She was still staring. Rocket saw her legs move—tensing up, as if she was about to attack or flee. He waved the blaster to get her attention. "Nuh-uh."

"Rocket?" Drax said through their comms. "What are you doing?"

Rocket plucked out his earpiece and flicked it away. It bounced against a rocky outcrop, onto the dry ground.

The Collector raised an eyebrow in mild interest.

"Noisy teammates," Rocket explained.

"Rocket!" Drax's voice came from the ship this time, amplified through the speakers all over. His voice carried easily through the massive hole. "Do not do this!"

The Collector was looking up past Rocket. Rocket peered over his shoulder to see what was so interesting. The sun glinted against the bridge. Gamora and Groot stood pressed against the glass, watching.

"I am Groot!"

"Rocket," Gamora said sharply. "Put down that weapon. Take Kiya and run. We'll delay him. It's not too late."

"Interesting." The Collector squinted at Gamora, then looked back to Kiya. "The two of you have grown close, have you not? Marvelous. You will be able to imitate her even more effectively."

"Did you hack into my krutacking ship?" Quill yelled, followed by heavy thudding. "*Open these doors!*"

That thudding in the background had to be Drax slamming into the bridge hatch. Rocket didn't have a whole lot of time.

Rocket scratched his head. "Look, Tivan, I'm gonna catch flak over this, so how about we get it done. Do you have my Groots?"

Finally, Kiya's face snapped to him. "You—you—"

"Me. Me." If she kept this up, he might actually start to feel guilty. She looked real upset.

"*I just got away from him!*" she screamed.

"My Groots," Rocket repeated.

"The girl," the Collector said.

"That's cute, but no. The Groots first. I showed you mine, you show me yours."

The Collector studied Kiya, as if confirming she was really there. "Your enhancements can't be functioning optimally, and prying out my tracker by yourself may have left lasting damage. Won't you let me patch you up?"

She'd been sweating before. Now, she was crying.

Thud—thud—

The viewport showed a glint moving inside the bridge. Had to be Gamora's sword.

"I'm *waiting*," Rocket said.

"Very well." The Collector gestured at his shuttle with a flourish. As if on cue—that man had *excellent* timing—the Groots climbed out. The first was the one they'd talked to in the arboretum. Rocket had seen the next three on holo, when the Guardians had asked for Kiya's location.

"Hi, guys," Rocket said.

They squinted at Kiya and gave Rocket a questioning look.

"I am Groot?"

"Ehhh, I'll explain later," he said. Knowing Groot, he wouldn't exactly *like* the explanation, but Rocket would deal with that once Kiya was on the shuttle. For now, he wanted all the Groots safely behind him. "Get in the ship. There's a big hole, lots of angry howling from the speakers, can't miss it. Trust me on this, guys."

They started to walk through the dry foliage toward the ship, casting glances at Kiya, the Collector, and Rocket. The other Guardians were still on the ship, yelling and bashing at the windows and doors. Rocket did *not* want to know what that bridge hatch looked like by now. It had to be seconds from breaking open. Drax did not mess around.

"The girl, please," the Collector said sharply.

Rocket wiggled his gun at Kiya. "Get on that shuttle. I don't wanna have to ruin the merchandise, but I *will* shoot you. Somewhere non-lethal.

It'll hurt a lot."

"I am Groot…?"

Kiya looked at Rocket, her face twisted in hatred. Her gaze dropped to his blaster.

She walked forward, her legs stiff, and climbed into the shuttle.

"Pleasure doing business." The Collector dropped into a curtsy.

Moments later, the shuttle teleported away, and they were gone.

49

AS SOON as the doors clicked open, Drax was outside.

He tuned out the yelling from the others. He had a single goal: It was small, furry, and traitorous—and it would soon be grievously injured.

"Rocket!" he bellowed.

He stormed through the Grootlings standing uncertainly by the edge of the ship. Spun toward Rocket, sending hot sand and crumbling rock spraying, and went straight for his target.

Rocket was holstering his blaster, walking back with a skip in his step and hum in his voice. At the sight of Drax, he slowed down.

"Look," he said, "Drax—"

Then he said nothing, because Drax had his hand around the twisty little rodent's neck and was lifting him up. Rocket squirmed and flailed in the air, kicking with his hind legs.

"Ggkkhhh—ghh—"

"You. Sold. Her. Out!"

"Agghhk—"

Furious little nails scrabbled at Drax's skin. They did no harm.

"You know what he did to her!" He slammed Rocket onto the hull of the ship. "She is a *child,* and you—"

Rocket's claws did Drax no harm; Gamora's roundhouse kick to his skull, however, did.

Drax stumbled aside, his grip on Rocket loosening.

"Release him!" she said. "Now!"

"He sold *Kiya.* Of all people, Gamora, I had thought *you* would protect her."

"Let us explain," she demanded.

"No explanation could excuse this." Drax glared at her, fury burning him up inside. Rocket's betrayal of the group—of the girl—was one thing. Gamora taking Rocket's side was too much. "To sink so low—"

"He didn't sell her out! Let us explain."

Quill and Groot came running out the ship, too. "Drax, it's a setup!"

"I am Groot!"

Drax shook his head. "I know what I saw!" Kiya had stepped on board that ship with the Collector and teleported away. The scorchmarks from the teleportation energy still lingered on the rocky ground. Nothing about that could be a setup.

Rocket squirmed within his grip.

"We're getting her back, Drax. We have a plan."

Drax glared at Quill, nostrils flaring.

He would hear this plan of theirs.

"Let Rocket go," Gamora said. "If our explanation isn't enough, you can always murder him later."

Rocket made a strangled sound of offense.

Drax hesitated. Then he bent over and set Rocket down. Rocket collapsed against the cracked ground, reaching for his throat and coughing as though his lungs were preparing to exit his body.

Drax crossed his arms. "Explain."

Two Grootlings crouched by Rocket's side, steadying him as he coughed.

"You couldn't've—asked me that—'fore?" Rocket said.

"If this was a setup, it was…convincing."

Quill looked exasperated. "That's the whole point."

"You all knew this?" Drax looked from teammate to teammate.

"We couldn't tell you," Quill said. "We didn't have much time, and historically speaking, your acting skills are not great. The Collector knows our tricks. We didn't want him to get suspicious."

"*Ex-plain.*"

Rocket was still hacking and coughing. "You got my fur all gross," he said, pointing accusingly at the smear he'd left on the filthy hull of the ship. "Kiya didn't know, either, all right? She could've given the plan away too easily. It needed to look convincing to the Collector."

"Actually…" Quill said.

"You told her?" Rocket glared. "I thought we all agreed! Wasn't worth the risk!"

Gamora looked unimpressed. "I agreed it was risky. I didn't agree not to tell her. I was *not* handing her to Tivan without her consent."

"It's only for a li'l bit." Rocket turned his glare on Quill. "You went along with it? Wusses."

"I went along with it because I agreed. Besides, have you met that girl? She'd have fought like hell if she'd thought it was real." Quill plopped onto the firm ground, legs crossed, pressing two fingers against his skull. "Okay, Drax, look. We needed a long-term solution. We—and Kiya—can't run from Tivan forever."

"Agreed," Drax said.

"Remember our buddy Ka-Lenn? He's dealt with the Collector regularly, and he's on the Kree Supreme Science Council, specializing in weaponry; these things have to be related. The Collector loves old weaponry, with a special status or history, as well as brand-new weapons. Unique ones. Prototypes."

Drax narrowed his eyes. He could not tell where this was going.

"At the hospital, Ka-Lenn was especially interested in Kiya's implants. Not in what kind of implants they were, but in how she was getting along with them. He helped us get away from hospital security, then saved our asses again from the Accusers. We thought he was helping us in order to keep us away from the Kree, so we couldn't rat him out. But what if he was keeping *Kiya* away? If he'd secretly sold the Collector high-tech Kree prototypes to enhance Kiya with, he wouldn't want her to fall into the hands of his fellow Kree. It could be traced back to him—and the Kree get very territorial about their technology. Can't have one of their own selling it off."

"I couldn't identify the implants' tech, but it did have a Kree flavor to it," Rocket said. "The implants were unmarked, which is unusual. They were elegant, but unfinished. Once I thought *Kree prototypes,* everything fit."

Gamora took over. She leaned against the side of the ship, her arms crossed, her head in the shade. "Rocket set up a trade: the other Grootlings for Kiya."

"I told the Collector we were on Vadin, no more than that," Rocket said. "Except I didn't know Annay was trying to slow us down by tipping off both the Accusers and the Collector about us. She must've let him know the location of the ship, so he could see through those bogus tips and find Kiya way sooner than we'd thought—once I confirmed what planet we were on." He shrugged. "My bad."

Quill nodded. "The Kree won't tolerate prototypes being in Kiya's or the Collector's possession. The Collector is fine duking it out with us—he enjoys it, even—but he won't be so happy when we sic the entire Kree Empire on him. There's an entire universe to collect; he can put his time to better use than fighting the Kree."

"The Kree get Kiya back, yank out her implants, and presto." Rocket climbed to his feet and dusted himself off. Dirt billowed away in clouds. "Better yet, we'll have done the Kree yet another favor after saving their asses just now."

"Which gives us leverage," Gamora said. "We need it, to keep Kiya safe."

"I see," Drax said slowly. "Where is Ka-Lenn now?"

"Oh, I tied him up and stuffed him in a closet." Rocket fluffed up his tail. "Didn't want him warning the Collector it was a setup. The Kree'll probably find him soon. He'll make up something convincing-sounding—he's too scared to lose his job."

"And you believe the Kree will rescue Kiya?" Drax said.

Quill nodded. "I'm about to contact the Accusers with what we know. They're honorable. They'll want their technology back, but I don't think they would harm Kiya. What crimes could they accuse her of? She's a teenage girl. She didn't steal the tech, didn't buy it, didn't want it, didn't even knowingly keep it hidden from the Kree—she had no idea it was theirs to begin with. I trust the Accusers to get her out of Tivan's museum alive, probably within a matter of hours. If they don't hand Kiya over to us after that, we can always pick a fight with them. I'd go up against Kree over the Collector any day."

Drax mulled it over.

Then he uncrossed his arms and crouched in the sand in front of Rocket, who glanced at him suspiciously. "I had thought you capable of selling out the girl. I owe you an apology, my small friend."

"Yeah, you do."

Gamora stepped closer. "*Would* you be capable, Rocket?"

"I'm capable of a whole lot, Gam."

"Yes. But would you have done it?"

Rocket's eyes narrowed as if it were a trick question. Finally, he shrugged. "Nah. Probably not."

"No?"

"She's your family, ain't she?"

"In a way."

"Well, I'm part of this stupid team, so I guess that makes her my family, too. And I don't sell out family," As an afterthought, he grumbled, "Just don't expect me to always *like* 'em."

"That is reasonable." Drax extended his hand. "I apologize."

They shook on it, Rocket's hand dwarfed in Drax's.

"Aw, good, we're all friends again," Quill said, clapping. "Now, if you'll excuse me, I have to make a few calls."

THE NEXT morning, Ka-Lenn stopped by the Vadin workyard early.

"Don't make that face, man," Peter said.

"It *smells,*" Ka-Lenn complained.

"You think?" Peter glanced at Gamora, who sat beside him on a gleaming stack of stirium sheets. She merely shrugged in response. The workyard stretched past her. Rows of ships stood parked haphazardly around the yard, bordered by a massive multilayered warehouse. Helper bots fussed back and forth, fetching requested supplies and tapping automated cranes into action. Peter supposed the workyard did sort of stink—of fuel, of metal dust, of grease, of aeroserin, and more—but he enjoyed it. It was a smell of promise.

Not far away, Rocket and Groot zipped around the ship, projecting holos of different cargo bay entryways to see which fit best and which features they wanted. Groot had merged with the Collector's Grootlings the day before. The process had only taken a few seconds.

Gamora focused on Ka-Lenn. "Tell us about Kiya."

He looked at her flatly. He had not been too impressed when Peter had suggested meeting up. Apparently, he took "getting stuffed in a closet" personally.

Still, they had enough to discuss that it wasn't hard to convince him.

"I offered you proof yesterday," he said, annoyed, "that she was recovered alive—"

"That's a low standard to meet," she interrupted. "How is she? Where is she? When can we see her?"

"I thought we had an understanding," Peter said. "From what I hear, Kiya isn't the only part of the Collector's museum the Kree retrieved after recognizing the technology as their own. A tip like that should be worth something."

Ka-Lenn rubbed his forehead. "You people are insufferable. Please tell me you'll leave this galaxy the moment that sorry excuse for a ship is fixed."

"That depends on your answer." Gamora stared at him in a way that would've sent lesser men quivering.

"Kiya is fine. She's completely unharmed. Apparently, her first reaction was 'What took you so long?' You must have rubbed off on her."

Peter could've sworn he saw pride in Gamora's face. A twitch of her lips, a glint in her eyes.

Ka-Lenn hopped onto a stack of stirium sheets across from them, drawing up and crossing his legs. "We're not removing Kiya's implants. For one thing, they're too deeply intertwined with her biological functions at this point. It might kill her. For another, we don't particularly *want* to remove them. She's one of the few subjects the grafting process worked well on."

"She's in constant pain," Gamora said.

"The implants failed her more than once," Peter added. "The rest of her body isn't set up for them."

"Only because she escaped too soon. We've talked it over with her. We'll perform a few surgeries to minimize the pain and complete the process. Admittedly, she isn't thrilled, but she agreed. After that, she'll stay in our care."

Peter barked out a laugh. "Yeah, that's not happening."

Ka-Lenn stretched, then slumped back to lean on his arms. He gave Gamora and Peter a once-over. "What are you going to do about it, exactly? We can't safely remove the enhancements, and my colleagues would be very upset if we let our property out of our sight. We could kill her, but she's a valuable subject. And she's agreed to stay, under certain conditions we're still discussing but will likely acquiesce to. I don't see how any of this involves you. Honestly, I'm the one with the right to be upset here: I wanted all of you out of my hair, and instead this child who could rat me out at any moment is going to stick around."

"I want to talk to her," Gamora said.

"That's nice."

"Who's performing the surgery?"

"Me and my team," he said without hesitation. "That means you'll want to keep me intact—I'm the girl's best chance of success."

"Perfect." Up until now, Gamora had been direct, but calm. Now she sounded outright vicious. She leaned in. Her hands wrapped around the edge of the stirium stack, and her eyes settled on Ka-Lenn's. "We have two proposals. The first proposal: If Kiya dies, or *anything* goes wrong during her surgery, I kill you. I don't care if it was an accident. I don't care if it wasn't your fault. I don't care if you spent hours trying to save her life, and it's the biggest regret of your career. I don't care if someone else walks in and shoots her out of the blue, before you can act. If she dies, you die."

"That..." He blinked. "That is tremendously unreasonable."

"Yes," Gamora said, "and it's what's happening. Kiya is inconvenient to you. I won't let you 'accidentally' slip up in surgery and eliminate that problem."

He looked away, glaring at nothing in particular.

"Cheer up, buddy," Peter said. "Our second proposal doesn't involve killing you at all."

"Why did I even come here?" Ka-Lenn wondered aloud.

"Because we can get you court-martialed! It's great!" Peter said, delighted.

"Are you done? You know, when you asked me to meet you at a workyard, I thought you might have repaired my car."

"Hang in there," Peter said, holding up one finger. "We were busy yesterday afternoon and evening. We've talked to the DiMavi government to let them know what happened, and suggest our plan of approach. They agreed. They were also grateful enough for solving all this and dropping Annay into their laps to give us honorary citizenship on top of a basket of local treats and alcohol. I quite like these people. We've also talked to some members of the Vadin Elder Council. They suspected DiMavi of the attack straight away, but given the number of DiMavi civilians injured and killed, well...it's enough to cast doubt, and they can't prove anything. They're also pret-ty embarrassed about being unable to keep either their own people or their DiMavi guests safe during a peace ceremony, of all things. They need a scapegoat."

"You?" Ka-Lenn suggested hopefully.

"Tempting!" Peter said.

Gamora was still shooting death glares at Ka-Lenn, but it didn't stop her from pitching in, "And unfortunately plausible."

"Yeah, given the involvement of the Grootling, we're easy targets." Peter smiled. "But hundreds of people saw our Groot on stage right beside him—so we're off the hook. They thought Groot ate him or something. They don't know it's really the same Groot. So here's the story we're feeding them, and that you'll enthusiastically back up: The people behind the attack are the same Kree bandits that attacked DiMave four years ago."

"That seems unlikely."

Peter shrugged. "Let's say they're still bitter over getting chased out of DiMave after the Maraud. They dressed up as Kree soldiers, got their hands on a biological weapon, and tried to make a mess out of the peace ceremony. We're running with it. It gives the Kree a safe, minimally political target, allowing them to save face and go after someone, and it gives the DiMavi some semblance of seriously overdue justice for the Maraud. Like I said: You're going to back it up. Because the moment you let slip there were DiMavi involved, we'll tell the Kree precisely how the Collector got his hands on their tech."

"See?" Gamora said. "That proposal did not involve killing you. We're true to our word."

"Hurray," he said gloomily. "And then you'll actually leave me in peace?"

"Once we have our Grootling, we'll never contact you again," Peter said.

"And another thing," Gamora said.

Ka-Lenn winced.

"I want to talk to Kiya."

50

GAMORA met Kiya in the military hospital outside the capital of Vadin.

She got a lot of wary looks as she sat in the guest recreation area on the ground floor. She couldn't tell whether the Kree patients, visitors, and staff recognized her as Gamora, deadliest woman in the galaxy, or as Gamora, one of the Guardians—who had recently either saved the day or mucked things up, depending on who you asked.

All those perceptions were true, anyway.

Kiya sat down across from her. "Say the word," Gamora said, "and I'll get you out."

"I meant what I said. I want to stay."

Gamora scrutinized her face for signs of duress or brainwashing, and found none. Kiya didn't seem afraid, either, aside from the undercurrent of wariness that had permeated their every interaction.

Kiya simply sat in her chair across the small round table, leaning back and twirling the glass of ninati juice before her.

"You wanted life to go back to normal," Gamora said. "This isn't it. You'll be trapped again."

"I know. But…" She kept playing with the juice. "*Normal* is gone. The

Kree can give me *safe.* That's good enough. They've agreed to my terms: They'll complete the enhancements that were already in progress, but not implant anything new. They'll inform me thoroughly before each surgery or assessment. They'll train me to use the implants optimally, but with a focus on self-defense. They'll let me visit my remaining family and friends on DiMave, as long as I'm with an escort. They'll let me continue my studies—they'll even give me my own greenhouse and supplies."

"And you will be trapped."

"On. My. Terms." Kiya looked up, shifting her focus from the juice to Gamora. "They can keep me safe from Tivan. As long as I'm in their care, he'll think twice about coming for me again. For now, that's enough."

"What if they change their minds?"

Gamora had dreaded Kiya inevitably leaving the Guardians, but she'd known it was for the best. She'd imagined the girl undercover, hidden, building her own family and her own life. That way, even if Gamora had to lose her immediately after finding her, Kiya would still be safe. She deserved a different kind of life from the one Gamora led.

Different, not *better:* There was nothing bad about Gamora's life with the Guardians. They were her family. They were her friends. She admired no one more.

The Guardians of the Galaxy simply weren't right for Kiya. Gamora had accepted that. Still, leaving Kiya here to be the Kree's guinea pig—that was worse than she'd imagined.

"The Kree agreed to let me stay in touch with the Guardians," Kiya said.

Gamora paused. "Oh?"

"With you."

She sat silently for a moment. "With me."

"You're the one who told me about the plan to hand me back to the Collector."

"I didn't tell you. I asked you."

"Which should never have been up for debate." Kiya dipped her head, and her voice took on a harsher edge. "I know why Rocket didn't want to tell me—but he should've."

"He should've."

Whatever anger Kiya felt, she either managed to dissipate it or tuck it away, because when she looked back up, her eyes were neutral. "I'll be able to call every week or two to let you know how things are going here, and to keep up on how the team is doing. If that's all right with you."

"Yes," Gamora said slowly. She hadn't realized how heavily her thoughts about Kiya—about *leaving* Kiya—had weighed until now, as they lightened and faded.

Kiya wanted to stay in touch.

That was all Gamora wanted.

"Yes," she repeated. "That's all right with me."

"Good." Kiya sipped her ninati juice.

"If they mistreat you, let us know. We'll come get you. It won't be the first time we we go up against the Kree, and it won't be the last." Gamora leaned in. One final time, she asked: "Are you *sure?*"

This time, Kiya didn't answer so quickly. For a moment, Gamora feared that maybe Kiya really did doubt her decision, that the Kree had threatened her. Then Kiya did something Gamora hadn't expected:

She smiled.

"It's not what I thought I wanted." Kiya seemed to be thinkingthrough her words as she said them. "But the life I wanted back isn't there anymore: I'd have to build it up from scratch. So maybe I should see what's out there, first."

"It's a big universe," Gamora said.

"Yes. I've seen a lot of the bad, now. But I don't want to run from the rest before I even get to know it."

Gamora cocked her head. She said nothing.

"How is Groot?"

"He's good. He's back to being himself. Only one Grootling left to find," Gamora said. "I asked him what you wanted to know—why he sacrificed himself for you in the bar on DiMave."

"What did he say?"

"I am Groot."

"Very funny. What did he *mean?*"

"He meant: I am Groot."

"Oh." Kiya's lips twitched with a smile. "Hey, I thought…wasn't Drax coming?"

"He'll be here. He had an Accuser to visit in the south wing. Something about a rematch."

"She survived the spores?"

"She was the only one who did. The Accuser armor protected her. She'll recover, in time."

"How many others…?"

Gamora gave Kiya a long look, then shook her head. "It wouldn't help to know the number."

Too many, was the answer. Even if only a single person had died from the spores, it was too many.

"But what happened is my responsibility."

"You played a part in it against your will, as a result of desperation. That's very different. It's enough to know that it happened; what you *do* with that knowledge going forward…that's your responsibility."

Gamora had done this. She'd chosen to fight alongside the Guardians of the Galaxy.

What Kiya would do—that was her own choice.

Gamora looked forward to seeing her make that choice.

WHAT?" Rocket said, following the others out of the shuttle. He squinted in the evening gloom, which painted the sky above the nearby trees a colorful pink-purple shade. "This is the middle of nowhere! Don't tell me this is where Ka-Lenn keeps his Grootling."

"Nope," Quill said. "Gamora's already picking him up."

"Then what *else* does Kree-Lar have for us?" He shook his leg as something crawled over his foot. "Ugh, nature."

"It's more about what we have for Kree-Lar."

Rocket scrunched up his face. "That ain't informative, Quill."

"I am Groot," Groot snickered.

He watched as Quill and Groot reached back into the shuttle and rummaged around.

"How'd your talk with Tivan go, anyway?" Rocket asked.

"Oh, you know," Quill called back. "Good alcohol, terrible company, obligatory tour of the known marvels of our universe. I feel we reached an understanding, though."

"Does the understanding include, *don't put your flarking paws on Groot ever again?*"

"Yes, actually." Quill and Groot walked away from the shuttle, each holding an identical rectangular object covered in black drapes.

"You got boxes," Rocket said dubiously.

"I negotiated for a peace offering," Quill corrected him.

Rocket pointed at Groot's box. "Your peace offering is making funny noises."

"I am Groot?" Groot raised the box and pressed his face flat to the top. He smiled. "I am Groot."

"What do you mean, *they're excited?*"

They walked toward the edge of the woods. Rocket followed, tromping through the grass and swatting away bugs.

"Who's *they?*" he asked. "Excited about what?"

Finally, Quill and Groot crouched and set down the boxes near the tree line. Quill took the cloth on Groot's box and plucked it off, quickly following it with his own. "Ta-da!"

Rocket stared at the contents.

They hadn't been holding boxes—they'd been holding cages.

And the cages held—

"*Rodents?*" he said.

"Raccoons," Quill corrected him. "Earth raccoons from the Collector's museum. We're setting them free."

Rocket looked up, his face a mask of horror. "They're disgusting."

"I am Groot," Groot admonished.

"How're they cute? Look at 'em! Look at those *hands!*"

"They're family, however distant they might be, and we're going to treat them right," Quill said. "I named this one Fluffy, and that one's Squishy, and that one's Stinky-Butt because on the way back from the Collector's— you know, I don't want to talk about it."

Rocket glared. This was ridiculous. This was embarrassing. This was outright offensive. He still couldn't resist pointing out, "You missed one."

"Oh! Yeah. I figured you get to name that one."

Rocket peered at the fourth raccoon. It seemed to be the runt of the set. It was gross and hairy and made an angry sound at them, or maybe at the world in general.

"I don't wanna name it," he huffed. "It's just an idiot animal."

"I am Groot."

"Ugh, no. Groot is a good name for a tree, bad name for a rodent."

"Raccoons aren't rodents, actually," Quill said.

"Changed my mind," Rocket announced. "I call it Peter."

"Awwww—!"

"Now get rid of them. I think Squishy's got some kinda disease."

"All right, let's get these babies to freedom," Quill said. "You want to open a cage?"

"Nope." Rocket watched the raccoons warily. Two of them hissed and snapped furiously at the cage bars. The other two seemed more resigned, but were still twisting and turning and feeling up the cage with those weird little hands that Rocket hadn't seen on anyone except himself in years.

"Suit yourself! Groot, on the count of three..." They ripped away the fronts of the cages and danced back. One raccoon shot out with such force that Quill made a half-leap away and ended up flat on his ass. The others scuttled out more slowly, sniffing the ground and inspecting their surroundings.

"I am Groot." Groot had the widest smile on his face.

"You are so embarrassing."

"Aw, look at them go," Quill said. "Goodbye, Peter! Goodbye, Fluffy! Goodbye, Squishy! Goodbye, Stinky-Butt!"

"I am Groo-oot!" Groot called out.

"Huh, that's right, ain't it?" Rocket looked up at Groot. "You—part of you—lived with them in the arboretum."

"I am Groot."

"I'm sure they'll miss you, too, buddy. Hey, Quill, did the Collector really just *give* them to you?"

"He has no more use for them." Quill watched the raccoons sniff around their new home. One of them promptly climbed a tree. "A while ago, I said there wouldn't be a team without Gamora. I also said that Kiya was hard to replace. The Collector feels the same way. She was the core of his tribute team: Without a Zen-Whoberian, he doesn't see the point in even trying to replicate the rest of us. It would be a poor knockoff—beneath his standards."

Rocket nodded slowly. "What was he gonna do with them, you think?"

"I don't want to know. This is better."

"Yeah." He shrugged nonchalantly. "I guess."

"If you care about that sort of thing."

"Exactly." He paused. "Hey, I think Peter and Squishy are—"

"And that's enough raccoon-watching for today, children," Quill announced. "Let's go back to the ship. Gamora should be done by now."

The three of them turned back to the shuttle, leaving the raccoons to their own devices.

"I am Groot. I am Groot?"

"I actually have no idea." Rocket wrinkled his nose. "*Are* we endangering the local ecosystem?"

"Probably," Quill said thoughtfully.

Rocket shrugged. "Ah well."

51

THIS is the last of it, right?" Ka-Lenn stood in the doorway of his research and storage facility, watching Gamora lead out the emaciated Grootling. "You have your Groot, Kiya survived the surgeries and is thriving, and my government is pursuing the bandits responsible for the Maraud. You'll leave me alone?"

Gamora focused on the Grootling by her side, her hand on his back. He walked unsteadily.

"I am Groot," he said quietly.

"Don't thank us," she said. "Not for this. We should have come sooner."

"I am Groot." He climbed into the newly repaired ship she'd landed in the field, where Drax was waiting for him.

Gamora did not follow. She turned, walking back to Ka-Lenn. Gravel crunched under her feet.

"We'll leave you alone," she told him.

"And you won't tell my superiors?"

"We won't. I keep my promises."

"I'd say it was a pleasure doing business with you, but it was primarily blackmail, so…"

"I never promised I wouldn't kill you for performing invasive surgery on an unwilling, unconscious girl, however."

He stepped instinctively back.

Gamora pulled her sword.

AND WE'RE all complete again." Quill thumped into the pilot seat.

Time to leave Kree-Lar and finish this thing for good.

Rocket twisted around in the navigator's seat to look at Groot behind him.

Groot took a few moments to look around the bridge. His eyes went from Rocket to Gamora, from Drax to Quill, before finally settling back on Rocket.

Contently, he said, "I *am* Groot."

"Man, you're such a sap."

"I almost miss those little Grootling buggers, you know?" Quill said wistfully. "Running around, destroying my ship, being all obnoxious and cuddly…"

"I am Groot?"

"I said I *almost* miss them."

"I prefer you like this, Groot." Gamora reached over to affectionately flick a stray branch growing from his elbow. "Back to normal."

"I am Groot."

"I would not personally describe the Guardians as normal," Drax said, his brow furrowing. "And as you pointed out, Gamora, I once lived a normal life."

It was something few of the others—perhaps only Quill—could claim.

"What?" Rocket said. "Why, we ain't normal?"

Drax studied Gamora. His forehead wrinkled further. "Did you not consider such a life?"

Quill looked up from the star map he'd been engrossed in.

"There's nothing to consider," Gamora said. "That life doesn't exist for me."

"You've never wondered?" Quill said.

"I wondered. I never wanted." She leaned back and settled comfortably into her chair. "Why would I? I like *this* normal. I like *our* normal."

"No, wait, but what ain't normal about us?" Rocket repeated.

"Our normal is pretty good," Quill said.

"I am *Groot*."

Drax nodded. "I am satisfied with it."

Rocket gave up. "I guess it's all right."

"I am Groot."

"Exactly." Gamora propped up her legs against the back of Quill's seat. "Let's fly."

THE END

THANOS
DEATH
SENTENCE

AN ORIGINAL NOVEL OF THE MARVEL UNIVERSE
STUART MOORE

THE CASTLE floated in space, three stories high and a quarter-mile wide. Frozen jewels shone from immense stone columns; enormous gargoyles stared down from the turrets. Twin carved faces—a huge skull and a beautiful young woman—flanked the thick wooden door that stood atop a stairway of worn slate. Smaller skulls spilled from every window and ran up and down the walls, creeping across the stone façade like ivy.

Thanos docked his wheezing single-flier ship and launched himself out of the cockpit, into open space. Cold stones cracked as he landed on the flat-carved meteorite that held the castle.

He rose to his feet, staring up at the huge carvings. Two faces of Death: the destroyer and the comforter. Age and youth. Horror and beauty.

He allowed himself a moment of hope. He had built this castle with his own two hands, as a gift to his dark love. Now she had summoned him back here. Did that mean she forgave him his trespasses, his failures? Could it be that she did love him, despite everything?

"Master?"

Thanos whirled, annoyed. At the edge of the castle wall, a small humanoid figure stood watching him. The figure wore a thinsuit and oval-shaped helmet, fitted to his elongated head. One of Captain Styx's lesser officers; as he shifted nervously back and forth, Thanos struggled to recall his name. Nil. That was it.

"I received your message," Nil continued, a slight quiver in his voice. "I'm afraid the, uh, the rest of the crew aren't coming. Even the ones that escaped. After the business with the, erm, the uh-uh-uh Gems—"

Thanos turned away, raised his hand, and without looking loosed a plasma blast in Nil's direction. Nil didn't even have time to scream. One moment he stood before the looming castle; the next, he was a wisp of vapor.

Thanos turned and strode up the stairs, leaving the last of Nil to waft off into space.

Inside the heavy double doors, the castle's main hallway was filled with air. Thanos allowed himself to breathe. He didn't require oxygen, but his senses felt stunted, limited without the Gems. He craved input: a sound, a taste, a stray scent.

A stench of mildew and decay washed over him. He looked around at the high, green-tinged walls, built of stone blocks weighing half a ton apiece. Thanos had salvaged them from the planet Agathon, from the oldest castle in the galaxy. The last Agathonian had watched, bloody and dying, as Thanos hauled away the stones one by one.

He reached out and touched the wall. It flaked and chipped against his finger. Slivers of stone fell slowly to the ground, hesitant in the meteorite's low gravity. He frowned. How long ago had he built this place? Not long enough, surely, for it to have fallen into such a decayed state?

He continued down the narrow corridor, past guttering torches mounted high on the walls. As he approached the throne room, his doubts grew. Was it truly Death who had called him here? He'd only heard her voice a few times before, on the rare occasions she'd deigned to address him. Could this be someone else? An enemy, perhaps?

Come to me.

He paused before the doors, willing his fear away. He had already lost ultimate power today. What more could an enemy do to him? What punishment, what fate could be more painful?

When he thrust open the double doors, his breath caught in his throat.

The room held hundreds of skulls. They lined the walls, covered the fixtures, even the columns reaching up to the distant ceiling. A rack of ancient weapons sat against one wall: knives, slingshots, heavy-gauge energy swords, dueling pistols salvaged from some backward world. The bones of long-dead foes littered the floor, cleared only to form a small pathway leading to the throne itself.

Mistress Death sat atop the high throne, resplendent in deep viridian robes.

Thanos stared, struck speechless by her beauty. The throne was constructed from a set of teeth and jaws 12 feet high. Thanos himself had pulled out the creature's heart and skinned the flesh from its bones.

Slowly Death turned dark eyes to stare at him. She uncrossed her legs—a divine, graceful motion—and rose to her full height. With quick, gentle movements, she began to descend the pile of skulls forming the throne's base.

He stood still, stricken with doubt, paralyzed by her beauty. Her skin shone white as marble; her face was flawless—eyes dark as pulsars set above perfect cheekbones, all framed by a regal silk hood in dark cerulean tones. Her lips were pale but full, with just a hint of blood pulsing beneath. She was as tall as Thanos himself and as slim as a single-stemmed rose.

We're alone, he realized. That was unusual. Death normally traveled with a guard of demons and animal-men.

"Mistress," Thanos said. "I come to you in a somewhat diminished state."

She stared at him with a blank, enigmatic intensity.

"I had hoped to present you with a great bounty," he continued. "An offering, a gift of billions of souls. But my grandfather..."

She stopped and held up a hand. Her eyes narrowed, as if to say: *No excuses.*

"Of course. Yes. I merely wish you to know: I have not abandoned you. I will never stop trying to win your love."

A slight smile tugged at her lips.

"Already I have begun setting new plans in motion. Masterworks of slaughter, weapons that will shake the stars." He clenched his fist. "I *will* be worthy of you, Mistress. I..."

Mistress Death held a slim, black-nailed finger up to her lips.

"Mistress?"

Her eyes locked onto his. Thanos found he could not look away. In her gaze, he saw worlds colliding, a massive starship punching a hole through the stars. Gray steel planes, bombs with fins, cities reduced to ash. Bodies torn apart; a woman's flesh melting from her face.

She stepped closer.

Thanos held his breath. Was it possible? Did she love him after all? He had come here empty-handed, his life's work in ruins. But he had *tried.* Had that proven his devotion? Was the mere attempt enough?

He reached out to take her in his arms. She was cold and warm, vacuum-death and starfire. Her flesh was paper-thin, her muscles wiry. Her hands reached out to encircle his neck.

This, he thought. This is everything. I will never stop, Mistress. I will bring you the stars, the soul of every sentient being that has ever lived.

Her lips parted. He closed his eyes and leaned in for the kiss.

Cold teeth bit down on his lip. Bone sliced through rocky skin, digging deep, drawing blood.

Thanos cried out. His eyes shot open to see Death's true face: a grinning skull, stark white against her deep blue hood. He could almost hear her cruel, silent laughter.

He struck out in anger. When he slapped her face, he expected to hear the clatter of bone, the shattering of enamel. But instead he felt flesh—the flesh of a woman, warm and yielding against his savage blow.

Thanos howled with rage. Psionic energy poured out of him; cosmic beams blasted from his eyes, fanning out in waves through the room and out into the halls of the castle. The stones of Agathon bent and cracked under his assault.

He was oblivious, lost in a raging blood fever. His lip ached, but that pain was nothing compared to the pain of betrayal. His love had spurned him, rejected his offer. Returned his affection—at the moment of his greatest vulnerability—with a vicious, personal attack.

She would pay, he vowed. He would bring her to her knees, hear her bones crack beneath his powerful fists. Then...then maybe she would understand...

He shook his head, his vision clearing. The room still stood, but in his rage he'd cracked the high throne in half. Skulls tumbled onto the floor, mixing with grains of rock that spilled down from the ceiling.

And Death was gone.

He turned sharply at a creaking noise. A heavy wooden door swung open on thick hinges. The room beyond was dark and indistinct. With a shock, he recognized it as Death's bedchamber.

A woman's hand appeared from within, finger curled, beckoning him inside.

He paused. Remembered the feel of Death's cheek as he struck her, the impact of his granite hand against soft flesh.

He strode to the door, crushing skulls beneath his feet. A strange excitement, some terrible masculine urge, came over him. If she awaited inside that room, if this were all some twisted game, he would force her to confront what she'd awakened. He would make her feel his power.

The room was dark, windowless. Skull-patterned wallpaper, just beginning to peel, lined the walls. In the center of the room, dominating the space, stood a high, canopied Victorian bed. Dark crimson curtains surrounded the bed, suspended from posts carved to resemble ancient snake demons.

He walked to the bed, his heavy steps shaking the room. He leaned forward to place his knee on the bed and thrust the curtain aside.

Nothing. No one here. He was alone.

Consumed by fury, he ripped and tore at the bedcovers. He yanked a curtain down, rending it from end to end. He snapped a post free of the bed, cracked the carved serpent in half, and flung its severed head across the room.

He sank onto the bed, struggling to clear his head. A strange sensation came over him, a deep fog of unreality. As if he'd entered into a fever dream, a sort of cosmic delirium. He almost laughed. Was there such a thing as an Infinity Gem hangover?

Then his thoughts grew dark again. Death was gone. She had *lured* him here, to this chamber that he himself had furnished. Everything in this room, all the trappings of the castle, were tributes of his love—

No. Not everything.

He crawled to the edge of the bed, swept aside a half-torn curtain, and stared back toward the door. A large wardrobe stood against the wall, its polished mahogany surface carved into four segments: two thin, hinged doors in the center, and a larger mirrored panel on either side.

He walked to the wardrobe, examined it. He had never seen it before. He stood before one of the mirrors, studying his image. His blue-gold battlesuit was torn; his boots were stained with mud. His lip was red with blood.

But still he was Thanos.